THE SAHARA EVENT

AN EDEN BLACK THRILLER
BOOK 7

LUKE RICHARDSON

RICHA BOOKS

Pomponius Mela circa 43 CE
BRITANNIAE
BRITANNICUS OCEANUS
EUROPIA
GALLIA
ITALIA
HISPANIA
ATLANTAE
ATLANTICUM MARE
MAURETANIA
AFRICA
The Richat Structure, Mauritania. Present day.
MOROCCO
N
S
W
E
WESTERN SAHARA
RICHAT STRUCTURE
approx 40km
MALI
OUADANE & AIRFIELD

Marrakesh, Morocco.
Present day.
N
W
E
S
MADRASA BEN YOUSSEF
MARRAKESH
MEDINA
PLACE DE ESPICES
JEMAA EL-FNAA
SQUARE
KOUTOUBIA
MOSQUE
The Sahara Event

Are you ready for the adventure of a lifetime?

64% of you read my books without me ever getting the chance to say thank you. I'd love to change that.

If you've ever enjoyed one of my stories, I'd love to welcome you into my *Adventure Society*. This weekly newsletter is your chance to travel to the places that inspire my stories, explore the real-world mysteries, and be the first to know when a new book is ready.

Most of all, it helps me write the stories you love as this way we're connected directly without relying on algorithms or online stores. Believe me when I say that direct connection is so important!

Will you join me for an adventure today?

lukerichardsonauthor.com/adventuresociety

Your next adventure starts here...

"He who fights with monsters should look to it that he himself does not become a monster. And if you gaze long into an abyss, the abyss also gazes into you."

Friedrich Nietzsche

1

———

Mauritania. Ten years ago.

Dr. Eva Glass leaned toward the window as the Sikorsky S-76 helicopter thundered across the Sahara. As her eyes focused, she caught a glimpse of her own reflection in the pane. Her brown hair, now streaked with gray, was tied tight, and her eyes wore the brackets of a long journey across continents. Her gaze shifted through the window and assessed the great expanse of sand stretching out beneath them, as it had since they'd crossed the Atlas Mountains hours before.

Reflecting on their work so far, Glass realized that this journey was just another arduous process in what had been a relentless few months. She cast her mind back, remembering clearly the afternoon, and the fossil, that had started it all.

To the untrained eye, the fossil was a normal trilobite specimen—one of those ancient marine arthropods with segmented bodies and bulging eyes that crawled across ocean floors hundreds of millions of years ago. It was the kind of thing that sat in a drawer for decades without attracting much notice. And this specimen would have remained there too, had it not been for Professor Jay Lawrence's relentless curiosity.

"I'm not sure how I can help you," Glass said, stepping into Lawrence's cramped office all those months ago. "As director of the Particle Physics Department, I don't have time for fossils and, frankly, they're not my area."

"I'm certain that's correct," Lawrence replied, placing his pen on the desk and flashing Glass his disarming smile. "I'm sure you're thinking that there are enough fossils amongst the staff at this university. I can assure you, on that, you are also correct." If it was Lawrence's intention to immediately charm Glass, he'd been successful.

"What does it say about my fading youth if you can read my face like those old rocks of yours?" Glass retorted, pacing into the room and lowering herself into the chair opposite Lawrence.

"All I ask is five minutes of your time, Director," Lawrence said, his smile widening further still as he shuffled through a pile of documents. "Although I fear after my five minutes is up, you'll want to know more."

As Glass looked at the documents, a spark of curiosity moved through her. Whatever Lawrence had here, it was probably more interesting than the funding application she was midway through.

"But I'll get to the point," Lawrence continued. "Unlike, as you put it, my old rocks, we don't have fifty million years at our disposal." Lawrence slid a sheet of paper from the pile and placed it in front of Glass. "Tell me, what do you make of this?"

Glass leaned forward, half expecting another tedious geological survey or grant proposal. Instead, she found herself looking at a series of diagrams showing the internal structure of something at a molecular level.

"This looks like crystalline structure analysis," she said, running a fingertip across the diagrams. "Very precise work."

"Do you notice anything unusual?" Lawrence said.

"Yes, actually," Glass said, looking more closely. "The molecular arrangement has been forced from its natural alignment."

"Yes, indeed." Lawrence leaned back, his chair creaking. "In your opinion, what kind of force would be required to do that?"

"Extreme heat," Glass said, her interest piquing. She looked up and met the professor's gaze.

Lawrence scratched his stubbled chin and nodded. "What sort of temperatures might we be talking about?"

"To completely restructure at the atomic level?" Glass paused, running the calculations in her head. "We're talking about temperatures in excess of a million degrees. Where did this come from?"

"This." Lawrence pushed a photograph across the desk. "Paradoxides Mauritanicus—a perfectly ordinary trilobite specimen from the Cambrian period. But since these readings came back, we've called her *Atomic Annie*."

"*Atomic Annie*, how very cute," Glass said, studying the photograph, which showed a long-dead creature with a segmented, oval-shaped body preserved in gray rock. Nothing about it looked remarkable to her untrained eye.

"She was originally catalogued as part of a routine collection in the 1960s," Lawrence said, tapping the photograph. "Standard procedure—photograph, measure, file away. She sat in our collection for decades without anyone giving her a second look."

"Then how did you?" Glass said, turning her attention back to the test results.

"Call it academic curiosity," Lawrence said. "But I certainly didn't expect old *Annie* to light up our instruments like a Christmas tree. We've since run the same tests on other samples from the collection and got similar results." Lawrence picked up the stack and laid several more documents out across the desk.

"It certainly looks as though all of these have been exposed to the same high temperatures," Glass said, looking from one document to the next.

"As I suspected," Lawrence said, leaning back in his chair. "And that's interesting, because..." Lawrence paused, clearly leaving a gap for Glass to finish the sentence.

"Nothing on Earth can generate that kind of heat," Glass said, her gaze snapping up to meet Lawrence's as the realization hit her.

"Again, as I suspected," Lawrence said, folding his arms. "I'm no expert, but as I understand it, volcanic activity peaks at around two thousand degrees."

"Lightning?" Glass said, looking up.

"Maybe thirty thousand Celsius, but for microseconds." He pointed at the readings.

"There is only one process I know of—" Glass said, her gaze sweeping across the readings. "Where are these from?"

"Mauritania," Lawrence said.

"Then there must have been—" Glass said, stopping herself as she realized the ridiculousness of what she had been about to say. She met the professor's gaze as the color drained from her cheeks.

"Rest assured, you are in a safe space here," Lawrence said, his voice dropping to a whisper. "We are just two academics engaging in a friendly discussion."

Glass paused, then, reassured by something in her colleague's gaze, continued.

"In my experience," Glass said, picking her words carefully, "the sort of temperature required to fundamentally alter the atomic structure in this way would only occur in nuclear fusion. But... as far as I know, there's no record of nuclear activity in that area. How old did you say this fossil is?"

"Five hundred million years," Lawrence replied.

"Did you run a radiation test?"

"Indeed. Full analysis," Lawrence said, fishing out another document.

"Although the sample shows clear evidence of nuclear processes, it's not particularly radioactive now. Much less than I'd expect, given the severity of the damage," Glass said, running a finger across the document.

"What does that mean?" Lawrence said.

"Accounting for the half-lives of the isotopes involved, we're looking at something that happened ten to twenty thousand years ago," Glass said. "Which is impossible as we didn't split the atom until 1938. Everything before that was theoretical."

"And controlled nuclear reactions didn't happen until 1942," Lawrence added. "In fact, look at this." Lawrence dug out another piece of paper and placed it on top.

"There are similarities. What is this?" Glass said, running a finger from one document to the next.

"Sand deposits from the Trinity site in New Mexico ..." Lawrence paused. Glass gasped, knowing exactly what was coming next. "... after the first plutonium device was detonated in July 1945."

"They're unmistakable," Glass said, inhaling sharply. She studied the data again, her mind running through the implications. "But ... are you seriously suggesting someone was conducting nuclear experiments while our ancestors were still living in caves?" Glass looked at the documents, her gaze now hard and focused. "That's impossible. The level of scientific knowledge required would represent an industrial civilization we've no record of."

"We don't use the word *impossible* in this department, director," Lawrence said, his tone friendly. "We look at the evidence and draw from that our own conclusions."

"Okay, professor." Glass nodded. "It is true that this fossil predates our understanding of nuclear fusion by at least ten thousand years. What's your theory?"

"Now, that's the question I hoped you would ask," Lawrence said, that warm smile once again flashing across his face.

2

———

Mauritania. Ten years ago.

"Thirty minutes out." The pilot's voice dragged Glass back to the present. She glanced at Lawrence, staring down at the desert from his seat on the opposite side of the cabin.

"We have it a lot easier than the French scientists who found our *Atomic Annie* to begin with," Lawrence said, somehow sensing Glass's gaze.

"Yes, indeed," Glass replied, stifling a yawn. "Although I bet they had less bureaucracy to deal with." She eyed their team filling the rest of the aircraft's seats—experts in geology, archaeology, geophysics, and a military escort at the Pentagon's insistence.

"The French simply packed up and went," Lawrence said, adjusting his headset. "No oversight committees, no risk assessments."

"You make it sound like a dream." Glass considered the labyrinthine approval process they'd endured to get here—presentations to university committees, to the National Science Foundation, and finally to a shadowy Pentagon research division. The fact that they'd ultimately received full funding—including the military escort—suggested *Atomic Annie* had attracted attention at the highest levels of government.

"Different times," she said, her eyes tracking the rise of the dunes below.

"We're dealing with potentially dangerous materials in hostile territory," one of the military escorts cut in, listening to their conversation through the chopper's comms system.

Lawrence turned slightly in his seat and flashed the man the look of a schoolmaster addressing a misbehaving child. "Dangerous materials? Our *Atomic Annie* stopped being dangerous a long time ago, Sergeant."

"That fossil shows nuclear signatures matching weapons-grade material," the sergeant snapped. "This is a matter of international security."

A chill that had nothing to do with the helicopter's air conditioning worked its way up Glass's spine. Although she knew their funding came with strings attached, the military coming along for the ride made her nervous.

"You know something that's always worried me," Lawrence said, his voice dropping into a conversational cadence. Quite the diplomat, he clearly realized discussing the ethics of scientific discovery with their compulsory escorts was a waste of everyone's time.

"What's that?" Glass answered, drawn in by Lawrence's easy tone.

"That this place was once a tropical paradise," he said, pointing at the desert. "We know that around the time our *Atomic Annie* was subjected to that radiation, this was a savanna with rivers, lakes and forests. It remained like that for hundreds of thousands of years until ..." his voice trailed to nothing.

"Why would that worry you?" Glass eyed a valley of darker stone running between the dunes some distance away—possibly one of the ancient rivers that Lawrence described.

"A life spent studying things from millions of years ago provides something of a unique perspective," Lawrence said, gesturing at the desert. "You realize how fragile all of this really is ... on a long enough timeline, of course."

Glass scowled, unsure if she agreed with the professor or not. Although Lawrence was a brilliant scientist, he veered toward lengthy, hyperbolic descriptions. Glass suspected—perhaps a little unfairly—that a lifetime working with rocks had taught him there was no rush to get to the point. She, on the other hand, worked with particles that sometimes existed for just fractions of a second. In her world, speed was everything.

"I'd say that one of humanity's greatest flaws is assuming what we see now will always be that way," Lawrence said, surprisingly concisely. He folded his arms and fell into silence. The chopper lurched, buffeted by the rising heat.

"Why does that worry you?" Glass asked, looking across the cabin as her stomach bounced with the craft's movement.

"Who's to know which part of our planet will turn into desert next?" Lawrence continued gravely. "It could be Europe, vast parts of Asia, or even the United States."

Glass pictured the desertification of places she knew and loved. Although they now had technology to hold back the desert—pumping water and conditioning air—the impact on the food chain, the natural world, and wildlife would be incalculable.

"I understand," Glass said, her gaze shifting over the sand.

"Two miles out and the instruments ... going haywire." The pilot's voice crackled through their headsets. The chopper bounced again.

"Just as we expected," Lawrence replied, pulling out a map and running his finger across it.

"What's the problem?" The sergeant barked.

"The compass is spinning like a carnival ride, GPS is—" Static fizzed, cutting the pilot's words.

"You'll have to do this last bit the old-fashioned way," Lawrence said. "Navigate by sight. Can you do that?"

"Of course," the pilot said. "As long as whatever ... doesn't start messing with the control systems."

"What exactly are we flying into?" The sergeant said, his voice tight.

"Exactly what we expected," Lawrence said, without looking up. "A massive electromagnetic anomaly centered on the—" The comms squealed with a sharp, piercing tone, then cut out.

A beat of silence passed, then the chopper dropped.

Glass's stomach lurched up into her throat. As quickly as the drop started, it stopped, forcing her into the seat.

"Woah—controls dipped," the pilot shouted, now backed by the sound of screaming alarms. "I've got manual control, but something surged through the avionics."

The chopper shuddered again, as though flying through a storm. They dropped again, the desert floor rushing up to meet them.

Glass gripped the armrest as the craft leveled out. She looked out the window, hoping for her lurching stomach to calm down. Through the heat haze, she saw something.

"There it is," Lawrence said, clearly seeing the same thing.

The geometric precision of the concentric rings was unmistakable.

"That's incredible," Glass breathed, leaning in close to the pane.

"The Richat Structure," Lawrence said. "One of the greatest geological mysteries of all time."

The great rings, over twenty miles across, spread out across the desert like a massive target carved into the earth. Ring after ring of weathered stone rose and fell across the land, each ring perfectly centered within the next. They passed across the outer ring, heading for the center.

"It's impossible," Glass said, amazed by the sheer geometric precision of the thing.

"Mainstream geologists believe it's an eroded dome," Lawrence said. "But from here—"

"It looks more ..." Glass stopped as she noticed the even spacing between each of the rings. "This looks ... purposeful," she said, struggling to process what she saw. Glass intellectually understood the scale of the structure from the satellite images they'd studied, but witnessing it firsthand was something else.

The chopper's shadow dropped into the expansive valley spread out between the rings. The sleek shape looked little bigger than a toy amid the landscape.

"It's ... it's impossible," Glass said.

"You know we don't use the word *impossible*, doctor," Lawrence said, flashing her an excitable look as they bounced and swerved. "And to think, this has been here for millennia. Hiding in plain sight until satellite photography finally revealed it."

"It's more beautiful than I'd ever imagined," Glass said, unable to look away from the rings: rust red outer bands, pale cream middle sections, and something that gleamed almost silver at the center.

They sped up over the next ring, the chopper shaking in an updraft. This time the vibrations didn't stop, though.

"Interference in the ..." the pilot said, his voice fading before returning. "Navigation, radio, even the fuel gauges are ..."

"This was not in the briefing," the sergeant grunted.

"What we're dealing with here is not in any briefing," Lawrence shot back. "This is the edge of human understanding."

The helicopter bucked, swinging from side to side as they sped out across the next valley, toward the structure's central rise.

"Bringing it down ..." the pilot said, his voice strained. "Prepare for—" The sound dropped out completely, leaving only the mechanical whine of the rotors.

Glass's stomach lurched as they dipped lower and lower, the geometric perfection of the inner rings filling the window.

"Hold ...!" the pilot shouted, the comms returning for a moment. He swung the craft toward the raised circular area in the center of the structure.

The helicopter's descent steepened as they powered across the final valley. Reaching the structure's central mound, an updraft sent the chopper into a momentary spin.

The pilot dragged the craft back into line, tilted the nose groundward and powered on. They banked hard, the occupants sliding against their seatbelts. Finding a suitable place to put down, the pilot leveled out and reduced power.

"What really is this place?" Glass muttered, looking down at the ground as they approached.

Lawrence turned away from the window and met her gaze. "That's what we're here to find out."

3

———————

THE SIKORSKY TOUCHED down with a bone-jarring thud, kicking up a cloud of sand that obscured everything beyond the windows.

"Welcome to the middle of nowhere," the pilot said, powering down the engines. "Hope you brought sunscreen." The engine noise dropped from a roar to a whine.

"Thank you, Captain," Lawrence said, removing his headset and unclipping his seatbelt. "Not a bad landing with all the technical difficulties."

"It'll take more than a few odd readings to put me off," the pilot replied.

The noise of the chopper faded into the desert silence. Their vision cleared as the sand drifted back down to the ground.

"Before we get out, there are a few things to remember," Lawrence said, climbing to his feet and addressing the group. "We are a peaceful research mission, here at the invitation of the Mauritanian authorities. We're not here to antagonize or upset any local people." Although he didn't look at anyone in particular, Glass got the impression his comments were aimed at the military men.

"If shots come my way, I'm not stopping to ask questions," the sergeant replied, making a show of readying his rifle.

"The only issue you'll have out there is the heat," Lawrence said, pointing a thumb at the door. "Keep Geiger counters on at all times and suit up if levels require it. We don't know exactly what we're dealing with here." He gestured toward the equipment bags. "We get our answers and we're back in Marrakesh by nightfall, preferably without glowing in the dark."

A ripple of nervous laughter moved through the cabin.

Lawrence slid open the door, and the furnace heat of the Sahara streamed into the cabin. He stepped down, the sand crunching beneath his boots.

Glass grabbed her bag, readied her camera and followed. The moment she left the chopper's enclosed space, she heard the soft, intermittent clicking of her Geiger counter. It wasn't the rapid-fire chatter that would signal immediate danger, but a slow, steady tick-tick-tick that registered radiation above background levels.

"The reading is consistent with *Atomic Annie*," Lawrence said, glancing at his own detector. "Only just above normal, so we're definitely in the right place."

"This place is incredible," Glass said, pacing away from the chopper. She snapped several pictures of the level expanse of rocks and sand that topped the structure's central mound. "And only discovered because of aerial photography."

"You mean, *we* didn't know about it until aerial photography," Lawrence said, cupping a hand over his eyes. "This is a sacred place, make no mistake about that."

The military men barged their way past the researchers to be the next out of the chopper. They fanned out, checking for enemies, which Glass supposed their training taught them to find everywhere.

The rest of the academic team followed, carrying bags filled with various sample collection kits.

"The local Amazigh people have stories about this place," Lawrence continued. "They call it the *place where the sky and earth meet*. Given what we're reading on these instruments, they might not speak metaphorically."

Glass nodded, watching her teammates spread out and begin their work.

"Let's move," Lawrence said, glancing at the military men. "The depression we saw on the satellite image is this way." He checked his counter, then headed off toward the mound's edge.

"It's hard to believe that this was once an ocean," Glass said as they approached the edge. A steep cliff fell away, affording them a view out across the circular depression. She took several photographs, zooming in on various rock formations.

"Look at those sediment patterns," Lawrence said, pointing at a section of the incline which sloped out beneath them. "That's textbook marine deposition. Ten thousand years ago, this whole depression would have been under water."

"But the Atlantic Ocean is hundreds of miles away," Glass said, lowering the camera. She looked around, not quite believing that the arid landscape could have changed so much.

"This entire region was part of a vast inland water system," Lawrence said, striding off in search of the depression.

Glass paused to take a few more photographs. When she lowered the camera, Lawrence had already disappeared.

"Professor?" Glass called, taking a few quick steps in the direction he'd indicated. Heat haze shimmered ahead of her, distorting the landscape into rising patterns.

"Lawrence?" she called again, taking another few steps.

A faint reply drifted back, followed by the scraping of stone against stone.

Glass quickened her pace, scrambling over the pile of rocks and saw Lawrence standing in a hollow, which had obscured him from her sight.

"Eva!" he said, looking up at Glass. "You need to see this!"

Glass scrambled down into the hollow, sliding over loose sand and stone. The air felt cooler here, sheltered from the sun. Drawing close, she realized what had caught his attention. What she'd initially assumed to be a shadow cast by the rim of the basin was an opening—a triangular hole cut into the rock.

"This is it," Lawrence said, looking into the opening with amazement. "This is what we came to find."

Glass paced up to the opening and peered inside. The passage was around five feet high and three wide. She snapped several photographs, using the flash to illuminate the gloom.

"What's in there?" Glass said, leaning into the passage and running her palm against the wall. "The rock, it's smooth. However this was made, it wasn't with primitive tools."

"The counter," Lawrence said, looking at the device.

Glass listened closely, realizing that the counter's lazy clicking had quickened—not alarmingly, but enough to notice.

"It's still within safe parameters," she said, checking the screen. "But definitely stronger than before."

They dug flashlights from their packs and ducked into the opening.

"Let's see what ten thousand years of secrets look like," Lawrence said, leading the way inside. After a few paces, the floor sloped downward, and the ceiling rose, allowing them to stand at full height.

"Do you know what technology could have built this?" Glass asked, sweeping her light across the walls. The rock showed no seams, no tool marks, no indication that separate blocks had ever been joined.

"This defies every principle I know," Lawrence replied. They walked together deeper into the tunnel, their Geiger counters maintaining a steady rhythm.

"How far does this go?" Glass whispered, sweeping her flashlight beam ahead.

"I think we're almost there," Lawrence said, as they emerged into a vast chamber—so large that the beams of their flashlights dissolved before reaching the far walls.

"What in the name of ..." Glass said, freezing as she registered the chamber's true size. The space was perfectly spherical, with crystalline veins running through the walls like a circulatory system. Some veins pulsed with a faint glow—amber, violet, a blue so deep it looked almost black.

"Now, this is impossible," Lawrence said, playing his beam across the curved walls. "In all my days, I never imagined."

"I thought we didn't use ..." Glass started, stopping when she saw a vast crystal tower in the center of the chamber. The structure twisted as it climbed from floor to ceiling, branching out at various heights to create platforms and walkways. One such walkway sprouted from the wall a few feet away.

Glass lifted the camera to her eye and hit the shutter several times, trying to capture the size of the chamber.

"This must be the source," Lawrence whispered, striding ahead and stepping onto the walkway. "Whatever this place is, it's been putting out low-level radiation for millennia."

"Are you sure this is ..." Glass said, stepping to the edge and looking down. A deadly drop loomed on either side of the narrow walkway before curving out into the center.

"We can't come all this way and not..." Lawrence said, advancing across the walkway.

The crystalline veins around them pulsed like a slow heartbeat.

Looking ahead of Lawrence's position, Glass noticed that one crystal, a single block around the size of a baseball, shone brighter than the rest. Mounted in some kind of elaborate cradle, it was positioned at the center of the chamber. As Lawrence neared, it glowed more brightly, as though vying for his attention.

"The radiation, it's coming from here," Lawrence said, looking from his Geiger counter to the crystal.

"Are you sure that's a good idea?" Glass said, lowering the camera and looking at the object. She advanced a few steps across the walkway, the perilousness of the drop on either side making her feel dizzy. "Maybe we should go back and suit up."

"It's still well within safe levels," Lawrence said, checking the counter again. He extended a hand, ready to pull the crystal from its cradle.

"But wait," Glass said, her gaze shifting nervously around the chamber. "It might be ..." she stopped mid-sentence, not knowing exactly what she'd intended to say.

"Whatever this place is for, however it's emitting such signatures, this is the key." Lawrence crouched, looking closely at the crystal. "It's glowing, as though it has its own power source."

"We'll come back with a full team," Glass said, "and document it all."

"We can't do that," Lawrence replied. "We may not get another approval. This could be our only chance. And if I'm right about this, there's no telling what we could learn." He extended his arm and closed his fingers around the crystal.

"Lawrence, wait!" Glass said, her hand outstretched.

Lawrence tugged on the crystal, pulling it from the cradle. A deep, bone-rattling rumble erupted from somewhere far beneath them—not just sound, but a vibration that rose through the bedrock. The central tower shook, several of the smaller offshoots crumbling. Dust cascaded from the ceiling like gray snow.

4

"Lawrence!" Glass shouted across the chamber. "What happened?"

Lawrence took a step backward, staring up at the crystal tower. The rumble intensified, transforming from a deep bass note into a roar.

"The whole place, it's destabilizing!" Glass yelled, retreating toward the passageway through which they'd arrived. The camera now hung forgotten around her neck. "We need to get out of here!"

The chamber shook again, more violently this time. Chunks of rock and crystal the size of house bricks fell from the ceiling, smashing the platform or tumbling past them into the void.

One massive stone slammed into the crystal tower, ringing like shattering bells. The collision sheared off a human-sized shard that fell end over end, plummeting directly toward Lawrence who remained stationary, looking trancelike at the object in his hands.

"Professor!" Glass shouted, breaking into a run. She sprinted across the walkway, dodging falling debris, and shoved Lawrence to the ground. The pair fell, sliding across the platform, stopping a few inches from the edge.

The crystal shard slammed into the spot where Lawrence had stood, exploding with the sound of lightning. Razor-sharp fragments scattered in all directions.

"We've got to get out," Glass said, climbing to her feet and pulling Lawrence up. She staggered toward the walkway, the ground shifting like a ship in a storm. She looked up at the towering crystal column, its light pulsing between white and blue.

"I'll go first," Glass said, reaching the narrow walkway and releasing Lawrence's arm.

She stepped out, arms extended for balance. Lawrence followed a step behind, clutching the crystal to his chest with one hand while using the other for balance.

With the sound of a shattering window, the walkway cracked, a jagged line shearing it in two.

Feeling the surface tilt beneath them, Glass charged. She lunged forward, arms outstretched. Her boots slid across the slick crystal as she closed the distance. As the walkway fell from beneath her, Glass bent her legs and sprang for the passageway. She hit hard, fingers clawing at the stone edge, legs dangling over nothing.

Her camera smashed against the rock, the impact tearing it from its strap. It fell into the chasm, clattering to the ground far below.

Glass hauled herself up, ignoring the sharp pain in her ribs, and spun around. The walkway was gone—nothing but glittering fragments falling into the darkness below.

"Lawrence!" she shouted, rushing forward, fearing that Lawrence had fallen with it.

"Help me," Lawrence shouted in reply.

Glass looked down and saw him, clinging to a jutting

crystal spur which projected from the chamber wall a few feet below.

"I think I can reach," Lawrence shouted, his feet scrambling for purchase on the smooth surface. He held the spur with one hand and clutched the crystal to his chest with the other.

"Hold on!" Glass shouted, dropping onto her stomach and leaning over the edge. She extended her arm, stretching toward him. "Drop the crystal and give me your hand!"

Lawrence looked up at her, then down at the crystal against his chest. The spur he clung to cracked, a web of fractures spreading like a spider's web.

"I can't. We need this," he shouted through gritted teeth. "You have no idea—"

"Lawrence, do it now!" Glass roared.

"This could be the—" Lawrence kicked, his boots swinging through the air.

"Forget it!" Glass screamed, stretching so far over the edge that her own balance wavered dangerously. "Grab my hand!"

With his free hand, Lawrence hurled the crystal toward Glass. It sailed through the air and thudded down behind her. He reached out, fingernails scratching at the stone. His boots kicked, scrabbling for any foothold.

"Grab my hand!" Glass said, pushing herself right up to the point of no return.

Their fingertips brushed. She felt the roughness of his palms, the desperate strength in his grip. Their eyes met. His lips moved, forming words she couldn't hear over the roar of collapsing stone.

With an almighty crack, the outcrop onto which Lawrence held disintegrated.

"Take care of it," Lawrence mouthed.

Then his fingers, slick with sweat and dust, slipped away from hers.

Glass squeezed, her nails tearing at his skin. But the weight was too much, the grip too slick.

"No, no, no ..." she gasped, as his hand slipped through hers.

Lawrence fell backward, slowly at first. His body spun once, twice, before the shadows swallowed him completely.

Another chunk of crystal smashed down beside Glass. The impact sent a shockwave through the ground, nearly pitching Glass into the void. She pulled back and scrambled to her feet. She fought for balance as loose rocks skittered past, tumbling down into the void.

"If I don't get out, we're both dead," she shouted, hoping Lawrence could hear, but knowing instinctively that he was gone. She back stepped, supporting herself on the wall of the passage. "I'll get help and come back."

She turned to run, then stopped. The crystal Lawrence had thrown lay by her feet, still pulsing with that strange internal light. For a moment she thought about leaving it, then remembered the fervor in Lawrence's eyes as he tried to save the thing.

"Damn it," she hissed, reaching for the crystal. She paused, her hand hovering nearby as though the thing might burn her. Another tremor shook the chamber, more violent than before. A crack split the ground, almost shaking the crystal from the ledge.

Glass lunged forward and snatched up the crystal. It was heavier than she expected, and warm—almost alive in her hands. For a moment she stood frozen, staring at it, as Lawrence had done. She shook herself into focus, shoved the object into her pocket and bolted into the passageway.

She sprinted, thrown left and right as quakes racked the

structure. Her flashlight beam swung wildly, catching glimpses of the tunnel ahead—walls cracking, dust cascading.

The smooth floor that had seemed so impossibly perfect on the way down was now treacherous with fallen debris. She leaped over a chunk of ceiling that had crashed down, nearly losing her footing on the loose stones beyond it.

A roar bellowed from behind her. The sound grew louder, closer, shaking the floor and walls. A blast of air rushed past her from behind, thick with dust.

The incline seemed steeper than she remembered, her legs burning as she ran.

Nearing the opening, she heard raised voices backed by the urgent winding-up thrum of the helicopter.

Glass launched herself through the opening, her hands outstretched to break her fall. She hit the sunbaked earth, rolling across the rough surface. She lay gasping, every breath filled with grit and dust.

Strong hands grabbed her and forced her back to her feet. Glass looked up as the military men dragged her back to the chopper.

"No, no, we can't leave without Lawrence!" Glass shouted, trying to change direction, but the men dragged her on. "He's down there! We can't leave him!" She pointed back to where a cloud of dust rose from the opening.

The men reached the chopper and bundled her inside. One shoved her into a seat while the other remained outside.

"We've got to go back for him!" Glass screamed, fighting against the man.

"No, we stay here any longer, and we're all dead," the soldier barked as another tremor moved through the ground.

Glass looked around in panic and saw the other scientists already strapped in, their faces pale. The chopper bounced and shook, rotors tilting precariously close to the ground.

"Help me!" she shouted, looking from one person to the next. "We've got to get Lawrence!"

"We can't," a scientist called out, his voice tight with fear. "The whole place is unstable."

"Ready for takeoff," the pilot said, gripping the controls.

The second military man climbed inside and slid the door closed. With a nod to the pilot, the helicopter's turbines increased in pitch, the machine shuddering. The skids lifted from the ground, sand and debris swirling in spirals.

Glass's stomach dropped as the aircraft tilted forward and gained altitude, the ground falling away. Through the window, she watched the collapsed entrance shrink to nothing more than a smudge against the rocky plateau.

The sergeant returned to his seat, leaving Glass to look out through the window. The helicopter turned sharply to the left, engines straining.

Glass slid the crystal fragment from her pocket. Here in the daylight, it looked like an ordinary piece of quartz, but in the chamber, it had been something else entirely. She removed a lead-lined sample container from her pack, slipped the crystal inside and sealed it shut.

"What's that?" one of the scientists said, leaning around his seat to better see the object.

"I don't know," Glass replied, her fingers tightening protectively around the case. "But I'll find out."

5

Isla de la Fortuna, Caribbean Sea. Present Day.

"I'M GOING to find you, and I'm going to kill you," came the voice through Eden's earpiece. She darted around two massive tree trunks, dodging a stream of bullets that hammered through the forest canopy, shredding the under-growth and splintering bark.

"Baxter!" Eden shouted, watching as the line of destruction raced toward her partner.

Baxter ran, moving in a straight line, oblivious to the danger cutting through the jungle behind him.

Eden covered the distance in five quick steps and launched herself into a tackle. She wrapped her arms around Baxter's stomach and drove them both sideways into a tangle of ferns. They hit the ground, rolling through thorny vines as the rounds punched through the jungle overhead.

"I was going to do that anyway," Baxter said, untangling himself from the vines and scanning the undergrowth.

"That's easy to say when you're not full of bullet holes,"

Eden said, jumping to her feet and crashing through a wall of broad leaves. "We need to get to the beach. That's our only way out."

"Just so you know, I never miss twice," came the mocking voice through Eden's earpiece.

Eden turned and saw Baxter pale as their tormentor's words registered. She charged to the left as the surrounding jungle exploded into a shower of shredded plants.

"We need to keep moving," Eden said, ducking beneath a tangle of low-hanging vines. "Stay out of sight."

"You can run, but you can't hide," the voice came again, the tone suggesting this was all one big game.

Eden tucked in behind the thick roots of a tree and paused. The noise of an engine cut through the undergrowth behind them. The sound grew, roaring closer and closer. Turning the other way, she focused on the gentle sound of the sea whispering against the sand.

"That way," Eden said, pointing toward the sound. "If we can get to the beach, we've got options."

"We'll be exposed out there," Baxter said, glancing back toward their pursuer. "At least here we've got some—"

A burst of gunfire whipped through the trees some distance away. The rounds chewed palm trunks and sliced the leaves into ribbons.

"They're trying to flush us out," Baxter muttered, pressing himself against a tree trunk as another burst of gunfire raked the jungle floor.

"They're doing a good job of it too," Eden said, wiping sweat from her eyes. A barrage tore the canopy overhead into confetti. "Right now, we don't have a choice. We stay in here, it's only a matter of time before they find their mark."

Eden turned and shoved her way through a dense tangle of ferns and wild ginger plants. The undergrowth was thick

—broad leaves slapped at her face while thorny vines clawed at her clothes and skin. She shoved aside a curtain of vines, then held it for Baxter to slip through.

"Tick tock, tick tock," the voice came again, followed by a sinister laugh.

Baxter shoved aside the next low-hanging branch, and the pair broke into a steady jog. Eden slipped in front, with Baxter crashing through the vegetation behind her. She scrambled across massive buttress roots extending from a pair of towering ceiba trees and dropped down on the other side. Moving a branch aside, she looked out at the crescent of sand stretching in both directions.

"That's a lot of space with nowhere to hide," Baxter said, dropping beside Eden and looking out at the beach. "What do we do now?"

The whine of the approaching engine erupted from behind them. The chattering of machine guns followed, sending twin streams of lead into the bark above their heads.

They dropped down low, tucking in behind the roots as chips of wood rained down.

An aircraft thundered overhead, flying so low its belly nearly clipped the upper branches. The plane sped out over the beach and into Eden's full view for the first time.

"The Bronco is built for stuff like this," Baxter said, nodding toward the aircraft. "It's a beautiful thing. They've seen action in Vietnam, Central America, and the Philippines. And that pilot knows what they're doing."

"I'd prefer to keep the plane appreciation for those that aren't shooting at us," Eden said, watching the Bronco bank into a curve in preparation for another pass. The aircraft's distinctive twin-boom design gave it an almost insect-like appearance, the pilot clearly visible through the bubble canopy. "You got anything useful to tell me about it?"

"It's a counter-insurgency aircraft," Baxter said, cupping a hand over his eyes. "Purpose-built for hunting ground targets in dense terrain."

"When I said useful, I meant useful to us," Eden said, throwing Baxter a side-eye. The Bronco completed its turn over the water, dropped in altitude, then started back in their direction.

Baxter opened his mouth to speak, but the voice on the comms interrupted him.

"Peek-a-boo, I see you!"

"Take cover!" Eden shouted, launching from their position and charging for a fallen palm tree a little further down the beach. Baxter followed one step behind.

The Bronco thundered across the surf, opening fire.

"Get down!" Baxter shouted, closing the distance between them and shoving Eden to the sand. Bullets thudded down, hammering dual lines through the space they would have charged into. The Bronco roared overhead, the sound of the engines filling Eden's ears.

"Looks like I got you back," Baxter shouted as the aircraft pulled up sharply across the jungle, already turning for another attack run.

"Not for long," Eden said through clenched teeth. "Get behind there." She pointed at the fallen palm tree, its trunk bleached white by the sun. They ran and then crawled in behind the tree.

"Twin M60 machine guns, rocket pods, and enough fuel to keep us pinned here all day," Baxter replied, peering out at the plane. "In the right hands, that thing's as deadly as they come."

The Bronco swung through its turn and leveled out, the

nose pointing directly at their position. Even at this distance, Eden could see the pilot's silhouette, methodically scanning the beach for movement.

"Time to run!" the voice teased as the aircraft accelerated again.

"Have you got anything positive to tell me?" Eden added.

"Urrm," Baxter said, clearly thinking hard. "It's subsonic, top speed maybe two hundred and eighty knots."

"Well, ain't that good to know," Eden said, rolling her eyes. "Lucky I can run at Mach three."

"Do you even know what that means?" Baxter raised an eyebrow.

"Don't change the subject. Do you know anything about the plane that might help us?"

"It's designed for close air support, not air-to-air combat," Baxter said. "That means the pilot has to fly low and slow. If we can force them into a bad position, they'll be vulnerable."

"What kind of bad position?" Eden said, ducking as the Bronco approached again.

Baxter flattened himself against the sand as lead struck their cover. Bullets sliced through the log like a chainsaw, sending splinters the size of knife blades up into the air.

"If we can force them to fly through smoke, debris, or something they can't see through, that'll buy us some time," Baxter said, looking up as the Bronco moved on. "Or get them low enough that they can't maneuver freely."

"You can't stay there all day!" came the voice of the pilot again, clearly reveling in their superiority.

"But without weapons, we'll have to get creative," Eden said, looking at a small jetty some distance away.

The aircraft swung into another turn, the twin turbo-props rising in pitch.

"They're lining up again," Baxter said, watching the maneuver.

"Then we'd better get moving," Eden said, calculating the distances in her mind.

"What? Where?" Baxter said, as the Bronco fired, and the beach erupted in geysers of sand.

"I've got a plan," Eden said. She looked at a buoy bobbing a few hundred feet from the shore, then back at the jetty, and the speedboat tethered to it. "Well, it's not really a plan—"

"But it's the best we've got?" Baxter completed.

6

———

"THAT'S NOT EVEN A PLAN, it's a sequence of worst-case scenarios," Baxter said after Eden had finished her explanation. "You've totally lost your mind this time, you know that?"

"I don't see you coming up with anything better," Eden said, backing up and shooting Baxter a glare. "And let me remind you whose idea this was in the first place." She cupped a hand over her eyes and scanned the coastline.

"This is definitely not the time to dish out the blame," Baxter muttered.

"I think it's exactly the time to be dishing out the—" Eden said, cut short as the Bronco bellowed overhead, bullets chewing through their already damaged cover.

"Well, unless you've got a better idea, I'd say we need to move," Eden said, wiping wood chips from her hair. "This tree isn't going to take much more punishment."

"Running out of time with nowhere to hide!" the pilot mocked, their voice hissing through the comms. The Bronco swung into another turn, the buzz-saw drone of its engines once again increasing in pitch.

"This is madness," Baxter said, eyeing the dense jungle canopy behind them. "Couldn't we just hide in the jungle and wait for them to run out of fuel?"

"Underneath all those bulletproof leaves?" Eden said. "That's not going to end well."

"Good point," Baxter said, peeking up as the Bronco swung slightly to the south, clearly planning to approach at a different angle. The craft dropped in close to the beach, its nose angled toward the shoreline.

"It's time to end this!" the pilot said, breaking into a laugh. "Do you want to surrender?"

"Coming in hot," Eden hissed, tucking in beside the tree trunk.

The plane dropped even closer to the beach, kicking up a blinding cloud of sand in its wake. At the last minute, the Bronco swung to the left, approaching at an angle that would leave them exposed.

"Move!" Baxter shouted, noticing their pursuer's shift in direction. He heaved against the fallen tree, exposing a hollow in the sand. He shoved Eden into the depression and lay on top of her. Bullets threaded another line in the sand right where they'd been.

The Bronco reverberated overhead, climbing slightly before turning out over the water.

"Getting desperate," Eden said, shoving Baxter away.

"Yeah, coming in that low," Baxter said, cupping his hand over his eyes. "That's not procedure—this is personal now."

"No, I mean you," Eden said, elbowing Baxter in the ribs. "Coming in for a cuddle like that. You really choose your moments."

Before Baxter could reply, Eden jumped to her feet and sprinted across the beach.

"Wait, this is madness!" Baxter shouted. He shook his head and then sprang to his feet and followed.

Eden accelerated, kicking up sand as she sped toward the pier. Covering the distance in a few seconds, she leaped onto the jetty. The uneven wooden planks shifted under her feet, threatening to send her sprawling.

"Get that started," she said, pointing at a speedboat tethered to a cleat.

Baxter jumped into the boat and crossed to the controls. He grabbed something from the compartment beneath the console and then turned to the ignition.

"The key's already here," he said, surprised at their first bit of luck in ages.

"Great, let's just hope it starts," Eden said, pulling out her knife and digging the blade into the base of the large fuel tank mounted to the jetty. Liquid poured out, streaming over her hand, then down across the jetty and into the water.

"Get in!" Baxter said, turning the key. The outboard engine, which looked to be held together with string, groaned before dropping into silence.

"Just a minute," Eden said, jerking the knife to the side, extending the hole to increase the flow.

"What do you mean, just a minute? We don't have a minute!" Baxter roared, turning the key again. This time the outboard coughed a plume of smoke into the air. "That really doesn't look healthy."

Clearly noticing their movement, the Bronco's pilot repositioned, bringing the aircraft down low.

"Coming in fast and low!" Baxter shouted, manually pumping fuel into the engine. "They're lining up to finish the job."

Eden crossed the jetty, cut the ropes which held the boat

in place and jumped in. She glanced up from the spreading fuel slick to see the aircraft's shadow racing closer. The pilot had them trapped on an exposed jetty with nowhere to run, and a boat that refused to cooperate.

"Come on!" Baxter yelled, turning the key again. The outboard shook, groaned, and then died.

"Maybe it's time to admit this wasn't such a good idea," Eden said, the Bronco growing larger by the second. The pilot opened fire. Muzzle flashes strobed from the craft's wing-mounted guns.

Baxter hit the starter again. The outboard engine coughed, sputtered, belched another cloud of smoke, then finally roared to life. He shoved the throttle, sending the bow high into the air, and an arc of water out behind them.

Eden grasped the side of the boat as they accelerated away. Gunfire smashed into the jetty, smashing the already weakened planks into woodchips.

"Did you find it?" Eden shouted, staggering toward Baxter.

"Got it!" Baxter said, passing Eden the flare gun he'd fetched from beneath the console.

Eden grinned for what felt like the first time all day. "Slow us down a moment. I've only got one shot at this." She aimed the gun at the growing oil slick.

Baxter killed the power, and the speedboat dropped into a steady drift.

The Bronco plunged lower still, turning the water into spray. Bullets blasted a line of white foam toward the boat.

Eden waited a beat, allowing the Bronco to approach the jetty, then fired. The flare zipped through the air in a streak of red and white, landing squarely in the fuel. Fire erupted across the water, racing along the slick's path. Thick black smoke billowed in a dense column, creating an impenetrable wall directly in the Bronco's flight path.

With no choice, the pilot forced the aircraft into a steep climb. The Bronco's engines screamed with the sudden demand for power, its belly nearly vertical.

"Hit it!" Eden said, spinning around to face Baxter. She braced herself against the console as Baxter shoved the throttle to the max.

Behind them, the Bronco topped out its turn and barreled around for another pass.

"Keep it steady! Head for the buoy!" Eden shouted, pointing at the yellow sphere bobbing in the water.

The Bronco lined up again, now clear of the smoke, which rose into the air in a thick black column.

"We're not going to make it!" Baxter yelled as the distinctive rattle of the aircraft's guns boomed overhead. Bullets thwacked into their wake, missing the stern by a foot or two.

"Almost there!" Eden shouted, her eyes fixed on the buoy now just fifty feet ahead. The large orange hoop on top of the buoy came into view. She reached over the side of the speedboat and seized the ring as the Bronco took aim. She held the ring aloft, waving it at the pilot. A familiar voice boomed through the earpiece.

"Damn it, a second later and I woulda got ya," Nora 'Sierra' Byrd said, as she aborted the maneuver, pulling the Bronco into a climb.

"Yeah, whatever," Eden said, taking a breath for what felt like the first time in minutes.

"Meet you at the beach bar for a sundowner in twenty," Byrd said, swinging the Bronco into a wide arc and powering away.

Eden watched the aircraft retreat, its wings waggling in the pilot's salute.

"Roger that, Captain, good show," Eden said, dropping the hoop into the boat and collapsing onto a seat.

Baxter turned the speedboat and accelerated away. "The things you call fun," he said, wiping his brow. "Next time, I'll just meet you at the bar."

7

Experimental Research Center, Los Alamos, New Mexico. Present Day.

DR. EVA GLASS strode through the corridors of the Experimental Research Center. She glanced down at the screen of the tablet which her assistant held in front of her.

"Why does the President want a report on this?" she said, her gaze rising to her assistant's. "What we do here is above everyone's pay grade."

"I think being nosy is part of the job," the assistant replied, glancing nervously at the device. "What reply shall I provide?"

Glass turned and strode past a group of technicians who knew better than to get in her way. Reaching the elevator at the end of the hallway, she looked into the facial recognition camera. The system processed her identity, and the reinforced steel door slid open.

"Send the usual obfuscation," Glass said, stepping inside the elevator and placing her palm on the secondary biometric scanner. Her assistant followed as the sub-levels appeared on the control panel—floors not listed on any official building plans. Glass selected Sub-Level Nine, and the doors slid closed.

"Like what?" the assistant said as the elevator descended.

"We're a long way from field trials," Glass said, throwing him a glance. "Although don't say that." She thought for a moment. "Tell them that after neutron activation analysis we have carbon-14 anomalies."

"That makes no sense," the assistant said, typing on the tablet's screen.

"Exactly," Glass replied. "The more complicated and nonsensical the better."

"And if they push for more?"

Glass watched the floor indicator drop—sub-level five, six, seven.

"Remind them of Los Alamos Directive 7744," she said, her voice hardening. "Presidential curiosity does not trump national security. Some things are too dangerous for even the Commander-in-Chief to know."

The elevator stopped and the doors opened, revealing an antechamber that looked more like the interior of a spacecraft than a government facility—all brushed steel and softly glowing panels. Two armed guards stood at the corridor's far end, their guns already leveled on the elevator. Recognizing Glass, they lowered their weapons.

"Consider it done," the assistant said, making no move toward the door. Even as one of Glass's closest confidants, this was somewhere he didn't go.

"And invent some kind of security breach and tighten up," Glass said, stepping out of the elevator. "I don't want another visit from Pentagon officials."

"As you require," the assistant replied, glancing at the

schedule. "And Director, you have a briefing with the new recruits. Five minutes ago."

Glass glanced at her watch, scowling as though the digits were purposefully lying to her. "I'll be there soon. Make the coffee strong enough to strip paint, I've got a feeling we're going to need it."

Glass paced down the corridor, stepping between the guards and completing yet another security check. With her access approved, the blast-proof doors swung open. She entered the chamber and crossed to a raised viewing platform. She looked down over the main containment area, then glanced at the screens which displayed real-time readouts of temperature, radiation levels, and electromagnetic field fluctuations. As always, her gaze settled on the circular pool in the center. The water glowed faintly from the underwater lights.

"Morales, status report please," Glass said, speaking into a microphone mounted on the desk.

Morales, her face obscured behind a hazmat visor, turned toward the director. "The power readings are up. It's burning through the containment water at an incredible rate. We're losing hundreds of gallons a day."

Another technician made a micro-adjustment to one of the controls. The readings on one of the screens spiked erratically.

"And the energy output?" Glass said, studying the monitors. The data streams told a story that seemed like science fiction—the water wasn't just being evaporated or consumed, but converted into pure energy at the quantum level.

"Off the scale," Morales said. "We could power this entire facility for a year. But even more interesting, when we added dissolved compounds to the water, it absorbed them too."

"What do you mean?" Glass looked up, confused.

"We tried sodium, potassium, magnesium, and organic compounds, with unchanged results. The crystal harvests whatever it comes into contact with at a molecular level."

"That *is* interesting," Glass said, stepping away from the console. She looked down at the pool which kept the crystal from directly draining the land around them. "Continue monitoring. I have new lambs to indoctrinate."

As the elevator once again reached the ground floor and the doors opened, Glass checked her watch. Making the new recruits wait a few minutes was always a good idea, she thought.

She strode into the conference room without breaking pace, conversations dying mid-sentence. She reached the center of the room and turned to face the group.

"Good morning," Glass said, placing her hands on her hips and eyeing each of the assembled people. Her gaze was met with uncomfortable stares from all except one—a small, middle-aged man sitting at the far end of the table. She knew him to be Dr. Alistair Irons.

"Welcome to the edge of the known universe," Glass said. "You've all signed the necessary documentation, so I will be crystal clear on what we're doing here. The Experimental Research Center exists for one purpose and one purpose only—to ensure that the United States of America remains the most technologically advanced nation on Earth."

She stepped backward and snatched a remote control from the lectern.

"Since 1947, this division has worked tirelessly to guarantee American preeminence in fields that the public can't even comprehend. Every discovery we make, every breakthrough we achieve, serves to protect every man, woman, and child on American soil."

She tapped the remote, and a montage of American historical images played across the screen on the wall behind her—the moon landing, the first atomic test, the Manhattan skyline, Mount Rushmore, troops raising a flag.

"Our founding fathers envisioned a nation that would lead humanity into a brighter future," Glass said, pacing. "At the Experimental Research Center, we make that vision a reality."

The screen shifted to show satellite imagery of various international research facilities.

"Make no mistake—our adversaries are working day and night to surpass us. Your work here isn't merely science—it's a duty of the highest order." She stood straight, almost at attention. "The President and Joint Chiefs have personally authorized your presence here." Glass stepped up to the table and looked around the room again. "Your specialized knowledge and unique talents were not selected by accident. You represent some of the sharpest minds on the planet, and now you will apply those minds in ensuring that when the history of the next century is written, it will be done so in American ink. Questions?" She folded her arms.

"Yes, just one." The bold English accent boomed through the room.

Both the presence of a question and the tone with which it was delivered surprised Glass. She moved her gaze toward the speaker, but didn't let the surprise change her posture.

"Yes, Dr. Irons?" Glass said.

Irons's hands lay beneath the table, his shoulders tensed. He held her gaze with unwavering intensity, the muscles in his jaw working as though wrestling with something.

"How do you justify developing weapons that will kill millions of innocent people?" Irons's voice was steady despite the gravity of his words.

"Dr. Irons, I think you may have misunderstood the nature of our research here." The blood drained from Glass's face, but she fought to keep her expression neutral. "We're developing technologies to improve and protect American lives."

"Protect?" Irons let out a bitter laugh.

Around the table, the other recruits shifted uncomfortably.

"You can't honestly believe that?" Irons asked, slowly rising to his feet. His chair scraped back across the floor with a sound of nails on a chalkboard. He seized a walking cane which had been leaning against the table beside him and took two steps.

"You know that once you create something, it is no longer yours to control." Irons lifted his hands beyond the level of the table, revealing a pistol. He raised the weapon, pointing it directly at Glass. "And I cannot let that happen."

8
———

Eva Glass straightened up and looked at the weapon. At first glance, she thought it was a regular handgun, but then she noticed its odd shape. The weapon was sleek and angular, with flowing lines that seemed almost organic.

Irons raised the pistol another few inches, his finger resting on the trigger. He advanced, using the cane for support.

The other recruits sat frozen, their eyes darting from the director to the weapon and back again.

Irons rounded the table and stopped a few feet from Glass. He leaned his weight on the cane with one hand, holding the weapon with the other.

"You've read my file," he said, his tone surprisingly playful. "You know exactly what I'm capable of."

Glass looked down at the weapon, and then at Irons. Though small in stature, an icy determination burned in his gaze. Glass didn't like it one bit.

"Is this supposed to impress me, Dr. Irons?" Glass said, nodding at the weapon. "What exactly am I looking at?"

"A polyether ether ketone composite, reinforced with

carbon nanotubes," Irons said, a smile flashing across his face. He moved his weight from the cane to his leg. "The barrel's lined with a ceramic-tungsten alloy encased in polymer. It was a labor of love to get it thin enough to avoid detection, but strong enough to withstand the firing pressure."

Glass checked the other recruits in her peripheral vision. They all sat motionless, their attention shifting between her and the weapon. She wondered whether they thought this was some strange initiation test, then wished it was.

"You are clearly an impressive—"

"The mechanism is entirely non-metallic with springs made from compressed carbon fiber," Irons continued, obviously enjoying the subject of his creation. "It fires ceramic-tipped Teflon rounds with polymer casings. They won't take down a whole unit, but let me tell you, it's certainly strong enough to punch through flesh and bone. Especially at this range." Irons tilted his head, indicating the gap between them.

"Impressive engineering," Glass said. Although her voice remained impassive, her folded arms tightened across her chest. "It's particularly impressive that you got it past our scanners. As I'm sure you know, they don't simply search for metals, but anything with—"

"You have a multi-spectral imaging system," Irons interrupted.

A prickle of irritation moved through Glass, the disrespect of an interruption possibly affecting her more than the actual danger.

"The system processes over fifty thousand data points, identifying anomalies down to five hundred microns in size," Irons continued, shifting his weight again.

"Indeed," Glass said. "It's clear that you have very detailed information on our security protocols. This is a serious leak."

"Whilst that is true, the leak is not your greatest concern right now," Irons said, moving the gun from side to side as though calling Glass back to the issue in hand. "But as you've asked, I used a patch that mimics the standard reading of skin, while masking anomalies beneath. The components came in separately—individually they're harmless, but together, *boom*." A smile flashed across his lips.

"And what do you want from this show of ingenuity, Dr. Irons?" Glass said, speaking slowly. "Your file indicates no political extremism, no concerning psychological—"

"I know what you're messing with down on Sub-Level Nine," Irons said, his voice hardening. "Once something that powerful is out in the world—"

"I don't know what you've been told," Glass said, the tremor in her voice betraying her. "But I've never heard of Sub-Level Nine. I fear you've been watching too many science fiction films."

Irons let out a harsh laugh. "Let me jog your memory. I'm talking about the crystal you recovered from Mauritania ten years ago. The one that produces energy in ways you don't understand and has a molecular structure the like of which you've never seen before."

"How could you possibly—" Glass started, Irons's words slapping her like physical blows.

"Let us not concern ourselves with that," Irons said, cutting Glass off with a shake of the weapon.

The other recruits stirred uneasily.

"Suffice to say, I know," Irons continued. "It is you who has no idea what forces you're playing with." His voice dropped to the whisper of someone talking in a holy place.

"Humankind has no business playing with such things." His finger tightened on the trigger. "You're playing God, and it has to—"

The doors hissed open, and six figures dressed in tactical gear flooded into the room. They fanned out, assault rifles raised.

"We do what is necessary to keep our country safe," Glass said, internally breathing a sigh of relief at the security team's arrival. Her posture remained as rigid as it had been before. "That includes fitting our facility with hidden cameras, monitored by a high-powered computer system, which is trained to recognize situations like this the moment they occur." Glass took a step back and leaned against the desk. "I'm afraid, Dr. Irons, you never stood a chance."

Surprisingly, the grin on Irons's lips remained. Then, even more surprisingly, it widened into a full smile.

"Oh, I know about your system," Irons said, lowering the gun. "In fact, my employer and I relied on the automated security alert, and the team of operatives who would respond." He glanced at his watch. "They took a little longer than usual, wouldn't you say?"

"Stop this madness," Glass said, her voice rising for the first time. "Take this man to the containment cell. We need to find out where he got his information before we hand him over to the authorities. I fear you've enjoyed your last day of freedom."

The security operators in the room remained motionless, their tactical gear and face masks making them look more like machines than men. Then, as if responding to some invisible signal, they pivoted, aiming their weapons at Glass.

"I gave you a direct order!" Glass roared, her composure ebbing away. "Stop wasting time and take—"

"I'm afraid you've misread the situation, Director," Irons said. "Do you really think I would get this far and not know the workings of your security system?"

Glass took a step back, crashing into the lectern. The operatives remained motionless, guns raised.

"I didn't just know about your security protocol, I was counting on it." Irons threw his plastic gun onto the table, where it broke into three. "Radio," he said, gesturing to one of the guards. The man unclipped a radio from his vest and passed it across.

Glass glanced at the gun on the table, which now appeared as harmless as a child's toy.

"We have the director. Secure the perimeter and initiate a lockdown," Irons said, speaking into the device.

"This is impossible," Glass said, locking eyes with Irons, who seemed to have grown in stature in the last few seconds. "There is no way to bypass our biometric scanning technology—"

"There is just one," Irons said, clipping the radio to his belt and shifting his weight again. "A genuine code red, flagged by the central system. It wouldn't be much of an emergency if the men here had to wait to be scanned in, would it?" Irons said, amusement lacing his tone.

"Lockdown activated," came a voice from the radio.

Red lights mounted above the door flashed, and grills dropped across the windows.

"You'll never get away with this," Glass said, the gravity of the situation finally dawning. "You're in the center of one of the most secure sites in the country. The whole place will be surrounded within minutes."

"As you know, Director, this facility is a black box." Irons leveled a finger at Glass. "That, I suppose, is the problem with keeping secrets."

9
____

Isla de la Fortuna, Caribbean Sea. Present Day.

"THIS PLACE IS SOMETHING ELSE." Eden looked from the sun which was now an orange semi-circle on the horizon, down to her glass which contained a healthy measure of Byrd's Barton 1792 bourbon. Half a mile out to sea, the *Balonia* bobbed on a gentle swell.

"It ain't bad at all," Byrd said, settling into the seat between Eden and Baxter. "It's not been an easy ride, though. A few years in the making, planning and building." She flicked a thumb at the collection of buildings behind her. "We've got accommodation, cooking facilities, and of course the hangar over there. Your support has helped a little bit too." Byrd turned her usually steely gaze on Eden.

When they'd first met, Byrd had been eking out a living with a small flight and parachuting school an hour's drive north of Mexico City. As they grew to trust her, Eden realized that such a place, if positioned on the coast, would provide excellent cover as a stopping off point for the *Balonia*. It was private enough that their comings and goings would remain unnoticed, and with Byrd flying frequently to the mainland, anything they needed was a phone call away. With some investment, and pulling some strings, they'd set Byrd up with what appeared to be the perfect site.

"It was nothing," Eden said, breaking off the gaze. "How are the neighbors?" She nodded at the adjacent island which lay across a small expanse of water.

"Had some trouble with them recently," Byrd said, lifting her glass for another sip. "But nothing I can't deal with. They saw the sharp end of my—"

"Remind me not to upset you," Baxter said.

"You couldn't upset me if you tried, Captain," Byrd cooed, lips curling into a flirtatious smile. "By the way, if you ever feel the need to further hone those aerial skills of yours, you know where to come."

Eden sipped the bourbon and was about to swallow when she saw Baxter turn beetroot red. He slipped down in the chair, his shoulders tight, clearly embarrassed by Byrd's tone.

Eden clamped her mouth shut as an involuntary laugh made its way up her throat. She tried to swallow, but the whiskey wouldn't go down.

"I'll ... I'll bear that in mind, thank you," Baxter said, raising the glass in an attempt to hide behind it.

"Stay as long as you want," Byrd continued, laying a hand on Baxter's forearm. "I'll keep you busy, that's for sure."

"That's a very kind offer ... but ... I'm ..." Baxter's voice trailed away, his face now a shade of purple.

Eden tensed her jaw, the bourbon burning her palate. The laugh tickled her throat, escaping one hiss at a time.

"You know what these old girls are like," Byrd said, removing her hand from Baxter's arm and adjusting her hair, which she wore in a fifties-style beehive. "There's always a lot of greasing that needs doing."

Eden put the glass down and covered her face, trying to hide her grin.

"Lemmie say this, it takes experienced hands to get 'em to their best," Byrd continued.

"Yes ... I can imagine ..." Baxter said, his gaze locked on the horizon, as though concentrating hard might allow him to teleport there.

Eden turned away from the pair, tears of hilarity streaming down her cheeks.

"You know," Byrd said, pausing for a sip of the bourbon, "it's rare to find a young man who appreciates a classic." She glanced at Baxter. "All the young'uns now just want speed. They don't care about the curves of the classic models."

Baxter muttered something that could have been agreement, before gulping down a healthy measure of the bourbon.

Eden tittered, wiping her eyes. The whiskey burned her mouth, the laughter still preventing her from swallowing.

"There's so much more to the vintage bodywork," Byrd continued. "I promise, once you get your hands on it, you really feel it, and you'll never look back."

Eden's shoulders shook as the laugh made its way through her diaphragm. She forced a breath, swallowed the whiskey, and roared with laughter. The sound came from her belly, but soon occupied her entire body.

"Well, I dunno what's ticklin' you," Byrd said, folding her arms and shooting Eden a sideways glance.

"The vintage body—" Eden tried to explain, but descended into inaudible giggling.

Byrd raised an eyebrow. "I don't see you laughing at my vintage body work all those times it's saved your skinny—"

"I'm sorry," Eden stuttered, wiping her eyes. "It's just the stuff you say, it sounds so provocative."

"Well, li'l lady." Byrd leaned forward and placed a finger on her lips, the gesture making her look like a seductive fifties pin-up. "I'm talkin' to the captain here about our mutual love of planes. I've no idea how that can be misconstrued."

"When you suggested I got my hands on your vintage body work, that did sound a little over friendly," Baxter said, his voice barely above a whisper.

Eden roared with laughter anew, and Byrd gasped.

"Well I never," Byrd said, launching to her feet and eyeing Eden and Baxter like naughty children. "You pair are somethin' else." Byrd snatched up their glasses and stomped over to the bar, which was set up in a small structure a few feet away. A colorfully painted sign hung above the door— *Byrd's Beach Bar. You can't buy happiness, but a large scotch helps.*

Byrd generously sloshed at least a double measure in each glass before returning.

Eden took a few deep breaths to control herself then accepted the glass.

"This beach bar is great," Eden said, finally recovering. She nodded at the wooden structure, countless bottles glinting from within.

"A non-negotiable," Byrd said. "It was the first part of my vision." She lifted the glass as though the liquid inside *was* the vision. "The people coming here are on a holiday, of sorts. They're gonna pay a lot of money for it anyway."

"Do they actually *pay* for what you did to us today?" Baxter said, glancing almost reluctantly at Byrd.

"That was so cool," Eden said, tilting her head up to

catch the sun. "Although people tend to do that to us for free."

"Yep. There's a growing market for things like that," Byrd said. "The more bonkers the experience, the more they'll pay."

"Some people have too much money and not enough fun," Eden said.

The sun's bottom edge dipped beneath the horizon, sending a column of gold skittering across the water.

"And that's where I come in," Byrd said, nodding at the hangar. "This place has gotta earn its keep."

"You weren't using live rounds though, right?" Eden said, shooting Byrd a look. "There were points back there where it actually felt real."

"That would be tellin'," Byrd said, gifting Eden one of her trademark winks. "But suffice to say, I got some friends in the movie business. They helped me with some of the effects."

"It felt realistic," Baxter said, shaking his head.

"You weren't in danger," Byrd said, winking at Baxter. "I wanted you back in one piece."

Baxter flushed red, and Eden giggled again.

"I dunno why you're laughing, li'l missy." Byrd turned her gaze to Eden. "You weren't in danger, until you started setting fire to stuff."

"Sorry about that," Eden shrugged, gazing out at the *Balonia*. Lights blazed in a few of the windows now, posing a subtle reminder that work was never far away. "You know me, I couldn't help myself."

"That I do," Byrd replied, taking a sip. "Hey, did I tell you I'm getting a Supermarine Spitfire next month?" Although Byrd was talking to them both, the conversation was clearly angled toward Baxter. "Imagine being chased down by the superstar of the Battle of Britain? Already sold out two months solid!"

Eden tuned out of the conversation, letting herself relax. Since their recent work in Cambodia, it had been a long trip across half the world. Whilst she'd enjoyed getting her training routine back, and focusing on her stewardship of the Council, the *Balonia* had become something of a luxury prison. So, when they realized they'd be passing Nora 'Sierra' Byrd's new flight school in the Caribbean, she couldn't wait to stop by.

"Original or replica?" Baxter said, leaning forward, his interest piqued.

"Restored original," Byrd said. "Still has the classic Merlin 66 engine. When that thing fires up, you'll feel it in your chest."

"No way!" Baxter said. "There can't be more than thirty airworthy Spitfires left in the world."

"Thirty-four at last count," Byrd said. "How my good friend Bourdell managed to get his greasy little mitts on this one, I have no idea. He's flying it down here himself. If you're around, Captain, I'll take you for the ride of your life."

"You just can't help yourself, can you?" Eden said, glancing at Byrd, then at Baxter, before the three of them descended into a fit of laughter.

10

―――――――

"Now, Director, I know that a tour of the facility is on our agenda today. I suggest we do that now." Irons nodded toward the door and lifted the radio to his lips. "All staff to the conference room."

The doors hissed open, revealing a huddle of twenty or so people, surrounded by more gun-toting operatives. Glass recognized her team, many still in their hazmat suits. She made a quick assessment of the assembled people—it looked as though Irons's men had successfully rounded up everyone.

"Inside," Irons indicated, flicking his wrist toward the door. Glass's team hesitated, looking from the armed men to their director.

"This will be over soon," Glass said, attempting to sound confident. "Site security are already en route. Whatever these people want, they don't stand a chance."

A gunman smashed the butt of his weapon into the back of one of the older technicians, who crumpled to the floor, a clipboard still clutched against his chest. As though snapping awake, Glass's team rushed inside, gasping and sobbing. The operatives inside the room positioned themselves around the perimeter to better watch their captives.

"Report," Irons said, lifting the radio to his lips.

"All clear," came an Irish-accented reply almost immediately. "Facility locked down."

"Good," Irons said, clipping the radio to his belt and accepting a tablet from one of his men. He swiped the screen, and the conference room doors closed and locked with a mechanical click.

"No one comes out of here without my authorization," Irons said, pointing his cane toward the sealed conference room.

Two guards positioned themselves facing the door, clearly ready to fire if necessary.

"This way," Irons said, leading the way down the corridor, followed by Glass, and six armed men. They reached the main elevator, and Irons beckoned Glass across. "This is your moment to shine, director. I know you are one of the only people capable of taking us to Sub-Level Nine."

"What? There is no—" Glass started, interrupted by a gun jabbing into her back.

Irons placed a hand on Glass's arm. Although the touch was light, the firm squeeze carried a threat.

"Fine," she said, stepping up to the control panel. "But it's not what you think. We're still in the early—"

"Spare me the official nonsense," Irons said. "I know exactly what you're doing, and I know exactly what that thing is capable of."

Glass completed the authorization procedure, and the doors slid open. They shuffled inside, and Glass sent them down to Sub-Level Nine.

The elevator eased to a stop and the doors parted. As protocol dictated, the guards stationed in the antechamber raised their weapons at the elevator. Recognizing Glass, they hesitated, giving Irons's mercenaries just long enough to fire. Muzzle flashes strobed and shots boomed in the enclosed space.

The guards reeled backward, slamming into the wall before falling to the floor.

"Open it," Irons said, pointing his cane at the doors that led through to the chamber.

Choking back nausea at the sight of her fallen colleagues, Glass did what Irons instructed. The blast proof doors hissed open, revealing the main chamber beyond.

Irons led the way through, moving as though he already knew every inch of the space.

"A very impressive operation," he said, reaching the viewing platform and gazing into the pool, the illuminated water shimmering. "It's even more impressive that you managed to keep it a secret ... almost, anyway." He grinned at the director.

"You realize, whatever you think you know about our work here, you've only scratched the surface," Glass said, the gunmen shoving her to the railing alongside Irons. "This place isn't kept secret to hide it from our enemies—it's a secret to protect everyone."

"Save the warnings, Director." Irons placed a hand on the railing and turned his attention to one of the screens. "The question isn't whether we understand the risks. The question is whether exploring such an object is in humankind's best interest. Did you ever stop to think about that?" Irons turned and met Glass's gaze.

The technicians continued working at their monitoring stations around the chamber, so absorbed in their tasks that they hadn't seen the new arrivals.

"What do you know about making such choices?" Glass

replied, forcing as much authority into her voice as she could muster.

"I know that in all of recorded human history, the concentration of ultimate power has never ended well," Irons said, his gaze following the chains from the ceiling-mounted lifting system, down into the water. "Just to think, that thing down there could be the most dangerous object in the world. If only you could work out how to use it." He glanced at one of the screens showing a video feed from the bottom of the pool where the crystal hung in its specially designed cradle. Irons pulled a handkerchief from inside his jacket and dabbed at his forehead. "It's ... well ... beautiful."

"What do you want with it?" Glass said.

"First, I have a small task to perform with it, then it'll be put somewhere it can never be found again."

"And waste all the potential we have here." Glass pointed at the pool. "This crystal is revolutionizing the way we think about—"

"Who appointed you the guardian of the world?" Irons said, levelling his finger at Glass as though it were a weapon. "The atomic bomb promised to end all wars and yet here we are, with thousands of warheads scattered across the globe. What makes you believe this, whatever it teaches you, will be any different?"

Before Glass could answer, Irons slammed his cane against the railing several times. The sound rang out across the vast chamber like a bell.

The technicians looked up, their fingers freezing at the keyboards.

"Attention," Irons bellowed. "Step away from your stations and move to the center of the chamber. Hands visible at all times."

Glass recognized Morales moving toward a hidden

alarm. A gunman swung his rifle toward her—not quite aiming, but the threat was clear.

"Security won't help you," Irons said, glancing at Glass. "Tell them to cooperate." The rifle barrel jabbed into Glass's back once more.

"For now, Dr. Irons is in charge," Glass said.

"For now," Irons said jovially. "How very funny you are, Director."

The technicians moved, their arms raised as instructed.

"Excellent," Irons said, starting down the stairs toward the pool. Another nudge told Glass that she was supposed to follow.

"Tell me, Director, what are we looking at here?" Irons said, reaching the edge of the pool and peering into the water.

"I thought you already knew all our secrets," Glass said, as Irons's men herded the technicians together in the middle of the space.

"Humor me," Irons said, throwing Glass a smile. "I want to hear it in your words."

"Within this containment device is a crystal recovered from beneath the Sahara over a decade ago," Glass said, stepping up to the railing which surrounded the pool. Blue light pulsed hypnotically beneath the water. The ethereal glow washed over Irons's face, leaching the color from his skin and deepening the lines around his eyes.

"And what has it taught you so far?" Irons said.

Glass remained quiet for a moment, watching the light pulse beneath the surface. "That everything we think we know about the fundamental nature of reality is ... provisional. That crystal doesn't follow any of the normal rules. Conservation of energy, causality, even its molecular structure is ... unusual."

"Meaning?" Irons leaned forward, gripping his cane tighter.

"With it, we are understanding things that weren't possible before," Glass said, her voice somewhere between wonder and dread. "Things that, quite frankly, shouldn't be possible."

"You're being deliberately vague, Director," Irons said, shaking his head. "Deliberately vague."

"Unfortunately, I am not," Glass said, looking up at Irons. "The crystal seems to operate outside our mainstream understanding of physics. But from what you've said already, I think that somehow, you know this."

"I have my sources," Irons said, gazing into the water like a man obsessed. "You recovered the crystal yourself, by hand?"

"That is correct," Glass said, once again shocked by Irons's information.

"If it's not dangerous, why keep it in the pool?"

"Director, don't answer," one of the technicians shouted. Glass turned and saw Morales step forward. "Don't tell him what we've learned."

Two operatives stepped forward, their guns aimed at the young woman's head. Morales stood firm, a fire burning in her eyes.

"Young lady, while your loyalty is very impressive, I'm afraid you've been playing for the wrong team." Irons smiled sweetly at Morales, then turned back to Glass. "Carry on, or your star pupil there gets a bullet in the brain."

Glass swallowed, her mouth suddenly feeling like the desert from which the crystal came. "The crystal seems to, how can I explain this, absorb energy from its surroundings. That's how we think it powers itself. Every time we investigate it, scan it, look at it, that happens. If it weren't for the water and the lead-lined tank, it would pull its energy from the land or even us." She gestured at the surrounding people.

One of Irons's operatives took an involuntary step back as though the few inches would make all the difference.

"But for limited periods of time, while the crystal is not active, it's perfectly safe to handle," Glass added.

"That's impossible," Irons said, leaning across the railing, the blue light washing his face again.

"We don't use that word in this department," Glass said. "As a dearly departed friend of mine once said, we look at the evidence and draw our own conclusions. And there it is." She pointed down into the pool.

"Amazing," Irons said.

"I am confident that in the next few years we can use it to—"

"Create the deadliest weapon in the history of humankind," Irons said, turning his gaze on Glass. His voice dropped to a malevolent whisper. "He who fights monsters should be careful lest he thereby become a monster."

"And if you gaze long into an abyss, the abyss also gazes into you," Glass replied, recognizing the quote. "Nietzsche. Though I suspect we have different interpretations of who the monster is in this scenario."

"Do we?" Irons smiled grimly. "You've spent years staring into that abyss, Director. Tell me—what has it shown you about yourself?"

The blue-white pulse from the depths lit Irons's hollow cheeks into skull-like shadows, and his eyes into dark pits.

"In this facility, we explore the fundamental forces of the universe. It's true that those forces can be used to create or destroy, which is why I will make sure that our discoveries are used for good."

"And there is our fundamental disagreement," Irons replied, gazing once again into the depths. "You believe that because you created it, or discovered it, it belongs to you. But, once you unleash whatever power this thing has, it is a force unto itself. At that point it is no longer yours to control." He paused, glancing hungrily at the pulsing blue light. "Prometheus didn't get to decide who received fire, Director. The moment he stole it from the gods, it belonged to all humanity."

The blue-white pulse seemed to intensify, as if responding to the words.

"But this isn't fire," Glass said, her voice barely above a whisper. "In the wrong hands, this is the power to unravel the very fabric of existence."

"Perhaps the abyss has been gazing into both of us," Irons said softly. "The question is which of us has become the monster—the creator who fears her creation, or the liberator who covets it." A beat of silence passed through the chamber, broken only by the distant beeping of a machine.

"Now," Irons said, looking at the technicians as though sharing a great idea, "let's bring the crystal to the surface."

11

———

"But… we can't do that," Morales said, her gaze moving from Irons to Glass. "Containment protocols require that—"

"Protocols written by people who are no longer in control of this facility!" Irons roared, driving his cane into the concrete. He snapped his fingers, and the men pointing their guns at Morales stepped closer. "Tell me, what is your name?"

Glass nodded to indicate that Morales should answer.

"It's Lucia, Lucia Morales."

Irons staggered closer to the young technician and peered up at her, his short stature forcing him to crane his neck.

"Well, Miss Morales," Irons said, placing both hands on top of the cane and leaning forward in an apparent attempt to take the weight off his leg. "It's all very well, admirable even, for you to consider protocols when weapons are pointed at you. Many people would not be so brave." Irons cast a glance at the rest of the technicians cowering behind the young woman. "But allow me to speak openly, you are now in a situation that your protocols never accounted for."

"The protocols are very clear," Morales said. "The safety of the—"

"Nonsense," Irons said, shifting his weight again. "Look around you. We are the only people here. As such, we must act as we see fit."

"I'm not..." Morales started, looking at the director for reassurance.

"For now, we must do what Dr. Irons requires," Glass said, disgust lacing her tone.

"Thank you, director, but I would like Miss Morales to understand," Irons said, rubbing a hand across his chin, "Allow me to lay a decision before you. You have experience operating the retrieval system, yes?" He waved a hand toward the pulleys and chains that ran down into the pool.

"Yes, I have," Morales said. "It's a complicated system with—"

"Excellent," Irons said, grinning. "Then I suggest you do that, or I'll have my men try to figure it out." Irons nodded toward the gun-wielding brutes. "They are good at operating guns, very good in fact, but their experience has its limits."

Morales's gaze flicked to one of the men, his rifle in a grip that would probably smash the retrieval system's control unit to pieces before he got it to work.

"Fine. I've operated the system many times," Morales said, stepping forward. "I'll need Dr. Henderson to monitor the electromagnetic field generators throughout the entire process." She pointed at another of the technicians, an older man with frameless spectacles.

"Very well," Irons said, looking at Morales for a long moment then turning to face the older technician. "You will assist Miss Morales. But understand this—any attempt at sabotage, any disruption of the process, and you won't survive the day."

Sharing a nervous glance, Morales and Henderson moved to the control terminal at the side of the pool. Irons instructed two guards to follow them, taking up a position where they could watch every keystroke and monitor readout.

Morales tapped the console, and the winching system, which ran on a pair of steel gantries, hummed to life. She pressed several buttons, engaging the hydraulics and powering up the electric motors.

Glass took a half-step backward. Irons and his men didn't notice—all focused on Morales and the winching system. She cast a glance over her shoulder at an emergency stop button on the wall some distance behind her. Hitting the button would cause a shutdown, stopping all operations in the chamber for several hours.

Morales pushed a lever on the terminal, and with a deep mechanical clunk, the chain began spooling upward.

Moving as slowly as possible, Glass took another half-step. When no one looked her way, she took another, then eyed the button again.

"That's it," Irons breathed, watching the chain with a reverence usually reserved for miracles. "Bring it up slowly."

The winch motor settled into a low, grinding hum.

Glass peered down into the water, the glow intensifying as the crystal approached the surface. Realizing time was short, she swung around and charged for the button.

She made two strides before the first gun howled. A line of sparks erupted from the wall ahead of her. Automatic fire ripped through the air, and the button disintegrated with a flash and a shower of plastic shrapnel.

Glass threw herself sideways, hitting the floor hard

enough to drive the air from her lungs. She bellycrawled behind a computer terminal as rounds glanced off the floor around her.

"Enough!" Irons roared, his voice cutting through the chaos. The shots ceased, their reports echoing away. In the silence, Glass realized the winch had stopped too.

"Continue," Irons said, snapping his fingers.

The crane whirred again, drawing the crystal ever closer to the surface.

"I warned you about desperate acts, Director," Irons said, leaning forward on his cane. "I realize it must be challenging to concede that you are no longer in charge. But I implore you, it is better for us all if you accept the inevitable."

"And what is the inevitable?" Glass said, peering from her makeshift cover.

"That there is nothing you can do to stop me," Irons said. "I have already won."

"Just a few more feet," Morales said, her tone as professional as ever. "Slowing the motor to minimize impact."

The winch's pitch dropped to a deep, laboring groan. Through the water, the crystal's glow intensified, casting patterns of light across the ceiling.

Irons looked down at the object like a medieval alchemist finally seeing the philosopher's stone.

"You understand how dangerous this could be," Glass shouted as the first part of the assembly broke the surface. "This isn't a weapon—it's a key to something we don't yet understand."

The high-tech cradle broke the surface—gleaming black metal, festooned with cables and monitoring sensors.

"Oh, I know that," Irons said, sounding as though the whole thing were a joke. He shifted his attention from the cube to Glass. "And I know exactly what I'm going to do with it. Something I've needed to put right for a long time."

"Put right?" Glass said to herself, slightly thrown by the strange turn of phrase.

Irons gasped as the crystal itself emerged from the water. Although only partly visible inside the cradle, the object commanded attention—pulsing with that impossible light—not quite blue, not quite white.

Irons staggered forward, his cane forgotten, and leaned out over the railing. His mouth hung slightly open, and for a moment, the calculating mastermind was gone—replaced by a childlike wonder.

"Bring it to me," Irons shouted, his arms extended as though reaching for a long-lost love.

The crane's motor cut out, and the crystal stopped rising. It hung a few feet above the surface of the water, swinging gently on its chains.

"Move it here, now!" Irons snapped, glaring at Morales.

The young technician worked the controls, and the crane started rolling along the gantries. The crystal swung gently, water dripping back into the pool.

"Careful now," Irons instructed, his voice unnaturally calm.

Morales nodded, making microscopic adjustments to the crystal's trajectory.

Glass ducked back down and took a moment to assess the situation. If Irons were able to remove the crystal from the facility, the possibilities could be catastrophic. He could take it anywhere—to a rival nation desperate for the ultimate leverage, a terrorist organization willing to pay billions, or worse, to some hidden facility where he could experiment with forces that shouldn't be unleashed.

Glass silently cursed herself. She should have left the

damned thing in the desert where it belonged. Watching the crystal swinging gently, she spotted a control panel mounted beside the pool. The words *Emergency Containment Flush* were printed in bold letters above a red button. Next to the sign, a small oxygen mask sat in a glass case, for use in an emergency evacuation.

"Just a bit closer!" Irons shouted.

The motor whirred again, inching the crystal and all its terrible secrets toward a madman whose intentions clearly weren't noble. Each click of the chain felt like a countdown to catastrophe.

Glass looked from the control panel to the crystal, now suspended mere feet from Irons's outstretched hands. His fingers twitched with anticipation, like a pianist about to strike the first note of a symphony.

A plan crystallized in her mind—desperate, probably suicidal, but the only option left.

12

———

GLASS EXPLODED from her hiding spot, covered the open ground in seconds, and hit the containment flush button. Klaxons wailed and warning lights pulsed. She snatched the oxygen mask from its case and pulled it down over her nose and mouth.

Not waiting for Irons's instruction, the gunmen spun toward her, rifles already rising. Muzzle flashes strobed, and bullets screamed across the chamber. Concrete exploded from the wall to her left in a spray of dust and shrapnel. A monitor to her right disintegrated in a shower of sparks and plastic.

"Stop shooting! The crystal!" Irons roared, his voice cutting through the noise like a whip crack. He waved both hands maniacally.

"Containment flush initiated," announced the facility's computer.

"Stop her!" Irons shouted, his attention diverted from the crystal.

Glass climbed onto the railing and jumped for the crystal. She sailed through the air above the pool, arms outstretched. For a terrifying moment, she thought she'd misjudged the distance as the cradle swung away from her.

Several of the guards closed in, their arms outstretched, trying to grab at her.

The sound of gushing water echoed through the chamber as emergency drains swung open at the bottom of the pool. The floor shuddered as thousands of gallons flowed out of the pool.

Glass extended her arms out as far as she could, unfurling her fingers to the maximum. Just as she thought she'd missed the cradle, her fingers caught the edge of the housing, the impact nearly shredding skin. The momentum sent the whole assembly into a sideways swing, the chains groaning under the sudden movement.

"No!" Irons roared, gripping the railing. He snatched the sidearm from one of his men and opened fire, clearly not thinking that his own bullets might damage the prize.

Glass hit the housing's release mechanism, and the crystal came free in her hands. It felt heavier than she remembered, having not held it like this for years. It pulsed with that same warmth, though, a strangely pleasant sensation that seemed to pass through her skin.

She glanced back at Irons, who was struggling to take aim. Clutching the crystal to her chest, she jumped into the pool.

With the water level already around the halfway mark, what should have been a controlled dive became a terrifying plunge. The surface churned and bubbled as the emergency systems pulled the coolant away at an alarming rate.

Glass straightened out, her body hitting the surface like a hammer on stone. She pulled the crystal in tight against her body, the impact threatening to tear it from her grip. She kicked down, trying to put as much distance between herself and the shooters as possible.

Muffled gunfire roared from above, Irons now clearly having instructed his men to fire. Shots whizzed sluggishly through the water in front of her, creating a strange vapor trail before altogether losing momentum and drifting to the bottom.

Glass kicked, fighting to orient herself as the current strengthened. The drainage port loomed ahead—a black tunnel that would either be her escape or her tomb.

The rubber mask clung tight as she tried to breathe. It was built for smoke or gas leaks — not for staying alive underwater.

Pushing the doubts from her mind, she streamlined her body and used the flow of water to conserve energy. The current strengthened as she neared the port. The heavy grate that would normally prevent anything from entering or leaving the pool had retracted with the emergency flush protocol.

The moment before the drain sucked her inside, Glass looked up and over her shoulder. High above her, she saw the blurred shapes of Irons's men. Muzzle flashes strobed like deadly lightning. The sound of the gunfire muffled and then disappeared altogether as the powerful flow pulled her into the drainage tunnel.

Glass kicked, the current bouncing her around inside the tunnel like a pinball.

The light from the chamber faded, plunging her into total darkness. The thunderous roar of the speeding water bellowed in her ears, totally disorienting her.

Her lungs burned as the breathing device struggled against the pressure. The tunnel twisted, slamming her against the wall and spinning her around.

Surrendering to the current, she tucked her arms in close to her body and let the system pull her through. Her lungs screamed for oxygen, the burn in her chest intensifying with each passing second. As panic clawed at the edges of her consciousness, the duct widened, emptying into a larger chamber. Here, she knew, the emergency system activated its second phase—massive, compressed air injectors which forced the water to ground level.

The first blast of compressed air caught her by surprise. Instead of horizontal movement, she shot through a vertical shaft with incredible force. The water and air mixture bounced her from side to side as she powered up. The pressure in her ears built to excruciating levels—humming and hissing.

The breathing apparatus seemed to have stopped working completely now. Her oxygen-deprived brain screamed with increasing desperation—spots danced in her vision, and a strange tingling spread through her hands and feet. The sound of the roaring water faded, replaced by a high-pitched ringing right inside her skull.

Her chest burned, each moment a battle against the growing urge to simply open her mouth and inhale the rushing water. The boundary between panic and surrender thinned to a hair's breadth.

The vertical shaft suddenly curved. The compressed air drove her forward, the combination of water and air reducing friction as she shot through the final stretch of the system.

Then, just like a dream, a spot of daylight appeared ahead. The circular opening grew larger with each passing second. Glass fought to remain conscious, her lungs burning beyond anything she'd ever experienced. The tube narrowed at the exit, concentrating the force of the expulsion into a jet. With a final surge of speed, she flew from the spout. For a breathtaking moment, she was airborne, sailing twenty feet above the surface of the containment lake. The sudden brightness blinded her after the darkness of the tunnels. She dragged the mask from her face and gulped desperately, filling her lungs before gravity reclaimed her once again. She took a moment to orient herself and prepare for impact.

Below, the containment lake stretched out—a concrete-lined basin, designed to safely hold the contaminated coolant until it could be processed. The surface rushed up to meet her, the impact knocking the hard-earned breath from her body.

She plunged deep, the crystal nearly tearing from her grip. She kicked frantically, waterlogged clothes working against her. With desperate determination, she tucked the crystal against her body with one arm and used the other to claw toward the surface. Her legs burned with effort, each kick weaker than the last. Black spots bloomed across her vision. The moment before her body betrayed her, forcing her mouth open to inhale air that wasn't there, she broke the surface.

She gasped and spluttered, treading water as best she could. Once her breathing had recovered, she paddled to the side of the pool and crawled out.

She lay gasping for a few seconds, then rolled over and sat up. She looked back at the facility—a nondescript concrete structure nestled against the hillside half a mile away. No alarms howled, and no guards ran her way.

Inside, she knew Irons was probably screaming orders, organizing search teams.

Glass struggled to her feet, water streaming from her

clothes. Right now, she needed to get herself and the crystal as far away as possible.

13

Isla de la Fortuna, Caribbean Sea. Present Day.

As the sun finally disappeared beneath the horizon, Byrd refreshed their drinks and put some music on. Sounds of the fifties boomed from a speaker system in the beach bar. She clicked a switch, and the lights festooned between the trees started to blaze.

"You know, for someone who doesn't like the company of others, you've made this place very welcoming," Eden said, accepting the glass with the silent agreement that this would be her last.

"Hey, it's not that I don't like the company of others," Byrd said, mock offended. "Not all others, anyway."

"Most people, then," Eden said.

"Alright, I'll give you that. It's just that when you've been shot at, let down, and spat out as many times as me, the list of people you trust is short."

Meeting Byrd's gaze, Eden noticed it held a depth which she'd not often seen from their larger-than-life friend.

Although Eden knew Byrd had spent time in the Air Force, they'd never spoken of it.

"You aren't so different," Baxter said, pointing at Eden. "When we first met, you were camping in the woods."

"I was not camping," Eden said. "I lived in a converted—"

"I think we understand each other better than you realize," Byrd interrupted, clinking her glass against Eden's. "Suffice to say, you guys are on that trusted list, so you're welcome any time."

The sound of an engine drifted from the direction of the *Balonia*, then a light snapped on. Eden saw a figure, silhouetted against the *Balonia's* lights, untie a speedboat from the stern. The engine raised in pitch as the boat cut an arc through the water, a beam of light from the bow sweeping ahead. Eden leaned forward, the sound like a death-knell to her relaxation.

"I reckon that's Winslow," Byrd said, lifting her glass toward the incoming craft. "I knew it was unlike him to miss Happy Hour."

"Agreed," Eden said, noticing two figures in the boat as it drew closer. "Athena too, I think."

"This proves what I've always suspected," Byrd said, a warm smile lighting her face. "That man can smell a single malt from half a mile away."

Eden smiled at the thought. Although she'd recently learned that Alexander Winslow wasn't her biological father, as she'd grown up thinking, strangely, she now felt even closer to him. During her teenage years the pair had fought—Eden wanting to join him on the adventures that took up so much of his time. Now, facing such dangers herself, she realized that everything he had done had been to protect her. Since taking

over from him as the leader of the Council of Selene, she realized staying out of danger was much more difficult than she'd
expected. Although Eden still had questions about her real
parents, she figured the answers would come in time.

The craft slid alongside the small wooden dock and the
engine died. Athena tossed a line around a cleat and
secured the boat, then climbed out. She turned and offered
a hand to Winslow, who rejected it and stepped up to the
dock unassisted. The pair walked quickly toward the shore.

The first cool breeze of the evening pushed in from the
sea, causing Eden to shudder involuntarily.

"Something tells me they're not here for the drinks,"
Eden said, watching the speed with which Athena and
Winslow moved.

"Someone clearly missed the memo about vacation
mode." Byrd set down her glass, her easy demeanor shifting.

Baxter stood, his posture automatically straightening as
Winslow and Athena neared.

"I'm sorry to break up the party," Winslow said, when he
was still a few feet away. "But we have something of a
situation."

"Damn it, how did I know you were gonna say that?"
Byrd said, standing and offering her hand to the newcomers.

"Just when I was starting to relax," Eden groaned,
putting the glass down and climbing to her feet. "It's not like
you to break up a party. What's the problem?"

"It had better be a good one. I've invested damn near
half a bottle on this." Byrd looked around the group.

"We've picked up a call from an old answering service,"
Winslow said. "It's super low-tech, but reliable as anything.
It's essentially an answerphone on which people record
messages, linked to a company that doesn't exist, of course.

Anyway, it's been out of use for almost a decade, so getting a message there is definitely bad news."

"And what *is* wrong?" Eden said, encouraging her father in the general direction of the point.

"It's hard to tell," Winslow said, nodding at Athena. "The message isn't very clear."

Athena removed a tablet from her bag and hit play.

"Los Alamos ..." the voice mumbled before a bolt of static cut it off. "Compromised ..." Another word broke through the static and before the line cut to silence.

"That's it?" Eden said, looking from the tablet to her father. "You rushed out here for that? It doesn't even say anything."

"What do you think it means?" Baxter said.

"Honestly, I don't know," Winslow replied, looking around.

"Why is this worrying you?" Eden said. "It could be anyone, right?"

"No one has that number. It's top secret and is only to be used in serious circumstances. If someone's using it now, then there's an issue," Winslow said.

"They said Los Alamos, that's in New Mexico, right?" Baxter said.

"The Oppenheimer place?" Eden watched her father closely.

"Yes, that's it. The laboratory has had a long and interesting history. Some of the stuff they work on is incredible, but also very dangerous in the wrong hands."

"And you think that's the issue?" Eden said.

"It could be, but there's no way of knowing." Winslow nodded, then shrugged.

"Where did the call come from?" Baxter asked.

"We traced it to a motel outside Los Alamos," Athena said. "It's been closed for nearly twenty years."

"Okay, that is weird," Eden admitted. She looked up at the oil black sky, glistening with countless stars. "Have you got a contact in the area you can send over to take a look?"

"No, this is too serious," Winslow said. "If someone knows that number—"

"Okay," Eden said, the last bit of relaxation draining from her thoughts. "We need to go. What's the best way to get there?"

"Now, young lady, that's a question I know the answer to." Byrd collected up their glasses and started toward the hangar with an easy attitude that was totally at odds with the prospect of a long international flight. "Go and get what you need. Wheels up in twenty minutes."

14

Experimental Research Center, Los Alamos, New Mexico. Present Day.

Dr. Alistair Irons gripped the railing and peered into the pool as the last trickle of water ran into the drain. He stared into the black hole, his jaw tightening as he processed the implications of Glass's escape. The opening gaped back at him, mocking him with the fact that even the most carefully laid plans could be undone by human unpredictability.

"I doubt that went as you expected," came a voice from behind him.

Irons turned, shifting his weight to lessen the pain. He saw the young technician, Morales, watching him with her hands on her hips.

"The director always likes to get her own way," Morales said, a mocking tone lacing her voice.

"Get over here," Irons bellowed, pointing at the floor before him.

One of the gunmen grabbed Morales by the arm and dragged her across the chamber.

"Get off me," Morales muttered, pulling herself away from the brute and walking on her own. She stepped alongside Irons as instructed, looking down into the now empty pool.

"Where does this go?" Irons said, pointing at the drain with one hand while leaning on the railing with the other.

"It goes to a—" Morales started.

"Don't you even think about lying to me," Irons said, leaning forward and looking up at the woman. To compensate for the fact that his diminutive frame forced him to look up at her, Irons scrunched his face into a malicious frown. "I need the truth, and I need it now."

"It goes to a containment lake," Morales said, pointing at the drain. "The water stays there until it passes through a decontamination process—that'll filter out any radioactive particles or chemicals, so that it can be returned to the environment."

"Interesting," Irons said, rubbing a hand across his chin.

"Yes, it is. The process is groundbreaking," Morales continued. "Even microscopic contamination could have serious environmental consequences if it reached the—"

"I don't care about that," Irons said, snatching his cane and thumping it against the floor. "Is it possible for a person to get out that way?"

"I ... the system wasn't designed for people. The pressure differentials, the distance ..." Morales looked from Irons to the drain. She swallowed, clearly struggling with the fact that they were discussing the fate of someone she respected. "I'd say it's unlikely. The force would be like getting shot through a cannon."

"But theoretically possible?" Irons said, eyebrows raising.

"Theoretically, yes," Morales hesitated before nodding

reluctantly. "It doesn't take more than a minute or two, but it's incredibly ..."

"Damn it," Irons muttered, his hand closing around the top of his cane. He thought about the crystal—all that searching and all that planning, literally disappearing down the drain. He lifted the radio to his mouth. "We have a potential breach. The object has been compromised. Send units to the containment lake immediately."

"What about the director?" One of the men said, stepping forward.

Irons turned and looked at the man for a long moment. The brute had the quiet focus of a man who didn't speak unnecessarily, and didn't miss when he pulled the trigger—both positive traits in Irons's opinion.

"What's your name?" Irons said, focusing on a scar which traced through the guy's brow.

"Kavanagh, sir," the man replied.

Irons wondered whether the man's Northern Irish accent suggested roots in the Special Forces before this foray into the dark side.

"Let me tell you this, Kavanagh," Irons said, his teeth clenched. "The director is irrelevant. That crystal is all that matters. Monitor the roads, airports, and any ways out of the state. Use our contacts in the local authorities, no one in or out." He paused, his fingers drumming against the cane's handle. "Prepare diving equipment. We may need to search the lake."

"Understood," Kavanagh said, already reaching for his radio.

"I don't care if you have to drain the entire lake with buckets!" Irons said, gesticulating. "That crystal is worth more than everything and everyone in this facility. Without it, our work here is meaningless."

The silence that followed was broken only by the soft hum of machinery and the distant drip of water. The technicians exchanged nervous glances, one of them absentmindedly wiping his palms on his lab coat.

"We will find the crystal." Irons started toward the elevator, his cane cracking against the floor. "Our plan remains unchanged. Now we return to the surface."

The technicians stared back at Irons, then at each other.

"Now!" Irons roared, gesturing toward the elevator.

Morales led the technicians up the stairs, passing Irons with a defiant scowl.

At the top of the staircase, Irons paused and glanced back at the empty pool. The cradle hung as though mocking him, the chains dripping. He turned and paced, his leg screaming in pain, back toward the elevator.

A collective gasp rose from the technicians when they saw the two guards lying in the antechamber, blood spreading across the floor.

"Keep moving," Irons commanded. "There's no time for your pity."

They crowded into the elevator, Irons positioning himself near the control panel. He watched the technicians huddle together on the opposite side, their eyes downcast. The only one who met his gaze was Morales, standing with her jaw set and her arms folded. The guards shoved them inside, and the doors slid shut.

"You, take us up," Irons said, pointing at Morales. She unlocked the system and started them toward the upper levels.

"Once we reach the central lab, you will await further instructions," Irons said, taking the opportunity to crank his captives' fear up another notch or two. "If you attempt to leave or communicate with the outside ..." he let the threat hang for a moment as the elevator door slid open, revealing the corridor.

"Out," Irons said, directing them through the doors. "Take these people to the conference room," he instructed two operatives. The men nodded and wielding their rifles like cattle prods, moved the technicians away.

"Not her," Irons said, pointing at Morales. "She may be useful later. She stays—"

A sharp electronic tone cut through his voice. Kavanagh removed a phone from his utility jacket and passed it to Irons. Irons stopped walking and glanced at the display.

"Take her to the lab and meet me there," he said, gesturing down the corridor. He paused for a few seconds, allowing the group to move ahead. When they were out of earshot, he answered the call.

"Dr. Irons," came the voice he had been expecting. It was neither male nor female and clearly enhanced by some kind of technology. "I was expecting a call from you to confirm your progress. I assume everything has gone to plan?"

Despite the technological masking, Irons recognized the subtle inflections of someone accustomed to absolute obedience.

"There has been a delay," Irons said.

"Define *delay*, Doctor," the caller said, the electronic masking failing to hide their tone of displeasure.

Irons watched Morales and the guards reach the end of the corridor and move into the lab.

"Director Glass escaped with the crystal," Irons said. "I have reason to believe she died in the attempt, but we are still waiting for confirmation. I'm confident that within the hour we will have found her and recovered—"

"Stop." The single word cut through his explanation like a blade. "You're telling me that after months of planning, after all the resources I've provided, after your endless assurances of total control—you've lost both the director and the object?"

"Temporarily—"

"Do not interrupt me, Doctor." The voice went quiet, which somehow made it even worse. "You told me that every contingency had been accounted for. You told me that the director would not pose a problem."

"Yes, I know. People, unfortunately, are unpredictable," Irons said.

"Yes, you have proved that," the voice replied.

"That's not what I meant. I was talking about—"

"Find her, find the object, and call me back within the hour."

The line went dead.

15

———

Approaching Los Alamos at 10,500 ft.

"When you said this was the quickest way to get here," Eden said, pacing into the flight deck of Nora 'Sierra' Byrd's vintage Dakota Skytrain. "I'm not sure you were strictly telling the truth."

While still working the controls, Byrd turned around in the pilot's seat, showing a flexibility that was both surprising and slightly disconcerting.

"Believe me, little lady, unless you've got a Gulfstream G650 in your underwear drawer, this is most certainly the quickest way."

Baxter snorted out a laugh from the co-pilot's seat.

"If you didn't happen to have a good friend with a collection of aircraft fueled and on standby, you'd either be on hold to every charter company in the Yucatan or flying commercial." Her point delivered with the whiplash speed she was known for, Byrd swung back to the controls.

Eden scowled but had to admit that the older woman had a point. She raised her hand to her neck and rubbed one of the many sore points—although the Skytrain was a classic, it certainly wasn't comfortable. Flying through the night with fuel stops factored in, the journey along the Mexican coast and up into the United States had already been an eight-hour slog.

"Yeah, well, I'd certainly rather take my chances with this old bird than spend six hours in a commercial terminal waiting for a delayed connection," Baxter smirked.

"Watch who you're calling an old bird, Captain," Byrd shot back.

"I didn't mean ... I ..." Baxter's face flushed red, the color visible in the low light.

Eden grinned, remembering their discussion at Byrd's Beach Bar the day before. She stepped close behind Byrd and peered out through the windshield.

"Whilst that's true, this thing isn't exactly subtle," Eden said, looking out at the rugged terrain of northern New Mexico, shifting from thick pine forests to sprawling, arid plains. Ribbons of dry riverbeds snaked through the land like glistening silver threads.

"We're catching some headwinds up here," Byrd said, tapping the altimeter. "Nothing nasty, but it's pushing us back a little."

"Probably thirty, thirty-five knots," Baxter said, peering into the sky as though he could see the movement of air. "Should we climb a little higher to clear it?"

"This beauty is built for low and slow," Byrd said, gripping the yoke tighter as turbulence rattled the airframe. "Coming up on our landing soon anyway." She glanced at the navigation screen—Byrd's only nod to the modern world in the vintage flight deck.

"There's Los Alamos," Baxter said, clearly relieved to keep the conversation professional.

Eden shuffled forward and looked in the direction Baxter indicated. Although still some distance away, the size of the site was startling. Rows upon rows of buildings, some squat and utilitarian, others vast and modern, sat clustered between rocky ridges. Lights glowed along the various roads that crisscrossed the site.

"Los Alamos County Airport is over there," Byrd said, banking the Skytrain gently to the right, the twin engines humming. "I'll radio air traffic control."

"I'm not sure that's a good idea," Eden said, as the single runway emerged from the heat haze.

"What do you mean?" Byrd said, her thumb freezing on the call button.

"That's the nearest airport to the facility, right?"

"Of course, the next one is—"

"Whoever's behind this might be watching the airport," Eden said. "And, to put it politely, they'll see us coming a mile off in this."

"She's got a point," Baxter said, watching a commercial jet on final approach to the airport.

"Agreed," Byrd said, banking the plane away from the airstrip. "This girl certainly doesn't arrive without an audience. It looks like we'll need a change of plan."

"Any ideas?" Eden said, watching as the commercial jet touched down, a cloud of smoke rising from the tires.

"Lucky for you, I've got a solution. My good buddy Bourdell got something that might just help you at a military surplus auction a few weeks ago." Byrd tilted her head toward the Skytrain's rear. "Third crate from the back. Captain, you go too."

Eden led the way. Baxter unbuckled his seat and followed. She found the crate and pulled it open. Inside, five tightly packed bundles sat in custom foam cutouts, each about the size of a large hiking pack.

"Experimental, handle with care," Eden said, reading the worn stenciled letters. "What is this?"

"Rogallo wings," Baxter said, pulling one from the housing. The pack was heavier than it looked, with thick shoulder straps and a bright red toggle.

"In English, please," Eden said, pulling another pack out and checking the harness system. "They look like they should be in a museum."

"I heard that!" Byrd said.

"They're like parachutes, but they fly, not fall." Baxter hefted two more packs out and checked them over.

Eden raised an eyebrow to indicate that he should continue.

"With a regular parachute you pretty much drop straight down—maybe one foot forward for every foot you fall. These beauties have a twenty to one glide ratio. We could jump miles from our target and glide right up to it."

"Got it," Eden said, glancing at Athena and Winslow who remained sprawled out on the Skytrain's horribly uncomfortable benches. "Probably time to wake up these two sleeping beauties."

Eden crossed the cabin and nudged Athena with her elbow.

"What? Who is it? I don't want to. You can't make me!" Athena shouted, shoving Eden away.

"Alright, you stay here," Eden said.

"What? What?" Athena said, brushing hair from her face as she finally opened her eyes. "We're here already? That was quick."

"It really wasn't," Eden groaned, having not slept a wink herself. "And it's not getting any better."

Winslow stirred on the opposite bench, lifting the hat from his face with a deliberate slowness that suggested he'd been awake the whole time. "Compliments to the captain."

"Received!" Byrd bellowed. "But I'm sorry to tell you, this ain't gonna be a smooth landing. For you guys, anyway."

Eden explained the plan as they helped each other strap the packs on.

"We wouldn't have this issue on a commercial flight," Athena groaned, supporting herself on the wall as Baxter double checked her pack.

"I heard that too!" Byrd said.

When they were all strapped and double checked, Baxter led the way to the cargo door.

"Testing comms," Eden said, switching her headset for earbuds.

"Got you loud and clear," Byrd replied. "Stand by for my call."

"Understood," Eden replied, glancing back toward the flight deck.

Eden tugged on the straps across her chest for the twentieth time, before checking her father's.

"I'll be fine," Winslow said, catching her eye. "Admittedly, it's been a while since I've flown without a plane, but I'm sure it'll come back."

"Just like riding a bike," Eden said, grinning.

"We're about to go dark," Byrd said. "I'll dive, and then you're out."

"She's going to cut the transponder," Baxter explained. "That'll give us a couple of minutes before anyone tracking us gets suspicious. In an old plane like this, electrical issues are common."

"That's reassuring," Athena said, rubbing sleep from her eyes and stepping alongside the cargo door.

"And the dive?" Eden said.

"That'll get us beneath the radar," Baxter explained, pointing at the cargo netting that ran along one wall of the cabin. "You might want to hold on."

The moment they'd all looped an arm through the netting, Byrd's voice came through the comms. "We're dark," she said, her voice unusually tense. "Hold on!"

The Dakota's nose dropped like a stone. Eden gripped the cargo net as her stomach bounced into her throat. The engines screamed, their pitch climbing to a painful whine. Through the window, the ground tilted and rushed toward them at a sickening rate.

"Get ready!" Baxter shouted, bracing himself beside the door. The Dakota's frame groaned and shuddered, rivets rattling in their housings. The hills that had been safely below them now rushed up on both sides, rocky peaks reaching eye level.

"We're using the valley to mask our descent from the radar," Baxter yelled, his explanation doing nothing to ease the terror of their near-vertical plunge.

Byrd pulled out of the dive as quickly as she'd entered it. The wings flexed visibly through the window, bending up with the strain.

"Get ready!" Byrd's voice cut through the chaos. "Ten seconds to drop!"

Baxter swung the cargo door open, and the air whipped inside the Skytrain with violent force.

They were now so low that a startled hawk plunged from their path. The sound hammered against Eden's eardrums—the twin engines screamed, and the wind shrieked in through the opening.

"Remember, clear the aircraft completely before you pull," Baxter said, looking at Eden, then Athena, then

Winslow. "The wing needs room to deploy, or you'll get tangled in the tail."

The Dakota bucked slightly in the mountain turbulence, the crags on either side whipping past at an impossible speed.

"Go!" Byrd said.

16

———

Experimental Research Center, Los Alamos, New Mexico. Present Day.

THE DOOR of the lab hissed open and Irons strode through. He paused for a moment to assess the scene. Morales stood between four guards, her arms folded tightly across her chest and her mouth twisted into a contemptuous frown.

"You won't get away with this, you know," she said, her gaze meeting his.

"And what exactly do you think *this* is?" Irons said, taking a step and leaning on his cane.

The doors slid closed behind him. He took another step forward and looked around the lab. A long steel workbench ran down one side, topped by various computer systems. At one end of the lab, a large window looked into the clean room next door.

"An attack, a hostage situation, corporate espionage—I don't know, and I don't care," Morales said, stepping forward. The guards flanking her moved too, their guns raised.

Irons smiled. Whilst the young woman clearly had no idea what was going on, she had guts.

"But whatever harebrained scheme you have planned, you're now stuck in one of the most secure facilities in the world." Morales lifted her chin, as though the argument was over.

"Things are not quite as you see them, my dear," Irons said, taking another step forward and trying to ignore the shooting pain in his leg. He paused and looked around the lab with an almost wistful expression. "Right now, your mind is scrambling to restore order, to find familiarity in what is a sudden paradigm shift. It's totally normal when everything you believe proves to be false." He moved closer, his cane tapping across the floor. "Get me a chair," he said, snapping his fingers at one of the guards. "I've got to get the weight off this leg."

The guard did what he was instructed, appearing a moment later with a chair, which like the rest of the lab, was white.

Without a word of thanks, Irons slumped into the chair and leaned his cane against the wall. Sitting down for the first time in far too long, he breathed a sigh of relief. He stretched out his injured leg and noticed Morales watching him closely. She looked angrily away, a few moments of silence passing between them.

"That's one of the things that so fascinates me about scientists," Irons said, leaning back into a stretch. "And I am qualified to say this, being one myself." He placed a hand on his chest. "In fact, my résumé is the only real thing about this whole situation. I believe my employer knew that you would run thorough background checks, so needed someone with the correct—"

"What's so fascinating about terrifying people who've

dedicated their lives to making things better?" Morales said, shooting Irons a hate filled glance.

"Is that really what you think?" Irons laughed and lifted his cane from the floor. "No, what fascinates me is all of this." He swept his hand from side to side, gesturing toward all the high-tech equipment. "You're so brilliant at seeing the trees—counting every branch, measuring each ring, analyzing the chemical composition of every leaf—that you don't notice the forest burning around you."

Morales opened her mouth as though to speak, then looked down at Irons for a long moment. "What do you mean?" she said, academic curiosity clearly getting the better of her.

"Your wonderful director has escaped with the crystal, yes?" Irons said, tensing the muscles in his thighs in a bid to relieve the pain.

"That is true," Morales said. "The crystal that just happens to be one of the most incredible things we've ever worked with. And I hope you never get it."

"Tell me, what's so interesting about that crystal? It's a regular chunk of quartz, no?"

"To a layman, maybe," Morales said. "But once you look at it closely, everything changes. Its structure, it's ... it's like nothing else on earth."

"I know that," Irons said, nodding slowly. "I understand it, I believe, better than you. It will help me achieve something I have wanted to do ..." Irons's voice trailed off, his gaze settling on the distance, as though looking at something outside the room.

"Say this works out for you? What do you plan to do with it?" Morales said.

"Don't you worry about that," Irons said, snapping back

to attention. "But tell me this: the crystal has an interesting radioactive signature, does it not?"

Morales looked at Irons, clearly torn as to whether she should discuss top secret information with an outsider.

"Once again," Irons said, recognizing the young woman's indecision, "you are reacting to things as they were, not as they are. As I say, I know all about the crystal, what it has taught you, and the secrets it holds that remain frustratingly out of reach."

"But how? This is a top secret—"

"Don't worry yourself about that," Irons said, holding up a finger and wiggling it from side to side. "Let's discuss this radioactive signature."

"Fine, you're right," Morales said, her tone like that of an angry teenager. "The crystal pulses with a radioactive signature like nothing we've seen before."

"Exactly," Irons said, nodding.

"Well, why did you—"

"You say it pulses?" Irons asked.

"Yes, we don't yet understand why," Morales continued, seeming to warm to the theme. "But every two to five minutes it emits a unique pattern of gamma radiation. The wavelength is unlike anything naturally occurring—"

"Precisely," Irons interrupted, his smile widening. "Unlike anything naturally occurring. Which means?"

"It's ... detectable," Morales said slowly, realizing what Irons had been getting at. "With the right equipment, you could track it."

"Indeed," Irons said, grinning and interweaving his fingers. "Your esteemed director was too busy escaping to realize she's carrying something which we can track all the way across the globe. Now, is that a radiation detector on the bench over there?"

Morales hesitated, her eyes darting between Irons and the device.

"I've asked you nicely," Irons said, his grin fading. "Don't make me ask again." The guards shifted their rifles slightly —a subtle but clear reminder.

"Fine," Morales said. She stomped across to the bench and snatched up the radiation detector, a handheld device about the size of a large smartphone. She carried it across the lab and placed it in Irons's outstretched hand.

"A fascinating piece of equipment," Irons said, activating the display. "Your team modified it, didn't they? Extended the range, increased the sensitivity."

The screen flickered to life, showing a topographical map overlaid with radiation readings.

"So, all I need to do is input the details of the radioactive signature here," Irons said, tapping away at the screen.

Morales watched him closely, her arms folded. Although she didn't say anything, she was clearly surprised at the ease with which Irons operated the high-tech device.

"And now we just have to wait, for how long did you say?" Irons said, looking up at the technician.

"Two to five—"

"Well, that was quick," Irons said, tilting the screen so Morales could see. A single pulse of light flashed on the screen some distance from their location. "It seems the director made it out, alive. Now be honest, did you overplay the difficulty of getting out through the drainage system?"

Morales paled, a tiny piece of her composure slipping away.

"That's okay, my dear, I would have done the same," Irons said, almost softly. He grinned and lifted the radio to his mouth. "I know the location of the crystal. We move out immediately."

17

Baxter went first, launching himself out through the cargo door. He disappeared into the roaring slipstream, his body immediately whipped backward by the wind.

"Move!" Athena shouted, pushing Eden toward the door.

Eden took a breath and then jumped through the opening. The wind hit her like a physical wall, spinning her violently. Sky, ground, aircraft—everything blurred into a nauseating kaleidoscope. The Dakota's tail flashed past, and the rush of air replaced the sound of the engines. She fought to stabilize, spreading her arms and legs wide. Her spin slowed and the ground rushed up toward her.

Checking her distance from the aircraft, she pulled the ripcord. For a moment, nothing happened. Then, with a violent crack, the pack exploded outward. The straps jerked tight against her shoulders and thighs as the wings yanked her vertically. The sound of the wind dropped from a roar to a whistle.

She glanced up at the Rogallo wing stretching out above her in a perfect triangle, the fabric and aluminum frame slipping through the air like a giant kite.

"Not bad for a first time," Baxter said, his voice coming through the comms. "Coming past."

Eden glanced to the right and saw him swing alongside her, banking effortlessly in a smooth curve.

"I'm taking the stairs next time," Athena said, swooping through the air above them.

"This is definitely one of the most unique landings I've had," Winslow said, soaring somewhere behind.

"My work here is complete." Byrd's voice came through the comms. "See ya on the flip side." The Skytrain powered into a climb, the wings rolling from side to side in Byrd's trademark salute.

"Slick, I don't think anyone noticed at all," Athena said.

As the rumble of the Skytrain's engines faded into the distance, Eden listened for other aircraft but heard only the passing air.

"Hard to believe this entire place was once a secret city," Athena said, pointing out the collection of buildings in the distance.

"Yes, quite," Winslow replied. "Almost ten thousand lived here during the Manhattan Project, and officially, the place didn't even exist. But that's nothing compared to what they keep hidden in plain sight today."

"I thought we were supposed to know everything," Eden said, swooping alongside her father. "Isn't that what the Council of Selene is for, being one step ahead?"

"Yes, of course," Winslow said. "But as you know, it's rarely as simple as that. It's impossible for one single organization to hold all the world's secrets, as you are no doubt figuring out for yourself."

"Sometimes it feels like we're just middle managers, trying to keep everyone happy," Eden said.

"I think that's quite true," Winslow replied. "But you're doing a great job of it."

"The motel is this way," Baxter said, barreling to the left.

"This is definitely easier than walking," Athena said, adjusting her bodyweight to follow Baxter.

Beneath them, a switchback road snaked up the hillside.

"That's one of the old supply routes," Winslow said, nodding at the road. "During the war, they'd bring everything in this way—equipment, materials, personnel—all under cover of darkness."

Ahead, the landscape grew increasingly desolate—volcanic formations jutted from the earth like bones, and the sparse vegetation gave way to empty stretches of sand.

"That's it," Baxter said, pointing at a low building in the shadow of some tall trees. The road snaked past the motel and out into the distance, looking as though it might continue forever.

"The Atomic Rest Motel," Athena said, reading the cracked neon sign at the front of the structure. "Rooms available."

"It looks like they've all been available since the 1970s," Eden said, looking at the single-story L-shaped building which opened onto a weed-covered parking lot. Warped plywood covered some windows, while others had been left open to the elements. "You're sure this is where the call came from? It doesn't look like anyone has been here in years."

"Certain," Winslow said. "They used a hard-wired phone too, so it's not easy to fake."

"That parking lot looks clear enough," Baxter said, banking toward the cracked asphalt. "We'll set down there."

Eden followed his lead, shifting her weight to line up with

the lot. They descended together, their shadows racing across the ground like four prehistoric birds. Twenty feet from the ground, Eden pulled on the control handles, slowing her forward speed and dropping into a gentle descent. She hit the lot with a thump, stumbling forward a few steps.

Baxter landed smoothly a few feet ahead, releasing the straps before the wing fully settled. Athena came in next, skidding on the gravel. Winslow overshot, landing beyond the lot in a patch of scrub brush, which tangled the lines and deposited him in a heap on the earth.

"Get these wings out of sight," Baxter said, slipping off the pack and folding the wings away. "Anyone flying over will spot them immediately."

Eden looked up—the sky was clear for now at least.

They dragged the wings toward the motel and shoved them through a smashed window.

Eden retrieved her handgun from a zipped pouch on the side of the parachute pack and stepped back to look at the structure.

"This place is perfect," Winslow said, stuffing his chute inside with Baxter's help. "Isolated, abandoned, and just a short dash to the lab."

"Too perfect," Eden muttered, studying the motel's lifeless windows.

"There's no signal out here. Not even emergency bands," Baxter said, checking his phone.

"Welcome to the Bates Motel," Athena said, placing her hands on her hips.

"I'm definitely not staying the night," Eden said, checking the weapon's magazine and racking the slide to chamber a round.

Baxter and Athena retrieved weapons from their packs.

Eden made to pass a weapon to Winslow, knowing already that her father would refuse.

"I'll let you young things do the shooting," he replied, shaking his head. Despite the dangerous situations they frequently found themselves in, her father seldom handled a weapon.

"I'll make sure to let the bad guys know that you're here in a peaceful capacity," Eden replied, raising an eyebrow. "I'm sure they'll happily keep their bullets away from you."

"Stay at the back," Athena said, stepping in front of Winslow.

They stalked toward the motel's old reception room, watching the building for any movement. Boards covered several windows, and an awning hung, tattered and ripped. The Stars and Stripes, bleached nearly white by the sun, flapped from a bent pole.

"The last stop before oblivion," Athena said, glancing up as a gust of wind hissed through the treetops.

Eden shoved the door open and stalked into the reception room. Baxter and Athena followed, fanning out on both sides. Winslow stepped inside a pace or two behind.

Something skittered nearby—a quick, scratching sound that stopped as suddenly as it started. Eden spun toward the sound, her gun raised.

"Probably a rat," Baxter whispered, scanning the room.

"I love what they've done with the place," Athena said, assessing the reception area's mid-century design gone to ruin. A curved desk dominated the center of the room, its Formica surface cracked and peeling. Behind it, room keys hung on hooks—most still in place as though expecting guests at any moment.

Another thud echoed from somewhere deeper inside the building.

"It's coming from that way," Eden said, pointing to the door behind the reception desk. "Probably an office. If a call came from anywhere, that's my guess."

"Old buildings like this always make noises," Baxter suggested, his tone lacking conviction.

Eden rounded the desk and checked the area behind. Discolored papers littered the floor, and an old cash register sat upside down. She took another step toward the door.

A distant metallic clang reverberated through the building.

"This place is creeeeeepy," Athena said. "Give me a haunted crypt any day."

"Agreed," Eden said, approaching the door. "The dead can't hurt anyone."

She nodded to Baxter as the pair stepped up to the door. She shoved, and the door swung open, revealing a small room. Filing cabinets with open drawers lined one wall. A desk sat beneath a broken window, illuminated by a shaft of dusty sunlight.

Eden paced in first, scanning the corners before gesturing for Baxter to follow.

"Look," Baxter whispered, pointing at a phone on the desk.

It took Eden a moment to notice that the phone wasn't covered with the same grime as the rest of the room. Wires extended from its base, not into the wall where a standard phone plug would be, but across the floor and out through the window.

"Someone connected it directly into the main telephone line," Baxter said, carefully lifting the handset. "It's been manually wired."

"That explains how—" A violent crash cut Eden off in

mid-sentence. She swung around as a figure burst out through another door.

The person, wild-eyed and disheveled, lunged across the room with startling speed. Baxter reacted first, raising his weapon, but the attacker was already upon them.

They collided with Eden, smashing her against the filing cabinet.

Eden kept hold of the gun, but with the person's arms wrapped around her, couldn't bring it to bear. She shoved backward, trying to free herself from the attacker.

"Eva!" Winslow said, his voice cutting through the noise. "What are you doing here?"

The figure froze, spun around and locked eyes with Winslow.

"Alexander Winslow, as I live and breathe," she said, straightening up.

18

———

"It's HARDLY GOURMET, but it'll keep you alive," Eden said, passing a full canteen of water to Eva Glass and dropping a few energy bars on the table.

"We also have those dehydrated meals, but they actually taste like sandals." Athena picked up one of the bars and unwrapped it. "You're much better off with these."

Glass took several deep swallows of water, her hands trembling.

Eden looked closely at the woman for the first time. She was athletic with dark hair turning to gray at the temples. She wore a trouser suit, which Eden figured at one point had been smart but was now tattered and stained. A bruise had spread across her jaw, and dried blood caked one of her torn sleeves.

"Start at the beginning," Winslow said, reaching across the table and touching Glass on the back of the hand.

Glass nodded, explaining the situation at the Los Alamos facility and her daring escape through the tunnels.

"After that, I ran," she said. "I found my way to a service road and waited for a delivery truck to pass. As usual, the driver wasn't paying attention, too busy helping himself to the food he was supposed to be delivering." Glass's gaze drifted out into the reception area. "While he was rummaging around in the back, I sneaked into the cab and hid behind the driver's seat."

"And he brought you here?" Eden said, wondering why a delivery truck would come to this abandoned place.

"The driver stopped at a diner off Highway 502, once again thinking with his stomach."

"Sounds familiar," Eden said, casting a glance at Athena as she took a bite of the bar intended for Glass.

"Gives me a bit more weight behind the punches," Athena said, retorting with a sharp elbow to Eden's ribs.

"While he was eating, I crawled out and saw an old Jeep parked at the edge of the lot. Those older models start up like turning on a light switch." Glass managed a weak smile. "Got it going and drove outta there. I circled back a few times to make sure I wasn't being followed, then found this place."

The team fell silent for a moment, processing what they'd heard.

"Training kicks in when you need it," Glass said, clearly attempting to make light of the situation.

"And how do you guys know each other?" Eden said, gesturing from her father to Glass. Baxter and Athena looked from one to the other, clearly thinking the same.

"A long time ago ... was it ... Prague?" Winslow said. "An off the books mission, of course."

"It was a lifetime ago, certainly," Glass replied, smiling warmly. "What did happen to those papers you asked me to look over?"

"That's still top secret," Winslow said, patting her hand.

"I get it, and that's how you knew about this weird phone system," Eden said. "And why no one's used it for years."

"Correct," Glass said. "The old systems work the best, in my opinion."

"Too right," Winslow said. "Nowadays, it seems—"

"What do you know about this guy, Irons?" Eden said, pulling them back to the topic.

"Dr. Alistair Irons," Glass said, giving a brief visual description. She spoke with no emotion, as though talking about a new recruit in a board meeting. "He's one of the world's leading plastic composite experts. He used to work out of Oxford, England."

"Used to?" Winslow said.

"Yes, he was injured in a lab explosion a few years back and hasn't worked since. When we got his application, I knew his knowledge would be useful to us at the E.R.C."

"Why is he doing this?" Eden said.

"I've no idea, really," Glass replied. "He talked a lot about technology making the world a more dangerous place, but didn't mention specifics."

"Could he be working for someone else?" Eden said.

"Almost certainly," Glass answered immediately, as though she'd had the same thought. "I mean ... it's obvious that he had access to vast resources. Knew all our security systems and had a well-trained team ready to move at the right moment." Her fingertips tapped on the table. "That suggests both finance and ... connections. Deep ones."

"Any idea who that might be?" Eden said.

"None at all." Glass placed her hands flat on the table. "Irons was many things, but forthcoming wasn't one of them."

"Well, do you know what?" Athena said, finishing her

snack. "It's so refreshing to hear escape stories that don't involve ancient relics or mysterious curses."

"Or a magic ring that changes the weather," Baxter added.

"What about a secret society that controls everything we do?" Eden said, looking at her father. "No offence."

"You're in charge now," Winslow shot back.

"Good point," Eden conceded. "But what we do now is definitely a lot less ... sneaky." The group looked at Eden as though they didn't believe a word she said.

"What's the situation at Los Alamos now?" Athena asked. "Isn't there a protection service that'll take control and—"

"It's out of control," Glass said, shaking her head. "What happens inside the Experimental Research Center is so secretive that we have our own security team."

"And that's the one Irons somehow infiltrated," Eden said, joining the dots.

"Correct. Even the President doesn't know exactly what we're up to," Glass said.

"What are you working on that requires all that secrecy?" Eden said, already knowing Glass's answer was going to be long and confusing.

"If I told you, I don't think you'd believe it," Glass said, shaking her head.

"We've seen our fair share of crazy stuff," Athena said. "I still can't sleep without seeing—"

"I think we need to know," Eden interrupted, placing her hand across the director's.

"Ten years ago we started this new project, and it's been ..." Glass paused, selecting her words carefully. "It's just been incredible."

Everyone waited, watching Glass closely. "What is it?"

Eden said, squeezing Glass's hand in a way she hoped would encourage her to get to the point.

"It's allowing us to pick apart our understanding of physics," Glass said.

"Oooh, like antimatter and promatter," Athena said. "I know that's powerful stuff."

"Sort of, but not exactly," Glass said, studying Athena's expression as though trying to determine if she was joking or not. "Although, it's not called promatter. It's just *matter*—the ordinary stuff that makes up everything we can see and touch. Antimatter is the counterpart, the mirror image."

"That's a *matter* of personal opinion, surely?" Athena countered.

"But it goes beyond that?" Eden said, driving her fingertip into the table.

"Yes. To put it simply—"

"Yes, please do put it simply," Eden said, steeling herself for an incoming monologue.

"The entire universe is made of particles," Glass said, blinking hard.

"Oh wow," Athena said. "I genuinely thought you were going to say something that we didn't already—"

"At least, that's what we believed," Glass said, her voice taking on a sharper edge. "For decades, science has developed these neat models—protons, neutrons, electrons, all the fundamental forces. Everything fit together and nicely explained how reality worked."

"I see a paradigm shift," Winslow said, leaning forward with his fingers steepled.

"Nowadays we call it a plot twist," Athena corrected.

"What we're working on doesn't follow any of these rules," Glass said, nodding. "It's opened our eyes to look at things in a different way. The possibilities really are myriad."

"Myriad, wow," Athena said, wide eyed. "That sounds like a lot."

"Okay, let's go back to basics," Eden said, driving her finger harder into the tabletop. "What exactly are we talking about here?"

"It doesn't just bend the rules," Glass continued, a sort of mania taking over her voice. "It completely ignores them, as though whoever or whatever created it is trying to show us something. Things that should be impossible—energy appearing from nowhere, particles spontaneously generating, distortions in spacetime that should not exist."

"Incredible," Winslow said. "It sounds like what you're working on will make the Hadron Collider at CERN look like a Commodore Amiga 500."

"I have a question," Athena said, raising a finger in the air. "What's a Commodore Amiga 500?"

Winslow inhaled and was about to jump into an explanation of the computer system from the 1990s, but Eden got there first.

"That doesn't matter right now," Eden said. "What exactly are we dealing with here? What's the THING?"

"It operates at a level more fundamental than matter or energy. It's as if ..." Glass paused, searching for words. "As if it exists partially outside the framework of reality as we know it."

"Sure, but what does that mean?" Eden said, attempting to stop the conversation from totally disappearing down an academic rabbit hole. "What actually IS IT?"

"I love this," Athena said, leaning forward. "It's like watching a science documentary live. Did I tell you how excited I am that we're not dealing with another mind-controlling relic from the distant past?"

"Yes!" Eden and Baxter said at the same time.

"Sometimes I feel as though we're children playing with something beyond our comprehension," Glass continued.

"Okay, stop, timeout!" Eden said, banging on the table and making the 'T' symbol with her hands. "I get that this thing is important, I get that it's mysterious, but what exactly is it? What is showing you these amazing scientific developments?"

A beat of silence passed between them while the hint of a smile passed across Glass's face.

"You had it right," Glass said, smiling and looking at Athena. She drew something from beneath the table, wrapped in a filthy piece of cloth. "We found an ancient relic." She unwrapped the cloth, revealing a crystal that seemed to pulse with inner light.

"Oh man, not this again," Athena said.

"Now that," Eden said, looking at her friend, "is what you call a plot twist."

19

"SHE'S HALF A MILE AHEAD," Irons said into the radio. "Hiding out in what looks like an abandoned motel. The Atomic Rest."

He looked up from the scanner and out the window of the Chevrolet Suburban as they sped through the barren landscape, following his instructions. Scraggly piñon pines and juniper bushes clung to the red dirt and the occasional rusted fence post marked property lines that no longer mattered.

The two identical Chevrolet Suburbans in front kicked up clouds of dust that hung in the air like a specter.

"It's not too late to stop this," Morales said from the seat beside him, her tone steady despite the gun pointed toward her. "You let me out, and I'll say that I didn't see you. I can probably talk the others into doing the same."

"Once again, my dear," Irons said, laughing as though the comment was genuinely funny. "You very much misunderstand me. I am not some two-bit thief attempting to steal something for my benefit."

"Why are you doing this?" Morales said. "You claim to be a scientist, so surely you welcome progress?"

"How wrong you are," Irons said, shaking his head. "Just like the rest of your team, just like me many years ago, you think you are serving humanity. Advancing knowledge. Making the world safer." His voice took on a sardonic edge. "Do you ever stop to consider what might happen when something goes wrong?"

"We have strict security protocols. Classification levels," Morales said. "We work in the safest—"

"Arrogant, foolish and short-sighted," Irons said, his voice cutting through. "What you create down there, in the perfect isolation of your lab, will exist far beyond your lifetime. How can you ensure future generations use this in the way you've intended?"

The lead SUV slowed, its taillights flaring red through the dust cloud. Irons's driver responded instantly, maintaining their precise formation.

"We're not simply creating the technology—we're establishing the frameworks for its responsible use," Morales said.

The convoy turned a corner, loose rocks pinging against the undercarriage.

"As the first to master a technology, we will have the chance to establish international oversight, regulatory bodies, safety standards that—"

"Don't make me laugh." Irons snorted in amusement. "All of those things crumble the moment someone decides they need an advantage. Did the Treaty of Versailles prevent World War Two? Did the Nuclear Non-Proliferation Treaty stop nuclear weapons from spreading?" He shifted in the seat. "Every generation of scientists makes the same mistake —they assume their successors will share their ethics."

"Three hundred feet," Kavanagh said over the radio, his Northern Irish accent unmistakable. "Looks like the motel's been closed for decades."

"Good, we end this now," Irons said.

"And you think you're better than that?" Morales said, meeting Irons's gaze with a passion that caused him to pause for a moment.

"Not at all. In fact, that is the reason we are here, because I am no better than that." Irons paused, considering how much he should tell the young scientist. Decision made, he lifted the radio.

"Stop here and proceed on foot," he said. "I don't want her to hear our approach."

"Understood," Kavanagh said. The leading SUV slowed to the side of the road. The doors swung open, and the men climbed out, readying their weapons.

"And this time, no mistakes," Irons said. "Get me the crystal."

"And the director?" Kavanagh replied.

"I don't care," Irons replied, watching the men start up the road. When they had stalked out of sight, he turned to Morales.

"I know you're heading blindly into a mistake, because the one I made was much worse. If I could take it back, I would do so in a heartbeat." He looked through the windshield, eyes glistening at the thought.

"And yet you send your thugs to kill?"

"That is true, but we must consider the greater good. I spent years telling myself the same lies you are. I used to believe, fervently believe, that my research would make the world safer. That I could control how it was used. That the benefits outweighed the risks." Irons looked back at the young scientist. "I learned the most painful way, that wasn't the case."

Irons leaned forward and slowly rolled up the leg of his pants.

Shock registered on Morales's face as she took in the full extent of his prosthetic—the complex assembly of titanium and composite materials strapped to his residual limb.

Irons knew from his own reaction, several years ago in a hospital bed, that it was the scarred flesh around the attachment point that shocked most—a patchwork of burns and surgical scars, mottled pink and white.

"I thought the same as you," Irons said, looking up at Morales, the shock still apparent on her face. "Then science took my leg, and my wife. All in the name of progress."

"Eyes on the motel," Kavanagh said. "It doesn't look like anyone's been here for years."

"She's there," Irons replied, studying the scanner. The crystal's pulse from two minutes ago told him the crystal was somewhere near the rear of the structure. He relayed the location to his men and lowered the radio.

"We were conducting what we thought was a routine stability test, the sort you do every day," Irons said, watching Morales's expression shift from defiance to horror. "Standard safety protocols, experienced team, everything by the book." He touched the scarred flesh around the knee joint, feeling the familiar ache that never truly went away. "I was so confident in the procedures, so certain that I understood the chemistry, that I never stopped to consider what might be wrong."

"I'm ... I can't imagine ..." Morales said, momentarily thawed by Irons's raw emotion.

"We had deadlines too, of course. Everyone wants the answers now. My wife, Anne, was leading the tests that day."

He paused, taking a slow breath. "The blast wave blew out half of the building's windows. Anne died instantly." His voice grew quieter. "They dragged me out of the rubble three hours later. I was the only survivor, and only because I was standing at the door."

"Tell me, Miss Morales—when your research goes wrong, how many of your colleagues are you willing to sacrifice for the greater good?" When Morales said nothing for a long moment, Irons continued. "That is why we put this right, now and forever."

20

"HOLD ON A SECOND," Winslow said, pointing at the object on the table between them. "This thing here violates every law of physics?"

"I know, you wouldn't believe it," Glass said, glancing down at the object. "Other than the glow, which we never really understood, it looks like a normal chunk of quartz."

"It is pretty, I'll give you that," Athena said, her gaze locked on the object.

"Yes, indeed, but it's when we looked deeper that things became truly interesting." Glass lifted the crystal, turning it side to side in her hands. "It emits a very specific type of radiation—like nothing we've catalogued before."

The team instinctively shuffled away from the table.

"Don't worry, the levels aren't high enough to be dangerous," Glass said. "Although we kept it in containment just to be sure. But it pulses at a frequency that doesn't match any known isotope."

"Why would Irons want this?" Eden said. "I don't understand what's so special about it."

"Studying it closely, we noticed several strange characteristics. The molecular structure is different, very different from normal quartz. It's almost as though someone forced it out of alignment. As though they've done it on purpose."

"Like encoded it, somehow?" Eden said.

Glass looked up at Eden, surprise flashing across her face. "Yes, sort of. But things got even more interesting when we realized that the crystal was somehow drawing power from the things around it. The water in the tank, for example."

"To do what with?" Winslow asked.

"We've no idea," Glass said. "It's doing something, but what, we never found out."

"Where did it come from?" Baxter said, speaking for the first time since the crystal's reveal.

"Actually," Glass said, looking up with surprising focus. "It came from a fossil."

"Oh man, this is worse than I thought," Athena groaned.

"A colleague of mine, Dr. Jay Lawrence, noticed something unusual in a trilobite specimen." Sadness now laced Glass's tone. "It's not often that our paths would cross in the academic sense, but I'd just published a paper on crystalline atomic bonds, so he somehow ended up at my—"

"And?" Eden said.

"To get to the point," Glass said, in a tone that suggested such a thing was beneath her. "Dr. Lawrence had a trilobite fossil that he thought had been exposed to impossible heat —over a million degrees. To put that in perspective, the surface of the sun is only about six thousand degrees."

"But that's impossible, right?" Baxter said. "Even a jet engine only—"

"You mean to say nothing on Earth could generate that heat?" Eden interrupted.

"Exactly," Glass said. "Not naturally, anyway."

"Right, hold on, so what does that mean?" Athena said.

"As we saw it, there were two options," Glass said, extending two fingers. "There are records of meteorites that have undergone that kind of atomic reconfiguration."

"A fossilized fish from outer space!" Athena said, wide eyed.

"Or—"

"The only thing capable of producing that much heat, that we know of, is nuclear fusion," Glass said.

"This is groundbreaking," Winslow said, leaning backward.

"Yeah, a fish from outer space," Athena said. "I didn't even know they had oceans there."

"I don't get it," Eden said, pointing at the crystal. "How does that link to this?"

"A controlled nuclear event in pre-history suggests an incredible understanding of science," Winslow said.

"An understanding precise enough to do something strange to this chunk of crystal?" Eden said.

"Precision implies intelligence," Winslow said. "Intelligence implies ..."

"Someone purposefully conducted nuclear-like experiments, or a process we don't yet know of, which generated enough heat to change this at the atomic level," Glass said.

"And long before we were supposed to even know about atoms, let alone splitting them," Winslow finished.

"Rewind," Eden said, trying and failing to make the connections. "I get the fossil, but how did that lead us to this crystal?"

"Working as part of an interdisciplinary team, we traced the origins of the fossil," Glass said, her eyes distant with memory. "The specimen had been part of a collection donated by a French geologist who'd mapped unusual formations in the eastern Sahara back in the 1950s."

"Let me guess," Eden said, pointing at Glass. "You went on an expedition."

"The Pentagon was interested enough to fund it, though officially we were conducting a geological survey," Glass said. "We flew out of Marrakesh and—"

"Wait," Winslow said, levelling a finger at Glass. "Where exactly were you?"

"I think you know," Glass said, her tired expression melting into a smile. "On the Adrar Plateau, near Ouadane in Mauritania."

"The Richat Structure," Winslow said. "Also known as the Eye of the Sahara."

"Another place I've never heard of," Eden said. "How is the world so relentlessly surprising?"

"The geological textbooks call it an eroded dome—a natural formation created over millions of years," Glass said, looking at Eden before returning her gaze to Winslow. "But what we found there tells a different story entirely."

"The place is enormous," Winslow said, gesturing with his hands.

"Yes, almost twenty-five miles from side to side."

"What you found there suggests it's ... artificial?" Winslow said.

"Is that so hard to believe?" Glass asked. "Consider the scale of what we build today. That's much smaller than say, New York City's five boroughs, or Greater London."

"But those are surface cities," Eden pointed out. "You're talking about something built beneath the ground, right?"

"Yes, the parts that remain are beneath the ground," Glass said. "Our working theory is that the structures on the surface were destroyed or decayed over time. What's left has been buried beneath accumulated sediment over the millennia."

"That makes sense," Eden said.

"Imagine if Manhattan was buried under ten thousand years of sand and erosion. From above, you might see odd hill formations. But dig down, and you'd find the subway system, the foundations, the infrastructure."

"Excellent, that basement cocktail bar on Bleecker Street would still be there," Athena said.

Eden's mind raced, trying to process the implications. "But that would mean—"

"It means that what geologists have been studying for decades is merely the top of something much larger," Glass continued. "It's the perfect camouflage—a seemingly natural geological anomaly hiding what might be the most important archaeological site in human history."

A loud thud sounded from somewhere in the motel.

"Just the wind," Glass said, glancing toward the window. "This place makes noises like that."

"An entire city," Athena breathed.

"More than a city," Glass corrected. "The place is inter-connected with crystalline veins, running through the rock like a root system. It's infrastructure on a scale that makes our power grids look primitive."

"Who built it?" Eden whispered.

"We don't know," Glass said. "The dating of the fossil's radiation suggests it was active around ten thousand years ago. But the construction of the place was far more advanced than that of a primitive human society."

"And that's where this came from?" Eden pointed at the crystal.

"Yes, at the center of the structure was a large chamber," Glass said, her hand moving toward the crystal. "Perfectly spherical, maybe three hundred feet across. The walls covered in veins that pulsed with light. That was mounted right in the center." She gestured at the crystal on the table.

"Why did you leave?" Eden said. "Why haven't I seen pictures of this all over the internet?"

"Because you spend most of your time watching people open boxes on YouTube," Athena said. "I've no idea why that's even a thing."

Glass took a sip from the canteen. "We'd just found the central chamber when the tremors hit. Lawrence was on one of the crystal walkways—these narrow bridges that connect the outer platform to the central formation—when everything started to collapse." Her voice caught and she took a moment to steady herself. "The walkway shattered beneath us. I just made it back, but my camera fell. I tried to reach Lawrence, but the structure ... gave way. He threw this to me before he fell." She pointed at the crystal.

"The whole chamber came down?" Winslow asked.

"I don't know. I ran to get help, but once I got to the surface, the military escort pulled me back into the chopper." Glass picked up the crystal, her fingers shaking. "Lawrence died for this. And now Irons is running the facility where we've spent a decade trying to understand what it is."

"Awful," Baxter muttered.

The window exploded inward in a shower of glass. Several canisters sailed through, hitting the floor with metallic clangs that Eden recognized instantly. The window in the reception area shattered next, with two more canisters flying through.

"Smoke! Get down!" Eden shouted, already on her feet.

21

EDEN GRABBED THE CRYSTAL, then flipped the table, shoving it against the door. A dull thud boomed through the wood as another canister bounced off the tabletop, ricocheting back into the reception area.

Baxter shoved Glass to the floor as thick gray smoke curled out of the canisters already in the office. The noxious gas spewed out, filling the space at lightning speed.

"Back door, that way," Glass said, coughing as the smoke filled her lungs.

Heavy boots thundered into the reception room as men swarmed inside. More gas spewed out, filling the room with thick gray smoke.

"Stay low!" Eden shouted, her voice barely audible over the chaos. Her eyes streamed and her throat burned. She reached out and grabbed her father with one hand, and Baxter with the other. Baxter grabbed Athena, and Athena, Glass. As a human chain, the group moved through the office and into the kitchen, where the gas had yet to permeate.

Eden took a breath of the clearer air as another canister

zipped past, smoke already pouring out in thick tendrils. Eden's hip slammed into the corner of a rusting table, sending a stack of plates crashing to the floor.

"Back door!" Glass gasped between coughs. She led them around a row of empty shelving units and shoved open a flimsy door with broken panes.

Coughing and spluttering, they rushed out into the fresh air. They ran across the open ground behind the motel and ducked in behind a rusted delivery van. Smoke rolled out behind them like floodwater, climbing through the boughs of a dead cottonwood tree.

Eden rounded the van and pressed her back against the corrugated metal side, feeling it flex under her weight. The truck sat on blocks, its wheels long gone.

She moved to the truck's bulbous nose and peered back at the motel. Shapes moved in the smoke as whoever was after them searched the building. Gas flooded out through every gap in the crumbling structure, billowing through cracked glass and seeping through missing tiles.

A gun howled through an open window, and a bullet pinged off the engine block.

Eden ducked back behind the truck, pulled out her weapon and sent a few shots back. Baxter fired from the other side of the vehicle, forcing the shooter out of sight—whether down or taking shelter, neither could see.

"Good one for advertising our position," Athena said, as two more operatives popped up and fired.

"You came here in a Jeep, where is it?" Eden said, looking at Glass.

"That way," Glass said, pointing off into the trees. "But I'm not sure you're going to like it."

"What do you mean I won't like it? It has four wheels and—"

A barrage of bullets raked the ground ahead of them, sending up chips of dirt.

Baxter swung out and fired back, hitting one shooter in the arm and another in the chest. "There's too many of them," he said, as another stepped forward to take a fallen man's position.

"Yes, it has four wheels," Glass said.

"Then let's go." Eden darted the way Glass indicated, moving from tree to tree until the cover was thick enough for them to run unseen. They sprinted between gnarled trunks, moving through the undergrowth as quickly as they could.

A crack of a rifle boomed from somewhere behind and bark exploded from a trunk to Eden's left. She wheeled around and ducked behind the tree as more shots zipped past. She popped out the other side of the trunk and squeezed off three quick shots. The gunfire ceased momentarily, then two more shooters joined the fray.

"How many?" Baxter said, his pistol barking from somewhere to Eden's right.

"Six, maybe more," Eden said as her weapon clicked empty. "Damn it, reloading." She ejected the magazine and slapped in a new one.

"Over there," Glass said, pointing to the right.

Eden turned toward a figure trying to flank them through the brush. She fired, and the figure fell, disappearing into a tangle of leaves.

"They'll have us pinned down in minutes," Athena shouted between shots. As though proving Athena's point, the tree Eden and Glass hid behind shuddered under the impact of multiple rounds, chunks of wood flying.

"Glass, where's the Jeep?" Eden said.

"Two minutes, that way!" Glass pointed between some thickly packed bushes.

"You go ahead," Eden said, reaching into her pack and pulling out a flashbang. "This'll get us a few seconds of cover, but don't hang around." She leaned around the tree and fired, hitting a man mid-stride. He went down hard, his rifle spinning away.

"Go now!" Eden shouted.

Athena turned, leading the way into the undergrowth. Winslow and Baxter followed, Baxter providing covering fire as they moved.

Eden counted the tactical team's muzzle flashes—five, maybe six shooters spreading out, once again trying to flank her. She counted twenty seconds, allowing Athena to lead the others away, then pulled the pin on the flashbang. She hurled it high, over the attackers' positions.

The flashbang detonated, a boom roaring through the forest. The men ducked for cover, looking around for the source of the noise.

Eden emptied her magazine, then turned and ran, crashing through the underbrush. She caught up with the others as they reached the clearing. The Jeep sitting in the center, its once green paint scratched and rusting, windows missing or smashed.

"When you said I wasn't going to like it, you really weren't wrong," Eden said, seeing the Jeep for the first time. Baxter jumped into the driver's seat.

"Does this thing even start?" Athena said, circling the vehicle while scanning the brush for any sign of their pursuers.

Eden reached the vehicle and eyed the nest of wires spewing from the ignition.

"This will run past doomsday and beyond," Glass said,

leaning over Baxter and touching two frayed cables together. Sparks flew, but the engine didn't catch.

"Given that this looks like it already survived one apocalypse, I'm not optimistic about a second," Winslow said.

"I'm not worried about doomsday, I'm worried about surviving today," Eden said, dropping to a crouch, her gaze focused on the tree line.

"This doesn't look good," Athena said as shapes moved in the bushes, clearly preparing their approach. "I'd love to stick around and get this thing working, but—"

Baxter pumped the gas and Glass touched the cables together again. This time, the engine roared to life.

The tree line erupted with gunfire, bullets punching through the Jeep's already damaged body. Sparks flew as rounds pinged off the bodywork.

"Get in!" Baxter shouted, wrestling the vehicle into gear.

Winslow and Athena piled into the back, Athena shooting into the bush to keep their pursuers low.

Baxter hit the gas, and the Jeep lurched forward.

Eden remained behind the vehicle and then pulled herself up into the open passenger door.

The tactical team fired with everything they had—automatic fire raking the Jeep's sides, the spare tire exploding, the remaining taillight disappearing in a shower of plastic.

Keeping low, Baxter accelerated through the clearing toward the dirt road beyond, the engine screaming but holding together.

"I told you!" Glass shouted over the noise. "Doomsday and beyond!"

22

"What do you mean you've lost them?" Irons roared into the radio, his knuckles whitening around the device.

The Suburban's interior fell silent. Even Morales, slumped in the seat beside him, held her breath.

"The director was not alone." Kavanagh's voice crackled back through the radio. "She had a team, well trained too. They fled to a waiting vehicle. We pursued and took fire. Two men down."

"You're telling me that her team is more effective than yours?" Irons said, slamming his cane against the floor. "I thought you were the best?"

"Intel told us the director was alone," Kavanagh replied curtly. "Operations like this succeed or fail on their intel."

"I don't want excuses!" Irons roared. "Get back here. We need to pursue." Irons cut the connection and threw the radio on the seat beside him, glowering at Morales. He rolled the leg of his pants back up, the moment of honesty between them dissipated.

"From where I'm sitting, it looks like that has taught you nothing," Morales said, nodding toward Irons's injury.

"Excuse me?" Irons said, baring his teeth like a feral animal.

"Twice now you've assumed that, as a scientist, Glass is going to behave in a certain way. And on both occasions, she's surprised you."

"I don't think that …" Irons started, then stopped. "What's your point?"

"This flaw is yours, not hers," Morales said as though stating a fact. "You haven't taken the time to understand the true nature of what you're dealing with."

"Glass needs to do what she's told or—" Irons drove his fist into the seat between them.

"You know that quote about insanity that everyone attributes to Einstein?" Morales said, folding her arms.

"Doing the same thing over and over and expecting different results," Irons said.

"Well, that's you right now," Morales said, her gaze as hard as steel.

"Yes, but we're not in a lab now," Irons said stubbornly.

"Agreed, but we should still think like scientists," Morales said, her tone almost pitying. "And you've forgotten the most basic lesson."

"Remind me," Irons said.

"We must understand the materials we work with. We must know how they behave in different situations, particularly under pressure."

"Spare me the lecture," Irons groaned, studying the scanner's blank screen instead of looking at her. "I've been doing this since before you were born." He looked up scornfully. "I've forgotten more about pressure dynamics than you'll ever know."

"Exactly, so allow me to tell you something you've probably forgotten," Morales said, grabbing a bottle of water from the armrest. "Water is the most basic compound we know, right? What happens when it freezes?"

"It turns into ice," Irons said, like a petulant teenager.

"The molecules arrange themselves in a hexagonal crystalline structure. Most other substances become denser when they freeze, but water—"

"Becomes lighter. Indeed, it is anomalous. This is high school stuff," Irons muttered, turning his attention to something through the windshield.

"And when pressure is applied to ice?" Morales prompted.

"It behaves differently," Irons said, thinking. "It will remain solid at temperatures where it would normally melt."

"Even above boiling point," Morales said.

"What's your point?" Irons said.

"Under pressure, the rules change." Morales leaned forward. "You're doing the same thing to Glass. The pressure you're applying isn't breaking her—it's transforming her into something that operates by different rules entirely."

"People aren't molecules," Irons said, repositioning his leg to ease the pain.

"True, but they follow patterns. And right now, you're creating conditions you don't understand. You're producing a version of Glass that even she didn't know existed." Morales nodded toward the silent scanner. "The same way pressure transforms graphite into diamond, you've transformed a careful scientist into someone desperate enough to do anything. That's not luck helping her escape. That's phase transition."

Irons fell silent. He stopped drumming against the handle of his cane as though turning something over in his mind. His gaze remained fixed on the headrest for a long moment, then snapped to look at Morales.

Something shifted in his expression—not quite respect, but recognition. It was the same look he might give upon discovering an overlooked variable in an equation. He shook his head as though dismissing the thought.

"But even diamond cracks if the pressure is substantial enough," Irons said, movement through the windshield catching his attention. He watched his men emerge from the treeline and stagger back out onto the road. Two operators supported a third between them, his legs barely carrying his weight. Another clutched his ribs, wincing with each step. They reached the forward Suburbans and climbed in.

"Sir, they need—" Kavanagh said.

"They need to do their jobs. As do you," Irons said, his voice dangerously quiet. "Eight trained operators, bested by a scientist. It's embarrassing. Get in. We need to up the pressure, high enough to crack diamonds."

BAXTER SWUNG the Jeep out onto the highway, sending a cloud of grit pinging across the asphalt. He accelerated away from the motel and down an incline into a wide open plain. To their left, a pair of sandstone mesas rose from the desert floor, layers of ochre, amber, and burnt sienna standing tall. He wrestled with the gearshift, finally getting it into place with a grinding whine.

"That doesn't sound good," Eden said from the passenger seat.

"It's all part of the charm," Baxter said, once again wrestling with the shift. "These things are bulletproof."

"Now that's not true at all," Athena said, glancing at the numerous bullet holes in the sides of the vehicle.

"We need to get out of here as quickly as possible," Eden said, looking down the length of the road, which stretched unbroken into the horizon.

"Yes, I'm working on that," Baxter said, pumping the accelerator. "I think we're going to need a new vehicle."

"When I said this thing would run until doomsday, I didn't mean quickly," Glass said from the center of the rear seat.

"And you have no idea what Irons actually wants?" Eden said, turning around in the passenger seat. "He's clearly serious."

"I can only imagine," Glass said, pointing at Eden's pack, which now contained the crystal. "As I said, that thing contains secrets we're only just starting to understand."

"Control, probably," Athena said. "In my experience, men like that want to control something. I don't think it really matters what."

"Maybe, but there are a lot of powerful objects," Eden said. "It seems like a lot of effort to go through—"

The engine coughed violently, cutting her off. The Jeep shuddered and nearly stalled before catching again.

"Come on, you can do this," Baxter said, wrestling with the gearshift.

"Is it possible that he knows something about the crystal that you've yet to discover?" Winslow asked.

"Only a small group of people know it even exists. Fewer still know as much as I told you," Glass said, clearly troubled by the possibility. "I don't see how he would—"

"The same way he figured out how to get into your department," Athena said. "That man must have someone on the inside."

"I trust my whole team," Glass said, as though the suggestion was insulting. "I've no idea how he knows what he does, or what he thinks he can do with the crystal."

"Right now it doesn't really matter," Eden said, her voice tight.

"I think it does. It changes everything," Winslow argued. "It's actually the basis of this whole—"

"No, that doesn't change the fact that we're traveling in a tin can that's struggling to exceed thirty miles an hour," Eden said, glancing at the speedometer.

"I think that's broken," Baxter said, tapping the dial. The needle fell loose inside the casing. "And, yes, I'm doing my best." The Jeep slowed, losing power, and then juddered forward with the motion of a running hare.

"I think you need to try harder," Athena said from the back.

"I really am," Baxter said, teeth clenched with both effort and frustration. "This vehicle doesn't run on hope."

"It would probably go faster if it did," Eden said.

"Well, it needs to go faster," Athena said, looking out the rear windshield. "Because we've got company."

23

EDEN TURNED and saw three black shapes cresting the hill behind them, gaining fast.

"How did they find us?" Baxter said, looking at the shattered rearview mirror.

"This is the only road for miles around," Glass said, her shoulders tensing.

"We can't outrun them in this heap," Baxter said, downshifting in an attempt to squeeze a little more speed out of the engine. The transmission protested with a grinding whine. "We need a Plan B."

"There's a town about fifteen miles ahead," Glass offered. "We could try to lose them there."

"We're not going to make fifteen miles," Eden said.

The side mirror exploded in a shower of glass and plastic.

"What are the chances those are just warning shots?" Athena said, pulling out her weapon and checking the magazine. She leaned out of the window and returned fire, the shots striking the road.

"No chance at all," Eden said, a bullet slamming into the

tailgate. She leaned out the window and returned fire, one round glancing off the windshield of the leading vehicle.

"Damnit, they're bulletproof," Eden said, ducking back inside to reload. "I mean properly bulletproof, not like this horse wagon."

"And they're accelerating," Athena said. "Thirty feet and closing."

Eden glanced in the side mirror and saw the leading SUV racing up behind them. The second and third vehicles hung back slightly, ready to ram or swerve if necessary.

"Maybe it'll be quicker if we get out and walk," Eden said, sending Baxter a side eye.

Further bullets struck home, pinging off the Jeep's chassis.

"If you want to try that, be my guest." Baxter fought the steering wheel, which, clearly unhappy with their speed, kept trying to wrench itself free and spin out the window.

"Twenty feet now," Athena said, firing into the SUV's front grille.

"Hold on a second," Baxter said. "Take the wheel." He pulled out his phone and tapped the screen.

"What! This isn't a time to catch up on your emails," Eden said, leaning over and gripping the wheel. She checked the rearview and saw a man leaning out the passenger side of the leading SUV, tracking them with a rifle. He fired, bullets pinging off the tailgate.

Baxter found what he was looking for, slid his fingers across the screen to zoom and then nodded.

"Just as I thought," he said, tucking the phone away. "There's a ranch track up ahead."

"How's that going to help?" Eden said, letting go of the wheel as Baxter took control again. "You wanna ride out of here on horseback?"

The leading SUV pulled out into the oncoming lane and accelerated. They drew level with the Jeep's quarter panel in seconds. The passenger finished reloading and leaned out the window again, rifle steady. At this range—barely the length of a car—he couldn't miss.

"One horsepower definitely isn't going to cut it," Athena said, taking aim as the SUV roared closer still. "They're trying to box us in."

Eden popped up through her window, weapon already raised. She squeezed off three quick shots. The first sparked off the SUV's hood. The second went through the window, causing the driver to swerve. The gunman's burst went high, flying uselessly over the Jeep.

"Nice!" Athena shouted.

Eden ducked back inside as return fire erupted. Bullets hammered into the Jeep's door, one punching clean through before slamming into the dash.

The second SUV surged forward too, coming up directly behind them.

"They're boxing us in!" Athena popped up behind the seat and fired on the pursuing vehicle.

"If they're aiming for the tires, they're not doing a good job," Winslow hissed, ducking lower in his seat.

Baxter yanked the wheel hard right as bullets perforated the tailgate. The Jeep fishtailed, kicking up a cloud of dust that momentarily obscured them from their pursuers.

"Down!" Eden shouted.

Baxter hunched over the wheel as he floored the accelerator. The engine roared in protest. A shot cracked through the rear window, punching through the headrest and out through the side window an inch from where Winslow ducked.

The leading SUV accelerated, now pulling alongside the

Jeep. The passenger leaned further out, swinging the rifle toward Eden.

"There's the turning to the ranch," Winslow said, pointing to a narrow road up ahead.

"You think that's a good idea?" Eden said, glancing at her father. "We go up there, there might not be another way out."

"We can't stay here," Winslow said, eyeing the ribbon of asphalt disappearing into the distance. "What is it you always say ... it's not a great plan—"

"But it's the best we've got," Baxter shouted, hauling the wheel to the right.

The tires howled as the Jeep slalomed, leaving two streaks of rubber on the blacktop. The vehicle bounced off the road and down onto the track. They accelerated again, the Jeep shaking violently as it thudded down the rutted dirt track.

"The ranch is a mile up here," Baxter said, pointing up the road.

"This is such a bad idea," Eden said, the Jeep hitting a pothole and almost bouncing from the track entirely. She leaned out the window as the leading SUV attempted to make the same turn. Going too fast, they screeched to a halt a few car lengths past the turning. The second SUV slipped inside, making the turn and taking the lead position.

"They're still coming," Winslow warned, twisting to look through the shattered rear window.

"No kidding," Eden said. The SUVs fell into formation and picked up speed. "Quickly too."

As though announcing their presence, another bullet smashed through the Jeep, punching a neat hole in the dashboard between Eden and Baxter. Baxter swung around a sharp bend and in behind a small stand of trees.

"Maybe we can get out of here on a combine harvester," Eden groaned, gripping onto the seat as the vibrations threatened to throw her into the footwell. "Farm vehicles are totally known to be great for high-speed chases."

A fresh barrage of gunfire erupted from behind, bullets clanging off the roll bar.

"There's the ranch," Baxter said, a rooftop coming into view. A rusty windmill turned lazily in the breeze, its metal vanes catching the sun. "And as I thought, that's the barn on the right."

"What's the barn got to do with it?" Eden said, looking at Baxter. "I was joking about getting out of here on a combine harvester. That's a really bad idea."

The Jeep crested the hill, momentarily hidden from their pursuers. They hit a dip in the track, the suspension bottoming out with a crunch. The ranch's gate loomed ahead—a wooden archway crowned with an enormous bull's skull, horns curling outward.

"No time to open up," Baxter said, pinning the pedal to the floor. The engine screamed as if sensing the coming impact. "Hold on!"

Winslow braced himself against the rear seats. "Are you sure? Maybe we should—"

"Too late!" Baxter howled.

The Jeep charged up the track, dust flying.

"Brace!" Eden yelled, gripping the dashboard.

The Jeep slammed into the gate. Wood splintered, the gate's bars exploding in all directions. Chunks of timber bounced off the hood and roof like artillery shells.

The massive bull skull tore free from its mounting and fell onto the damaged windshield, coming to rest directly in Eden's sightline. The empty eyeholes fixed her with an accusatory stare, as though the long-dead beast was scowling at her for disturbing its rest.

Baxter fought the wheel as the Jeep slewed sideways, tires struggling for traction on the loose dirt. The bull skull broke free and bounced across the yard, scattering a trail of fragments as it went.

Baxter hit the brakes, sending the Jeep into a controlled slide, finally coming to rest a car's length from the barn doors.

Eden peered out, genuinely surprised that the Jeep remained in one piece.

"They're coming around the corner now," Athena shouted, twisting in her seat. "They've slowed."

"They've realized the obvious," Eden said, letting go of the dashboard and swinging open the door. "We've got nowhere to run. This place must be a thousand acres or more. There's nothing but scrubland in every direction."

The pursuing vehicles moved slowly now, advancing with the deliberate patience of a predator who knew their prey was cornered.

"This way," Baxter said, leaping from the vehicle and charging toward the barn.

Eden grabbed her pack and followed, casting a dubious glance up at the structure, its timbers gray with age, roof partially collapsed at one corner.

"We won't need to run. Follow me!" Baxter shouted over his shoulder. He reached the barn doors, yanked one open and disappeared inside.

Eden followed, with the others stumbling in behind her.

Athena pulled the door shut, plunging them into gloom. Shafts of sunlight shone through gaps in the roof like stage lights, dust motes swirling in the golden beams.

Eden blinked, and as her eyes adjusted, shapes emerged

from the shadows. Farm equipment lined the walls beside bales of hay and piled-up fence panels. A narrow ladder led up to the loft area in the roof. In the middle of the space, a tarpaulin covered something massive.

"Help me with this," Baxter said, grabbing the tarp with both hands.

Eden ran across and pulled. The cover slid off in a cloud of dust, catching the light like golden smoke. For a moment, Eden couldn't see anything, then the dust cleared.

"You've got to be kidding me," she said, looking at Baxter with a grin.

24

"That," Baxter said, "is our ticket out of here."

A small aircraft—a vintage Cessna with faded paint and patched panels—sat in the center of the barn.

"What ... how did you know that was here?" Eden said, turning in astonishment from the plane to Baxter.

"Ranch owners use them for dusting crops or just to get around." Baxter paced up to the aircraft and placed a hand against the fuselage in the same way a jockey might greet a horse. "I looked at the satellite images and saw an airstrip through those doors." He pointed to a set of large doors at the other end of the barn.

"And I thought you'd lost the plot," Eden said, pacing toward the other doors. "I'll get these open while you start her up."

"They're entering the yard," Glass said, looking out through a cracked window. "They've slowed."

Baxter swung open the aircraft's door and heaved himself into the cockpit.

Outside, engines roared as the SUVs closed in on the barn.

Eden and Athena ran to the barn's rear doors and heaved them aside, revealing an airstrip of hard-packed earth, now overrun with grass and weeds. At the end of the strip, a windsock hung limp from a pole.

"That doesn't look like a comfortable take off to me," Athena said, shaking her head.

"It doesn't look like we've got a choice," Eden said, turning as the vehicles outside crunched to a stop. One engine purred into silence, followed a moment later by two more.

Eden rushed across the barn and peered through a gap left by a missing plank. The doors of the leading Chevrolet Suburban swung open, and four men climbed out, weapons raised.

"I'll keep them back," Eden said, firing through the opening. The first shot caught one gunman in the vest before he could take cover. She adjusted her aim, but the others remained behind the SUV's bulletproof doors.

"We're not going to hold them off for long," Eden said, glancing at Baxter inside the Cessna. He cranked a lever, pumped something, and then turned the key, which had fortunately been left in the ignition. The Cessna's starter motor whined, and the propeller made a single, reluctant revolution. Then, ground to a halt.

"Damn it!" Baxter shouted. "The battery's weak."

"I'm not surprised. This thing must have been around since the Second World War," Eden said.

"1955, actually," Baxter shouted back. "You can tell because—"

A sharp crack echoed through the barn. Splinters of wood exploded from the doorframe.

"Get back," Athena shouted, motioning for Winslow and

Glass to move further into the barn. They ducked behind a mower, rounds pinging off the metal.

Athena pulled out her weapon and aimed it through a broken window. She carefully returned a few shots, sending the men cowering back inside the SUVs.

"How many have you got?" Athena said, looking at Eden.

"Five, maybe six shots left. You?"

"Three, maybe," Athena said. "Once we stop returning fire, they'll be on us."

"Take mine," Baxter said, leaning out of the Cessna and throwing his weapon to Athena.

Athena caught the gun one handed as another volley smashed the wood into chunks, bullets rebounding from a stack of oil drums with metallic pings.

"You still sure this is the best idea?" Eden said, firing again, then glancing at Baxter. He hit the starter. The propeller turned through two sluggish revolutions, then stopped.

The men returned fire immediately, clearly growing more confident.

"It's not looking good," Winslow said, ducking low.

"Come on, you can do this," Baxter said, as though soothing the old machine. "I need some more time. You can do this."

"That thing will take a miracle to get started," Glass said, looking at the cockpit.

"If anyone can start it, it's Baxter," Athena yelled, firing another bullet.

"Credit where it's due, he knows a thing or two about dealing with stubborn machines," Eden said, throwing Baxter a grin before firing again.

"He's got a skill for stubborn people too," Athena said, looking squarely at Eden.

"I am not stubborn," Eden said. "I won't accept that."

Another barrage of gunfire tore through the wall, splintering wood and kicking up dust. One round punched through the Cessna's tail section, leaving a neat hole in the aluminum.

"I hate to rush you, but time is something we don't have," Eden said, as another salvo whizzed overhead. She fired again, her gun clicking empty. "Nor are bullets." She dropped behind the oil drums. "I'm out!"

A new volley of fire concentrated on her position, bullets thudding into the floor and zipping around the barn.

"It's me they want," Glass said, her voice cutting through the tension. She stood and started toward the door. "If I go out there, they might leave you alone. I'll say you were passing by, and I thumbed a lift."

"No way." Eden launched to her feet, dropping her now useless weapon.

Athena leaned around the door jamb and fired three precise shots. One man took a bullet to the leg and dropped, the others ducked back out of sight.

"We can't keep this up for long," Athena said. She fired again, then the gun clicked as she too exhausted her ammunition. "I'm out!"

Baxter hit the starter again. The propeller thrummed but still didn't catch.

"If I don't go out there, they'll kill us all," Glass said, walking toward the door like King Canute on his way to stop the tide. She passed through a shaft of sunlight, the beam illuminating her face in a way that made her look almost angelic.

"No, if you go out there, they'll—" Eden said, lunging to intercept her.

"Yes, and if I don't, they'll kill us all." Glass spun around and grabbed Eden by the arm. "The most important thing here is to stop Irons getting the crystal. If you escape with the crystal, even if it's at the expense of my life, that's a fair trade." The fierceness of Glass's voice shocked Eden into silence.

Outside, the men shouted, clearly realizing why the return fire had stopped. Another barrage of shots smashed through the door. A moment of silence passed, then footsteps crunched on gravel.

"There must be a way," Eden said, looking from Glass to the lifeless Cessna and back again.

"Listen to me closely," Glass said, her grip tightening. "There's no knowing what damage Irons will do if he gets that crystal." Glass pointed at the bag strapped tightly to Eden's back. "That thing is powerful beyond our understanding. It's imperative that it stays out of his hands."

A bullet punched through the wall, showering them in wood fragments. Neither woman flinched, locked in the moment.

"There is only one way to stop Irons getting the crystal and exploiting it for his own gain," Glass continued.

"Whatever it takes, we'll do it together," Eden said.

Another bout of gunfire cut through the barn, rounds thudding into the planks of the loft overhead.

The Cessna's propeller spun again. The engine sighed and dropped into silence.

"You have to take the crystal back," Glass continued, looking at the door. "Take it back to the Richat and bury it in the chamber."

"But how? You said the place collapsed," Eden said.

"One way in collapsed, but there's another," Glass said. "I know someone who can help you. You must go and see a woman called Yasmine Amana in Marrakesh, she will guide you. Show her the crystal and tell her I sent you."

Before Eden could argue, Glass turned, and with her hands extended above her head, pushed the barn door open and stepped into the yard.

"Target acquired!" one of the men shouted.

"It's me you need, no one else," Glass replied.

Eden rushed to the door and peered through a gap in the planks. The men surrounded Glass, guns raised.

A voice spoke through a radio. Then, a single gunshot cracked through the air like thunder—the sound of an execution, not a warning.

Glass's knees folded in beneath her and her hands fell to her sides. She dropped into the dust, blood pooling around her. The men moved in, quickly searching her body. Clearly not finding what they sought, one man spoke into the radio. He looked up at the barn and then signaled to his comrades. They fanned out, closing in on the barn door.

The Cessna's engine caught with a spluttering cough before roaring to life. Blue smoke billowed from the exhaust stacks as the engine settled into a rough idle.

"Yes!" Baxter shouted, pumping the air with his fist.

Eden didn't even notice, Glass's final words running through her mind—*Marrakesh, Yasmine Amana, return the crystal.*

25

"NEGATIVE, she does not have the crystal," Kavanagh said, standing over Glass's prone figure.

"Check again," Irons snarled, looking from the body to the barn beyond.

Kavanagh knelt once again and ran his hands across the director's pockets. "Negative, it's not here," came the reply.

"It's still in the barn," Irons said. "Get in there and fetch it."

The men fanned out, aimed their weapons at the barn and approached the door.

The distinctive cough and sputter of an engine trying to catch drifted from the structure. Blue-gray exhaust fumes seeped through gaps in the walls.

"Stop wasting time!" Irons roared into the radio.

The engine's sputtering suddenly strengthened to a steady rumble that made the rotten planks rattle against their fixings.

The leading man yanked the door open while his team surged inside, spreading out to cover different parts of the space. The engine noise exploded into a full-throated roar.

Irons saw movement through the open door, something big with spinning propeller blades. Suddenly, the sound made sense.

"Shoot that plane!" he roared into the radio, spittle flying.

A light aircraft burst from the rear doors of the structure, trailing a thick cloud of exhaust. The Cessna bounced like a wounded bird, its faded fuselage visible for a moment before dust obscured everything. The aircraft lurched left, then right, fighting for control on the makeshift runway.

Gunfire erupted from inside the barn, sparks flying from the aircraft's tail where the bullets hit home. One of the windows shattered, but the plane kept moving, gaining speed despite the damage. The front wheel lifted, looking as though the craft would leap into flight, then dropped back down to the ground.

The plane increased in speed, bouncing once, then twice. Then, impossibly, it lifted from the ground completely. The nose came up, the main wheels followed, and the battered aircraft rose into the sky.

"Get back here!" Irons shouted, his fist clenched as the light aircraft climbed away, becoming smaller with each second. "They won't get far in that thing. We need to follow them!"

The aircraft rose, flying in a straight line away from the ranch.

The men appeared, sprinting back through the barn, rifles bouncing against their chests. They jumped back into the leading two Chevrolets.

"Bring the body," Irons shouted, pointing at the figure still lying on the ground. "We can't leave a trace."

Two operatives jumped back out and dragged Glass's body across the yard. Irons recognized Glass's once well-pressed suit, now tattered and stained. Something dark matted her gray-streaked hair—blood or water, he couldn't tell.

Another man popped open the trunk and together they manhandled what had once been the director of the Experimental Research Center inside.

Seeing the body for the first time, Morales let out a cry. She clamped her hand against her mouth at the sight of her former mentor.

"She's irrelevant," Irons said, his voice flat. "Breathing or not, she's worthless to us without the crystal."

"This is murder," Morales said, her voice tight with barely controlled rage. "You killed her!"

"Your concern is touching but misplaced," Irons said, folding his arms. "She chose her path when she took the crystal from me. The consequences are hers to bear." Irons lifted the radio. "Follow that plane. They won't get far out here, and I want to be there when they land."

"You're a madman! You're sick!" Morales said, glaring at Irons.

The leading Chevrolet pulled away, kicking up dust as it powered back down the track toward the highway.

Irons said nothing, thinking that whoever was helping Glass had got lucky. But they were running out of time. Sooner or later, their luck would run out, and he would be there to collect what was his.

"Glass spent ten years studying that crystal. Ten years of being careful, methodical, and safe. You're treating it like some kind of trophy to mount on your wall," Morales said, her voice cracking.

"Do you have any idea who signs your paychecks?" Irons said, turning to face the young woman. "That's who really controls the crystal. Not Glass, and certainly not you. You have no idea what her superiors would have done when they discovered the secrets inside."

"Her superiors?" Morales let out a bitter laugh. "You mean the government? They trusted her judgment. That's why she was the director."

"But do you trust theirs?" Irons shook his head slowly. "Trust is such a fragile commodity. Do you know what happens when weapons of unimaginable power are *trusted* to government oversight? They end up in the hands of whatever administration happens to be in power, used for whatever war they're fighting that decade."

"Your solution is to steal it yourself?"

"For now, yes," Irons said, shifting his weight and wincing as his prosthetic pressed against the seat. "Your loyalty is all very well until someone higher up decides they need what you have."

"Eva Glass would never have let that happen." Morales's face flushed with anger. "We are scientists, working to further the understanding of—"

"Glass would have had no choice!" Irons's voice rose sharply, causing the men in the front seats of the Chevrolet to glance back. "Do you think people care about her decades of careful research when there's a war to win?" He leaned closer, his voice dropping to barely above a whisper. "When you are dead and gone, your creation lives on. Who will protect it then? I've seen what happens to scientists who put their discoveries ahead of all else." His voice croaked with something close to regret. "They lose everything."

The phone in Irons's pocket buzzed. He pulled it out and recognized the number immediately—or rather, the lack of one. His employer never left digital traces.

Irons turned toward the window and answered. "Yes."

"You've had more time than you asked for, Doctor," the

electronically masked voice said. "I'm waiting for good news."

"We have eyes on the object," Irons said, glancing into the sky. "It's airborne, but we have the trajectory and—"

"Airborne?" the voice snapped. "As far as I was aware, you were in a secure facility, and now—"

"There were ... complications," Irons said, keeping his voice as low as possible. "But we're minutes behind them. When they land—"

"Who has it?"

"The operatives are currently ... unknown," Irons said. "They extracted it during our operation. But we are tracking visually." He looked up at the plane, now just a distant dot in the sky.

"Unknown operatives." The voice somehow got colder. "In an airplane you didn't know existed, from a facility you said was completely secure."

"The situation is under control," Irons insisted, sounding feebler each time.

"It doesn't sound like that is the case," the voice said. "In fact, it sounds like the situation is a long way from being under control." A beat of silence passed down the line. "Dr. Irons, I'm beginning to think you've mistaken my patience for weakness. We had a deal. You have two hours to obtain the object. Not tracked, not located—physically secured. If that's not the case, the deal is off."

Irons swallowed, knowing immediately the implications. Without the deal, without the crystal, it was over. "Understood."

The line went dead.

WHILE IRONS SPOKE on the phone, Lucia Morales looked down at the scanner on the seat between them. The dot blinked from the screen—refreshing as it did every time the crystal pulsed.

She stared at it for several seconds, waiting for it to move across the map like the plane, but the dot remained stationary. Realization struck like ice water. The dot was still flashing above the ranch.

In the chaos of the chase, Irons hadn't thought to wait and see whether the crystal was actually on board the plane.

Morales glanced at Irons. He was turned toward the window, voice low and tense, completely focused on his call. She reached over and spun the scanner around to face her. Of course, she knew the device. In fact, she had helped design it. She tapped the frequency adjustment button three times, then pressed the reset control.

"Understood," Irons said, ending his call. He swallowed, placing the phone on the seat between them.

The dot on the screen flashed, now showing the radioactive signature moving southeast at high speed, back toward Los Alamos. Tracking a different radioactive signature altogether, probably a routine uranium shipment heading to the containment facility, the scanner would now take them in totally the wrong direction.

26

———

"So let me get this right," Eden said, scrambling down the ladder from the hayloft where the group had watched the men chase after the pilotless plane, then run back to their SUVs, before powering away. "That plane will fly in a straight line until it runs out of fuel?"

"That's right," Baxter said, following her down the rickety ladder. "I set the trim tabs to keep her level, locked the rudder with a bit of rope, and wedged the control yoke in position with a bit of wood. She'll maintain that heading and altitude until the tanks run dry."

"How long does that give us?" Athena said, jumping the last few steps.

"An hour or two," Baxter said. "It'll come down somewhere in Arizona or Colorado, depending on the winds."

"Won't it crash into something?" Eden asked.

"Not likely," Baxter said, looking into the sky where the Cessna was now just a speck. "Between here and Colorado, there's maybe three towns with more than a thousand people. The rest is empty desert, canyon lands, and scrub. Hundreds of miles of nothing."

"It looks like they bought it," Eden said, watching the convoy which was now just a cloud of dust powering down the highway.

"We need to move in the opposite direction. Fast," Winslow said.

"Then we need to find our way to Marrakesh," Eden said, explaining what Glass had told her. She stepped out into the yard and looked at the spot on the gravel where Glass had fallen, a bloodstain marking the dirt.

"One thing's for sure, we're gonna need another ride," Athena said, pointing at their shot-up Jeep. "That won't make it another mile."

"You know, I genuinely thought you were getting us out of here on that plane," Eden said, looking at Baxter.

"You didn't expect me to fly an aircraft without a full service history?" Baxter said, looking at Eden in genuine shock. "The list of things that could go wrong is—"

"Oh, I'm totally with you," Eden said, dead serious, "but if flying an un-serviced aircraft is the most dangerous thing we do this week, then we're doing well."

"Don't ask for trouble," Athena said.

"Hold on, what's that?" Winslow said, pointing toward the highway.

Eden cupped a hand over her eyes and looked in the direction her father indicated. A vehicle swerved from the highway and down the track toward the ranch, a cloud of dust rising above it.

"Someone's coming," Athena said, instantly alert. Her hand moved to her gun, then stopped when she realized it was empty.

"Friend or foe?" Eden murmured, watching the vehicle.

"Only one way to find out," Baxter said, stepping to the center of the yard and waving at the incoming vehicle.

The truck slowed as it approached the ranch, its engine clattering as if it contained more loose parts than attached ones. It rolled through the smashed-up gate and stopped. The driver cut the engine.

Eden and the rest of the crew approached the vehicle as the driver's door swung open and a man stepped out. Wearing faded jeans, a plaid shirt with the sleeves rolled up, the man regarded them with the dispassionate interest of someone who was used to seeing unusual things.

"Saw that old Cessna go over," he said, his voice carrying the distinctive drawn-out vowels of the region. "Thought that was mighty peculiar, seeing as we buried old Jake near about three years ago now." He walked around to the front of his truck and leaned against the grille, watching the group.

"Yes, sorry about that," Baxter said, stepping forward. "We had a bit of a situation. I'm—"

"I don't think Jake would complain much. He'd like the old girl to get some air through her wings," the man continued, ignoring the outstretched hand.

Eden eyed the truck, noticing the bed was filled with makeshift wooden pens containing several pigs that watched the proceedings with curiosity.

"It wouldn't be anything to do with the folks been stirring up dust with those black Suburbans? I saw 'em heading for the interstate like their tails are on fire."

"Yes," Eden said, "and thanks to them we could do with a ride out of here." She pointed at the Jeep, with its complement of bullet holes.

The farmer looked at her for a moment, then around the rest of the group.

"You passing through?" he said.

"Yep, passing through," Eden agreed.

"Everyone's just passing through," the man said thoughtfully, as though the phrase carried more resonance than its literal meaning.

"It's a bit of a strange—" Eden said, considering what they could safely tell the man.

"Don't tell me nothing," he said, holding up a hand. "I don't wanna have to lie if I get asked. But, I'll tell you something for free—sometimes the law ain't the same as what's right. And those boys in the Suburbans?" He spat into the dirt. "I seen their type. Private security, government contractors, whatever they call themselves these days. Dirty business."

He looked at his truck, then back at Eden.

"I'm heading to Alamosa. Got to deliver these hogs anyway." He scratched his chin thoughtfully. "Tell you what —I'm gonna go check in old Jake's barn there as I suspect someone's been rootin' around. It'll take me about five minutes to look around proper. If you folks happen to find your way into the back of my truck while I'm gone ..." He shrugged. "Well, I wouldn't know nothing about that, would I?"

"That's very generous—" Winslow started.

"No, it ain't," he said, already sauntering toward the barn's open door. "Cos I don't know anything about it."

"One quick question," Athena said, taking a step toward the truck.

"Shoot," the farmer said, turning around.

"Do pigs bite?"

"Not too much," he shrugged, turning and pacing into the gloom.

27

———

Marrakesh, Morocco. The following day.

THE BLACK MERCEDES V-Class cut through the traffic that surrounded Menara Airport. Eden peered out through the tinted windows, watching the city slide past in the fading light.

"Five thousand, two hundred miles," Winslow said quietly, leaning in close to his daughter. "That's roughly the same distance the Phoenicians traveled when they circumnavigated Africa, and yet we've done it in a little over a day."

The journey from the dusty back roads of New Mexico to North Africa had been a blur of desperate measures—the farmer's truck to Alamosa, followed by a hastily chartered flight to Dallas where they'd freshened up and bought supplies while waiting for the Citation CJ3+ jet that brought them to Marrakesh.

"I just hope it's quick enough," Eden said, touching the bag in which the crystal was stored.

"I'm sure of it," Winslow said, touching her hand. "We've done all we can."

"Have you found anything useful about Yasmine Amana?" Eden asked, leaning forward and tapping Baxter on the shoulder.

"Not much," Baxter said, glancing up from the tablet computer on which he'd spent every minute of the journey. "She runs a small shop in the Medina that specializes in artifacts from pre-Islamic North African cultures. She's not written or published anything publicly, and isn't affiliated with any official organizations, that I can see. Nor was she present on any of the expeditions Glass led here."

"There's got to be a connection," Eden said, her eyebrows inching together in thought. "Glass used her last moments of life to send us here. That's no accident."

"A lot of knowledge exists outside academic circles," Athena said, watching two men weave through the traffic on a donkey cart loaded with brass lanterns. "Just because she's not a recognized authority doesn't mean she doesn't have valuable knowledge."

"I know that," Baxter said, looking up from the screen. "I wasn't suggesting—"

"In fact, academia represents a tiny section of humankind's collective knowledge," Athena continued. "It's only in our western centric attitude that academia seems so important."

The driver leaned on the horn as they rounded the donkey cart with only inches to spare.

"She's right, of course," Winslow said, turning to Baxter. "Until relatively recently, most human knowledge was transmitted orally."

"Exactly," Athena nodded, watching a mother adjust her daughter's hijab. "My grandmother never wrote a word but could identify every plant she saw."

"We're close," Eden said. They overtook a pair of idling

buses, and the minaret of the Koutoubia Mosque came into view. The rose-colored stone caught the last of the day's light; a flock of birds wheeled around its golden spire.

"I'm not dismissing oral tradition," Baxter said, closing his tablet with a sigh. "It's just strange that this woman, who was clearly very important to Glass, barely exists online."

"Not necessarily," Winslow said, clearly warming to the subject. "Morocco has an extraordinary tradition of preserving knowledge outside conventional channels. The University of Al-Qarawiyyin in Fez is actually the oldest continuously operating university in the world. Founded in 859 CE—over two centuries before Oxford."

"But that's still an academic institution," Baxter pointed out.

"Yes, but it grew from the Moroccan tradition of oral knowledge transmission," Winslow continued. The traffic ground to a halt and Winslow pointed through the open door of a local madrasa. Inside, students sat in a circle around their teacher, no books in sight. "For centuries, the most respected scholars weren't necessarily those who published the most, but those who memorized vast amounts of information and could recite it perfectly."

The driver accelerated and then hit the brakes as a horse and carriage clattered out in front of them.

"Alright, thanks for the history lesson," Eden said, holding her hands up in mock surrender. "I get it. You're saying that Yasmine Amana might know something about the crystal that's never been written down."

"That's my guess," Winslow nodded. The Mercedes slowed, crawling alongside a towering archway.

"Like a lineage of knowledge keepers who've preserved information about whatever civilization created the crystal?" Eden said, looking down the narrow street beyond the archway. A group of robed figures moved in the gloom, almost invisible from the street.

"That would explain why Glass never mentioned it officially," Athena said, turning from the window. "If there's a secret society of knowledge keepers, the last thing they'd want is academic attention."

"That's quite a leap," Baxter said, though his tone suggested he found the theory plausible.

"It's possible, though," Winslow said. "Consider how many secret groups there have been throughout history—from our own Council of Selene to the Eleusinian Mysteries of ancient Greece to the more esoteric orders like the Templar Knights. Knowledge has often been guarded jealously and passed down only to the initiated."

The driver sounded the horn, gesticulating through the window for a group of taxi drivers to shuffle out of the way. He pulled into the space before hitting the brakes.

"I stop here," the driver said, speaking for the first time since they'd left the airport. "No vehicles inside. That way." He pointed through the archway.

Baxter passed some money across, and the group climbed out.

Looking up at the medina's walls, which had stood for nearly a millennium, Eden realized that this certainly seemed like the sort of place where secrets could hide in plain sight. The call to prayer rose from a nearby minaret, answered moments later by another across the city. The overlapping voices merged into a single, haunting harmony.

"I guess we're about to find out why Glass sent us here," Athena said, stepping out of the vehicle and closing the door.

Eden looked up at the minaret of the Koutoubia Mosque as its loudspeakers joined the fray.

"This way," Baxter said, glancing at the directions on his phone and then setting off into the gloom. "The shop is about five minutes through the medina."

Eden looked at the path ahead, the only light coming from a pair of lamps hanging outside a shop. Something moved, although from where she stood, she couldn't see what it was.

"Could the shop be a cover?" Eden asked, following Baxter and Athena, Winslow a step behind. "A good excuse to handle ancient artifacts and make connections through the archaeological community, maybe?"

"It's possible," Baxter said, not sounding sure.

Music drifted from an open window above, topped by the raucous sound of laughter.

They turned a corner and passed under another archway. The passageway opened onto a vast square. Hundreds of lamps strung on wires cast a yellow glow over the huge space, creating long, distorted shadows.

"Jemaa el-Fnaa," Winslow murmured, his voice barely audible above the cacophony. "The Assembly of the Dead."

"Charming name," Athena remarked, scanning the crowd for anyone looking their way.

"Once a place of public executions," Winslow continued. "The severed heads of criminals and political enemies would be displayed on spikes as warnings. Some say the square is built on a massive burial ground."

Smoke from food stalls rose in thick columns, twisting through the light before dissolving into the night sky.

"Stay close," Baxter said, leading them through the throng.

A man with a tray of gleaming brass teapots balanced impossibly on one shoulder hustled past them, his face half-hidden in shadow. A group of women draped in vibrant fabrics pushed the other way, their laughter rising above the general din.

"The oral tradition still at work," Athena said, nodding at a storyteller plying his trade. He sat beside a lantern, which projected his animated gestures against a nearby wall.

"Snake charmer," Winslow said, pointing at another man. The man, his face half-concealed by a turban, played a melancholy note on a flute as a cobra rose from its basket.

"In the old days," Winslow whispered, leaning close, "it was said that these performers could summon djinn—spirits—with their music. The boundary between our world and the supernatural was thought to be thinnest in places like this."

"I can believe that," Athena said, mock shivering. "It's creepy."

They passed the food stalls, smoke billowing from grills laden with sizzling meats.

"Down there," Baxter said as they reached the square's far side. He led the way into a narrow alley that was barely wide enough for two people to walk side by side. Unlike the busy main thoroughfare, this passage was quieter, its high walls casting it into almost complete darkness. Doorways punctuated the walls, most unassuming wooden entrances that gave no hint of what might lie behind them.

Eden took the lead, glancing up at the walls which leaned toward each other overhead. They followed the passage as it twisted left, then right, then left again, each turn taking them deeper into the medina's heart. The sounds of the main square faded behind them, replaced by the muffled echoes of voices from somewhere inside.

The passage narrowed further still, forcing them to walk single file. Above, the strip of sky had darkened to deep indigo, and the walls seemed to swallow what little light remained.

They passed under a low arch, forcing Eden to duck, then emerged into another passage that branched in three directions. Baxter consulted his phone, then pointed left. The route sloped downward, the stones beneath their feet grooved from centuries of footsteps.

"There it is," Baxter said finally, pointing to a small door set into the wall. A candle burned from a sconce beside the door, the flame dancing.

Eden stepped up to the door, thinking that the scene had probably remained unchanged for hundreds of years. Suddenly the idea of an ancient society, passing important information down through the ages, didn't seem that implausible.

She raised her hand to knock as the door swung open.

28

EDEN BLINKED, her eyes struggling in the low light. A mountain of a man filled the doorway, his shoulders straining the seams of his traditional djellaba robe. He leaned forward, ducking beneath the low door frame to look out into the street. His gaze shifted across the visitors, starting with Eden and ending with Winslow. Then, without a word, he moved aside and beckoned them in.

With a swift backward glance, Eden stepped through the doorway. Baxter came next, ducking beneath the low frame, followed by Winslow and Athena. They emerged in a space that appeared more like a mythological treasure cave than a shop. Unlike the cramped tourist bazaars that lined the main thoroughfares of the medina, this space was unexpectedly vast, suggesting that it occupied several combined buildings. Display cases lined the walls, stacked with artifacts that ranged from silver jewelry inlaid with amber and coral, clay vessels painted with symbols and patterns, and ceremonial daggers with handles carved from bone or horn. Ancient textiles hung from the walls, and thickly woven rugs covered the floor.

"This place is incredible," Eden said, stepping up to a large wooden table in the center of the room. An assortment of books lay open, some of which looked centuries old, their pages yellow and fragile.

The shopkeeper closed the door with a gentleness incongruous with his imposing size and stepped into the center of the room. He clasped his hands across his stomach and watched his guests.

"What's that symbol?" Athena said, pointing at the distinctive outline of a hand with the fingers stretched upward, etched into many of the artifacts.

"That's the mark of our guardian," the man said, following Athena's gaze. His voice was a low growl which almost required straining to hear. "The Hamsa—what some call the Hand of Fatima." He crossed to a large Hamsa stitched into a tapestry on the back wall and traced its edge with a fingertip. "It has been our protector since long before the coming of Islam or Christianity to these lands."

"The protective hand," Winslow murmured. "It appears in cultures throughout the Middle East."

"It's beautiful." Eden looked around the shop and saw the symbol carved on amulets of various sizes and materials, embroidered into textiles, carved into wooden panels, and etched onto metal artifacts. Some were ornate and encrusted with gems, others simple and unadorned.

"It is powerful too," the shopkeeper added. "Our ancestors knew that true protection comes not from weapons or walls, but from maintaining balance within ourselves and with the world." He looked directly at Eden, his gaze surprisingly firm. "When the soul exists in harmony within a person, they become a worthy guardian of knowledge."

"We need to speak with Yasmine Amana," Eden said, returning the shopkeeper's stare.

"Yes, I sensed that was your purpose here," he said, as though the request was a casual one. "You will, when the time is right. My name is Hamid." He placed a hand against his chest and then glanced at a small cooker in the corner on which a brass kettle sat, a stream of steam rising from the spout. "And you are just in time for tea."

"This is incredible," Winslow said, moving up to the table with the reverence of a holy man. He looked closely at one of the books, shaking his head slowly.

A breeze slipped through a high latticed window, swinging the copper lanterns on their chains and making the shadows dance.

"I'm afraid we don't have time," Eden said, taking another step toward their host. "This is a matter of urgency."

"Ah, the young," Hamid said, once again meeting Eden's gaze. Although his eyes radiated a kindness, his tone was firm. "Tell me, do you truly believe that the speed of your actions has any impact on the pace at which things happen?"

"You have an incredible collection," Winslow said, clearly changing the subject before Eden could reply.

"These coins are pre-Islamic, if I'm not mistaken. They are museum pieces."

"Many museums would like them, but they are pieces of our people's history," Hamid said, as though correcting a mistaken child. "Lalla believes they must remain with the people to whom they were born."

"Lalla?" Athena asked.

"Lalla Yasmine," Hamid explained, moving gracefully toward the kettle. "Lalla is a term of respect in our culture."

"You are Berber?" Eden asked.

"Amazigh," Hamid corrected gently, "Berber is what others call us, derived from the Latin for barbarian. We have always been Amazigh—the free people." He removed the kettle from the stove, pulled a fistful of mint from a hessian bag, crushed it between his hands and dropped it into a large silver teapot. He carefully added several spoonfuls of sugar and a dash of amber liquid from a vial on the shelf. He poured water into the pot, releasing the fragrant scent of the mint.

"Our lineage stretches back to before the Arabs came, before the Romans, before even the Phoenicians gazed upon our shores," Hamid continued, setting the pot aside and turning his attention back to his guests. The breeze intensified, causing a pair of lamps to clang together. "I fear dark forces brought you here."

"What do you mean?" Eden said, noticing Hamid's attention settle on the bag strapped to her back. His gaze hardened, as if seeing the crystal through the layers of fabric. "I have something I must show Yasmine—"

"I know," Hamid said, raising a hand to silence her. "But it is not yet time to talk of that. Save your explanation for Lalla Yasmine. First, we must have tea." He turned to a cabinet and selected five small glasses with delicate gold patterns around their rims. He placed the glasses on a brass tray etched with the Hamsa and poured the tea. The steaming liquid flowed from the spout in a graceful, steaming arc.

"It is our custom to share tea before matters of importance," Hamid said, moving around the room and placing the tray on a low table surrounded by cushions. He settled on one of the cushions, folding his legs in beneath him, and took one glass for himself before gesturing for the others to help themselves.

Eden's jaw clenched, thinking of their mad dash halfway around the world and the fact that every second they sat here drinking tea was an advantage for Irons.

"Of course, it would be our pleasure," Winslow said, fixing Eden with the same look he'd used when she was twelve and about to say something catastrophically rude. He tilted his head toward the table in a gesture that ended any argument, then moved to take a cushion opposite Hamid.

Eden stifled a sigh and reluctantly followed suit, sinking onto the embroidered cushion beside her father.

"In this land, tea is never merely a drink—it is a sacred pact between host and guest," Hamid said, holding his glass at eye level before bringing it to his nose. The lantern light caught the amber liquid, casting honeyed reflections across his face.

Athena and Baxter exchanged glances before taking cushions on either side of Eden and Winslow, completing the circle around the low table.

"They say that we must drink three glasses—the first is bitter like life. The second sweet like love, and the third gentle like death." He smiled slightly. "But for now, we share only the first glass—the beginning of our journey together."

They each lifted a glass from the tray.

"To safe journeys," Hamid said, raising his glass and taking a sip.

Eden did the same, the sweet mint flooding her senses. Despite her impatience, she found herself strangely appreciative of it.

Athena drank quickly, eyes never leaving Hamid's.

Baxter swirled the liquid contemplatively before drinking.

Hamid cradled his glass, finishing the tea in two deliberate sips. He returned the glass to the tray, turning it slightly so that the intricate gold pattern caught the light.

"Now," Hamid said, his voice deepening as he folded his hands in his lap, "before you may speak with Lalla Yasmine, there is a matter of trust to be settled."

"What do you mean?" Eden asked, setting her empty glass back on the tray.

The others finished their tea and placed the glasses down.

"The tea you just drank," Hamid said casually, "was infused with the venom of the desert scorpion. While the dose is not immediately lethal, without the antidote it will cause paralysis within thirty minutes, followed by respiratory failure within the hour."

29

"WHAT?" Eden said, shooting to her feet. "You poisoned us?" her voice rose in anger and disbelief, her momentary relaxation vanishing.

"I did," Hamid acknowledged, nodding once. "Including myself." He gestured to his own empty glass. "It is *el-mahak* —the test of worthiness."

"Why would you do this?" A knot of fear twisted in Eden's stomach.

Athena rose unsteadily to her feet and took a step back. Her facial expression cycled from anger to fear and back again.

"Those who seek the knowledge must first prove they value wisdom above their own lives," Hamid replied. "Fear not, the antidote is nearby. If you are worthy, you will find it before the venom takes effect."

"This is madness," Eden said, taking a step closer to the big man, her fists balled. "Who are you to—"

"I am with you. I have drunk the same tea." Hamid held up a placating hand. "My role is to guide worthy seekers, not to judge them."

"You will tell us or—" Athena said, raising her fists.

"Where do we even start?" Baxter staggered to his feet and peered around at the vast rows of shelves lined with objects.

"I would advise you to save your energy," Hamid said, casting Athena a sharp look. "Every movement speeds up the effect of the poison."

"People have already died because of this, and if we don't speak with Yasmine, more will—" Eden stopped talking as a strange tingling sensation spread across her mouth. She raised her fingers, her lips rubbery.

"Desert scorpion venom works quickly," Hamid observed dispassionately. "First comes the peripheral numbness, then increased heart rate." He glanced at the old brass clock mounted high on the wall. "We have perhaps ten minutes before breathing becomes difficult."

Winslow struggled to his feet and braced himself against the table. His normally steady hands trembled, and a thin sheen of sweat spotted his forehead.

"We need to find that antidote," Eden said, looking at her father. She turned, her gaze sweeping around the vast shop. "It could be anywhere in here."

"I can't feel my fingers," Athena whispered, staring at her hands. She opened and closed her hands three times as though testing they still worked.

"Of course, it affects different people at different speeds," Hamid said, still seated on the cushion. "To remain calm is the highest form of strength, and the hardest to master."

Eden fought to focus as an unwelcome warmth spread up her arms. A disconcerting prickling sensation followed, as though a thousand tiny needles poked at her skin. She focused hard, searching the shop for any clues about where the antidote might be.

"The hands," Eden said, her speech slurring as the numbness spread.

"Yeah, I can't feel mine either," Athena said, looking down at her palms in disbelief.

"No, the Hamsa, the hand symbols. They're everywhere," Eden said, gazing at a large sliver one high on the wall. "Look, they're made out of brass, wood, ceramics... everywhere."

"Yes, the Hamsa," Winslow nodded, beads of sweat rolling down his temples.

"Could that be a clue?" Eden said, pointing at a large one carved from rosewood on a shelf beside Athena. "Hamid said they offered protection. Could they protect us against the poison?"

Athena leaned over and moved the rosewood Hamsa to the side, revealing an empty space behind. She stumbled slightly, catching herself against a display case.

"That does make sense," Winslow said. "The symbol has been associated with warding off danger for centuries."

"It's done a pretty rubbish job of protecting us so far," Athena said, moving across to a Hamsa made from hammered steel and pulling it to the side. "There are so many, we can't check them all."

Baxter zigzagged across the room and fumbled with the latch on a glass case containing several ornate golden Hamsas in various sizes. His hands shaking violently, he turned the objects around.

"There's got to be more to it than that," Eden said, supporting herself on the table. "We can't look behind them all. We don't have time."

"Could it be about the ways the Amazigh people would need protecting?" Winslow offered.

Eden looked around the room again. The copper

lanterns now left trailing halos of light as she moved her head.

"That one could represent water?" Baxter said, staggering toward a Hamsa covered in blue crystals, arranged like crashing waves. "That would protect them from drought." He turned it around, revealing an empty space behind.

"That one looks like fire," Athena said, pointing at another, embroidered into a rug spread across the floor, silver and gold threads flickering through it. "That would protect from the cold." She dragged the rug to the side, revealing nothing but the floorboards.

"We need more time," Baxter growled, squinting around the room.

"The speed of time is something you certainly cannot change ..." Hamid said impassively, his eyes half-closed as though in a trance.

"My vision's ... blurring," Athena said, coughing. "Hold on, could that be earth or rock, maybe? Protection from the elements."

"... but you can change how you move through time," Hamid continued, more to himself than anyone else.

Athena swayed across to another Hamsa, this one glazed orange like the African soil. She moved it to the side, revealing nothing. "Are you sure this—" She coughed violently, her whole body shaking.

"The tree that bends with the wind outlasts the one that stands against it," Hamid said, his voice now just a hiss of air.

Hearing Hamid's words, Eden had an idea. She placed a hand across her heart, struggling to focus. "No ... wait," she said. "Maybe we need to think in a less literal way." She looked at a glitzy Hamsa mounted on the wall. Spots danced at the edges of her vision. "It'll be more ... more spiritual."

"I think ... I think you're right," Winslow said, steadying himself on the wall. His arm shook and then gave way, sending him crashing into the plaster. His knees buckled and he slid down into a sitting position.

Eden made to rush toward her father, instinct overriding her focus.

"No," Baxter said, taking a step forward and placing a hand on Eden's upper arm. "We need to find the antidote. That's the only way to save him—to save any of us."

"True wisdom lies not in resisting the inevitable, but in finding your path within it," Hamid continued, though his words now fell on deaf ears.

"What might this spiritual protection look like?" Baxter said, helping Eden stand as another wave of dizziness threatened to topple her.

"Pure ... untouched ..." Eden croaked.

Athena pointed at a crystal-clear glass Hamsa hanging in an alcove, its surface catching and refracting the lantern light into rainbow patterns.

"Maybe that one—it's transparent, like pure spirit." She stumbled toward it, using display cases for support. Her shaking hands knocked over a brass incense burner as she reached for the glass Hamsa. She grabbed the Hamsa and pulled it from the wall, revealing nothing but stone behind.

"We're running out of time," Baxter wheezed, his breathing labored. Spots swam across Eden's vision as she searched the room again.

"No, of course, that makes sense," Eden said, pointing at the Hamsa Athena had removed. "It wouldn't look like that. Spirit isn't fragile. It endures. It's ..." Her increasingly unfocused gaze landed on a small, plain Hamsa near the door.

They had walked within inches of it but not even looked at it, their attention drawn to the more ornate objects around the shop. Now, with her vision fading, the dull blue-gray metal seemed to pulse with quiet certainty.

"It's that one, I know it," Eden said, moving toward the object.

"That one?" Baxter frowned. "That's just like the thousands of others around the medina."

Eden stumbled up to the object, supporting herself against the wall as another wave of dizziness swept over her. She paused, letting the dizziness pass for a second, then staggered another few steps and carefully lifted the amulet from its hook.

"Spiritual protection isn't about grabbing attention, it's about quiet strength," Eden said. Where the amulet had hung, she saw a small hole hollowed into the stone. A tiny vial of clear liquid sat in the hidden nook.

"I've found it!" Eden wheezed. Placing the Hamsa on a shelf, she wedged her numb fingers into the gap and pulled out the vial.

Athena rushed across the room, looking at the vial, which fit easily into Eden's palm. "That can't be enough for us all. Surely that's the dose for one person."

A heavy silence fell over the group as they all looked at Eden. She looked down at the tiny bottle, then to her father, then to Hamid.

"We have to share it," she said, her hand closing tightly around the bottle. "Maybe there's enough, or maybe this will buy us enough time."

"Or ensure we all die," Baxter said.

"We came together," Eden said, pointing at the small cabinet beside Baxter. "We live or die together. Get five glasses."

"Eden's right," Winslow said, his voice weak. "All or nothing."

"Why five? He poisoned us," Athena said, pointing at Hamid, who sat peacefully on the cushion. The big man mumbled something, although his words were no longer audible.

"We don't leave anyone," Eden said, crossing to where Baxter laid the glasses out. She carefully divided the contents of the tiny vial into the five glasses and drank one. The liquid was tasteless, leaving only the lingering mint of the tea on her tongue.

Almost immediately, the tingling in her fingers receded. Her heartbeat steadied, and her vision sharpened. The relief was so intense her knees nearly buckled.

She crossed to her father and helped him drink it, color returning immediately to his ashen face. She carried the remaining glass to Hamid.

The big man's eyes cracked open as she approached. She tilted his head back and poured the liquid between his lips. He inhaled and emitted a low groaning noise.

"You found it," he said, opening his eyes a little more. "And you chose to save even the one who poisoned you. That is ... unexpected."

"I wouldn't have," Athena said, stepping forward despite her weakness. "You could have killed us all! What kind of—"

"A necessary one," Hamid said, raising a hand to call for calm.

"Necessary?" Baxter's voice cracked with fury. "We came here for help, and you—"

"Most choose the ornate amulet, believing that strength of the spirit must be as conspicuous as the danger it guards against." Hamid coughed, wiped his mouth and straightened up. "Few understand that true safety often lies in what others overlook." He moved his gaze across them all. "And even fewer would choose to share uncertain salvation rather than secure their own survival." He struggled to his feet, supporting himself with the wall for a few seconds.

"That doesn't justify putting us in danger," Eden said, folding her arms. "Plus wasting our time."

Hamid paced across the shop and placed the amulet back on the shelf, as though casually tidying the shop. "Now we must go," he said, turning and meeting Eden's gaze. "Lalla Yasmine is waiting."

30

———

ALISTAIR IRONS STARED out the window as the Bombardier Global 6000 circled Marrakesh, preparing to land. The jet— large enough to transport his team plus their equipment— banked gently, giving him a perfect view of the city below, spread out like a constellation of lights against the surrounding desert.

The modern districts of the city blazed with streetlights, vehicles and shops, while shadows cloaked the ancient medina, punctuated only by pools of light. Looking down upon the labyrinth, Irons's gaze followed the narrow pathways and passages that had grown organically over a millennium, each generation adding their own.

"It's a rat's nest down there," Kavanagh said, studying a map of the medina.

"Yes, it is," Irons replied as the plane tilted further, offering them a view of the famous Jemaa el-Fnaa square with its hundreds of food stalls, merchants, and gathered crowds. "And so we'll catch them like rats."

"Sir?"

"Rats in a maze make the mistake of thinking they're

safe," Irons said, studying the square below. "We don't need to chase them through every alley. We just need to control the exits."

"Setting up a perimeter would take hundreds of men," Kavanagh said, studying the screen of his device. "There are hundreds of ways out of the medina, from streets to private homes. Watching them all would be impossible."

Irons sat rigid in the seat, the scanner on the table before him showing the crystal's last pulse. He looked from the scanner's display to the medina, concluding that the signal came from somewhere in the northeastern quarter.

"Yes, but all roads lead to Jemaa el-Fnaa," Irons said, as the square vanished from sight. "Half the team head to the northeast and herd the targets toward the square. The other half take positions in and around the square and wait."

"Understood," Kavanagh said, scrutinizing the map.

"Two minutes to landing," the pilot announced, the jet's nose tilting groundward.

Irons glanced across the cabin where Morales sat on the opposite side of the aisle, now positioned next to one of the guards, her wrists zip-tied to the armrest. She'd cost them six hours with her scanner trick, but fortunately, Irons had figured it out eventually. In five minutes they would have made up for lost time—time that almost cost them the whole damned mission.

The landing gear deployed with a mechanical whine.

Back in Albuquerque, they'd been closing in on what the scanner claimed was the crystal's radioactive signature. Irons had positioned his three SUVs for an ambush, all surrounding a section of road which passed through the mountains.

"Visual on the convoy," Kavanagh said from the leading vehicle. "Sir, you need to see this."

Irons clamped the binoculars to his eyes and focused on their oncoming prey. As his driver had said, he immediately noticed that something didn't stack up. This wasn't a random convoy, hastily transporting something across the country. This was a well-planned, fully armed military operation. An armored truck rumbled at the center of the convoy, bracketed by four black SUVs with what looked like government plates. Two motorcycles ran ahead, their riders in full tactical gear.

"I've seen this before," Irons said, as the pieces in his mind clicked into place. He lowered the binoculars. "They're transporting special nuclear material."

"Do we abort?" Kavanagh asked again.

"The scanner. It's been giving us a false signal," Irons said, suddenly realizing the deceit. He looked down at the device beside him and then across at Morales, whose expression remained emotionless. "Yes, abort now. And get out of here before they see us."

The plane jolted as they dropped through turbulence, dragging Irons back to the present. The sudden movement sent white-hot pain through his leg. He gripped the armrest, fighting to keep his expression neutral as his nerves screamed. As the pain faded, he looked across the aisle at Morales.

"That was a clever trick," he said, keeping the pain from his voice as best he could. "You almost had us open fire on a federal convoy." He looked down at the scanner, which had now been recalibrated to the crystal's signature.

"That would have taught you a lesson," Morales said, speaking for the first time in hours.

The Bombardier sailed across the airport's perimeter fence, landing lights shining through the windows.

"I've already been taught many lessons in this lifetime,"

Irons said, rubbing his leg in an attempt to ease the ache. "Now's my time to act on one of those lessons."

"Have you though?" Morales asked, watching him impassively. "Because right now you're chasing something you don't understand, just like you did ten years ago."

The landing gear met the tarmac, the chirping of the tires muted by the top of the line insulation.

"Oh, I understand far more than I ever did before," Irons said, forcing himself to stop rubbing his leg, should Morales interpret it as a sign of weakness.

"Since you've dragged me all the way here, why not tell me what you're planning? I suspect you plan to kill me, anyway." Morales said, her voice carrying the same clinical detachment she might use when discussing a failed experiment.

"I'm bringing you here as your help will be useful. You're an expert after all," Irons said. "As for what I'm doing, I'm doing something I should have a long time ago. Something that I need to put right."

"The person you're working with, they're funding this whole thing," Morales said, gesturing at the plane and entourage of men. "That means they want this crystal too. What's their endgame?"

The plane rumbled down the runway, losing speed. It turned onto the taxiway and past the terminal building, heading for one of the private hangars. Irons's team started unbuckling, checking weapons, and talking in hushed tones about the operation ahead.

"Surely it can't be as simple as a bag full of cash?" Morales said, pressing the issue.

"Money?" Irons almost laughed. "You're right there, I'm not doing this for money."

"Then what?" Morales said, leaning forward as the Bombardier slowed to a crawl.

"That crystal, as you know, has some incredibly special properties," Irons said, leaning back in his seat and stretching out his leg. "My employer, if we can call them that, is allowing me to use it for one special personal project before I hand it over." He gestured to his leg. "There is something I need to do, something I need to put right. What happens to the crystal after that is none of my concern."

The plane rolled to a stop inside the private hangar. Several rugged four-by-four vehicles and half a dozen off-road motorbikes waited at the edge of the tarmac for the next part of their mission.

"You're delusional," Morales said. "That object operates on principles we don't even have the mathematics for. You can't just plug it in and—"

"Don't worry about that, I know what I'm doing," Irons said, unclipping his seatbelt and pulling himself into a standing position. He picked up the scanner, which pulsed again.

"Do you really—" Morales started.

"Now it's time for you to put your skills to use." Irons nodded and one of his men opened a briefcase in front of Morales.

"What is this?" Morales said, looking at the stack of notes and documents inside.

"This is my work on the crystal. You'll see that I got significantly further than you." He bent down, his face just inches from Morales. "You have twenty-four hours to study these notes. I need you up to speed because you are going to help me."

31

Shaking off the final effects of the poison, Hamid paced to the back of the shop and pulled aside an intricately woven drape depicting the night sky with constellations Eden didn't recognize. The movement revealed a small door set into the wall. He slid aside an iron bolt and pulled the door open, exposing a narrow passageway beyond.

"For centuries, the guardians of knowledge have moved through Marrakesh unseen," he said, taking a lantern from a hook beside the door. He opened the lantern's small glass panel and touched a match to the wick. The lantern flared to life, casting patterned light across his face.

"What is this place?" Eden said, peering into the passageway. Light from the shop spilled through the door but died after a few feet, leaving the rest of the passage in total darkness.

"The knowledge of these thoroughfares continues to be a closely guarded secret," Hamid said, as though that answered the question. He ducked his large frame through the doorway, then paused to look back at the group. "Stay close, the way is not always straightforward."

Eden shot a glance back at her friends and then followed. Athena ducked through, with Winslow closely behind and Baxter last. They followed Hamid down the passage, the light from his lantern casting strange, long shadows across the walls and floor. High above them, a distant strip of sky provided a subtle silver glow.

Eden considered using the small flashlight she carried, or even the light function on her phone, but for some reason that sort of light didn't feel right in this ancient place.

The passage twisted to the left, revealing a vaulted roof arching overhead. Carved niches punctuated the walls, some holding unlit oil lamps, others empty.

Hamid led the way down uneven stone stairs, worn smooth in the center. At the base of the stairwell, the passage opened into a basement. Various wooden crates and woven palm baskets sat stacked against the walls.

"We move beneath shops and restaurants, always out of sight," Hamid said, his voice even quieter than usual. He gestured up as footsteps thudded across the boards overhead.

Hamid passed a sack of saffron beside several drums of argan oil, then weaved around a large stone basin that was still used to collect water.

"Watch your step," Hamid said as they ducked through an archway and started up another set of stairs. At the top, he turned abruptly right and passed beneath a lintel.

"Look, an eight-pointed star." Winslow paused, pointing at the tiny detail which was almost hidden in the gloom. "This appears throughout Islamic architecture, but the Almohad craftsmen of the twelfth century gave it this partic-ular stylized form."

"How long has this network existed?" Eden asked, rushing a few steps to catch up with Hamid who moved instinctively, knowing each indentation and twist of the passage.

"That is like asking how long people have kept secrets," Hamid replied.

They rounded another corner, and the passage sloped downward, delivering them to the top of a narrow spiral staircase. The walls changed from rough clay to smooth plaster, though much of it had flaked away over the centuries.

Without a pause, Hamid led the way down the staircase, his big frame fitting surprisingly well into the opening. At the bottom, the passage widened into a vaulted chamber. He raised his lantern to reveal a domed ceiling pierced with star-shaped openings.

"An old hammam," Hamid said, the echo of his voice showing the true size of the space. "It was abandoned at the time of the Great Plague, and the bathers never returned."

Several marble basins were set into the floor at different levels, their edges carved with flowing geometric patterns. Some tiles remained across portions of the walls, their colors lost to grime, others had fallen away to reveal the stone beneath.

"This place is extraordinary," Winslow said, approaching one of the basins and running a finger across the carved edge. "This design, I think it's probably late twelfth century." He stood and moved to the wall, carefully touching the remaining tiles. "These tiles, they're expensive work. I doubt this was a public hammam."

"What do you mean?" Eden said.

"This was private. Maybe for a wealthy merchant family or even minor nobility." He turned to Hamid. "This place should be explored. It could tell us—"

"Some doors are closed for a good reason," Hamid said,

the seriousness of his tone stopping Winslow in his tracks. Hamid turned and disappeared through a door in the far wall, forcing the others to catch up. They moved into a narrow passage, dropping into single file.

Eden stumbled up a set of stone steps in the near darkness, catching herself in time.

"Caution is our greatest ally," Hamid said, the glow of his lamp floating somewhere above.

Eden started to climb, with the others a step behind. The passage leveled out, and they moved through a short corridor made from rough brick. The corridor extended perhaps twenty paces before emerging into a small courtyard, open to the night sky.

Eden blinked, her eyes adjusting to the moonlight which seemed especially bright after the subterranean tunnels. The courtyard floor was simple packed earth with a few stubborn weeds growing through the cracks. On the opposite wall, two heavy wooden doors with metal studs stood side by side.

"We are close," Hamid said, lifting his face to the sky, "But I fear time grows short."

"I tried telling you that before that whole poisoned tea episode," Eden said, quietly enough for Hamid not to hear.

"While fools argue over the method, the wise agree on the progress," Hamid said, looking hard at Eden. The light from the lantern danced across his face.

Hamid stepped up to the door on the left and produced a key from within his robe. He unlocked the door, swung it open and indicated that Eden should pass through.

Eden did as she was instructed, passing into the gloom beyond. Athena stepped forward to follow, but Hamid placed his hand across the opening, blocking her path.

"Lalla Yasmine will speak only with the one who has passed the test," Hamid replied, looking directly at Eden.

"What do you mean?" Baxter asked, his muscles tensing. He took a step forward, standing level with the shopkeeper.

"What Lalla has to say, is for her alone." Hamid pointed at Eden. "That door is for the rest of you." He nodded at the other door a few feet away. "You'll find it open already."

"No way," Athena said, standing at her full height, although only reaching the big man's chest. "We stay together."

Hamid shook his head. "Some knowledge can only be passed from one vessel to another." He gestured toward Eden. "The Hamsa chose her. She, and only she, has proven herself worthy of Lalla's wisdom."

"What Lalla Yasmine knows affects all of us, and possibly the entire world," Eden said, looking into the gloom beyond.

"Perhaps that is true, perhaps it's not." Hamid folded his arms across his barrel chest. "But it's alone or not at all. The choice is yours." He glanced over his shoulder at Eden.

"That's not really a choice," Athena said, mirroring Hamid's stance. "I don't like it one bit."

"Of course it's a choice," Hamid said. "You weren't forced to drink the tea, nor to follow me."

"Eva Glass died to send us here," Athena said, trying to meet Hamid's gaze, but he looked off into the distance.

"And yet you hesitate to take the final step," Hamid said. "Either you trust the path or not. Half-trust is no trust at all."

"How do we know you're telling the truth?" Baxter said, looking from one door to the next.

"You don't, of course," Hamid said, as though it was a punchline to a joke. "You don't even know if Lalla Yasmine is real. Faith requires uncertainty."

"Faith gets people killed," Athena shot back.

Eden met her father's gaze. Winslow held the look, clearly thinking it over, and then nodded.

"We have to do this," Eden said, looking back into the gloom. She felt the pull of curiosity drawing her to something back there. "We've come so far, we have to see this through. I'll be back soon."

"That door is for you," Hamid said, pointing once again to the other door. "We will return as soon as the necessary has been said." He stepped through behind Eden, swung the door shut, and turned the key.

32

Baxter, Athena and Winslow shared a glance as the key turned in the door through which Eden had disappeared.

"Who does that guy think he is?" Baxter said, pointing at the iron-studded wood. "We've come up against some nasty people in our time, but never anyone so—"

"Chilled out?" Athena offered, shrugging. "The guy didn't even care that he'd poisoned himself."

"No, that's not it," Baxter said, turning to face the small courtyard's other door. "He's just so—"

"Wise?" Winslow suggested. "Did anyone else think that everything he said had two meanings?"

"Smug," Baxter finished, turning to face the others.

"Agreed," Athena said. She kicked a loose stone, sending it skittering across the packed earth. "Where did he learn all that nonsense? Give me a book of proverbs and I'll take him on, head-to-head."

"Glass is dead, we got poisoned, and Eden's gone with him alone," Baxter said, looking at the door through which Eden had disappeared.

"Yeah, and now we're following the orders of a man who

talks like we're all on some kind of spiritual journey," Athena added.

"You never know, perhaps we are," Winslow said.

"We've got a madman breathing down our necks, a trail of dead bodies, and a crystal the power of which no one actually understands," Baxter said, taking a few steps backward.

"Exactly, so we're going to need more than a tea ceremony and a philosophy lesson to get through this one," Athena said, folding her arms.

"Our best move now is to head back to our place and wait for Eden there," Winslow said, approaching the other door.

"Why don't we rip that door off its hinges and follow them?" Baxter glared at the door through which Eden had disappeared as though it were personally responsible for all recent events.

"Eden can handle herself," Winslow said, placing a hand on Baxter's upper arm. "Plus, she knows where we're staying. Sometimes the hardest thing to do, is nothing."

"Don't you start," Athena said, rolling her eyes.

"I don't like it," Baxter said, shaking his head.

Winslow stepped up to the other door and swung it open, revealing a narrow alleyway on the other side. The passage was open to the sky, allowing moonlight to filter down between the buildings.

"We're certainly not solving anything standing here," Winslow said, stepping through the door and starting down the passage. Athena came next, huffing loudly. With one more glance over his shoulder, Baxter followed.

The passage twisted sharply to the left, then right, threading its way through the medina's historic structures. Laundry lines stretched between windows above them, white sheets and colorful fabrics hanging still in the wind-less night. They turned the next corner and found another door blocking their path.

"There's only one way to go," Winslow said, glancing back at the others. He pushed the door, and it swung open on surprisingly silent hinges. He led the way through and paused, eyes struggling in the bright light of a busy city square.

Food vendors lined the perimeter, their carts sending up clouds of aromatic smoke as they grilled meat skewers, fried flatbreads, and stirred bubbling tagines. Groups of Marrak-shis sat at low tables, some playing cards, others chatting animatedly. A few tourists wandered between the stalls, cameras clutched to their chests.

"What is this place?" Athena said, shuffling forward while instinctively scanning the crowd for threats.

"This looks like Place des Épices—the Spice Square," Winslow said. "But that's at least half a mile from the shop. I certainly didn't think we walked that far."

"Impossible," Baxter said, pulling out his phone to check their location. The screen showed that they were exactly where Winslow thought, and nowhere near where they'd started.

Baxter turned back to the door they had passed through, only to watch it click closed. He tried the handle, but the door wouldn't budge.

"Those tunnels are confusing," Winslow said, shaking his head.

"Either way," Baxter said, watching the crowd suspi-ciously, "Eden is somewhere in this maze with people who've already poisoned us once tonight."

"Our place is ten minutes that way," Athena said, looking up from her phone and indicating a direction. After another grumble from Baxter, the group set off in a tense silence.

With Hamid's lantern now illuminating the space, Eden saw they stood in a vast room with rough stone walls.

"This way," Hamid said, gesturing across the space. They descended a flight of well-worn stone steps. At the bottom, instead of opening into another room, the passage turned sharply left.

The passage curved its way for what felt like several minutes. It branched several times, each time Hamid choosing the way without hesitation. Finally, they climbed another set of stairs and emerged in an ornately tiled passageway with white-painted walls. The tiles formed intricate geometric patterns in cobalt blue and emerald green. Arabic calligraphy in gold leaf adorned the upper portions of the walls, the flowing script catching light as the lantern moved.

"Nearly there," Hamid said, leading them into a wide antechamber decorated in the same style. Arches soared overhead with brass lamps hanging on long chains, unlit at this hour.

Hamid stepped up to a large arched doorway, then paused and turned. "Lalla awaits," he said, placing a hand against the wood. He pushed gently, revealing a vast open space beyond.

Eden stepped through and paused, looking out at a vast rectangular courtyard. A large pool dominated the courtyard's center, its surface mirroring the night sky above. Intricate mosaic tilework covered the walls, star-and-octagon patterns running through the panels in a kaleidoscope of color.

She stepped forward, still looking around at the space. The door behind her thumped closed. She turned to see that Hamid had not followed her through. For a long moment, nothing moved. Then, on the opposite side of the courtyard, another door opened. Light spilled from it, golden and warm against the moonlight.

A slender figure emerged, silhouetted against the light. As she moved toward the reflecting pool, Eden saw a woman of indeterminate age in deep indigo robes, a simple headscarf framing her hair. She carried a lantern like Hamid's, its flicker surprisingly bright, and moved with the effortless ease of someone at home here.

She reached the side of the pool where a large rug and two cushions lay. Padding across the rug, she sat, sinking into the cushion without the use of her hands. She placed the lamp on the floor beside her, the light seeping through the mottled glass and dancing across the pool's surface.

"Welcome to Madrasa Ben Youssef," the woman said, her voice carrying easily across the water. "For seven centuries, this place has been a sanctuary of knowledge in Marrakesh. The greatest scholars of their age once studied here." The woman swept her hand through the air, indicating the intricate designs surrounding them.

Watching the gesture, Eden got the impression that she wasn't simply suggesting people learned within these walls, but from them. She shook the thought from mind and stepped forward. "You are Yasmine Amana?"

"That is correct," the woman responded, patting the cushion beside her. "Come. The night grows short, and I fear we have a lot to discuss."

33

———

EDEN CROSSED THE COURTYARD, her boots echoing from the tiles. Remembering the culture she'd experienced in many Arabic countries, she undid and took off her boots before sitting on the cushion beside Yasmine.

The older woman looked up at her, the slightest smile on her lips. Despite the silver streaks of hair that framed her face at the edges of her headscarf, her actual age remained impossible to guess. She carried herself with the vitality of a young woman, yet her eyes held wisdom that suggested decades more.

"Eva Glass told me to come and see you," Eden said, meeting the other woman's gaze. "She died getting us here."

Yasmine held her gaze for a long moment, studying her. To Eden, it felt less like a look and more like an assessment —as if the older woman saw beyond the physical.

"Let me tell you something," Yasmine said, turning away and staring out across the pool. A gentle breeze passed through the courtyard, sending ripples across the pool's surface. "The mind is an incredibly powerful thing—"

"I really don't need another lecture," Eden said, her

voice rising despite her attempt to control it. She shifted on the cushion as if to stand. "I've rushed across the planet, chased by a—"

"As I do not talk for my own entertainment," Yasmine said, turning her gaze on Eden, "I can assure you, this is not another lecture."

"I just want to get to the point," Eden said, letting out a breath. "A woman has already—"

"The conversation is not at fault if you cannot follow its threads," Yasmine said, turning away from Eden and dipping a henna-patterned finger into the pool.

"What's that supposed to mean?" Eden said.

The sound of a vehicle carried from outside the madrasa, a reminder that the rest of the world was still out there, Irons included.

"It means, in this case, that sometimes death is merely a transition, like water becoming vapor." Yasmine wiggled her fingers, and a ripple spread across the pool. "Other times, death is something else entirely."

"Stop." Eden's hands clenched into fists. "I didn't watch someone die, then travel five thousand miles to hear your theories about the afterlife. Eva Glass sent me to you for help." Eden swung off her bag and opened the top. "She told me to show you this. She said that you would know how to stop it from falling into the wrong hands."

"Not yet," Yasmine said, raising a hennaed hand toward the bag. "Words shape intention and reveal truth. They are the real eyes to the soul. Tell me, did Eva Glass use those exact words?"

"She said—" Eden paused, trying to remember Glass's exact phrasing through the chaos of their escape. "She said, *you would know what to do.*"

"In that, she is correct. But how can I tell you if you will not listen?" Yasmine leaned back into the cushion and exhaled.

"I *am* listening," Eden said, frustration boiling over. "But you're not telling me what I need to know."

"If you do not yet know," Yasmine said, her soft tone cutting through Eden's much harder one, "how can you possibly know what you *need* to know?"

Eden grumbled in frustration and closed her eyes.

"I am simply trying to tell you that the mind is an incredibly powerful thing. The answers are all around you, but so far you have not seen them."

"What do you mean?" Eden said, looking around the walls, as though the answers might flash in neon writing.

"Let me give you an example." The older woman leaned forward and looked at Eden. "Why do you believe that there was poison in the tea?"

Eden looked at the other woman for a second. "Hamid told us, and then I felt it in my lips and hands." Eden raised a hand to her face, remembering the tingling sensation that had passed across her face.

"Hamid told you what the effects would be, you saw it happening to him, then your subconscious mind did the rest." Yasmine dipped a finger into the pool, ripples spanning out across the surface. "As I said, the mind is incredibly powerful—it creates your reality."

"So there was no poison in the tea?" Eden said.

"Unless you count mint, sugar and water as poison," Yasmine said with a vague sense of amusement. "When a person sees a rope in darkness and believes it to be a snake, does their heart not race the same?"

Eden narrowed her gaze, thinking through the events of the last few minutes.

"And here's something to think about," Yasmine continued, an eyebrow raised as she traced a circle in the water. "You struggle to believe that you were wrong about the poison—"

"I felt it," Eden said. "We all did."

"Yet you readily accept the reality that a stranger would poison you. What does that say about how you see the world?"

Eden opened her mouth to speak and then snapped it shut. She exhaled, fighting the urge to stand up and walk away. A few moments of silence passed between the women, backed only by the distant rumble of the city and the burbling water.

"The water really is surprisingly cold," Yasmine said, her fingers dancing through the pool again. "Try it."

Eden looked from the woman to the water, trying to work out if this were another trick. Realizing the quickest thing to do would be to get on with it, she leaned forward and dipped a finger in the water. She had to admit that, considering the heat of the day that had faded a few hours ago, the water was incredibly cool.

"I suppose the antidote we found was water?" Eden asked, watching the stars dance in the pool's reflection.

"Yet you believed it would save you," Yasmine said.

Eden withdrew her hand, water droplets falling from her fingertips like liquid silver.

"The mind is far stronger than you know," Yasmine said, closing her eyes and drawing a deep breath as though performing a meditation. "This is the first lesson you must understand: perception shapes your reality."

"I don't like being played with," Eden said, her voice hardening. She folded her arms and sat up straight. "We are here because lives are on the line, and you and Hamid are treating it like a joke. Glass is already dead, and many more will follow if—"

"Oh, you misunderstand entirely," Yasmine said. "It is not our fault that you came to this unprepared. The poison in the tea was a demonstration to reveal your character, your companions, and your willingness to sacrifice for others." She opened her eyes and looked at Eden. "You did well. You are here, no?"

"Glass said that you would help us," Eden said, shifting on the cushion and bringing the conversation back to its purpose. Yasmine didn't interrupt as Eden explained what had happened at Los Alamos, then took off her bag and pulled out the crystal. She placed it on the rug between them.

"The Eye of the Sahara," Yasmine said, leaning forward, her gaze locked on the object. The crystal's multiple facets danced in the lamplight, its surface pulsing with its inner radiance. "This was taken from us many years ago, and after all this time, your people still have no idea what they're playing with."

"The Eye of the Sahara?" Eden said, looking down at the object. "Glass never called it that."

"No, she wouldn't have." Yasmine's fingers hovered over the object, yet didn't quite touch it. "The name was sacred to us, known only to us. Eventually it was passed to the structure from which this never should have been taken—what you now call the Richat Structure."

"You've seen it before?" Eden asked, nodding at the crystal.

"Not in this lifetime," Yasmine said. "But I knew I would."

"And what does it do?" Eden said, a little unsettled by Yasmine's reaction.

"That you will learn when the time is right," Yasmine said. Eden really tried not to roll her eyes but failed. "From what I know, your scientists treated it like a book in a language they can't read—setting it on fire for warmth. I'm glad it will now be returned to us." Yasmine looked up from the crystal, as though pulling herself from a spell. "Put it away now, I have seen all I need."

Eden did what she was instructed.

"You will face challenges delivering this home," Yasmine said, looking at the water once again.

"I know, that's why I have to do it quickly," Eden said. "Before Irons finds us."

A motorbike started up, grumbling for a few seconds before fading.

"Haste serves no purpose if you stumble blindly into the waiting trap," Yasmine said. "If you are to survive this ordeal, you must see. Really see." A breeze passed through the madrasa, sending ripples across the water. "Pass me your hand."

Eden held out a hand, and Yasmine took it in hers. Eden noticed the intricacy of the geometric henna patterns which started at the tips of Yasmine's fingers and swirled up her arms, disappearing beneath her robe.

"Let's see what we've got here," Yasmine said, removing a small knife with a horn shaped handle from beneath the folds of her robe. Before Eden could pull her hand away, Yasmine passed the blade across the tip of Eden's middle finger, drawing blood.

"What ... why did you do that?" Eden tried to pull her hand back, but Yasmine held it with surprising strength.

The older woman muttered a few words Eden didn't understand, then held the hand out across the pool, letting the blood drip into the water. Eden watched, transfixed, as the droplets spread and danced through the water into something that resembled a red thread. The thread spiraled outwards, creating intricate knots that twisted together. Eden thought she caught a glimpse of something in the crimson patterns, a shape or symbol, but it vanished before she could grasp it.

"Your blood remembers what you cannot," Yasmine said, letting go of Eden's hand.

"I suppose this is another trick."

"That depends on whether you believe it to be true. If I told you I can see the genetic memory of your ancestors flowing through these drops, would you believe me?" Eden was about to speak when Yasmine continued. "It doesn't matter. I now see what I must share with you."

34

LALLA YASMINE RELEASED Eden's hand and reached beneath her robe. She withdrew a cylindrical object about the length of her forearm. It was made of the same blue-gray metal as the Hamsa in the shop, its surface etched with markings that Eden assumed to be the Amazigh writing system, Tifinagh. As the object moved, the markings caught the lamplight with a shimmer that looked almost like liquid.

"This has been in our keeping for a long time," Yasmine said, running her fingers over the inscriptions. She twisted the cylinder's ends in opposite directions and separated the two sections, revealing a hollowed interior lined with what looked like silk.

She slid her fingers inside and removed a roll of parchment from the protective casing. The material was yellowed with extreme age, yet remarkably intact. She unrolled it on the rug beside the lamp, revealing what appeared to be an ancient map.

"This," Yasmine said, her finger hovering above the map, "is a work of the Roman cartographer Pomponius Mela, created in the first century. He was one of the earliest geographers to accurately describe Africa beyond the Mediterranean coast."

"This map has survived that long?" Eden said, leaning in to examine the faded lines and inscriptions. The map showed a stylized representation of northwestern Africa, with mountains, rivers, and settlements.

"Of course not," Yasmine smiled. "Parchment turns to dust after a few centuries, even with the best care. This example is only around three hundred years old but was copied from an earlier version. Each generation of guardians has recreated this, and our countless other important documents, before the previous versions become unreadable."

"So it might not even be accurate," Eden said, disappointed.

"It certainly is," Yasmine said, as though Eden's suggestion was ridiculous. "We have a master copy recorded, which new versions are always checked against." She flicked her hand toward the courtyard's far corner, as though suggesting it was stored that way.

Eden followed the gesture but saw nothing, aside from the swirling tiles and ornate carved columns.

"We would never entrust something this fragile to parchment or papyrus," Yasmine continued, her fingers sweeping over the map. "Of course, we knew these lands long before Mela, but you people in the modern world seem to have an obsession with the written word."

Yasmine moved her fingers down across the map, tracing the Atlantic coast of North Africa. The lamplight flickered, casting shadows across the ancient markings. Reaching what would be modern Mauritania, she paused. Her finger rested beside a single word, written in faded Latin script.

Eden leaned closer, squinting at the text. The letters

seemed to shift in the dancing light, before resolving into clarity. She sat bolt upright, looking hard at the other woman.

"Atlantae," Eden said, her words more of a gasp. "It can't be... can it?"

The courtyard seemed to go completely silent—even the burbling water faded to nothing. Yasmine didn't speak for a long moment, letting the weight of the revelation settle.

"The truth is," Yasmine said, placing her hand on top of Eden's, "It can't *not* be. When the Romans found the ruins of a city, they clearly didn't understand the significance."

"You're telling me," Eden said, looking back at the map. "That's really it? The location of Atlantis?"

"Will you doubt everything I tell you?" Yasmine said softly. "Or is it just that you've been trained not to see what's directly in front of your eyes? The Romans knew. They marked it on their maps. And my people—we never forget."

"The Richat Structure," Eden said. "The Eye of the Sahara. It's not just a name. It's literally—"

"The last remnant of the greatest civilization this world has ever known," Yasmine finished. "And you're holding the key to powers they wielded ten thousand years ago."

"That makes sense," Eden said, thinking back to Glass's description of the underground structures. "Glass said there were buildings, transport infrastructure, and some sort of power generation."

"Yes, but she didn't know what you now do," Yasmine said. "She didn't put the two most obvious things together."

"Plato described Atlantis as a series of concentric circles," Eden continued, her thoughts now running at a hundred miles an hour.

"And what did he say about the location?" Yasmine asked.

"He said it was beyond the Pillars of Heracles—what we now call the Strait of Gibraltar," Eden said.

"Which is there." Yasmine traced her finger from the Strait of Gibraltar down the coast to the position of the Richat. "But that's not all. Plato also wrote of great mountains to the north that sheltered the civilization from harsh winds. What do we call the mountain range that runs across North Africa today?"

"The Atlas Mountains," Eden said, remembering the snow-capped peaks they'd seen from the plane on the way into Marrakesh. "But wait, Atlantis was said to be in the ocean. This is in the desert. It must be hundreds of miles from the Atlantic."

"How arrogant you are." Yasmine laughed, as though genuinely amused. "You see things as they are and assume they have always been that way. Is it so hard to believe that the Sahara was not always a desert?"

"I suppose ... I just ..."

"Ten thousand years ago, this whole region was a lush savanna with lakes, rivers, and abundant with life." Yasmine gestured to the map, drawing a circle around the desert. "Ancient navigators would have traveled by water from what is now the Richat Structure all the way to the Mediterranean. Today it's called the Tamanrasset River, though it's now been dry for thousands of years."

"And the crystal ... Eye of the Sahara?" Eden asked, pointing at her bag.

"That was both their greatest achievement and their undoing." Yasmine carefully rolled the map up again and slipped it back into the tube. "The concentric circles were not merely architectural—they were functional. They were designed to harness the power of the land and focus it on a single point, but with progress came imbalance, and where imbalance flows, destruction is never far behind."

The sound of metal banging against metal echoed from somewhere beyond the courtyard.

Yasmine looked up at the night sky, as though the sound had dragged her back to the present.

"Humans always seek to turn discovery into destruction," she said, her gaze returning to the pool. "Water, for example, can sustain life or drown it. The difference lies not in the water itself, but in how we interact with it."

"We need to destroy this threat, then no harm can be done," Eden said, folding her arms.

"You talk like a man," Yasmine said, her tone now playful. "Always pushing for a result before you've truly understood the problem."

"You mean like mankind?" Eden asked, slightly uncomfortable with the sudden shift in conversation.

"No, men, males, the patriarchy," Yasmine said, her eyes gleaming in the lamplight. "My grandmother used to say we were descended from Tin Hinan herself—the mother of us all. Whether true or not ..." She shrugged, running her fingers along the tile joints. "Power without wisdom brings only destruction. This is easy to forget ..."

"I appreciate the history lesson—"

"This is not history," Yasmine interrupted, her voice sharpening. "And I don't mean to say that men cannot share feminine traits. But I encourage you to think differently—it is not that you must destroy something to succeed, but understand—"

Another crash reverberated from beyond the courtyard walls, followed by the splintering of wood and the clatter of metal striking stone.

"Our time grows short," Yasmine said, looking at Eden in

a way that suggested she was totally absorbed in their conversation. She once again took Eden's hands in hers. "You must remember, sometimes what you seek is right in front of you, all you must do is see it."

She held up the finger Eden had placed into the water. "I'll make sure Hamid gets some ointment for that burn. It will heal by first light."

"Burn?" Eden laughed, then stopped. A tingling sensation spread across her fingertips. "But the water was cold. I felt it. It was ..."

She stared at the finger, the skin reddening.

"That's impossible." Eden's gaze snapped to the pool. For the first time, she noticed the gentle wisps of steam rising from the surface.

"Of course not," Yasmine said, giggling like a child. "But your mind made it cold."

The distant sound of heavy boots on tile echoed from inside the building now, punctuated by another crack—a door being forced open.

"Time to go," Yasmine said, climbing to her feet. "Someone is coming for you, and all is not good."

The door swung open, and Hamid charged into the courtyard. "Men, inside the madrasa. We need to leave, now."

35

"Lalla, I have prepared transport for us to reach the Richat. The journey will take several days," Hamid said, racing across the courtyard. "I fear these men are here to stop us, we must leave now."

A distant crash echoed through the madrasa, followed by thudding footsteps. Eden and Hamid turned to look at the noise, but Lalla Yasmine didn't even seem to notice.

"We can't leave now. We've got to get my team," Eden said, rising to her feet.

"No," Yasmine said, taking Eden's hands in hers. "You will see your friends when this is done. Hamid is now your guide on this journey."

Eden remained, frozen in position, looking at Yasmine. The older woman squeezed Eden's hands gently. In her eyes, Eden saw something far more powerful than the rifles heading their way.

"Your friends are safe, but you have work to do," Yasmine said, her voice rising over the coming noise.

Yasmine said a few words to Hamid, who nodded before turning and running across the courtyard. He ducked into an arched alcove and yanked open a door, revealing a spiral staircase corkscrewing upwards.

"This leads to the roof," Hamid said, squeezing through and racing up the stairs. "From there, we can cross to the neighboring buildings."

"Now, you must go," Yasmine said, releasing Eden's hands and nodding the way Hamid had gone.

Eden held the older woman's gaze for a second, then pulled her boots back on and sprinted to the staircase. She climbed the first couple of steps, then pulled the door closed behind her. Hurrying upward, she passed several small, latticed windows. Through the first she glimpsed a library, its shelves of leather-bound volumes lit by a single oil lamp. The next revealed a prayer room with rugs arranged in neat rows. Finally, she emerged onto the madrasa's roof, breathing deeply.

"We must not stop," Hamid said, looking out over the medina's rooftops. In the distance the distinctive minaret of the Koutoubia Mosque rose like a lighthouse on a stormy sea.

Hinges shrieked, and footsteps pounded into the courtyard below.

Eden crept to the edge of the roof and peered down. Yasmine had disappeared, along with the rug and cushions. Several men, dressed in black charged into the courtyard, rifles pressed to their shoulders. They swept the guns from right to left, barrel mounted flashlights cutting through the gloom.

"Such forces do not mobilize without powerful hands pulling the strings," Hamid said, studying the men below. "Follow."

He led the way to the edge of the roof where a gap of perhaps twelve feet lay between the madrasa and the next building. At first, Eden thought Hamid was going to jump, but thankfully he retrieved a narrow plank which had been leaning against the wall and dropped it over the void.

"How convenient," Eden said, looking at the makeshift bridge. "Maybe the spirits put that there to help us?"

"No," Hamid said, deadpan. "I put it there earlier." He stepped out onto the plank, the wood immediately sagging under his weight.

"Good idea, saving the spirits a job," Eden said, watching the wood bend further and further as the big man paced toward the center. "I'm sure we'll give them plenty to do later."

The plank groaned as Hamid approached the far side. With a final trembling crack from the wood, he reached the other building and stepped onto the rooftop.

"We have no time to waste," Hamid said, looking toward the noise of the approaching men.

"That's easy for you to say." Eden stepped out onto the plank, which immediately sagged. She reached the middle, the wood groaning as it bent lower and lower. A crack split the air, which for a moment Eden thought was the plank splitting in two. She braced herself, ready to jump, when the wall a couple of feet away disintegrated under rifle fire.

"Run!" Hamid shouted.

Eden sprinted, the plank buckling with each step. The wood splintered under her left foot as she launched herself forward, diving toward Hamid. She hit the rooftop and scrambled in behind a full-size olive tree in a large pot. Another burst of automatic gunfire followed, rounds smashing the pot to shards and spilling soil across the rooftop.

"They knew their way to the roof," Hamid said, from behind the neighboring pot. He pulled a weapon from beneath his djellaba and returned fire, forcing their pursuers to dive for cover.

Eden glanced out and saw that the building they were on was far humbler than the madrasa. Constructed from concrete and cinder blocks, potted trees dotted the rooftop and drying laundry swayed in the breeze.

With their pursuers out of sight, Eden darted from her position, grabbed the end of the plank and threw it down between the buildings. It slipped, then fell, crashing to the lane beneath.

"Let's hope we don't need to go back that way," Eden said, turning away and darting back across the rooftop.

Hamid rose to his feet and ran backward, firing as he moved. They hurried to the far side of the building and ducked in behind a decorative parapet.

Eden looked at the next building, about six feet away, and prepared to make the jump.

"No, this way," Hamid said, grabbing her arm and pointing further across the rooftop.

"Oh great, you have a plan?" Eden said, glancing back at the madrasa where four men assessed the gap between the buildings. Although too far to jump, it was only a matter of time before they figured out a way across.

"There is always a plan, whether we know of it or not," Hamid said, leading the way to the other side of the building. He swung open a rusted metal trapdoor set into the roof. Inside, a ladder descended into the darkness.

A man carrying a ladder appeared on the madrasa's roof, clearly having found it in a storeroom. The men positioned the ladder over the gap and one of them started across.

"Quick, down here," Hamid said, ducking as another volley of gunfire peppered their position.

"You don't have to tell me twice," Eden said, swinging

onto the ladder as rounds pinged from the metal. She climbed down, the room getting darker with each rung. After a surprisingly long descent, she landed on solid ground.

She pulled out her penlight—a tiny flashlight she always carried—and clicked it on. Sacks of grain and flour were stacked against one wall and bundles of dried herbs hung from the ceiling.

Hamid followed, pulling the trapdoor closed, muting the gunshots. He slid a thick bolt across and descended.

"The family who owns this house are part of our network," he explained, jumping down the last few rungs. The impact of his landing shook a cloud of dust from the piled sacks.

"Network?" Eden asked, ducking beneath a hanging bundle of mint the size of a small tree.

The sound of boots on the roof indicated that their pursuers had crossed.

"Those who protect the old knowledge," Hamid replied, weaving his way between another tower of grain sacks and stopping before an object draped in a large canvas cloth at the room's far edge. He dragged the cloth away, revealing the oldest motorcycle Eden had ever seen.

"That's not getting us anywhere," Eden said, looking down at the ancient two-wheeler. The motorcycle might have been blue once—or possibly green—it was hard to tell under the layers of dust and rust. The exhaust pipe was held on with what appeared to be coat hangers, and the kick-stand was a piece of rebar welded at an angle.

"This Motobécane has carried me through these streets for thirty years." Hamid rubbed the fuel tank lovingly. "The body may decay, but the spirit remains strong."

The footsteps overhead stopped at the hatch, the door rattling as someone tried to pull it open.

"That won't hold them for long," Eden said, glancing up as the metal twisted from its hinges. "You'd best get her started."

Hamid slipped the key into the ignition and fired it up. The engine coughed, sputtered, then did something Eden totally hadn't expected, started with a roar.

"Not bad," Eden said, sprinting across to the door and heaving it open.

Hamid walked the machine out into the narrow alleyway, the bike's light washing the scene in a soft glow. He threw his leg over the saddle, the suspension groaning.

"Get on," he said, shuffling forward.

The trapdoor crashed and screeched as the bolt finally gave way.

Eden climbed onto the narrow space behind Hamid, wrapping her arms around the big man's waist. Hamid twisted the throttle and the Motobécane lurched forward, powering them away into the city.

36

———

"WHAT ARE WE GOING TO DO?" Baxter asked, his voice tight with frustration. He paced across the rooftop terrace of their riad, the traditional Moroccan house built around a central courtyard. Like most riads in the medina, it had been converted from a merchant family's home into an intimate hotel, its thick walls and inward-facing design providing privacy and coolness even in the heart of the bustling city.

He gripped the railing and looked out over Jemaa el-Fnaa square, which continued to buzz with activity despite the late hour.

"She's been gone for hours," he said, turning so sharply that he sent one of the silk cushions tumbling from its chair. He left it there, pacing back between a pair of oversized plants.

"A wise man knows when to fight and when to rest," Winslow said, bringing a glass of scotch to his lips.

"Did you make that up?" Athena said, adding a little more wine to her glass.

"I don't know how you can be so relaxed," Baxter said,

looking at the pair who sat at one of the tables, drinks in hand.

"No, I read it in this book," Winslow said, pointing at the book open on the table in front of him. "*Zen and the Art of Not Giving a…,* it's called. I saw it on the bookshelf downstairs and remembered what you said about wanting to be as wise as Hamid."

"I definitely didn't say that," Athena said.

"Anything could happen to her out there," Baxter muttered, reaching the end of the roof terrace, and pausing to look down into the lane.

"You said something like that," Winslow said, turning the page. "Look at this one: *your words, become your thoughts, become your actions.*"

"Sounds like gibberish to me," Athena said, scooting along beside Winslow and looking at the book. "But it would be good to play Hamid at his own game. Let me have a look at that."

"How long do we just leave her?" Baxter said, pacing back across the rooftop.

"For now, there's nothing we can do," Winslow said, looking up at the younger man. "Saving your energy is the best course of action."

Athena flipped a few pages, then stopped. "*Worry is like a rocking chair—it gives you something to do but never gets you anywhere,*" she read out loud. "I like that one."

Baxter reached the other end of the rooftop and looked out at the silhouette of the Koutoubia Mosque, its minaret cutting a dark line against the sky. A clanging noise drifted up from the street as someone pulled a cart of scrap metal through the medina.

"What if she's in danger?" Baxter said, turning to face Winslow and Athena.

"Oh, I'm certain she is in danger," Winslow said. "Eden faces danger all the time. In fact, everyone on this planet faces danger all the time, but worrying about it will get you nowhere."

"She could get hurt, and we would never know," Baxter said, turning and starting back the other way.

Athena flipped another page. "Oh, this one's perfect for you," she said, looking at Baxter. "*The prisoner who paces his cell does not walk toward freedom, only deeper into his own captivity.* Does that sound familiar?"

"I'm not a prisoner," Baxter said through gritted teeth.

"No, but you're acting like one," Athena shot back. "Eden will be fine. I trust that."

Winslow set down his glass with a soft clink against the mosaic-topped table and rose to his feet. He walked across the rooftop and placed a hand on Baxter's shoulder. The younger man stopped mid stride and locked eyes with his senior.

"As you know, my daughter is one of the most skilled and resilient people I've ever met," Winslow said. "I know you care about her, we all do."

Below them, a cat yowled, and the faint sound of Arabic music drifted from a food vendor's stall.

"*Patience is bitter, but its fruit is sweet*," Athena said, snorting with laughter. "That's Aristotle, apparently. What did he know about learning ancient secrets from people who talk in riddles?"

"Probably quite a lot, given that he was one," Winslow said.

"Good point," she said, flipping the page again. "Although he probably wasn't forced to drink snake venom," she muttered.

"Eden will be fine," Winslow said. "She will deal with whatever she needs to tonight and contact us soon."

"But we don't know what—"

"You're worried because you care about her." Winslow gave Baxter's shoulder a reassuring squeeze, then glanced down at his watch. "With that said, I'm going to get some rest. It's been an incredibly long two days, or is it three?"

"Time is an illusion," Athena said, taking a sip of wine. "Did that sound wise?"

"Here's a phrase I believe in," Winslow said, looking from Athena to Baxter. "Rest is a weapon, use it."

"Ohh, I like that one," Athena said, thumbing through the book. "Is that Aristotle too?"

"No," Winslow said. "That's from The Bourne Identity."

Athena looked up aghast. "No way did Alexander Winslow just quote Matt Damon."

"It's Robert Ludlum, technically," Winslow said. Seeing that Athena clearly didn't understand, he added, "the author who wrote the book, before it was a film."

"It was a book?" Athena said with genuine surprise.

Winslow sighed, threw up his hands, and started toward the stairs. At the top, he paused, resting a hand on the wrought-iron railing. Baxter stood silhouetted against the square's twinkling lights.

"You should get some rest too," Winslow said, offering a comforting smile before disappearing down the stairs, knowing full well that sleep was something Baxter would not manage tonight.

Irons sat at the window of his fourth-floor suite in the Hotel Atlas, looking down at the nocturnal comings and goings of Jemaa el-Fnaa square.

"It's the perfect killing ground," Irons murmured, using a pair of binoculars to focus on one of the distant exits. "Wherever you are in Marrakesh, all roads lead here."

He rubbed his damaged leg with his free hand, trying to find a position that relieved the pain. He had been on his feet far too much over the last few days, leaving his skin blistered and raw.

For a moment he thought about Morales under armed guard in the next room. In order to help him piggyback the ancient system, she had a lot of catching up to do. She was young, passionate, and clearly capable—a good find. If only she could leave her loyalty for the director to one side, she would be an asset.

He lowered the binoculars and checked the scanner. The crystal's radiation signature was on the move again, traveling through the medina's northeastern quarter at quite a speed. That meant one of two things—either whoever had the crystal was on the run, or they were dead, and his team had it for themselves. Either, for Irons, meant progress.

"Team Alpha, report," he said, speaking into the radio.

"We pursued two targets from Ben Youssef Madrasa and across the rooftops, sir," came Kavanagh's reply. Boots on stone echoed in the background. "Lost visual when they descended into a residential—" The radio crackled with interference before clearing. "One male—large, approximately six-four, local dress. The female, five-six to five-eight, athletic build, dark hair. Age approximately thirty. Sending helmet cam stills now."

Another voice spoke in the background. "Take the left side. Check that door."

"They're on the move, that's good," Irons said, excitement lacing his voice. "We will be waiting."

Another white-hot pain shot through his thigh and into his hip. He dropped the radio and clamped a hand on his leg, forcing his breathing to remain steady.

"They exited the building before we caught up with them," the operative continued, his voice bellowing from the radio. "We're heading to the bikes now."

The wave of pain passed, and Irons bent down and scooped up the radio. "Yes, you need to do that," he said, his jaw still clenched against the pain. "Pursue them toward the square. We have a welcome party set up and ready." In the background, Irons heard several motorbikes kick into gear.

His laptop chimed with an incoming image—two figures on a rooftop, captured by his team's cameras. The photo was grainy, taken at a distance in moonlight, but clear enough. He enhanced it, zooming in until the faces sharpened into focus.

"Who are you, and what do you want with my crystal?" Irons said, leaning in and staring at the photo. He focused on the man first. Dressed as one of the city's own, he could have been one of the restaurateurs or market sellers who filled the streets of Marrakesh.

He turned his attention to the woman. She had an athletic build, with dark hair pulled back in a practical style. The way she stood suggested training—military perhaps, or some kind of secret service.

Irons thought he should probably close the picture and move on—they would be dead within the hour anyway—but curiosity nagged him. He felt, deep in the recesses of his mind, as though he'd seen the woman before, but he couldn't remember where. He thought about it for a few seconds, then opened an encrypted email system, attached the image and sent it to an address that was just a string of numbers.

His contact, a guy working out of Zurich, sold intelligence services to anyone with sufficient funds, no questions asked. With back-door access to the most comprehensive facial recognition databases, he would find the answer.

"Triple the usual fee if you can find their identities within the hour," Irons said, hitting send at the same time the radio buzzed.

"Moving to position now," came the call from one of the men in the square.

"Excellent," Irons replied. He picked up the binoculars and swept the rooftops surrounding Jemaa el-Fnaa. He selected positions for three snipers—one on the roof of Café de France, another above the north entrance, and the third on the old post office building.

Turning his attention to the shadows at the edge of the square, Irons saw several figures moving in the gloom. They spread out, taking positions behind market stalls and in doorways, ready to act quickly when needed. At the far end of the square, he clocked the three Ford Ranger pickup trucks. The vehicles sat with their lights off but engines running, ready to box anyone in should they get that far.

"Sir, motorcycle spotted, heading south on Rue el Ksour. Old Motobécane, two riders," another voice came through the radio.

"Let them come," Irons replied, excitement building. "The square is where this ends."

Irons let a breath go with the thought that it would soon all be over, allowing him to move to the next step of his plan. He opened his wallet and pulled out a photograph.

His wife, Anne, sat in their garden in Oxfordshire, surrounded by the roses she'd spent years cultivating. It had been high summer—the lavender behind her in full bloom, creating a purple haze in the background. Anne wore the yellow sundress he'd bought her in Paris, her red hair loose around her shoulders. Anne looked fascinated by a butterfly which had just landed on the bench beside her—a Small Tortoiseshell with black and yellow wings. Gazing at her expression now, Irons recognized it as a look of pure wonder, a look of love for the world around her.

"Soon our waiting will be over," he whispered to the photograph. It was the same promise he'd made every night, but now it really felt as if it was coming true. "Soon we will be back together. I can do this, my love, please have faith in me."

He clutched the photograph to his chest as emotion welled. He tucked it carefully back into his wallet and looked at the scanner as it pulsed again, closing in on his position. The crystal was coming his way.

37

"Hold tight," Hamid said, yanking the throttle.

"What do you think I'm doing?" Eden said, gripping Hamid's shoulders as the bike weaved from side to side, avoiding potholes and drainage ditches. "Is it too late to ask about our plan?" Eden said, shouting over the roaring bike.

"All is in hand," Hamid said, cutting past a donkey chewing at a sack of hay. "We have a four-by-four prepared by a friend in Gueliz. We start the journey tonight."

He yanked the handlebars hard right, aiming the Motobécane down a passageway which was barely wide enough for the handlebars. They swung around a corner, and a flight of stairs came into view.

"Wait, stop, stairs!" Eden shouted.

"Sometimes the shortest route is not the easiest," Hamid bellowed as they flew from the top step. The front wheel dipped, bouncing from the stairs as the suspension crunched. They hit the bottom of the flight, some part of the bike falling away with a clang. They accelerated again, the bike miraculously still in working order.

"How far is the Richat Structure?" Eden gasped, catching her breath after the bone-jarring descent.

"One thousand, one hundred miles, give or take," Hamid replied, swerving around a pile of construction debris. "Through Agadir to the coast, then south through Western Sahara to Mauritania."

"That's got to be what—three, four days of driving?"

"Two days to reach the Mauritanian border if we drive in shifts and don't stop except for fuel," Hamid shouted. "Another day across the desert to the Eye itself."

"That's too long!" Eden said, thinking about the madman hot on their tail. "Irons will catch us for sure!"

"It's the only option," Hamid said, accelerating toward what looked like a solid brick wall. When they were just inches from the wall, an opening to the right appeared. He swerved the bike, leaning at an impossible angle, the tires shrieking across the cobbles.

"Flights are monitored, and finding a pilot and plane are incredibly—"

Gunfire cracked from behind, echoing from the towering walls. Bullets smashed a line out of the bricks to the left, one pinging from the Motobécane's exhaust.

"We've got company," Eden said, tightening her grip around Hamid's waist.

Hamid righted the bike and accelerated again, giving Eden the chance to glance over her shoulder. Two off-road motorcycles powered down the lane behind them, each carrying a driver and a passenger.

"The men from the madrasa," Eden said, recognizing the tactical gear. "How did they find us?"

The passenger on the leading bike leaned around the driver, raised an assault rifle and fired. A stream of bullets struck the shutter of a closed shop, sparking from the corrugated steel and whining into the darkness.

"A hunter who has tasted blood does not forget the scent," Hamid replied, downshifting as they approached another turn. "And we are leaving quite a trail."

The pursuing bikes accelerated closer, their modern engines easily gaining on the vintage Motobécane. The crack of rifle fire came again, this time closer.

"Incoming!" Eden shouted.

Hamid weaved sharply left. The bullets zipped wide, striking the wall in a shower of mortar and stone.

"They're closing in," Eden said, glancing back as the bikes fanned out. The bright lights, now side by side, forced her to squint like an animal in the headlights. The bikes closed the distance, now close enough for Eden to see the rider's helmets through the wall of light.

"The mouse does not outrun the hawk by speed alone," Hamid said, yanking the handlebars hard to the right. The ancient Motobécane's rear wheel slid on loose gravel as they careened around a corner into an even narrower alley.

The pursuing bikes hit the brakes, dropped into single file, and accelerated again. The leading bike fired, bullets this time striking a hanging shop sign. The metal clanged like a bell as the sign swung wildly on its chains.

Eden leaned out, squinting through the dust and exhaust. Twenty feet ahead, a wooden scaffold bridged the narrow passage. Above it, the buildings leaned drunkenly toward each other, their upper floors nearly meeting.

"That'll do," Eden shouted into Hamid's ear. "Don't slow down!" She pulled her feet onto the seat and rose into a crouch.

"What are you—" Hamid said, as another bout of gunfire zipped past them.

Eden glanced over her shoulder, the leading bike now practically on top of them. The driver hunched forward, completely focused on the pursuit, the passenger raised the rifle for another shot.

Eden jumped from the seat, her hands closing around one of the scaffold's thick wooden crossbeams. She gripped on, growling with exertion, as Hamid and the motorcycle continued forward. Checking he was clear, she swung like a gymnast on the bars.

The lead rider, focused on following Hamid, didn't have time to react as Eden released her grip. She slammed down feet-first as the bike sped beneath the scaffold, striking the passenger in the chest and propelling him from the bike. He hit the cobblestones hard and rolled, the rifle bouncing away. The following bike broke, swerving to avoid their fallen colleague.

"Sorry about your friend," Eden said, finding the hand holds and gripping on. "He had to go."

The driver glanced back, momentarily surprised that his partner was no longer there. He reacted quickly, jabbing an elbow backward, aiming for Eden's ribs. Anticipating the move, Eden twisted to the side and caught his elbow beneath her arm. The driver struggled to pull his arm back, but Eden squeezed, pinning the arm in position. She swung to the side, forcing the driver off balance.

The bike swerved from side to side, the driver attempting to force Eden off balance. She pressed herself flat against the driver's back as a stone wall whizzed past. Then, the driver did what Eden had expected and released the handlebars to grab for his sidearm.

"That was a mistake," Eden said, using his shift in concentration to wrap her left arm around his throat in a chokehold. The driver clawed at her arm, totally forgetting about his weapon. With no hands on the bars, the bike wobbled, losing speed.

Eden released his arm and grabbed the handlebars, yanking them hard to the left. The bike lurched toward a wall.

The driver jerked backward, trying to smash his helmet into Eden's face. She tightened her chokehold, cutting off his air.

"You don't need this." She hooked her fingers under the rider's chin and found the helmet clip. She released the clip and yanked the helmet off, hurling it behind them where it shattered against the ground.

The rider slammed on the brakes, clearly hoping to throw Eden off. Bracing herself against the rider's back, she squeezed his throat tighter. The bike fishtailed on the uneven stones.

"This is your stop," Eden said, using the moment of instability to her advantage. She released her chokehold and grabbed the man by the back of his vest, pulling him sideways off the bike.

He fought to maintain his balance as Eden's weight forced him from the seat. Shoving the rider hard to the right with one hand, Eden yanked back on the throttle with the other. The bike lurched forward as she gave him a final shove.

"Thanks for the lift!" Eden said as the driver tumbled from the bike. She centered herself on the seat, took the handlebars in both hands and accelerated. More powerful than Hamid's vintage Motobécane, she closed the distance quickly.

"One down, one to go," Eden said, pulling up alongside Hamid. Glancing at the big man, she thought she saw the trace of a smile.

The roar of another engine echoed from behind them, growing rapidly louder. Eden glanced back to see the second pursuing motorcycle zip around the corner, its headlight finding them like a searchlight.

"The scorpion does not abandon its prey," Hamid said, downshifting as they approached another tight turn. "Turn left!" He banked hard into a narrow alley between two traditional houses. Eden followed, her stolen bike's superior handling making the turn easier than expected.

More gunfire erupted, this time close enough that Eden could hear the bullets striking stone. One round struck a hanging lantern ahead of them, sending it spinning and crashing to the ground in a shower of glass and sparks.

"There!" Hamid pointed ahead to where the alley opened into a wider street. "Jemaa el-Fnaa, we'll lose them in the crowds."

38

"WHERE ARE YOU, EDEN?" Baxter said, watching Jemaa el-Fnaa square's late night action. Whilst he knew that Winslow, Jason Bourne, or whoever, was right—*rest is a weapon*—right now, an instinct told him to keep watch.

A breeze rolled across the square, swinging the lanterns on the roof terrace of the building across the street. The lanterns' movement catching his attention, Baxter saw something moving across the rooftop.

He stood motionless, allowing his eyes to adjust. At first, he thought the object was one of the many cats that called the streets home, or even a monkey looking for food. But when the figure moved again, passing in front of a lantern, he realized its true size. A man stalked across the rooftops, heading in Baxter's direction.

Baxter remained stationary, watching the figure cross onto the rooftop of the next building. Dressed in black with something slung over his shoulder, this certainly wasn't a tourist looking for a photo-op.

The figure scaled a dividing wall and moved onto the building next to Baxter's position. Crouching low, they approached the edge of the rooftop, which directly overlooked the square. This position, Baxter figured, afforded them a clear line of sight both over the square and the narrow street that fed into it. The figure dropped, lying flat against the rooftop.

"It's an ambush," Baxter whispered, recognizing the position as a perfect chokepoint. "They'll have men on the ground chasing someone here. One shot, then escape into the chaos." Although he hated to admit it, the plan had a certain finesse.

The sound of motorcycle engines drifted from a few streets away. Something in the urgent rise and fall of the engines, as though the riders worked through the gears, carried a sense of urgency.

"Eden," Baxter said, his heart working its way into his throat. He turned and glanced at the staircase behind him, leading into the riad and out into the street. He considered waking Athena and Winslow, but the insistent whine of the approaching motorcycle engines told him time was not on his side.

Baxter looked back at the figure. The man unzipped the bag and removed a sniper rifle, assembling the weapon in near-total darkness.

His decision made, Baxter slipped over the balustrade and dropped onto a narrow ledge that ran along the building's exterior. Although the sniper's rooftop was only a story below his, dropping that distance would advertise his approach.

Baxter edged along the outside of the railing until he found a bundle of electrical cables running down the wall between the buildings. Using them like a rope, he lowered himself, hand over hand, covering most of the distance before releasing his grip and dropping the final few feet. He landed silently and immediately ducked behind an air conditioning unit.

The sniper now lay a few strides ahead, the scope clamped against his eye. He adjusted the weapon, angling it toward the approaching bikes. The man's hands moved across the weapon, performing the final checks Baxter knew so well—this guy was a professional.

The motorcycles roared closer—at least two, maybe three, moving fast. Their different pitches rose and fell as they weaved toward the square.

Baxter walked on the balls of his feet, closing the final distance using a cluster of satellite dishes as cover. He halved the distance before realizing he would have to make the final few strides in the open. If the man should sense him coming and turn, he would not only be seen, but probably shot.

The motorcycle engines growled closer still, now just one or two turns from the kill box.

Baxter exploded from cover, closing the distance in three strides. At the last moment, perhaps sensing the vibrations through the rooftop, the sniper rolled, reaching for his sidearm.

Baxter launched, driving his shoulder into the man's torso and sending them both crashing against the rooftop. The sniper rifle rolled away, falling from its stand and tumbling down into the street. It slammed into a canvas awning some distance below, waking a pair of cats who charged away with a screech.

The assassin twisted, pulling out his sidearm and backing up, trying to create enough space to level the gun at Baxter.

Baxter grabbed the man's wrist and slammed it against the roof. The assassin grunted, knuckles cracking on concrete, but his grip remained true. The assailant pushed back with surprising strength and swung the gun toward Baxter's neck. The gun barked, but the shot went wide, pinging off an air vent and up into the air.

The assassin drove his knee upward, catching Baxter in the ribs and forcing him to roll sideways. The man scrambled to one knee, bringing his weapon around for another shot.

Baxter bounced back onto his feet and lunged forward again, grabbing the man's gun and forcing it wide. Another shot cracked, the muzzle flash illuminating both men.

The assassin swung around, driving his elbow into Baxter's temple, then smashed the gun barrel into his jaw. Stars exploded across Baxter's vision. He staggered back, falling onto a satellite dish. He gripped the sides of the rusting metal dish, then forced himself up. He launched forward at the same moment a pair of bullets pinged into the dish.

Baxter slammed into the man, driving them both toward the roof's edge. Glancing over his shoulder, the assassin registered the drop. He tried to break free, but Baxter wrapped his arms around the man's torso. Muscles straining, he shoved them both toward the edge.

The sound of the motorcycles drew close enough to identify three distinct tones. One older rattled with the tone of breaking bones, the other modern engines screamed at a high RPM.

Baxter pulled back, creating some space, and drove his shoulder into the man's chest. He pushed again, driving them both toward the drop. With the assassin a foot or two from the edge, Baxter released his grip and stepped away.

The assassin tried to raise the gun, but Baxter threw a kick into the man's stomach, knocking him backward. The assassin stepped back, his foot hitting nothing but air. His expression changed from rage to confusion. He reached out, trying to grab Baxter as he teetered over the void. Baxter stepped away, out of the reach of the brute's swinging arms. Then, gravity did the rest.

The man fell backward, arms swinging uselessly as he plummeted three stories. He punched straight through a canvas awning, the fabric ripping from edge to edge, and slammed onto a charcoal grill below, sending burning coals exploding outward. The vendor and his customers scattered, screaming, as embers and flaming meat flew.

"I hope you like your meat well done," Baxter said, peering down at the motionless assassin at the center of the burning mess. He looked up just in time to see the motorcycles rounding the corner.

39

———

As the vehicles drew closer, Baxter recognized Hamid leading the charge on a vintage bike. A moment later, Eden appeared on a much newer machine. Then behind them, gaining ground rapidly, came a third motorcycle carrying two riders. The passenger on the pursuing bike shouldered an assault rifle. The rider attempted to take aim, but clearly struggled to get a shot with all the bouncing and weaving. Hamid took a sharp turn around an overturned cart, forcing the pursuer to slow.

Baxter assessed the scene. While the shooter struggled for a shot right now, sooner or later he would get lucky. As though answering Baxter's thoughts, the rifle flashed, bullets smashing into the ground just behind Eden's rear tire.

Looking out across the rooftops, Baxter realized other shooters probably lay in wait too.

"Definitely should have kept that gun," Baxter said, eyeing the assassin lying motionless on the grill.

He turned and saw an archway spanning the lane at the

point at which it opened into the square. From the center of the archway, a massive copper lantern hung on a chain.

"That's a mad idea, but it might even work." Baxter broke into a run, looking from the approaching bikes to the lantern. He sprinted out across the archway, sending a flock of doves into flight. The arch stretched barely a foot wide beneath his feet. Three stories down, people fled through the archway's opening, shouting in panic. The bricks beneath his feet seemed to sway as he reached the center, nothing but air between him and the cobblestones far below.

The passenger on the pursuing bike opened fire again, the bullets smashing into a wall and shattering a window.

Baxter dropped into a crouch and lowered himself down the side of the arch. He took the lantern's chain in one hand, then the other, climbing down hand over hand. As the pursuing bike gained speed, the passenger steadied the rifle for a clear shot.

Baxter lowered himself down another few feet, closing in on the copper lantern.

Hamid's bike roared through the archway below. Eden followed a heartbeat later, hunched low over her handlebars. Neither rider glanced up—their eyes locked on the escape route ahead as gunfire cracked behind them.

Baxter reached the lantern and clung to a lip that ran around the top, keeping the great brass object between himself and the shooter. The pursuing bike roared closer—thirty feet, twenty, ten.

Baxter watched the bike grumble toward him and then let go. He dropped through the empty air, tensed in preparation for impact. For a moment, he panicked that the bike had slowed or swerved. His stomach lurched as the ground rushed toward him. Then, the bike appeared, right beneath his feet.

Baxter slammed into the passenger with bone-jarring force. The impact drove the man forward, throwing the bike into a sideways skid. The rifle clattered to the cobblestones as both rider and passenger fought to maintain control of the machine.

Baxter shoved the passenger further still, forcing both men against the handlebars. The bike swerved wildly, the driver trying to compensate for the unexpected weight and impact.

"What the—" the passenger growled, reaching for a knife sheathed at his hip.

"No, you don't," Baxter said, clocking the glinting steel as the blade slid free. He seized the man's wrist, pushing the blade down.

The bike swerved hard left, forcing a young woman to yank her child out of its path. An old man jumped right, his walking stick clattering to the ground.

The passenger twisted his wrist, angling the knife point toward Baxter's stomach. Baxter wrenched the arm outward, but the passenger's grip shifted as he shoved the blade toward Baxter's thigh.

"It's not that easy," Baxter hissed. He twisted his hips, letting the blade slice through empty air. He lifted the man's knife hand and slammed it against the driver's helmet. Once, twice, the knife fell loose on the third impact, bouncing off the foot peg.

The passenger reached back with both hands. Baxter ducked low and wrapped his arm around the man's throat, using his other hand to grab the driver's shoulder for leverage.

The passenger thrashed, throwing several backward headbutts, but Baxter ducked. As the passenger weakened, he released the chokehold and shoved the passenger to the side, using the bike's momentum to throw him clear. The man hit the street and rolled, finally stopping at the feet of a camel chewing some hay.

"Fancy doing this the easy way?" Baxter said, shuffling forward and grabbing the driver's shoulders. The driver immediately jabbed an elbow back, catching Baxter in his already bruised ribs.

"I thought that might be your answer," Baxter said, reaching around to grip the handlebars.

The driver fought for control, jerking the bars left and right, trying to throw Baxter off balance. The driver made the move Baxter had been waiting for—his right hand dropped from the handlebars, reaching for the sidearm holstered at his hip.

Baxter grabbed the man's wrist before the gun cleared the holster, slamming it against the fuel tank. The driver tried again with his left hand, attempting to draw across his body.

"Not happening," Baxter said, looping both of the man's hands behind his back.

The motorcycle, now with no hands on the bars, wobbled dangerously as it sped toward a barbecue stall. The driver's eyes bulged, his gaze focused on their impending crash. In a desperate move, he leaned forward and bit down on Baxter's forearm. Baxter ignored the pain, using the driver's lack of balance against him.

"Time to go," Baxter said, shoving the driver off the seat.

The man slipped off the bike, but at the last minute grabbed the handlebars. The bike veered sharply. Baxter smashed his fist against the guy's fingers, sending him crashing to the ground and rolling beneath a tarpaulin-covered cart.

Baxter shuffled forward, brought the bike under control, and accelerated toward Eden and Hamid.

40

Eden heard a bike coming up fast behind her—another engine roar cutting through the chaos. She glanced over her shoulder, expecting to see another gun-toting goon speeding her way. Instead, Baxter powered alongside her on the stolen off-roader. He slowed the engine and offered her a grin.

"I'm really glad to see you," Eden said, returning Baxter's smile. "How did you find us?"

"You're not exactly quiet," Baxter said, shouting over the roaring engines.

Hamid's ancient Motobécane chose that moment to backfire, belching a cloud of thick smoke. The engine coughed, died for a terrifying second, then caught again with a sound like grinding metal.

"The wounded horse still carries its rider to safety," Hamid called back, patting the fuel tank as though comforting a dying animal. "Though perhaps not for much longer."

"We need to get—" Eden started to say, before the crack

of a rifle cut her off. The bullet glanced off the cobbles and smashed into a closed up juice cart.

"More shooters on the rooftops back there," Baxter said, jerking his bike sideways as another high caliber round zipped past. The bullet glanced off the catch on a snake charmer's basket, popping the lid open. Several cobras emerged, their hoods flared, sending the charmer scrambling away.

"Let's not stick around for the welcome party," Eden said, twisting the throttle and swerving around one of the juice stalls. The juice seller ducked out of sight as automatic gunfire smashed his watermelons and pineapples into chunks.

"Shooters on the ground too," Hamid said, unusually getting straight to the point. "Trying to corner us."

"Only a fool goes into a place with one exit," Eden said, powering back toward the center of the square. "Follow me!"

"That sounds like my line," Hamid shouted, coaxing a little more speed out of the Motobécane.

Eden hunched lower over the handlebars as muzzle flashes erupted from the rooftops and the shadows around the square—three, four, five positions. She weaved through a line of tourist horse carriages abandoned for the night, bullets shattering ornate lamps and tearing through leather seats. Wood cracked and split under the barrage.

Baxter and Hamid's engines screamed behind her, their tires skidding as they whipped from side to side.

"We need to get back into the souk," Hamid said, wildly gesturing toward the arched gateway ahead. "We can lose them in there."

A burst of automatic fire chattered into the cobblestones as two men ran from the shadows, shouldering rifles. Bullets shattered another ornate glass lantern and punched holes in a vendor's carpet display.

Eden swerved around a donkey cart loaded with oranges, which sat abandoned—its owner probably fled at the sound of gunfire. Bullets stitched across the cart, pulping fruit and filling the air with citrus mist.

"Not likely," Eden said. "Look!"

Headlights swept through the gloom as a black pickup truck swung around the corner, skidding to a stop in front of the entrance. Doors flew open and two men leaped out, weapons raised.

"Go left!" Baxter roared, skidding into a desperate turn. Bullets hammered into the ground, the crossfire coming from multiple directions. Another pickup truck sped into position, blocking the exits in that direction too.

"Nope," Eden said, slowing the bike momentarily. "It looks like we're stuck."

"The path is not always straight," Hamid said, pointing at a row of barbecue stalls right in the center of the open square. Made from canvas stretched over metal frames, the stalls were exposed on all sides. Long tables filled half the inside space, with a large grill occupying the other.

"Whilst that's true," Eden said, glancing at Hamid. "It's not especially helpful."

"They've stopped shooting," Baxter said, looking up at the rooftops on which several sniper rifles were probably aimed their way.

"That's because they know we're trapped," Eden said as another pickup truck came into view, tightening the net. "I think we all know what happens now." Her fingers closed over the brake, ready to stop and face whatever came next.

"No," Hamid said, with surprising force. He once again nodded at the barbecue stall. "We need to go inside that stall." He gunned the Motobécane's engine, swept the bike around and shot into the stall.

"I just don't see how—" Eden started, but Hamid was already too far away to hear. Eden and Baxter shared a glance, then followed.

"I'm not sure why this is helpful," Eden said as Hamid rolled his bike inside the stall. She looked around, the canvas covering fluttering in the breeze. "It's basically a tent but exposed on all sides."

They drove through the stall, passing long tables strewn with abandoned food.

Hamid slowed, clearly searching for something amid the debris. Finding what he was looking for, he stopped the bike.

"Get off the bike," Hamid said, killing his engine and kicking down the stand.

"Have you totally lost your mind?" Eden said, looking out into the square. The trucks moved forward, closing in.

Hamid knocked out two metal supports, bringing part of the awning crashing down in front of them and obscuring them from the oncoming shooters.

"At least that's got us a little privacy," Eden said, looking at Hamid as though he really was crazy. The canvas swayed above them, offering glimpses of the night sky through its various holes. "But the last time I checked, canvas isn't bulletproof."

"I haven't got any better ideas," Baxter said, killing his engine and kicking down the stand. Eden did the same and they both dismounted.

The bikes fell silent, replaced by the ominous rumble of approaching pickup trucks. Doors slammed, boots thumped against cobblestones and the metallic click of weapons being readied drifted through the canvas.

"Okay, what's going—" Eden said, stopping as Hamid dropped to his knees.

For a moment she thought he was praying. Then, he grabbed a stained piece of tarpaulin lying on the floor. He dragged it to the side, revealing an iron grate set into the ground.

"Help me," Hamid grunted, hooking his fingers through the bars.

The footsteps stopped just beyond the canvas. A radio hissed as instructions were given or received. The men stopped, clearly waiting for the command to continue.

Eden and Baxter grabbed the grate too and the three heaved together. The grate groaned, then suddenly gave, swinging up and back with a screech. A black hole gaped, cool air rushing up from the depths with the stink of ancient stone and stagnant water.

"The old cisterns," Hamid said, already swinging his legs into the hole. "Built by the Almohad to store water. They run beneath the entire medina."

"I could kiss you," Eden said, as the big man jumped down into the tunnel. She dropped through the opening next, falling about eight feet before landing in a pool of shallow water.

Baxter splashed down beside her, immediately pulling out a small flashlight. The beam revealed a vast underground tunnel with columns rising from ankle deep water.

"By the way, I'm changing our plan," Eden said.

"Where are we going?" Baxter said, striding on. "Did Lalla Yasmine tell you what to do?"

"We need to get to the airport." She turned to Hamid. "We now have a pilot, and I can sort us a plane."

"Understood, that way," Hamid whispered, pointing off into the shadows. "And no kissing required."

"Yes, but where after that?" Baxter said.

"Atlantis," Eden said, striding off through the water.

Baxter blinked a few times and then froze. He looked at Eden. "Maybe all that shooting has ruined my hearing, but I'm sure you just said—"

"Yes," Eden said, turning around and looking him dead in the eye. "We're going to Atlantis."

41

———

Irons climbed out of the Ford Ranger and assessed the smashed-up food stall. Although part of the canvas had fallen, obscuring the scene inside, the stall was isolated from all other structures.

"We've got them trapped, as you ordered," Kavanagh said, stepping alongside Irons. "They went in almost five minutes ago and haven't come out."

Irons took a reassuring glance at the scanner. He reminded himself of the facts—the crystal pulsed with its unique radioactive signature at least every five minutes, and the last pulse it emitted was inside that tent.

"I'm going to collect my crystal," Irons said, putting the scanner on the back seat of the Ranger and grabbing his cane.

"Sir, I really don't think that's a good—"

"Nothing will happen to that crystal," Irons said, pulling his Walther P99 Compact handgun from the holster beneath his jacket. He glanced at the surrounding men, each of them training their weapons on the structure. "If anyone comes out before me, kill them."

Kavanagh looked as though he were about to argue, then nodded.

Irons clicked off the Walther's safety, then using his cane with one hand and holding the gun in the other, limped away from the truck. He crossed the distance slowly, making for a join in the canvas.

The men shuffled aside to let him through, their weapons never wavering from the target. No one spoke as Irons limped up to the canvas, each step sending a bolt of pain through his leg.

"This is all for you, Anne," he whispered, picturing the photograph in his mind's eye. The image, he'd found over the years, did something to dissipate the pain.

Reaching the canvas, Irons paused. He lifted the weapon and stepped through the opening.

"You have something that doesn't belong to you," Irons bellowed, stepping into the center of the barbecue stall.

The flashlights of his men outside knifed through the canvas seams, casting beams of light through the smoky air. A pair of lanterns hanging from the steel structure washed the interior in a dull glow. But so far, the stall looked to be empty.

"You are completely surrounded," Irons said, circling one of the long tables. He peered behind the smoldering grill, topped by several skewers of now thoroughly burned lamb—nothing.

He moved around the three motorbikes standing in the center. An ancient motorcycle sat nearest, oil dripping from its cracked engine, with the two modern off-roaders behind. But still, the place was empty.

"I suggest you come out now," Irons continued, the confidence slowly draining from his voice. He did another full turn, seeking any nook in which someone could hide. Nothing.

"How is that even possible?" Irons groaned, already processing the implications.

He limped around the bikes, passed the grill, and then something came into view. Behind the grill, in the floor of the make-shift restaurant's kitchen, a large grate had been dragged from its mounting, revealing a hole in the ground.

"Dammit!" Irons roared, slamming his cane hard against the cobbles. The aggressive movement sent a shockwave of pain through him, causing him to bite his tongue. The taste of copper filled his mouth.

"Sir, what's happened?" Kavanagh said, pacing through the canvas.

Irons didn't respond. He stared into the hole, his hands trembling—whether from rage or the constant pain, he didn't know. Finally, he looked at the other man and pointed into the hole.

"Two men stay here, watch this entrance," he ordered. "The rest of you, find every well, every grate, every possible exit from wherever that goes."

"That could be dozens of exits, sir."

"Cover them all!"

Back in the truck, Irons glanced at the scanner which, now flashing, told him the crystal had moved away from the square.

Irons pulled out his phone and performed a quick online search. The results confirmed his suspicions in just a few seconds.

"Damn medieval cisterns," he growled, both hands clenching. "We stood here, we surrounded them, and they still escaped."

Once again, he thought about the photograph until his

phone beeped. His heart sank, thinking he would have to give another update to his ever-impatient employer, but it was the results from the photographs he'd sent.

"Hamid ben Yacoub," Irons said, reading the message. "Born in Marrakesh, 1971. Antiquities dealer..." he scrolled through the message, detailing a man who on the surface ran a shop in the medina, but in reality, was a whole lot more interesting. He scrolled through to the next part of the message. He paused, tapping the phone against his chin.

"Eden Black," he said, looking out through the windshield. "How very interesting to find you meddling in my business." Irons's gaze hardened suddenly as he realized these people weren't running scared. They were going somewhere purposeful, and in that moment, he knew exactly where.

"Change of tactics," he said into the radio. "We're moving out now!"

42

———————

THE ENGINES of the De Havilland Twin Otter droned as they crossed the border from Western Sahara and into Mauritania. Sitting in the co-pilot's seat, Eden looked out at the Sahara, which stretched endlessly in all directions—an ocean of sand and stone rippling in shades of amber and rust.

"Nice work on the plane," Baxter said, tapping the dashboard. "You know this is one of Byrd's favorites. Apparently, she used one last week too—"

"It's amazing what a bit of money and influence does," Eden said, not wanting to get Baxter started on the topic of planes. In truth, sourcing the aircraft had been no issue at all. In a country of winding roads and vast distances, Marrakesh Airport housed multiple charter companies willing to look the other way for a stack of cash.

"Not far," Baxter said, glancing at the dials.

Eden glanced back at Hamid, somehow cramped yet serene in the small aircraft seat.

"The sand keeps many secrets," Hamid said, his voice

crisp through the headset. He gazed meditatively out at the desert with the amazement of someone seeing it for the first time. "We must respect what we see here. It has outlasted many civilizations and will remain unchanged long after we are gone."

"That's very poetic," Eden said. "But let's stay focused on stopping Irons."

"Oh, I am," Hamid said, looking at Eden. "One does not exclude the other, be assured of that."

"The conversation is not at fault if you cannot follow its threads." Repeating Lalla Yasmine's phrase, Eden thought about Hamid's words until they bumped through a rare patch of cloud.

"You're quiet," Baxter said, stealing a glance at Eden. "Is it about the meeting with Yasmine?"

"Sort of," Eden said, shifting in her seat. "I just wish I understood it all a bit more. I feel..."

"Out of your depth?" Baxter said.

"No, just..."

"Drowning in worry?" Baxter offered.

"It's not that..."

"Ill-prepared?" Hamid offered. "The moth understands nothing of the flame—"

"Guys, stop, please," Eden snapped, casting them both a look. "You're not helping. In fact, you're so far from helping that you wouldn't recognize help if—"

"In the desert, we say anger is drinking poison and expecting your enemies to die," Hamid said.

"Don't mention poison," Baxter said, glancing at Hamid, whose folded arms almost filled the cabin.

"I can't deal with all this mystery. Just tell me how it is, in a way that makes sense," Eden moaned as a caravan of camels came into view, their shadows stretching long across the dunes.

"Yes, maybe just write it all down in an easy-to-read format," Baxter said, glancing routinely at the dials. "All this visiting at midnight stuff—"

"The young pilot speaks like someone who has never tried to preserve a truth across generations," Hamid said, leaning between the seats. "How would you ensure a warning survived ten thousand years? Stone crumbles, metal corrodes, paper burns. But stories ... stories endure."

"But stories can also change," Eden said, glancing back at Hamid. "How do we know that what Lalla Yasmine says is correct?"

"Sacred stories, the truly important ones, are preserved word for word," Hamid said, his voice taking on the cadence of a teacher. "Among my people, there are tales that have remained unchanged for thousands of years."

"That might be so, but there's a lot at stake here." Eden checked her phone. "That trick with the cistern isn't going to hold Irons off for long. Time is running out."

"Time moves differently in the desert," Hamid said, settling back and knotting his fingers together. "What seems urgent in the city, is less so out here."

"Physics doesn't care about philosophy," Baxter countered.

"Yeah, a second is a second, right?" Eden said, already regretting going down this particular conversational rabbit hole.

"You will see." Hamid chuckled softly.

Baxter checked their position. "Well, I can tell you now that in twenty human minutes ..." He stopped and leaned forward. "Oh my ... wow. Look at that!"

Eden followed his gaze through the windscreen and gasped.

The concentric rock circles of the Richat Structure sprawled out before them, impossible in their perfection. The outer ring stretched nearly twenty-five miles across, each inner circle rising like an amphitheater carved by giants. From the ground, the formation may have seemed natural, but from ten thousand feet, the pattern was so precise it defied logic.

"My grandmother said this was a crown fallen from the head of a giant, turned to stone by the sun." Hamid craned his neck to get a better view. "At the time I thought it was just a story, but now I am not so sure."

"It's incredible," Eden said, looking out at the shapes which seemed so vast compared to their tiny plane.

Baxter banked the plane to fly around the structure, rather than across it.

"Why are you turning?" Eden said.

"Remember, Glass said something down there interfered with the chopper's systems. I don't want to invite trouble."

"It's amazing that this place hasn't been thoroughly researched," Eden said.

"Sandstorms, equipment failures, local opposition," Hamid said.

"Local opposition?" Eden glanced over her shoulder.

"Yes, you will see," Hamid said darkly.

As they rounded the structure, Eden thought about Glass's description of what had happened here. Dr. Lawrence hadn't made it out alive, and years later Glass had died protecting their discovery.

"Whatever lies down there, it's already cost too many lives," Eden said, a chill moving through her.

"There's Ouadane," Baxter said, pointing at a collection

of weathered stone buildings clinging to the edge of the plateau beyond the structure. "Beginning descent."

Looking down as they flew low over the village, Eden saw movement between the buildings. Various blue-clad figures emerged from doorways and a pair of pickup trucks cut a line through the narrow streets, kicking up dust.

"It looks like we've got a welcome party," Eden said as the trucks sped through the small marketplace, weaving between colorful fabric awnings. A group of children playing in a courtyard stopped their game to point at the plane.

"Let's hope they're actually welcoming," Baxter replied, swinging the DeHavilland around to line up for landing.

"I'm not drinking any tea," Eden said, folding her arms.

Hamid barked out a laugh, then leaned forward and clapped Eden on the shoulder. "Worry not, all the tea is good."

The Twin Otter bounced, slicing through a pocket of turbulence. Eden's stomach lurched as they dropped twenty feet in an instant.

"Aren't we forgetting something?" Eden said, gripping the armrests. "Where's the runway?"

"See those white-painted rocks." Baxter nodded at the dusty strip of sand ahead. "It's between those." He worked the controls, and the plane dipped lower.

"That's not a landing strip, that's a sand pit!" Eden said, their shadow racing across the ground.

"It's the best we've got," Baxter said, clenching his teeth as the wheels slammed down, rattling the airframe. The aircraft bounced before settling onto the rough surface. Dust billowed around them, obscuring everything beyond the windscreen. The Twin Otter rattled and shook, every rut and stone transmitting directly through the landing gear.

Baxter hit the brakes, sending the aircraft into a skid. They slewed through the sand, first one way, then the other. Finally, they slowed and stopped, a plane-length from a sand dune which had encroached across the strip.

"Welcome to the edge of the world," Hamid said, unbuckling his seatbelt. "May we find what we seek, before it finds us."

43

———

THE TWIN OTTER's propellers whirred into silence as Baxter shut off the engines. He scanned the dashboard, looking for signs of any damage during their bumpy landing.

"Not bad at all," he said, sliding off the headset and unclipping his harness. "These beauties are hardy. I can see why Byrd likes them."

Eden rolled her eyes at Baxter's mention of Byrd, then swung the door open. The desert heat streamed in, instantly prickling her brow. As the drone of the engine fell away, she tuned into the sounds of the village. A donkey brayed from somewhere between the buildings, mixing with the sound of laughing children and the rhythmic thud of someone pounding millet in a mortar.

The dust from their landing settled and Eden saw two old Toyota Land Cruisers racing toward them. The vehicles burst out of the village, swerved around a pile of concrete blocks, and skidded to a halt at the end of the airstrip.

The doors swung open, and three men climbed out. Their traditional blue robes swept out behind them as they paced to the front of the Land Cruisers. The leading man, clearly one of the village elders, pointed at the plane and shouted something in what Eden assumed was Hassaniya or Tamazight.

"They don't look pleased to see us," Eden said, climbing out of the plane and stretching.

"Let me handle this," Hamid said, struggling out of the plane and pacing across to the welcome party. The elder watched him approach, shouting and wagging his finger.

"This isn't looking good," Eden said as Hamid tried but failed to speak over the elder's tirade. The other two men shifted uncomfortably, clearly torn between respect for their elder and curiosity.

Eden took a few slow paces forward.

"Maybe we should let Hamid—" Baxter said, keeping pace.

The elder's voice rose to a near-shriek, spittle flying. One of the younger men stepped back, clearly shocked at his elder's outburst.

Hamid raised both hands. He tried speaking again, but the other man cut him off with another high-pitched barrage.

"No," Eden said, moving forward. "Of course we need to respect the local customs, but lives are on the line here." She closed the distance quickly, the villagers watching her approach with a mixture of intrigue and confusion.

"What's the problem?" Eden said, stepping alongside Hamid and looking from one man to the other. Although she stood at a respectful distance, her tone and stance showed a confidence she didn't totally feel.

The elder turned toward her and his expression darkened further. For a moment, he simply stared, as if her presence confirmed his worst suspicions.

"You! Another outsider come to take what isn't yours!"

he barked, switching seamlessly to French, which Eden spoke with some confidence.

"Please, Uncle," one of the younger men said, trying to take the old man's arm. "Let's discuss this calmly—"

"No! This is not happening again!" The older man shook him off with surprising vigor.

Shutters swung open and villagers leaned out of their homes to watch the action.

"This man says we should not have come," Hamid translated. "He says that bad things happen every time outsiders come."

"But we have come to return—"

"We didn't ask for your help! We have *never* asked for your help!" the man cried, his wild eyes locked on Eden. "For ten summers our crops have failed, since the day the last people came."

One of the younger men, who Eden now noticed wore a faded Barcelona football jersey beneath his traditional robe, stepped forward. "Uncle, please. Hamid's family has helped us many times. We owe—"

"We owe the ancestors!" the elder's voice cracked like a whip. "Not outsiders who come with their ..." he gestured at the plane, "... machines and their greed."

The argument exploded into rapid Tamazight; all three villagers now involved. Eden listened closely, catching the occasional French word she understood: "... forbidden ..." "... cursed ..." and "... danger ..."

"What are they afraid of?" Eden asked Hamid.

"You come here with ..." He pointed at the plane, as though he didn't know the word. "... and you mess with things you don't understand. The French came in 1987. They mapped everything, took samples. Six months later—

drilling rigs. My brother's grazing land, destroyed. Many wells, poisoned."

He stepped closer, and Eden could see the deep lines etched in his face, each one like a story of hardship.

"The Americans ten years ago. Research, they said. Then our wells go dry, and crops die in the fields. You are a curse!" He spat the word like poison.

One of the younger men tried to interject, but the elder silenced him with a look.

"Now you come. I don't care what you promise this time. More machines? More fences? More of our young people are leaving because the land is ruined."

The elder suddenly raised both hands, attracting the attention of the whole group. He took a step toward Eden, his eyes burning with rage and genuine fear.

"I have seen what happens when the outsiders come. The land remembers. The desert takes its revenge. And we ..." he gestured to encompass the village, "... we pay the price."

He barked several words in Tamazight then, without waiting for a response, turned and strode to his Land Cruiser. One of the young men hesitated, glancing between the elder and Hamid, then followed.

Both men climbed inside. The engine roared to life, and tires kicked up the dust as the vehicle lurched forward. The truck fishtailed before finding traction and speeding away toward the village.

"What did he say?" Eden asked.

"He says that anyone who helps us is no longer welcome in Ouadane," Hamid replied, his expression grim.

The second young man, the one wearing the football jersey, backed away several steps, then paused. His hand went to his pocket—a nervous gesture—and Eden caught a glimpse of a photo tucked there.

Hamid spoke gently in Tamazight, forcing the young man's jaw to tighten. He glanced at the village, where the dust from the elder's departure still lingered.

"Khalid," Hamid said, switching to French. "I promise you, what we do today will help. We plan to return life to your land. I knew your grandfather—"

"Don't speak of my grandfather," Khalid interrupted, but his voice cracked. He stood frozen, caught between worlds.

A long moment passed, the desert heat pressing down on them. A child cried somewhere in the village.

Finally, the young man's shoulders dropped. "My daughter needs medicine, but the clinic in Atar requires payment." He looked directly at Eden for the first time.

"We can help," Eden said, glancing at Baxter. "We can give you money for the medicine."

The young man took a deep breath, clearly on the edge of a decision.

"How about this? We buy your truck." She nodded toward the rusty Land Cruiser, which certainly wasn't worth more than the scrap value.

"You don't have to come," Hamid said, following Eden's lead. "You stay here, and we will take the truck."

"I ... I'm not sure ..." The young man gestured helplessly toward the village.

"You can tell the others we stole your truck," Baxter said, looking at the buildings to see that the villagers had grown bored with the conversation and turned back to their daily tasks.

"For your daughter's medicine, and for the truck," Eden said, digging some notes from her pack—far more than the rusty vehicle was worth.

The young man stared at the money, pride clearly warring with necessity.

A strong wind pushed across the desert, whipping up a cloud of sand.

Finally, the young man accepted the bills. He split the pile into three smaller folds and slipped them away inside his robes.

"The fuel gauge doesn't work," he said, producing the keys and handing them to Hamid. "But I filled it yesterday. Should get you there and back if ..." He paused. "If you come back."

"We will come back," Eden said, meeting the young man's gaze. "We will return the truck."

"Don't make promises that are out of your power to keep," the young man said, giving a bitter smile. Then, as though shaking the whole episode off, he turned and paced back to the village.

44

———

"That went well," Eden said, watching the man disappear between the buildings.

"At least we got what we needed," Baxter replied, pointing at the rusty vehicle.

"This is the time for action, not talking." Hamid paced up to the Land Cruiser and jumped into the driver's seat. The engine coughed and clunked a few times before finally coming to life.

Hamid rolled the Land Cruiser across to the plane and they quickly loaded their supplies into the flatbed.

"I'm not certain we got a good deal," Eden said, pulling at a curl of paintwork which revealed at least three different colors underneath. She opened the passenger door and climbed in.

"At least we won't argue about the music," she said, eyeing the place where the radio should have been, now a hole spewing wires.

"At least it starts," Baxter said, climbing into the two-person passenger seat beside Eden and slamming the door.

"In the desert, comfort comes second," Hamid said,

crunching the stick as though aiming for gear three and a half. "This truck has survived where many newer vehicles have failed." He hit the gas, powering them away from the airstrip.

"How far?" Eden asked, shouting above the grumbling engine.

"Thirty kilometers," Hamid replied, his voice tight. "But the road—"

"Don't tell me, the road is long and winding?" Eden said.

"No, the road—" Hamid tried.

"Is yellow and made from bricks?" Eden said.

"There is no road!" Hamid shouted, bashing the wheel. "Other than what we make for ourselves," he added.

As if to emphasize his point, the Land Cruiser bounced through a rut, bottoming out the suspension with such force that Eden's head hit the roof.

Eden rubbed her skull and decided that teasing Hamid clearly wasn't worth this sort of rough justice. The three settled into silence as they followed the pair of worn ruts, leading into the distance.

"I don't suppose the air con works," Eden said, desperately breaking the silence. She flicked one of the switches on the dash and the knob came off in her hand.

"That's your answer," Baxter said, leaning out of the window to get a breath of air.

"They really don't want us here, do they?" Eden said, pointing back toward the village.

"I can't blame them," Baxter said. "It sounds like they've had a rough deal."

"Agreed, but do you really think..." Eden trailed off and pointed at the bag which she held between her knees.

"What?" Baxter said.

"Do you really think their crops died because Glass took the crystal?" Eden said.

"The truth is the truth, whether you understand it or not," Hamid said, by way of an answer. He swerved around a pothole which could have swallowed the truck.

The twin ruts that had provided something of a track disappeared, forcing Hamid to slow the truck. They crawled up a gentle ridge, bouncing and shuddering across loose rocks. The engine strained as the tires spun against the incline. At the top of the ridge, the outer ring of the Richat Structure stretched before them. The slope was not gradual as it had appeared from the air, but a steep cliff made from rough stone.

"This place is incredible," Eden said, looking at the layers of colored sediment. The ridge curved away in both directions, eventually disappearing into haze.

"The desert provides for those who know how to look." Hamid pointed to the left where the cliff face was broken by what might have been an ancient landslide. He swung the Land Cruiser toward the slope, working their way around the larger rocks. They reached the top of the precipice and before Eden could even suggest that it might be too steep, Hamid wrestled the Land Cruiser into gear and set off down the slope. Muttering what could have been either prayers or profanities, he swung them in a switchback route down the landslide.

Reaching the bottom, Eden was once again astounded by the true scale of the structure. Ahead of them, hazy in the distance, the next ring rose like a frozen wave. The ground between the rings wasn't the flat sand she'd expected, but a mixture of exposed bedrock, intricate channels, and scattered boulders.

"This was once underwater," Hamid said, picking up

speed on the level ground. "And everything above was fertile and green."

"And now it's like this," Eden said, trying to imagine the barren landscape covered in vegetation, water flowing between the rings. Beneath the merciless sun, with heat-waves shimmering, it seemed impossible.

"The wise see an oasis in every wasteland," Hamid said, glancing at Eden.

The group traveled in silence until they reached the second ring, its wall rising above them like a natural fortress.

"The path has been provided for us," Hamid said, pointing to a narrow series of switchback curves worn in the gentlest part of the slope.

"Seek and you shall find," Eden replied.

"Indeed, but what is easily found is rarely worth the journey."

The Land Cruiser grunted and groaned, the engine temperature climbing steadily as Hamid worked the accelerator. Several times they lost momentum entirely—wheels spinning, spraying cascades of grit and small stones out behind them.

"Come on," Eden muttered under her breath, bracing herself against the dashboard.

Finally, the worn tires found purchase, sending them bouncing over the uneven terrain. Reaching the top of the second ring, Eden peered out behind them, once again struck by the elegance and scale of the place. The three sat in silence as they rumbled across the rise, the Land Cruiser's engine settling into a steady rhythm after its struggle up the slope.

Within minutes the next descent appeared—a yawning drop that made their previous climbs look like gentle slopes. The edge fell away into nothing, disappearing into the haze.

Eden's stomach lurched as they approached the precipice.

"As you say, the path will appear," Hamid said, driving along the precipice until he found a suitable path. He selected a low gear and let the Land Cruiser roll over the edge. The vehicle's nose dipped beyond the point of no return, revealing how steep the descent was.

"Take it slow," Eden whispered, supporting herself on the dashboard as they rolled down.

"We must trust the path," Hamid said, riding the brakes as they bounced down the slope. Rocks scattered from beneath their tires, clattering down ahead of them like an avalanche. The steering wheel jerked as the front wheels hit patches of sand and rock, threatening to send them sideways.

"That way," Baxter said, pointing to what might charitably be called a path—a slightly less vertical line through the scree.

"The desert shows us the way," Hamid said, swinging the wheel hard left. The Land Cruiser's rear end swung out, slipping and sliding.

For a heart-stopping moment, Eden expected the truck to tumble down the slope in a tangle of metal. Somehow the aged tires bit and Hamid straightened their course. They zigzagged down, switching back and forth between the larger obstacles. But the hard work took its toll—steam billowed from under the hood, the smell of burning rubber seeping in through the vents.

"Almost there," Hamid said. Whether he was talking to them, himself, or the truck, Eden couldn't tell.

With a final lurch that threw them all forward, they hit

level ground. The truck limped forward, cutting furrows through the sand.

Through the heat haze ahead, the next incline materialized. At first, it was just a darker smudge against the shimmering air, but as they drew closer, the shape became solid. Rising from the center of the depression was a massive monolith—not the gentle hill she'd expected, but a towering rocky edifice.

The engine coughed—once, twice—then rattled into a harsh metallic clatter, as if someone were shaking bolts in a tin can. They lurched forward a couple of times before the engine cut out. A moment of silence passed, broken only by the faint tick of cooling metal.

"Better to pause willingly than to stop forever," Hamid said, tapping the dashboard.

"What does that mean?" Eden said.

"The engine needs to cool." Baxter pointed at the gauge that was well and truly in the red. "What was it you said about these old trucks outlasting newer models?" Baxter asked Hamid.

Without a reply, which Eden realized was something of a habit, Hamid swung open the door and climbed out.

Baxter wrestled the door open and exited too, followed by Eden. Although it was hot out here, inside the stationary truck would soon be worse. The silence that surrounded them was absolute—no wind, no insects, not even the distant cry of birds. It was as if they'd entered a place removed from the normal flow of time.

Hamid pried open the truck's hood, releasing a cloud of steam. He stepped back and swung his hand through the vapor, then looked closely at the ticking engine.

Eden walked a few steps away from the truck, to stretch her legs and escape the metallic smell of overheated machinery. As she walked, something crunched under her boot. She knelt and brushed away the sand, revealing a perfect spiral shell no bigger than her thumbnail. She picked it up, then saw another, and another.

"This really was once underwater," she said, rolling the shell between her fingers. After millennia in the desert, the shell still felt solid in her palm.

A sound boomed across the landscape. Distant at first, like static on a dead radio channel.

Eden turned, half expecting Hamid to have restarted the truck. He remained outside, looking up at a brown smudge that hung above the horizon, visibly growing second by second.

"The desert gives with one hand and takes with the other," Hamid said, his tone darker than before. "Get in the truck!"

45

WHAT STARTED AS A LOW RUMBLE, seeming to come from everywhere, soon boomed across the landscape like some massive, invisible beast. The cloud, which had been a thin line on the horizon moments before, now towered hundreds of feet into the air, blotting out the sky with churning darkness.

"Sandstorm," Baxter said, already moving back toward the Land Cruiser. "Move, now!"

No sooner had Baxter finished speaking, than the wind hit them, pushing Eden's clothes against her and whipping her hair around her face. Sand pummeled her skin with stinging force. The temperature dropped as the storm's shadow raced across the sky, swallowing everything in its path.

Eden looked from the coming wall of sand to the rock wall before them. There was no chance they'd reach the cliff before the sand engulfed them.

"The truck!" Baxter shouted over the rising wind. "Get in, we need to move."

A gust caught the Land Cruiser's open hood, slamming it shut.

"But the engine hasn't cooled," Hamid said, gripping the side of the vehicle. He pulled his scarf up over his nose and mouth and used the vehicle to drag himself back toward the driver's door.

"No choice," Eden shouted, doubling over against the wind. She dug her feet into the sand and shoved her way forward. The wind shoved her like an invisible hand, forcing her to fight for every inch of progress.

Just as she reached the Land Cruiser, the wind changed direction, rolling her to the side. She grabbed the truck's hood, gripping a small crack in the metal as the storm threatened to drag her away. She looked up and saw Baxter, reaching out of the passenger door, but still too far away.

Keeping as low to the ground as possible, Eden used the wheel arch to pull herself forward. The wind thrashed beneath her, attempting to pluck her from the sand and throw her up into the air.

Baxter looped the seatbelt around one arm and climbed from the truck. He inched toward Eden, his hand outstretched.

"Grab my hand," Baxter shouted.

Eden reached out and grabbed Baxter's fingers. They clenched hands, then wrists, then used the seatbelt to pull themselves back inside the truck and shut the door.

Hamid pumped the accelerator, and the starter motor whined. The engine caught with a reluctant cough, almost inaudible against the howling wind. The truck rocked, sand seeping in through tiny cracks around the windows and doors.

Eden grabbed a scarf, pulling it up over her nose and

mouth. She leaned forward and cupped a hand over her face as the sand stung her streaming eyes.

Hamid hit the gas, and the Land Cruiser lurched forward. The storm shoved them sideways, Hamid wresting the steering wheel back.

The storm intensified, hitting the truck like a physical wave. The cliff face towering above them, disappeared in a brown, howling chaos. Sand hammered against the windshield. The vehicle shook as winds buffeted from every direction, lifting it from its suspension and slamming it back down again.

"I don't even know which way we should go," Eden said, leaning over the dashboard and squinting into the swirling sand.

"When in doubt, keep going straight," Hamid shouted, his voice almost lost in the howl. The wipers scraped uselessly against the glass, leaving dusty streaks that only made visibility worse. He pushed the pedal to the floor and the Land Cruiser lurched forward before hitting a pocket of soft sand and slowing again. A crosswind hit the front end, pushing them into a spin.

Hamid swung the wheel, attempting to correct their course. The tires dug through the sand, then hit something hard, which whipped them back the other way.

Sand now poured through the ventilation system, filling the air as though they were trapped inside a desert-themed snow globe. The Land Cruiser shot forward, bounding across the sand for a few feet before the wind slammed it back.

Eden pushed the scarf tighter over her nose and mouth as breathing became even more difficult. The storm changed direction, showing her a glimpse of a towering shape through the sand.

"There! I can see it!" she shouted. "Dead ahead."

The Land Cruiser bounced violently again, the suspension thumping.

"What we seek is straight ahead!" Hamid shouted, having clearly not heard Eden.

The cliff face materialized through the swirling sand like a shipwreck emerging from murky depths.

They hit a pocket of solid ground, and the Land Cruiser raced toward the cliff. Hamid swung the wheel at the last moment and pulled them alongside the rock wall. The wind caught the back of the vehicle, sending it into a spin and smashing the vehicle's left side into the stone with a grinding screech.

Eden peered through the windshield at the great cliff, which stretched away in both directions, vanishing into the sandstorm like the hull of some hulking vessel. With the cliff offering a modicum of protection, the wind dropped slightly.

A boulder the size of a football tumbled down the cliff face, its shadow preceding it by a split second.

Baxter grabbed Eden by the shoulders and pulled her backward as the windshield exploded, the boulder smashing into the dashboard. A hail of glass and twisted plastic filled the truck.

The boulder bounced out again, slamming into the hood and causing a cloud of steam to rise from the engine. Sand poured into the truck like water through a burst dam, filling the truck's interior with choking, blinding grit.

Eden doubled over, coughing violently as the grit scraped down her throat. Every instinct told her to gasp for air, but each breath only brought more choking sand. She clamped her eyes shut, struggling against the grit that had already worked its way under her eyelids, turning every blink into agony.

"Out! Everyone out!" Baxter shouted, covering his face with his hands. A loud thump boomed through the truck as another boulder smashed into the roof, buckling the metal above their heads.

Baxter shoved the door open and darted out into the maelstrom. He battled his way in close to the cliff face where the towering rocks blocked some of the storm's fury. Eden shuffled out next, followed by Hamid, who scooted over the central console and lumbered into the swirling sand.

With an almighty crash, a rock the size of a car fell from the overhanging clifftop. It struck the top of the truck, punching the roof with the force of a sledgehammer. The metal buckled, the driver's side door frame twisting so violently that the window exploded in a shower of glass. The Land Cruiser groaned under the impact, its aged suspension giving way as the chassis bent.

Another boulder, then another, hammered down as the storm tore loose rocks from the cliff above. Each impact drove the vehicle lower, metal screeching against stone. The passenger seat where Eden had been sitting moments before disappeared under a section of collapsed roof.

"Looks like we're not going back that way," Eden said. She looked up at the cliff and saw a dark triangular shadow set into the wall. Taking a step closer, the shadow morphed into an opening.

"There!" she screamed, pointing at the opening. "A cave! There's a cave!"

She stepped away from the wall, and the storm's fury hit her with the force of a freight train. She staggered backward, nearly knocked off her feet by a gust that felt strong enough to uproot trees. She bent double, pushing herself against the cliff face. Sand whipped around her legs, and she felt as though she was wading through concrete.

"Stay together!" Hamid shouted from somewhere behind her.

Eden reached out and grabbed Baxter's hand, their fingers locking together. Together they fought their way forward, their backs to the cliff as the wind attempted to pull them apart.

Eden ducked as a piece of debris—maybe torn metal from their destroyed truck—spun past her head and smashed into the cliff, burying itself several inches into the rock. She struggled on, not wasting a moment. Just as it seemed they were closing in, the wind whipped around, once again changing direction.

Eden reacted, dropping into a crouch and pushing the fingers of her free hand into the rocks as though she was climbing the cliff. Baxter and Hamid did the same, using cracks in the rocks to anchor themselves in position.

Finally, Eden dragged herself into the opening. She kept moving, deeper and deeper into the cave's shelter. The howling of the storm dropped with each foot they advanced.

When the air no longer tried to drag her away, Eden stumbled a few more paces and collapsed to the floor. Baxter fell a moment later, followed by Hamid, all of them gasping and coughing.

46

EDEN LAY AGAINST THE STONE, fighting to catch her breath. She pushed up onto her elbows, wiped grit from her eyes, and coughed until her lungs cleared. When her breathing returned to normal, she looked around.

Beyond the narrow entrance, through which they'd escaped the storm, the space expanded to the height of at least two people. Light seeped in through the raging sand, cloaking the space in gloom. The moment her eyes had adjusted, a beam of light lanced across the space, followed by a second.

"Alright, guys," Eden said, shielding her eyes and glancing at Baxter and Hamid, who pointed their flashlights at her.

She swung her backpack off her shoulders and reached inside for her flashlight. As she opened the flap, soft light spilled out. She paused, momentarily confused by the strange light, then pulled the Eye of the Sahara from its protective pouch. Light spilled from the crystal, bright enough to pattern her face in its warm glow. What had once looked like an ordinary piece of quartz now sparkled as though alive.

"The Eye knows its home," Hamid said, noticing the glow. "It will show us the way."

"I hope so," Eden said, holding the crystal out in front of her and pulling the bag back onto her shoulders. "We need all the help we can get."

Hamid led the way deeper into the tunnel, ducking through an area where the craggy ceiling dropped to a few feet, and then through a few twists and turns. The passage turned again, the roof lifted high overhead, and the walls spread wide.

"This place is vast," Baxter said, sweeping his beam down the passage. "It looks like it goes on forever."

"Not forever, no," Hamid said, as though that was exactly the answer Baxter wanted.

"What is this place?" Eden said. The tunnel before them extended in a perfectly straight line, descending at an exact, unwavering angle.

"There are no tool marks, not even a scratch," Baxter said, crossing to one of the walls and running his hand along the stone.

"It's like a subway tunnel," Eden said, judging the size from one wall to the next.

"It is one of the many access routes to what lies beneath," Hamid said, his beam lancing ahead.

"I've never seen anything quite like this," Baxter said, searching the walls and ceiling for a crack, but finding none. "How could someone build this?"

"Perhaps the real question is not how someone built this, but how we forgot." Hamid sent a playful glance in Baxter's direction, who hurried a few paces to catch up.

"The air pressure is changing too," Eden said, yawning as her ears popped.

"We're getting deeper underground," Hamid said.

"I didn't have you down as a Jamiroquai fan," Eden replied.

Hamid turned and leveled a long look at Eden. "Your jokes are walls, Eden. Walls keep out understanding as surely as they keep out danger."

"Your ignorance of Jamiroquai is telling," Eden shot back. "Clearly, you missed the funk revival of the late nineties."

"Exactly how old were you in the late nineties?" Baxter said, grinning at Eden.

"Old enough to recognize a slap bass guitar when I heard one," Eden said.

The three progressed, walking side by side down the passage.

"Why is it always secret tunnels?" Eden said, the silence reaching the point of frustration for her, which wasn't very long at all. "I get that they're a feat of engineering and all that, but I've seen so many now."

"The world does not arrange itself around your experience," Hamid said.

Eden and Baxter looked at Hamid, then at each other.

"There have been a lot, though," Baxter said. "Under the Giza Plateau, those Templar ones in Portugal."

"Not forgetting that bunker beneath the mansion in Washington State," Eden said, glancing at the Eye of the Sahara which glowed gently. "Actually, I wish I could forget that one."

A front of air moved up through the tunnel, pushing against them as though the structure was exhaling.

"Did you feel that?" Eden said, holding up her hand. "That must mean this passage connects to something."

"Yes, every path leads somewhere," Hamid replied, without breaking his stride. "I just hope we are prepared for the destination."

"That all depends on how far it is," Eden said, rubbing one of her calves, which ached from the steep and constant descent. "Did your grandmother give any hints about the distance?"

"While our people have known about this for eternity, we have never visited," Hamid said, focused on the tunnel ahead.

"Eternity seems like a bit of a stretch," Eden said. "That's a figure of speech, right? Like saying *I'm starving*, when you haven't eaten since breakfast."

"The difference between *eternity* and *since breakfast* is perspective," Hamid replied, his tone even more wistful than usual. "To the mayfly, a day is a lifetime. To my people, a thousand years is merely the beginning."

"But with all this knowledge, you don't actually know where this tunnel goes?" Eden said, pointing up at the walls.

"Where it goes is not our business," Hamid said, turning to cast Eden a glance. "We are the guards of this place, not explorers."

"I wish I could be a guard and not an explorer," Eden said, looking at the Eye. "Imagine sitting still all day, looking after something. Preferably in a place where nothing happens."

"You'd hate that," Baxter said, shooting her a grin. "You've got the attention span of a—"

"Oh, look at that, an opening," Eden said, rushing toward a dark shape at the side of the passage ahead.

Drawing closer, she noticed there were two tunnels, one on each side, like an intersection.

Hamid and Baxter set off behind her, their flashlight beams bouncing. They reached the intersection and paused, looking down the two new passages, left and right.

"That tunnel looks as though it curves," Eden said, peering into the tunnel crossing theirs.

"You're right," Baxter said. "Could it be a giant circle?"

"Atlantis was supposedly formed of concentric rings," Eden said, looking from one side to the other. "And that would match the geology on the surface too."

"How wide is the central plateau?" Baxter asked, glancing at Hamid.

"Around four miles, which would make a circular tunnel like this over twelve miles in circumference," Hamid replied.

"We need to pick our direction carefully," Baxter said. "Or it's twelve miles to end up back at the same place."

"Ask the Eye which way," Hamid said, nodding at the crystal in Eden's hands.

"You think that'll work?" she said doubtfully.

"We are not here by accident," Hamid said.

Eden raised the Eye of the Sahara and stepped slowly into each of the passages. Walking down the curved tunnels, left or right, the crystal maintained its steady pulse, but when she continued straight ahead, the light intensified.

"Unless my eyes are making things up—"

"Your eyes see clearly," Hamid said. "But remember—a moth is also drawn to the flame that will consume it."

"Thanks for that," Eden said, taking another step down the passage. "I think the Eye wants us to go that way." She pointed down the straight tunnel which led them deeper beneath the structure.

"Or something down there wants what we have," Hamid said darkly, peering into the distance. "Desire flows both ways."

47

THEY PUSHED DEEPER into the structure, passing frequent openings which led from both sides of the tunnel—some only wide enough for a person to enter, others vast enough to drive a truck through.

"This isn't just a tunnel system," Eden said, peering through an opening. "This is the city." She looked out at a vast space with multiple levels carved into the walls at different heights, connected by what looked like spiral ramps. She lifted the Eye of the Sahara toward the opening, but the crystal maintained its steady glow. "Not that way," she said, turning back toward the descending tunnel.

"Those must be living quarters," Baxter said, directing his light into another opening. "It looks like this place housed a massive population."

Eden peered in beside him and saw small rooms rising in tiers, hundreds, or even thousands, disappearing into the darkness above.

"It's like that place in Turkey," Baxter said, his voice echoing off the ancient walls. "Derinkuyu. Found by someone renovating a house. Imagine knocking down a wall in your basement to find an entire underground city."

"Just to think, it's been here all this time, waiting to be discovered," Eden said, checking the Eye of the Sahara again.

"That's the attitude of the Western explorer," Hamid said, clearing his throat.

"I didn't mean—" Eden started.

"Like Columbus *discovering* lands where millions already lived," Hamid continued.

"That's not—"

"Isn't it?" Hamid said, gesturing at another space, which was so large their lights barely penetrated it. "My grandmother's grandmother knew these tunnels. We have stories and songs about this place, yet you talk about it *waiting to be discovered.*"

Eden opened her mouth, then closed it.

"The intent matters less than the pattern," Hamid said. "When the French came, they renamed this place. When NASA photographed it, they did the same. Each time ignoring what went before."

They walked on, passing a vast circular chamber with stone benches carved in concentric rings around a central depression, like an amphitheater. Eden tested the Eye at the entrance, but it showed no change, so they moved on.

"Yes ..." Eden said. "You're right."

"We don't seek to be right," Hamid said, his voice softening. "We seek to be heard."

Eden glanced at Hamid, and for once had nothing to say. Not used to such a sensation, she turned her attention to the Eye and then continued forward. They passed a vast hall with hundreds of small alcoves. Eden paused, holding up the Eye. For a moment it flickered, as if considering, then resumed its insistent pull toward the center.

"This would have been the city's lower levels, right?" Eden whispered, glancing back the way they'd come.

"Yes indeed," Hamid said. "Like the great cities of today, this place existed both above and below the ground."

"And this is only one small section of it," Eden said, thinking about how big the structure appeared from the air.

"At the time it was the biggest city in the world, by far," Hamid said, shining the beam of his flashlight into a small passage to the right.

"How many people lived here?" Baxter asked.

"The stories speak of thousands, perhaps hundreds of thousands," Hamid replied. "But numbers mean little."

They reached a junction, with two more passages branching off at right angles. Eden paused to check the direction, before continuing straight on.

"I wouldn't want to be lost down here," she said, leading the way. "We've no idea how vast this place is. We could be lost for weeks."

"We wouldn't last weeks," Baxter said, unclipping his canteen and shaking to reveal it was already half empty.

"The desert provides nothing, we must be prepared," Hamid said, tilting his head forward as though noticing something.

"I'm prepared, as long as it's not much further," Eden said, rubbing her calves again. "This tunnel has to reach something, at some point." She glanced over her shoulder, trying to calculate the distance travelled.

"Look at that," Baxter said, pointing ahead. Following Baxter's gaze, Eden saw that their beams scattered into a wider space ahead.

"Now that looks like we're getting somewhere," Eden

said, all tiredness forgotten. She charged ahead, then turned to the others. "Come on, keep up."

Out of the gloom, a circular chamber appeared. About forty feet wide, the walls rose to a domed ceiling, and the floor appeared to be made from the same smooth rock.

"Wait," Eden said, stopping in the mouth of the tunnel. Baxter and Hamid froze on either side of her.

"What is it?" Hamid said, peering into the chamber. "It looks fine to me."

"We've been in places like this before," Eden said. "There's always something nasty waiting for us."

"The imagination can be more dangerous than what it perceives," Hamid said.

"We've been shot at, crushed, burned and dropped into hidden pits," Baxter said. "She's right."

"Perhaps the greatest danger lies in not moving forward," Hamid said, shrugging.

"Easy for you to say," Baxter muttered, his flashlight sweeping methodically across the floor. "You weren't there when we nearly got crushed by stone blocks."

"Or drowned in the Hall of Records," Eden said, studying the chamber for anything that looked as though it could trigger an ancient defense mechanism. Seeing nothing, she dropped into a crouch and ran a hand along the floor near the entrance.

"Feels smooth, no pressure pads or tripwires." She rose to her feet and scanned the walls for the telltale holes that might conceal dart launchers. "Nothing there either."

"What about the ceiling?" Baxter said, aiming his flashlight upward.

"It looks solid," Eden replied. "No obvious weak points or hanging blocks. In fact, there are no marks at all. No hidden switches or panels. Nothing."

"An empty chamber holds nothing but our own delays," Hamid said. "We did not travel this far to admire smooth walls."

"Fine," Eden said, extending a foot and testing the ground. When nothing moved or rumbled or changed, she placed her other foot beside the first. She remained stationary for a few moments, ready to dart back if necessary. "So far, so good," she whispered.

Hamid watched them with what appeared to be amusement, although for once he offered no advice.

Eden took another step forward, again carefully assessing the floor.

Baxter followed close behind, scanning the walls and ceiling for any movement.

Despite his amusement at the pair's caution, Hamid followed.

"Wait, look at that," Eden said, pointing at something on the far wall.

Baxter panned his light to the position Eden indicated, illuminating a large symbol at the chamber's focal point.

"The Hamsa," Eden said, recognizing the symbol they had seen so many variations of in Hamid's shop. "Why do I get the impression this thing's following us around?"

"The Hamsa has been here for thousands of years, so I can assure you, it is us who have finally arrived to where it knew we would come," Hamid said. "You speak like someone who believes the world revolves around her progress."

"Alright," Eden said, taking another cautious step. "It's just a figure of—" she raised a hand, remembering Hamid's words last time she had claimed something to be a *figure of speech*. "I'm just ... just saying."

"Your words, reflect your thoughts, reflect your understanding," Hamid said.

Eden looked at Hamid for a long moment. Realizing she had no retort to give that wouldn't involve another philosophy lesson, she turned back to the symbol.

"You know, maybe this chamber is actually different," Eden said, reaching the halfway point. "It could actually just be a room underground, without loads of ancient killing devices."

Clearly afraid he was missing something, Hamid took a few steps.

Eden reached the base of the far wall and looked up at the enormous Hamsa. She stretched her hand toward the symbol, and then hesitated, studying it carefully.

"Still nothing," Baxter said, joining her to look up at the symbol.

Eden leaned forward and brushed her hand over the symbol. Dust came away, revealing the depth of the carving.

"No clicks, no grinding sounds," Baxter continued. "I think we're—"

A low rumble filled the chamber, cutting his words short. Eden whipped her hand away from the symbol as though she'd just been bitten by a snake.

The sound came from everywhere at once, shaking the walls and rumbling the floor. The reverberation doubled, then tripled in intensity. Dust cascaded down in thick curtains.

"Oh man, that doesn't sound good," she said.

48

———

"Move!" Baxter shouted, grabbing Eden's arm and pulling her away from the wall. "The place is coming down!"

The rumbling intensified to a deafening roar. Dust filled the chamber with a choking cloud so thick that it swallowed their flashlight beams.

The vibrations increased, almost shaking Eden off her feet. She crouched, placing a hand flat on the ground, ready to dart in any direction she needed. She peered up at the roof, expecting to see it split into cracks, but it remained solid. The ground vibrated, shockwaves moving out like falling rock.

"We need to get out," Eden yelled, pointing in the direction of the tunnel through which they'd come. "That's the only way in or out of this place. This is a dead end." The ground shook again, rolling like a ship on a stormy sea.

Eden inhaled and then coughed as the dust filled her lungs. She pulled her shirt up over her mouth and nose to breathe more easily.

"Maybe that is the only way out, maybe it isn't," Hamid

said, assessing the situation as though it was entertaining rather than deadly.

Behind the curtain of dust, another stone block slammed against the ground.

"That's not helpful," Eden said, glancing at Hamid, who was now little more than a shadow. Another thud boomed from somewhere across the chamber. Eden looked toward the sound but saw nothing. Dust swirled around them on all sides. A grinding, churning noise moved up through the floor.

"We need to go now," Baxter said, stepping back toward the passage. He moved carefully, checking each step as though the floor was about to disintegrate.

"Wait!" Hamid shouted, his voice cutting through the chaos. "Those who act in haste run toward the danger they seek to escape!"

"What's that supposed to mean?" Baxter yelled back. "Those who stay where they are get crushed!"

"I'm with Baxter on this," Eden said, darting toward the door during a lull in the noise.

"When the mind reacts in fear, you cannot see the truth," Hamid boomed, now completely obscured by the falling dust. "Think, Eden, what did Lalla Yasmine teach you?"

"This is not the time for a philosophy lesson—" Baxter shouted, freezing as something else crashed down, the impact shaking the whole chamber. The rumbling grew louder still, now so intense that it seemed to vibrate right through their bones.

"Lalla Yasmine," Eden said, dropping to a crouch in the clawing dust. She paused, taking a moment to think as another shudder moved through the floor beneath her.

"We'll be buried alive!" Baxter shouted.

Another tremendous crash shook the chamber, sounding like half the ceiling collapsing somewhere nearby. Eden instinctively raised her hands above her head, as though an extended arm would protect against thousands of tons of rock.

"The mind creates its own reality," Eden said, thinking about her midnight meeting with Lalla Yasmine.

"What? What are you talking about?" Baxter shouted, his voice cut off by a grinding, crunching noise.

"That's what Lalla Yasmine told me," Eden said. "The mind creates its own reality based on the information it receives."

"That's very interesting, but let's talk about it when we're not—" Baxter said, interrupted as another boom rippled through the floor. He raised his voice above the noise. "The walls are coming down! We have seconds—"

"Fear creates the reality you experience," Hamid said, his tone so calm it sounded almost meditative. "Look with your eyes, not with your terror."

"This is madness! We need to move," Baxter said, swiveling from side to side.

"Hamid's right." Eden rose to her feet and looked around the dust-filled chamber.

"The place is coming down," Baxter protested, his flash-light beam whipping around but illuminating nothing but dust. "We'll be crushed or buried alive!"

"That's your perception," Eden said, stepping back up to the carved Hamsa. "Think about it. All you can see is dust. All you can hear are grinding stones. Your mind is doing the rest."

"Yes!" Hamid roared. "You are learning!"

"You're both completely mad!" Baxter shouted.

Eden fought the instinct to flee as the rumbling

continued around them. She extended her hand and touched the symbol, feeling no cracks at all.

"The hand, it's completely as it was when we arrived," Eden said, turning back to the others, who she could only see by their flashlights.

"What does that matter when ..." Baxter started, stopping mid-sentence.

"I think the captain realizes too," Hamid said, in the tone of someone delivering a joke.

The great crashing noise increased, rumbling the chamber and forcing them all to crouch. For a moment they remained silent until the noise faded away. Then, as though the chamber realized the game was up, the vibrations faded into silence. The dust drifted to the ground, clearing the air.

"Will someone tell me what just happened, please?" Baxter said, looking around.

"We have been tested, the same way as Lalla Yasmine showed us with the tea," Eden said, more to herself than anyone else. "We felt poisoned because we believed we were poisoned. Our minds created the symptoms."

"What? We weren't poisoned?" Baxter said, looking at Eden like she'd grown a second head.

"I'll explain later. For now, let me think." Eden looked around the chamber, seeing it clearly for the first time. No debris lined the floor, and no cracks filled the walls. Even the dust was dissipating too quickly, as if it had been more illusion than substance.

"But the sounds, the shaking—" Baxter started.

"Were real," Eden said. "Just not what we thought they were. We heard mechanisms, not destruction. Ancient machinery designed to create the illusion."

"Close, but not quite," Hamid said, pointing back at the passage through which they had arrived. A massive slab of stone now sealed the entrance completely. Not fallen randomly but fitted into grooves, like a giant valve, sealing them inside.

Baxter rushed up to the slab and shoved against the rock. The stone didn't even tremor.

"It's too heavy." He braced his shoulder and heaved again, his boots slipping on the floor.

"Save your energy," Hamid said. "I fear you will need it later."

"This hasn't collapsed. It was engineered this way," Baxter said, turning his attention to the seams where stone met stone. "We walked straight into a trap."

"It's not a trap," Hamid corrected. "It's a test. Those who fled in fear would have been crushed by that closing door. We, those who remained calm and observant, survive to continue forward."

"Forward to what?" Baxter asked, frustration creeping into his voice. "We're sealed in a stone box hundreds of feet —" A soft hissing noise interrupted him. He looked around and pointed up at the ceiling. "More bad news."

A stream of sand poured into the chamber from an opening high in the ceiling—not a trickle, but a steady flow as thick as a tree trunk. It fell in a vertical column, piling up in the center and then spreading out in a cone shape.

"Time is of the essence," Hamid said, watching the flowing sand with amusement. He turned and pointed at the Hamsa.

"We have maybe fifteen minutes before the chamber is filled," Baxter said, his face paling.

"I would say no more than ten," Hamid said, sand already building up against the walls.

"It's accelerating," Eden said, looking up at the golden

stream. "This whole chamber, it's shaped like a giant hourglass."

Baxter paced away from the encroaching sand. The stream from above widened, doubling its flow. The cone in the center grew, expanding toward the walls like a slow-motion wave.

Eden turned her attention to the Hamsa, the first grains of sand flowing over her feet. "Hamid, you were right about one thing," she said. "The hand doesn't follow us, it leads."

49

"Yes, we're close," Irons said, pressing his face to the window of their Mi-17 Hip commandeered military transport helicopter. The desert scrolled beneath them in endless waves of amber and rust. He shifted his weight, the familiar discomfort in his leg a constant reminder of why he was here.

"Anne would have loved to see this," he whispered, touching the shape of the wallet in which he kept the photograph. His wife had always been fascinated by ancient mysteries, dragging him to museums and archaeological sites during their precious time together.

He thought again of the awful day on which Anne had lost her life. It was a day that Irons knew he would never forget, as it cost him both his leg and his wife—March 17th, 2019.

Irons had walked through the facility that day with what he now recognized as the confidence of a man heading for a fall. They were on the verge of a breakthrough, and he was pushing his team hard. They'd been working night and day, chasing a family of compounds that promised a plastic you could bend like rope and trust like steel—lighter, tougher, cheaper.

Irons stepped into the lab and saw that Anne was exactly where he knew she'd be. Jacket on, visor down, working. One tray held silicone molds for testing; another held a neat procession of labeled vials.

Seeing him enter, Anne had glanced from her work and smiled—the last smile she'd ever give. Then, her smile dropped to confusion as a bright white flash punched through the lab.

Irons felt the pressure hit him like an invisible fist. It lifted him up and slammed him against the wall. Windows shattered as the fireball rolled, peeling the ceiling away.

Sound lagged, then arrived all at once—alarms howling, glass shattering, something heavy clanging end over end.

"Anne!" Irons shouted, his voice a raw hiss of air. He tried to stand, but his leg didn't respond. He shoved and clawed his way across the floor. His palms slipped in spilled and burning liquids, his fingers slicing on glass. As soon as he saw her, he knew she was gone. Her eyes were open, confused, already far away. Shattered glass glittered in her hair.

The floor trembled and shook. Irons opened his eyes and realized he was back in the chopper, the craft jolting wildly.

"Readings are going crazy up here," the pilot's voice came through the headset. The helicopter lurched, rearing upward and forcing Irons back into his seat. His leg throbbed.

"Something's interfering with the electronics—" Static overtook the comms, hissing through the speaker in an eerie way that almost sounded like voices.

"Maybe we should land and approach on foot," Kavanagh said, his face paling.

"Are you joking?" Irons said, looking down at his damaged leg. "I won't get more than a few hundred feet down there. We continue."

"Compass is spinning like a—" came the pilot's voice again, before descending into another eerie wall of static.

"I've read about this, it's to be expected," Irons said, steadying himself against the vibrating hull. He picked up the scanner and looked at the screen for a long moment. "Yes, as I thought."

"What's that?" Morales said from her seat across the aisle.

"The frequency of the pulses has increased," Irons said, turning the device to show the scientist. "That not only tells us they are ahead, but the crystal is reacting to the network down there."

"I really advise against this," Morales said, gripping the armrests as the chopper bounced again. "This has never been tried before. Even your notes are... unclear—"

"I know what I'm doing," Irons said, placing the scanner down beside him. "Although you've not seen everything, you know what's at stake." He grinned at the young scientist, who returned the expression with a look of pure contempt. She hadn't been happy about being confined to the hotel back in Marrakesh, but at least that gave her time to get up to speed.

"I will not—" Morales started.

"You will do what you are told," Irons said, his voice dropping into a snarl. "You have work to do."

The chopper wheeled to the left, a strange clunking noise issuing from the turbines.

"Whatever you're planning, I hope that thing fries your brains," Morales spat.

"Oh, now, now, that's unnecessary," Irons said sweetly. "This could be the most educational trip of your career. You're at the forefront of—"

"What is that?" one mercenary said, pointing out through the window. All the passengers turned as the Richat Structure emerged through the heat haze. A silence settled over the craft as the team, even the battle-hardened mercenaries, gazed in awe at the structure.

"That's impossible," Kavanagh said, crossing himself despite twenty years of bloody combat.

"The original wonder of the world, no less," Irons said, shaking his head. For all he knew about this place, nothing prepared him for seeing it with his own eyes.

"Take us down to the central structure," he instructed the pilot. "That's where we'll find the access point."

The aircraft swung and yawed like a wild animal, each gust of desert wind threatening to send them into an uncontrolled spin.

Irons thought about the pyramids at Giza, Stonehenge, Easter Island—monuments scattered across the globe by civilizations that claimed no knowledge of each other. But this, he realized as he looked at the structure, was the source —the original blueprint that had inspired them all.

"Sir, we're losing systems quicker than I can—" the pilot said, fighting for control.

"Use your damned hands, man," Irons replied, never taking his gaze from the structure. "You're supposed to be the best in the business. Get us down there!"

The helicopter lurched. The main rotor shuddered, issuing a sound like tearing metal.

"This is going to be—" the pilot shouted, wrestling with the controls. "Brace for impact!"

Irons gripped the armrest as the cabin tilted violently. Through the window, he watched the desert floor fill the window with terrifying speed. The main rotor swung slowly overhead, no longer providing lift but at least slowing their fall.

At the last possible moment, the pilot leveled them out. They hit the ground, skipping across the surface before finally grinding to a halt.

"Good work," Irons said, unclipping his belt and reaching for his cane. Around him, his men checked their weapons and equipment.

"This is it, Anne," Irons said, once again touching the shape of his wallet in his pocket. He pictured her in his mind's eye, as though she were there with him. "Soon I'll put things right for you, just as I promised."

"Everything alright, sir?" Kavanagh said, standing over Irons and clearly alarmed to hear him talking to himself.

"Of course," Irons said, struggling to his feet. "Unload the equipment. We have work to do."

50

———

"SOMETHING TELLS ME, this is our way out of here," Eden said, wading through ankle-deep sand to reach the Hamsa. The hissing of the falling sand grew louder as the stream widened.

Baxter stepped up behind her, his flashlight beam sweeping over the symbol.

"I didn't notice these markings before," Eden said, pointing at a symbol on each of the fingers.

"Maybe they open something," Baxter said, looking closely at the symbols. "You know, like a giant combination lock."

"Only those who possess understanding may pass," Hamid said, lifting one foot and then the other in a useless effort to stay above the rising sand. "The ancients understood that knowledge without wisdom is more dangerous than ignorance itself."

"This one looks like the sun," Eden said, blowing sand from the symbol etched into the thumb. "Although there's something else around it." She leaned in close, running her fingers over the carving. "They look like concentric circles."

"Could those symbols be sunbeams?" Baxter said, glancing over his shoulder at the falling sand, which now crept up the walls at an alarming speed. He turned his attention back to the carving.

"Maybe, although I'm not sure," Eden said, changing position and brushing at the index finger.

"That's a crescent moon, I'm sure of it," Baxter said, pointing at the symbol.

"Look deeper," Eden said, tracing it with her finger. "There's more. You see this curve beneath? It looks like a wave."

"Nothing here is as simple as it seems," Hamid said, the sand reaching his knees.

"That's really helpful, thanks," Eden said, throwing Hamid a glance.

"It's like a double-exposed photograph, with two images in one," Baxter said.

"And this one looks like an eye," Eden said, focused on the middle finger.

"Some people call this place the Eye of the Sahara, because of how it looks from above," Hamid said. "They don't know the true Eye of the Sahara is what you have there." He pointed at Eden's backpack, into which she'd placed the crystal whilst they figured out what to do next.

"And this looks like stars, a constellation pattern," Eden said, pointing at the ring finger.

"And that's mountains," Baxter said, indicating the little finger.

"But what they mean, and how they'll show us the way out of here, I have no idea." Eden cast a backward glance at the accumulating sand. The conical pile in the middle of the room now equaled her height, rivulets of sand spreading toward the walls.

"The sun rises over the mountains, the moon watches with its eye, and the star guides us home," Hamid said.

"Where did that come from?" Eden said, turning as Hamid moved toward them, kicking up clouds of sand.

"It's an old saying," Hamid said, raising his voice over the hissing sand.

"Sun, mountains, moon, eye and star—it has all the elements we need," Baxter said, pointing at each in turn.

"If your old saying actually gets us out of here," Eden said. "I'll take back everything I said about the usefulness of your proverbs."

"It is not the fault of the words that you fail to grasp the meaning," Hamid said, folding his arms.

"Will everyone stop saying that?" Eden groaned, reaching up and shoving the sun symbol. The whole finger slid into the wall, grinding against the stone.

"Is that a good sign?" Baxter said, watching a trickle of sand escape the joint, running down the wall.

"Let's hope so." Eden struggled to the side and shoved the mountain. The symbol popped into the wall in the same way as the previous one.

"Nothing's happening yet," Baxter said, glancing back at the mound of sand, which now towered over them all.

"Oh, really?" Eden said, throwing him a glance. "I thought the ancient door had opened really quietly."

"Nothing will happen until the sequence is complete," Hamid said.

Eden moved to the crescent moon on the hand's index finger. At first, the symbol resisted her touch, then sank into the wall with a grinding sound.

"Now the eye," Eden muttered, pressing the middle finger. The symbol depressed easily, sending another stream of sand to the floor.

"One more," she said, reaching for the star on the ring finger. "This could go really well—"

"Or very badly," Baxter added, glancing back at the looming pile, which now almost reached the ceiling.

"Thinking makes it so," Hamid said, his voice tight.

Eden shoved the star. At first it wouldn't budge, then it snapped in so fast she nearly lost her grip on the wall. For a heartbeat, nothing happened, then all five symbols shot back out with a harsh mechanical crack.

The three looked at each other, listening for the sound of ancient machines coming to life.

"Wrong sequence," Baxter said after a few seconds of nothing.

"Dammit," Eden said, wiping dust from her face. "Hamid, what I said about your proverbs stands."

"Perhaps the saying was never meant to be literal." Hamid shrugged. "Perhaps it was—"

"We don't have time for this!" Eden snapped, the sand now running over the symbol's palm.

"There are over one hundred possibilities with five symbols," Baxter said.

"Thanks for that." Eden shot Baxter a glance and turned her attention back to the symbols. "There's something here. It's so simple, but I just can't get it."

"I'm just saying that it's important to understand ..." Baxter said, his voice trailing off when he realized no one was listening.

Eden closed her eyes and forced herself to focus. She looked again at the symbols. The underlying images slowly moved into focus, glaring at her as though the pressure of the situation had physically sharpened her vision.

"Wait a minute," she said, looking from one symbol to the next as something in her mind's eye aligned. With great effort, the sand now surrounding her at chest level, she turned and looked at Hamid. "So far, everything has been a lesson, right?"

"Yes, exactly," Hamid said. "It's a test, to make sure those who enter are worthy of the knowledge."

"Maybe to gain access to whatever is in here, you must know the story of how it was destroyed. That way, you prove you understand what you're dealing with," Eden said, pointing back at the hand. "The real story, not the myth."

"What do you mean?" Baxter asked.

Eden pointed at the middle finger. "This is not necessarily an eye, look at the pattern. They could be the concentric circles of the Richat Structure as we see it today, or Atlantis as it was then." She traced the symbol with her finger. "This is where it all began. Their greatest city." She moved to the thumb. "This isn't the sun, as we thought, but the rings of water and land that Plato described."

"Yes," Baxter said, leaning in close to the symbol. "That makes sense, sort of …"

"The story is encoded here, we simply need to tell it in the right order," Eden said.

"That would prove we are worthy," Hamid said.

"And the mountains?" Baxter lifted his arms to prevent the sand from trapping them at his sides.

"They expanded their civilization right up to the Atlas range," Eden said. "That's the third stage."

"Named after Atlas, the king of Atlantis," Hamid said quietly. "The connection has always been there in the name."

"And this constellation," Eden said, the answers coming more quickly now. "They navigated by the stars, spreading their knowledge across the world." With the sand now surrounding her neck, she reached out and touched the index finger. "The wave here, hidden beneath the crescent moon, is how it all ended. It ended in one night, not gradually, but in catastrophe. A flood that turned their green paradise into the Sahara."

"So, the sequence is ..." Baxter said, struggling to speak above the sand.

"The story of rise and fall," Eden said, speaking rapidly, as the sand threatened to engulf both her and the symbol. "Eye, rings, mountains, stars, flood. Creation to destruction."

"The ancient Greeks called it hamartia—the fatal flaw born from incomplete understanding. We must act," Hamid said.

"Here we go then," Eden said, reaching for the eye symbol with trembling hands. She pushed the symbol and it clicked inwards, as it had before. Next, she reached for the thumb with the rings, shoving that one in too.

The sand passed her chin as she depressed the mountains on the little finger. The symbol clicked beneath the surface of the wall, the sound of grinding stone offering no clues as to whether the sequence was correct. Tilting her head back in an attempt to stop the sand streaming into her mouth, she reached for the ring finger and pressed. The symbol with the stars sank into the stone. They all turned and looked at the wave on the index finger.

"You are pressing the symbol of a destructive wave while sand crushes the air from your lungs," Hamid groaned, the sand closing around his neck. "The ancients were not without a sense of humor."

"Hilarious," Eden said, spitting sand from her mouth. She stretched for the symbol, grit coating her tongue and teeth.

"Quickly," Baxter groaned, tilting his head back.

"The end of Atlantis," Eden whispered, shoving the

wave. The symbol clicked, locking into place. Then, the entire hand sank into the wall with a sound that Eden felt, rather than heard.

"Something's happening," Baxter said, his teeth clenched.

A grinding noise vibrated up through the floor, shaking the sand into spirals. A series of clicks sounded as ancient tumblers fell into place. The floor shuddered again, and the sand stopped falling. Then, the sand drained away, sliding into numerous openings around the chamber walls. It ran out, streaming in all directions.

"I guess we got it," Eden said, extending her hands and pushing against the wall to keep herself from sliding off her feet. Hamid and Baxter struggled up to the wall beside her, holding on too.

"Look," Baxter said, pointing as the wall on which the hand was carved pivoted inwards. The sand drained away more quickly now, falling to beneath their waists, then to their knees.

"And there," Hamid said, pointing behind them. The passage through which they arrived had now opened up again too. "The way is open for us to go forward and then return. Now, we must go."

51

EDEN SCRAMBLED THROUGH THE OPENING, bringing her flashlight to bear on the passage ahead. The tunnel continued for at least a couple of hundred feet, before opening into a wider space. She paused, brushing the sand from her clothes as Baxter and Hamid climbed through behind her. All three took a moment to steady themselves, coughing sand from their lungs.

"What is this place?" Baxter said, turning his attention to the passage ahead.

"We are approaching the core," Hamid said, flexing his ox-like shoulders and then striding on. "This is the center of the civilization. The place from which the Eye came."

The three paced down the tunnel, the space wide enough for them to walk side by side.

"Glass talked about these crystalline veins, look," Eden said, the beam of her flashlight catching something set into the wall. The light reflected, sparkling back across the passage. "They look like they're designed to carry something."

"Maybe a conduit for some kind of power," Baxter said,

tracing one of the crystal channels as it ran up and across the ceiling. "There are loads of them, look." Similar channels ran across the walls, all running in the same direction.

"We must keep moving," Hamid said, striding ahead. "The answers will come soon."

As they pressed forward, the passage opened out, its ceiling soaring high above them. The conduits lining the walls grew larger too, some now broader than a person.

And then, suddenly, the walls fell away, and they stepped into a space as large and grand as a medieval cathedral. Eden stopped cold, unable to believe what she was seeing.

"This place," she said. "It's just as Glass described. A perfect sphere." She swung her beam around the chamber and saw that the passage had brought them out about halfway up one of the chamber's walls. The walls arched away in every direction, disappearing into the vastness.

"But Glass told us the place collapsed, taking Professor Lawrence with it," Baxter said, looking around.

"They were not wise enough to pass the test," Hamid said, as though delivering bad news. "Remember, the mind creates its own reality."

"It looks like there was once one of those walkways there," Eden said, pointing her flashlight at a point where crystals jutted from the wall and the central tower.

"True, there's no knowing what this place looked like when Glass was here," Baxter said.

"We could always go down there and look for her camera," Eden said, peering over the edge. The chamber's wall swept outward in a smooth, continuous curve.

"There are other passages too, look," Baxter said, pointing across the space. "There must be dozens of ways to get here."

Eden followed his gaze and saw countless similar passages, opening into the chamber at regular intervals. Crystalline conduits, like the ones they'd followed, spread out at the opening of each passageway. She followed the conduits, noticing how they crisscrossed the walls like a circulatory system.

"This place, it's some kind of machine," Eden said, looking at how the thing was designed. "Like a giant circuit board."

"But for what?" Baxter said.

"It's for focusing unimaginable amounts of energy into a single point," Hamid said, and pointed back the way they'd come. "These lines spread for hundreds of miles beneath the ground. They take the Earth's natural energy and focus it here." He raised his hand and pointed at a structure right in the center of the chamber. A vast crystal tower, shaped like a helix, rose from the floor to the ceiling. The tower's base was easily fifty feet in diameter, narrowing as it rose before expanding again where it met the ceiling.

Eden focused her flashlight on the structure, which refracted the beam back out around the chamber.

A few feet to their left, a narrow walkway ran from the chamber's wall to a platform built into the center of the tower. Countless other walkways spanned the distance around the chamber's sides, some intact, others fractured into shards.

"When the Eye of the Sahara is placed there, the circuit is complete," Hamid said, pointing at the platform. Looking closely at the structure, Eden saw a cradle that seemed to be around the same size as the Eye, positioned right in the center.

"That sounds easy enough," she said, swinging the bag from her shoulders and withdrawing the Eye of the Sahara.

The crystal pulsed more quickly now, the light dancing like an aurora.

"The Eye reacts to coming home," Hamid said, gazing out across the chamber. "And look, the chamber responds."

Deep blue lights pulsed through the crystalline channels near where Eden stood, racing out across the chamber. They spread and multiplied as the channels twisted and crossed.

"Let's get this thing back where it belongs," Eden said, watching the lights swirling into shades of blue and mauve. "Then we all get to go home, right?" Holding the crystal out in front of her, she started toward the walkway.

"Wait," Baxter said, grabbing her arm. "Nothing about this suggests it's going to be easy. Maybe I should—"

"No," Eden said, holding Baxter's gaze. "Returning this is my job."

"It looks like this entire structure was built for … who knows?" Baxter said, pointing out at the central tower, which now pulsed more ferociously. "We have no idea what's going to happen when you reconnect it."

"There's only one way to find out," Eden said, pulling away. "Whatever happens, it's clear that we're in the right place." She raised the Eye of the Sahara, and the light patterned across her face.

"Just … be careful," Baxter said, understanding that he had no choice but to let Eden go.

"Careful is my middle name," Eden said, stepping up to the nearest causeway. She paused and looked across the six-foot-wide span of crystal that bridged the gap between the chamber wall and the central structure.

"No guard rails, this definitely wouldn't pass modern building regulations," she said, peering over the edge at the chamber floor, which curved away far below her. She gripped the Eye of the Sahara more tightly and started across. The crystalline conduits running beneath her pulsed, bursts of energy shooting toward the tower.

The Eye grew warm as Eden progressed. Whatever power the object had, and whatever its purpose here in the chamber, the two worked together.

"The patterns are changing," Hamid shouted.

Eden looked up and saw streaks of red now shooting through the blue. She glanced over the edge and saw the base of the chamber far below, mirroring the pattern. For a moment, the sight of the ground so far beneath her and the dancing colors caused her vision to swim. She snapped her attention back to the platform ahead and continued.

"Almost there," Baxter said, his voice tight with anxiety. "Put it in the cradle, then come straight back."

"Actually, I kinda like it out here," Eden said, rolling her eyes. "I think I'll hang around a while."

She looked up at the vast turret of crystal, the lights blazing more brightly than before. She hurried the last few steps and crossed onto the platform. Stepping to the center of the platform, she saw the true precision of the place for the first time. Constructed from some kind of metal, the cradle sat at the exact center point of the whole chamber, and probably the center of the whole structure.

"I get the impression that once I put this in here, there's no going back," Eden said, raising the Eye and taking another step toward the cradle. The crystalline conduits around her pulsed, flaring into bright yellow bursts that crackled like contained lightning.

"Quickly," Baxter said, his voice tense.

"It looks like a perfect fit," Eden said, looking from the Eye to the cradle. Tiny shimmering veins inside the cradle pulsed, as though preparing themselves for reunification.

Eden glanced over her shoulder at Baxter and Hamid, still standing in the mouth of the passage. Baxter frowned, his face tight with concern. Meeting Baxter's gaze, Eden understood exactly what he was thinking—he would prefer himself in danger knowing Eden was safe. She held the gaze for a heartbeat, then turned away and lifted the Eye of the Sahara above the cradle.

The Eye blazed in her hands, almost unbearably hot. The air around it shimmered as though radiating some strange energy.

"Here goes ... everything," she whispered, lowering the Eye toward its ancient home.

The crystal passed an unseen threshold above the cradle and an invisible force engaged, dragging it close. The Eye pulled against her grip, nearly slipping from her hands.

The chamber responded with a deep rumble, rising from the foundations. Lightning crackled between the conduits, arcing across the walls in brilliant white chains.

The thunder of boots on stone echoed like gunfire, and a voice boomed through the chamber.

"Stop, or your friends are dead."

52

"WHY DOES this always happen right at the key moment?" Eden groaned, looking from the Eye to the cradle, just inches apart. Even though she'd never heard the voice, she knew instinctively who it belonged to.

She paused, considering her options. She could slide the Eye into the cradle and face whatever consequences came her way. As though responding to her indecision, gunfire tore across the crystal tower, showering Eden in glittering debris.

"Turn slowly," the voice commanded. "Keep your hands raised."

Eden dragged the Eye of the Sahara away from the cradle, fighting the force that pulled it in the opposite direction. The crystals around the chamber snapped into a strobing frenzy, flashing as though angry with her decision. She clutched the Eye against her chest and turned slowly.

Armed men fanned out, guns trained on either Baxter, Hamid or Eden.

"I'm here to finally claim what's mine." A man emerged from the passageway, pausing to look out at the chamber. He leaned on a cane and moved as though walking caused him significant pain.

"You must be Dr. Irons," Eden said, recognizing the man from Glass's description. She took a step forward, ignoring the countless rifles that tracked her movement.

"Secure them," Irons said, nodding at Baxter and Hamid.

One of Irons's men lowered his weapon and unclipped a zip tie from his belt. As the mercenary approached, Baxter pivoted and drove his shoulder into the man's chest. The thug stumbled backward, staggering toward the precipice. Baxter ducked, spun and swung an elbow into the next man's stomach. The thug dropped to his knees, gasping for breath.

Reacting to Baxter's break for freedom, Hamid grabbed the nearest attacker's rifle. He twisted the gun upward, then drove a fist into the man's midsection. The guard bent double, and Hamid relieved him of the weapon before raising it at the other men.

The mercenaries responded with the distinctive clicks of multiple weapons. More men pushed forward, instantly replacing the fallen.

"A good show, gentlemen," Irons said, turning his attention to the fray. "But I'm afraid, on this occasion, you're very much outgunned."

Hamid and Baxter eyed the surrounding men, their situation becoming clear.

"I suggest you lower your weapons," Irons said. "The fact I'm even allowing you to live, is probably more than you deserve."

"Do what he says," Eden said reluctantly, reading the situation from the other side of the chamber.

"A closed door costs less than a broken shoulder,"

Hamid grumbled, lowering his weapon. The thugs surged forward, securing their arms and removing their weapons.

Irons took another few steps, one of his feet barely touching the ground. He reached the edge of the causeway, leaned on his cane and looked across at Eden.

"And you must be Eden Black," he said, his voice bubbling with fake warmth. "Your reputation precedes you."

"How did you know—" Baxter said, stopping as Eden sent him a glance.

"The price of fame is tough to bear," Hamid offered.

Whilst Eden always attempted to stay incognito, using as much influence as she could through the Council of Selene to remove online records, she knew that something always slipped through.

"I must thank you for showing me the way," Irons said, a rodent-like smile crossing his face. "I suggest that you too remove your weapon and throw it down there." He pointed into the abyss. When Eden didn't move, he continued, "My men are already twitchy, and I would hate for someone to slip. Bullet holes are so unbecoming."

"Oh, you mean this one?" Eden said, sliding the handgun from its holster and glancing at it as though seeing it for the first time.

"That's the one, my dear," Irons said. Although the man appeared physically weak, his baritone voice boomed across the chamber like a vintage television announcer.

"You're right about one thing," Eden said, eyeing the mercenaries. "These guys really are twitchy. What are you feeding them, energy drinks and candy?"

"Believe me, doing what you're told is the best thing for all of us," Irons said, his voice laced with fake sweetness.

Painfully aware that Irons had the upper hand, Eden

flung the weapon over the edge. It spun down into the void, clattering against stone somewhere far below.

"A good decision," Irons said, pausing to shift his weight. "You never know, with an attitude like that, you may actually survive this. That's not a guarantee, of course, but it's certainly possible."

"I live to serve," Eden said, "especially when it comes to helping maniacs like you."

"Poking a sleeping bear is a fool's errand," Hamid said, glancing at Eden.

"She does this all the time," Baxter said, shrugging. "Issues with authority, I'd say."

"I have no problem with authority," Eden said, shooting Baxter a playful look. "But I do have a few concerns about handing a dangerous artifact over to Dr. Crazy Pants."

"You have already been incredibly helpful," Irons said, either mishearing or ignoring the insult. "You showed me the way here and opened the chamber back there. I am incredibly grateful." He looked around in the manner of someone being introduced to a new restaurant.

"Don't mention it," Eden said, noticing that the crystal conduits had now dropped back to their previous dull blue glow. "I always say that the best places are the hardest to find."

"Yes indeed," Irons said, pointing at Eden. "You didn't disappoint. I have to say, I wish I'd realized sooner that you were coming here. All that chasing around was such a waste of time."

"What a silly boy," Eden said, waggling her finger at Irons.

"Why must you kick the quiet hive?" Hamid said, shaking his head.

"It's all part of the fun," Baxter said, nodding toward Irons. "This guy seems to take it pretty well."

"Now, I think it's best if I take it from here." Irons gestured at the mercenaries standing beside him. "Fetch the crystal. If she does anything, kill her."

"I told you," Hamid said. "You have agitated a—"

"You want it so much, why not come and get it yourself?" Eden casually hefted the Eye of the Sahara.

The two mercenaries stepped toward the causeway. They peered down into the abyss and froze.

"These men will come and fetch it," Irons said, once again ignoring Eden's comment. "Any wrong move, and they will shoot. Do you understand?"

"Not being funny, but I wouldn't trust these guys," Eden said, nodding toward the men who stared fearfully at the deadly drop. "How do you know they'll even make it across?"

Irons pointed at Eden and snapped his fingers. The men looked at their boss, then back at the causeway.

"It doesn't look too safe, boss," one man said, clearly the braver of the two.

"Do you think anything about this is safe?" Irons roared, turning his gaze on the man. "You're not paid to be safe. Stop wasting time. Now get over there and—"

"Oh, temper, temper," Eden said, looking from Irons to his men. "These poor guys are right to be concerned. You wanna be careful or you'll have the union on your back."

"Move!" Irons roared.

Clearly realizing that their boss's foul mood was more dangerous than the causeway, one man stepped forward. The other followed a few paces behind.

"Listen, I've got no idea what harebrained scheme you have in mind—" Eden said, raising an eyebrow.

"That is correct, you have no idea," Irons said, his expression darkening. "Your defiance, whilst refreshing, is wholly misplaced."

"I told you," Hamid said, nodding.

"She can't be told," Baxter offered. "It's best to sit back and enjoy the show."

"Unfortunately for you, the cards are stacked in my favor," Irons said, shifting his weight and leaning further onto the cane. "The best you can expect is to survive this whole ordeal."

The thugs took another slow step across the causeway. Watching them, Eden saw the leading man's knees wobble.

"Okay. Say we admit you're in charge now," Eden said, shrugging. "What's the plan?"

"I'm afraid my patience is far too thin for such explanations," Irons said, glancing at his watch. "I have no intention of being drawn into long dialogues, thus allowing you to figure out an escape plan." He shifted his weight, wincing as his leg touched the floor.

"You've gotta be joking." Eden's hands clenched into fists in mock anger. "Boasting about your plan is a key part of the bad guy persona. Now I feel let down by decades of Hollywood antagonists."

Ignoring the comment, Irons looked at his men advancing slowly across the causeway. "Hurry up!"

The men did as instructed, taking more frequent tiny steps. Eden grinned at the ridiculous sight—the brutish men taking tiny, rapid steps with their arms outstretched for balance—like rhinos attempting ballet.

"You know, refusing to explain yourself is actually pretty smart," Eden said, taking a moment to assess the situation. With countless weapons trained on her, no cover within reach, a perilous drop on all sides, she had to admit that for now they were stuck. "Most megalomaniacs can't resist waxing lyrical about their grand plans."

"Megalomaniacs waxing lyrical," Hamid said. "I like that."

Growing more confident as they neared the far side, the approaching brutes raised their rifles. Irons watched with the detached interest of a scientist observing an experiment.

"I have one question, though," Eden said. "How did you know where to find me? You've been one step behind this whole way."

"That, I can tell you," Irons said, his grin widening. He reached into his jacket and withdrew a smartphone-sized device. "The crystal pulses with a radioactive signal like nothing else in the world." He turned the device around, showing Eden the screen.

"I thought it might be something like that," Eden said, annoyed that they hadn't thought of a way to block the signal.

"You might as well have sent up flares telling us where you were going." Irons gurgled a laugh, as though the whole thing was genuinely amusing.

"Did you know that?" Baxter hissed at Hamid.

"Of course," Hamid said, shrugging.

"And you didn't think to say anything?"

"Knowledge offered unasked buys only suspicion."

"Gentlemen, please," Irons said, looking at Hamid and Baxter. "It's of no concern now." He looked back at the thugs as they stepped from the causeway, relief clear in their expressions. The leading man adjusted his rifle, training it squarely on Eden's chest.

"If you don't hand the crystal over immediately, one of these men will put a bullet through your heart while the other pulls it from your dead hands." Irons gestured at the mercenaries, now just feet from Eden's position.

"What a beautiful description. Have you ever considered creative writing?" Eden said, watching the leading mercenary's finger slide inside the trigger guard. "Let me think about that for a moment."

"No need to think about it. No negotiation, no last requests, no dramatic last words," Irons said.

"That's not really a decision," Eden said.

"You have two seconds to hand over the crystal," Irons said, theatrically checking his watch. "Tick tock."

Eden glanced down at the rifle, then across to Baxter.

"One second remaining." Irons said, taking an uneasy step forward.

The mercenary's trigger finger began its slow, inexorable squeeze. Eden watched the microscopic movement, the gradual compression of metal against metal.

"Fine!" she said, holding out the crystal, its surfaces dancing with light. "Take it!"

53

———

"A WISE DECISION," Irons said, watching the crystal like an addict eyeing their next fix. "Now, pass it across, very, very, slowly."

One of the mercenaries took a step forward, his hand extended.

"That's it." Irons spoke as though coaxing a child out of a hiding place. "Pass it to my associate there. No sudden movements, no heroics. We're all civilized people here."

"Nothing says *civilized* like the business end of a gun," Eden said, watching the mercenary with his weapon raised. Knowing she had no other choice, she extended her arm and placed the crystal into the mercenary's hand. The moment the crystal left her palm, the lights around the chamber flashed red for several seconds, before dropping back to blue.

The man slipped the Eye into a pocket on the side of his tactical vest.

"Good, very good," Irons said, his tone glowing with mock pride. "Now, walk back to us, slowly. No funny business."

"What is this *funny business* he speaks of?" Hamid said. "This man really does have a strange way of speaking."

"Funny business, I wouldn't dream of it." Eden stepped toward the causeway. She paused, indicating that the thugs should go first.

"No, you go first," Irons said, pointing at the causeway.

Forcing herself to smile, as though she hadn't thought about leading the men onto the causeway first, and then pushing them over the side, Eden started back across. She walked quickly, casually, making the span in a few steps. Once across, the armed men surrounded her, searched her for weapons, bound her wrists and shoved her alongside Baxter and Hamid.

"That didn't go quite to plan," Eden said, glancing at Baxter and then Hamid.

"No one can plan for events outside of their control," Hamid replied, nodding as though Irons turning up was little more than a minor inconvenience.

The two guards made it back across the walkway, this time their movements more akin to that of ice-skating elephants. The leading man passed the crystal over to Irons at a speed that suggested he was pleased to be rid of the thing.

"Do you even know what that is?" Eden said, watching Irons cradling the object like a parent reunited with their lost child.

"Oh yes, of course," Irons said, holding the crystal inches from his face. A pink and mauve glow swirled hypnotically across his skin. "I have sought this for years. It will give me the power to do something most consider impossible." He turned the crystal and examined it from various angles. "With this I can take the impossible and make it real." He turned and looked at one of his men.

"Bring the rest of the team here, we don't have time to waste."

A radio crackled as one of the men relayed Irons's instructions.

"All good here?" Eden whispered to Hamid and Baxter. "Nice attempt to take them down."

"Thanks," Baxter said. "Shame it didn't work."

"The chance persists every moment we are alive," Hamid whispered, muscles straining as he pulled against his bindings.

"Staying alive is always plan A," Eden said, noticing movement from the passage behind them. "Look, someone's coming."

They turned to see sweeping flashlight beams advancing down the tunnel. As the lights grew closer, the scale of the party became clear. The sound of footsteps followed, then the drone of electric motors and the rumble of wheels.

"It looks like you've got a whole army down here," Eden said, looking at Irons, who continued to gaze lovingly at the Eye of the Sahara.

"Yes, my love, we will be back together soon," he muttered to himself, stroking the object as though it were alive.

"I've seen some crazy things in my time, but this might just take the crown," Eden said, raising an eyebrow.

"A man who speaks to stone as if it were flesh has lost his way," Hamid said, shaking his head. "Whatever drives him, it has consumed his reason."

"For once, you've actually expressed what I was thinking incredibly concisely," Eden said, turning back to the passageway.

"What a compliment," Baxter said. "She never says nice things like that to me."

"Jealousy keeps score while losing the game," Hamid replied, grinning.

"Wait a second, did you just tell a joke?" Eden said as the first figures came into view—four heavily armed men. Flashlights mounted on the barrels of their assault rifles swept through the gloom. A pair of motor-powered carts followed the men, each secured with a tarpaulin.

"And what have they got there?" Eden said, watching the vehicles, which were each roughly the size of a small mining cart with thick rubber wheels.

"Whatever he's got there, it looks important," Baxter said, nodding at the angular shapes bulging beneath the tarpaulins. "And high-tech too."

A technician walked behind each trolley, manipulating a joystick on a handheld control.

"Do you get the impression that we're in over our heads?" Eden whispered, shaking her head. "Whatever Irons is planning, he's better prepared than us."

"The prepared wolf still falls into the tiger's pit," Hamid said. "Irons has tools, yes, but not wisdom."

"Is that supposed to be reassuring?" Eden said, turning to look up at the big man. "Next time I want encouragement, remind me not to come to you."

At the convoy's rear, four additional guards flanked a young Hispanic woman in a rumpled lab coat. She stumbled forward, clearly exhausted from her ordeal.

"I'm guessing that's one of Glass's team." Eden nodded at the woman. "I think if anyone can help us, she's the one."

"She certainly doesn't look like she wants to be here," Baxter replied.

Irons looked up as the small convoy reached the end of the passage. He eyed the equipment as though seeing it for the first time.

"Excellent," he said, straightening up and looking out at the chamber. "Get this all set up. We power up as soon as possible."

The technicians pulled the tarpaulins from the carts, revealing a ring of metal pylons connected by thick cables on the first cart and a bank of monitors and control systems on the second.

"Good to see you, Dr. Morales," Irons said as the guards shoved the woman in the lab coat toward him. "Are you ready to rewrite history?"

"I've told you, without testing we've no idea what—" Morales said, her expression hollow with fatigue.

"You've told me many things," Irons cut her off. "And I tell you this: what you have in skill, you lack in belief. Fortunately, I don't need your belief. I simply need you to check the equipment."

The technicians positioned the carts at the tunnel's opening, then ran cables from one to the next. They set about drilling into the crystalline conduits and attaching more cables to the carts.

"What are they doing?" Eden hissed, confident that her voice would be cloaked by the drilling.

As the men worked, white light shot through the crystal veins, each one strobing as though in distress.

"It looks like they're tapping into the ancient system's power source," Hamid said. "I expect they're planning to use it for something specific."

"Ahh, *something specific*," Eden said, shaking her head slowly. "Thanks for the absolutely useless info."

Red light pulsed through the chamber now, zooming from each of the openings, down to the floor and then up the central tower.

"Connect the power cells," one technician called out. "We need a steady flow at four hundred megajoules."

"That sounds like a lot," Baxter said.

"Is it possible to overload this place?" Eden said.

"Certainly," Hamid said. "Although what would happen—"

"Let me guess, you don't know." Eden watched the young scientist, who Irons had called Morales, moving between the equipment.

Morales looked out at the chamber, the crystals flickering at a crazy rhythm. She shook her head as though forcing herself to concentrate on the matter at hand, then adjusted settings on various screens.

"I need to talk to her," Eden said, pointing at the woman. "Anyone got any ideas?"

Irons stood at the center of it all. He held the Eye of the Sahara aloft like a conductor with his baton, waiting for his orchestra to finish tuning.

"Sir, we're detecting instabilities," one technician reported nervously.

"Expected and accounted for," Irons replied. "Continue setup. Dr. Morales, report."

"Reaching operational level," Morales said, glancing up from the screen. She looked out across the chamber as the lights turned from red to yellow. "I need to stress again—we have no idea how this structure will react to modern amplification technology."

"Then we'll make history by finding out," Irons said, smiling. "One way or another."

54

———

Dr. Alistair Irons paced toward the causeway, the crystal held against his chest. He paused at the edge and looked across the chamber as a bolt of white-hot energy raced around the walls.

The chamber groaned with something, Irons thought, that sounded like pleasure. It was as though the whole place had been waiting for him, biding its time to come together in this moment of glory.

"Report," Irons shouted, turning to see Morales tapping furiously at one of the control panels. The machine—the stabilizer—issued a hiss, belching a stream of cooling vapor from the port on the back.

"The stabilizer is responding to the ambient energy field," Morales said, the glow of the screen washing her face. "But I don't understand these energy ratings, they're off the charts." She looked up at Irons, her hair falling over her face. She brushed it aside without missing a single keystroke.

"That sounds bad to me," Eden said, struggling against the zip ties that Irons's men had secured around her wrists.

"This place has been collecting energy for thousands of years," Irons said, ignoring Eden's interjection and sweeping his hand through the air. "It's now time to put it to good use." A bolt of light ran up the central tower, its bright white tentacles reaching out like a giant spider.

"Anywhere else in the world," Morales said, shaking her head, "I'd think this was pure fantasy."

"Keep going," Irons said, repositioning his cane in an attempt to take the weight from his bad leg. "This is a place of wonder. Today we will not only make history, but visit it." He turned and gazed out across the chamber, his focus moving beyond the walls. "Before the day is out, we will put something right, something I've needed to do for a long time."

"Ready to power up," Morales said, looking up at Irons. "But once we go, we could lose control—"

"Don't worry about that," Irons said, extending the crystal high above his head. "We have everything we need. Start the power-up sequence. I will get in position."

"That sounds really bad," Eden groaned.

Gripping the crystal in one hand, and using his cane with the other, Irons started across the walkway.

Morales hit a few more keys and the system issued a sound like a turbine starting. Beginning low, the sound rose in pitch, building up through the frequencies, until it faded once again from the audible spectrum.

Irons moved across the bridge, his cane tapping. Pulling the crystal close against his chest, he didn't even think about the drop on either side. Today, he knew, things were going his way.

"The power is already at thirty percent," Morales shouted as a pair of technicians rolled out another cable. "I've never seen anything move so fast."

Irons took another few steps, nearing the platform. He paused and gazed up at the tower which reared above him, impossibly large and imposing. The millions of glittering surfaces reflected a brief flash of light. Colors sped and swept across the tower, moving and bursting like fireworks. He looked down at the crystal, colors swirling inside.

"The ancients knew that the future held not just one possibility, but several," Irons said, picturing Anne's face in his mind's eye. "Anne always said the universe had a sense of poetry."

"This is incredible," Morales said, shaking her head. "The ancient systems, they're synchronizing with our equipment like they were designed that way."

"Maybe they were," Irons said, glancing over his shoulder. "In this place, anything is possible."

"We're at fifty percent," Morales said. "This sort of power would shred anything in the modern world."

Irons continued, tapping his way toward the central platform.

A bolt of power shot through the chamber, lancing from one side to the next in a great snap. The guards cried out in surprise, sweeping their weapons one way and then the next. Irons remained wholly focused on each step, his gaze fixed on the cradle.

He stepped off the walkway and onto the platform. The crystalline heart of the chamber pulsed brighter, as though welcoming the Eye home. Energy cascaded around the conduits, forcing Morales to glance up from her work.

"Sixty percent," she said. She no longer tapped at the screen, but stood back and watched the readings climb. "The interaction between our equipment and the ancient power grid is creating some kind of amplification effect."

"I know," Irons said, closing in on the cradle. "That is

exactly what I intended. This place was built to manipulate forces we're only beginning to understand. We're simply ... borrowing their amplifier."

Another bolt volleyed through the chamber, this time arcing from the floor to the ceiling in a span of several hundred feet. The crack rolled around the walls several times, shaking dust into the air.

Irons reached the cradle and stopped. He looked back at Morales, and then at his men who gazed across the chamber with their guns raised, as though mortal weapons were any defense here. Then he looked at his prisoners, who also watched with amazement.

"You've no idea what you're messing with. You could kill us all, or worse," Eden said, shaking her head. The other two stood in morose silence.

Irons gazed up at the tower as another bolt shot across the chamber.

"Eighty percent," Morales said, her tone more urgent than before. "Dr. Irons, I really suggest we stop this now. If we push this any further, we're at risk of—"

"Making the greatest discovery of all time," Irons roared, his arms outstretched. "We will not go back. We will move boldly into the future ... and the past."

Irons shuffled forward and extended his hand, lifting the crystal toward its cradle. A shimmer moved through the air like a heat haze, momentarily distorting his view of the chamber's far wall.

"Excellent," Irons said, lowering the Eye into position. "The veil grows thin. There is no going back."

The distortion rippled outward in concentric waves, and for a moment, Irons could see *through* it.

"Yes!" he roared, his grip tightening on the crystal, which now hung inches from the cradle. A bolt of energy streamed from the crystal to the cradle, as though pulling the two together. "Increase the power!"

Burning white light strobed through the crystal conduits, zooming around the chamber so fast it appeared almost constant.

"We're at ninety percent of the theoretical—" Morales shouted, her voice cut off as a bolt of energy snapped through the air. "The ancient power grid is amplifying our output beyond anything we could have calculated. If we push it higher—"

"We must push it higher," Irons bellowed, his eyes blazing. The air between the crystal and the cradle fizzed with power as an unseen force pulled them together. "Success belongs to the bold. If we stop now, it was all for nothing."

"But if it goes wrong," Morales said, red lights now flickering across the controls. "The damage could be—"

"We will not fail." Irons turned and shot Morales a glance, his eyes as wild as the lights of the pulsing crystals. "Now, as I instructed you, set the coordinates for Oxford, England. Laboratory Seven, University Physics Department."

"But Doctor, that makes no sense," Morales said. "This machine is for power generation. It's not some kind of teleportation device."

"Oh, it's far more than that," Irons said, smiling.

He turned, paused for a second, then shoved the crystal into the cradle. The two clicked together, crackling with raw energy. A crack boomed through the chamber and a shockwave rolled outward, rippling the air. Through the undulating distortions, Irons saw things that shouldn't exist—the chamber as it had been thousands of years ago, filled with robed figures. The image dissolved into a kaleidoscope of impossible forms that he couldn't fully perceive.

Every crystalline vein in the walls blazed to life, dazzling everyone inside. Chunks of crystal and rock fell from the ceiling, crashing down and shattering into glowing fragments. The walkways and passages groaned and swayed under impossible pressure.

"Have you set the location?" Irons roared, his voice somehow cutting through the noise.

"Yes," Morales replied, tapping frantically at the system.

"Now the date!" Irons screamed, holding on to the cradle as the platform swayed beneath him.

"What do you mean, set the date?" Morales said. "This makes no—"

"Where we're going is not part of this timeline," Irons bellowed, his eyes blazing with manic triumph. "Set the date for March 17th, 2019!"

55

"MARCH 17TH, 2019," Eden said, turning to Baxter and Hamid. "Irons can't seriously be—" A great blanket of sparks cascading around the chamber like electric rain cut her sentence in half. The crystalline veins pulsed brighter, the air itself rippling with supercharged heatwaves.

"This is worse than I feared," Hamid said, shaking his head. His face pale, he spoke with uncharacteristic speed. "He seeks to walk backward through time itself."

Irons stood in a kind of trance gazing at the Eye of the Sahara. The crystal glowed with a light far brighter than any other in the chamber. It burned brighter and brighter until the light actually grew larger than the crystal.

Captivated by the scene, Eden watched as the ball of light emerged from the Eye, blossoming outwards.

"Something's happening," she said, pointing at the light.

"This is impossible," Baxter said, ducking as a bolt of energy crackled overhead. The bolt of light slammed into the wall behind them, the crystal veins absorbing it instantly.

"The line between possible and impossible grows thin in

places like this," Hamid said, nodding at the towering crystals.

A massive shard fell from the ceiling, plummeting past them to shatter on the platform twenty feet away. The fragments skittered across the stone, glowing like dying embers.

"My grandmother always said that the predecessors could navigate time like a river—upstream to the past, downstream to futures that might be."

"And you didn't think to mention this?" Eden said. "I thought Irons was crazy, but this is something else."

The ball of light in front of Irons expanded, now at least four feet across.

Eden gazed into the light and saw shapes moving there, like the shadows on an overexposed photograph.

"And Irons wants to go back in time?" Eden said, turning back to Hamid as she tried to process the impossibility of it.

"How would that even work?" Baxter said. "Get back!" He flattened himself against the wall as another bolt of energy hammered past, leaving a burning smell in its wake.

"These crystals aren't merely power sources," Hamid said, nodding toward the ball of light, which was now almost as tall as Irons. "They contain the code to manipulate reality as we perceive it. With enough energy, you can manipulate the past, and the future. But it's dangerous, incredibly dangerous."

"I have no idea what you said." Eden ducked as a chunk of crystal the size of her fist whistled past. "Other than the bit about it being dangerous."

"You're saying it's theoretically possible for Irons to go back in time?" Eden said. "What's the catch?"

"The energy required is catastrophic," Hamid said. "To force that shift, the Eye must harvest power from everything around."

"Harvest, what do you mean?" Baxter said.

"That sounds bad," Eden said, looking at Hamid. Deep in her stomach, she already felt as though she knew the answer.

"The power comes from everything," Hamid said. "The land, the vegetation, the people, every living thing for miles."

The floor lurched. With her hands still tied, Eden staggered into Baxter as the entire platform tilted several degrees.

"The people in the village," Eden said, struggling for balance. "That's why the Eye not being here affected their crops."

"Yes, indeed." Hamid nodded. "The land was out of balance. I fear that what Irons does now will be much worse."

"He'll kill everything," Eden said, struggling for balance. Light from the Eye blazed across the chamber, throwing strange shadows in every direction.

Hamid continued. "And if he changes something significant in the past—"

"He'll create a paradox," Baxter finished. "Reality tears itself apart trying to reconcile the changes."

"Or chooses one timeline and erases the other," Hamid said. "We might simply cease to exist, replaced by the new timeline."

Eden twisted her wrists against the cable ties, feeling them bite deeper into her skin. "We need to get free, and we need to—"

A howl filled the chamber, and a great spark lanced down, striking one of Irons's men in the chest. The bolt lifted him off his feet and threw him directly at Eden.

Eden leaped sideways, hitting the floor hard. Pain

exploded through her jaw as she landed, her bound hands offering no way to cushion the impact. The man sailed over her and slammed into the wall behind. Blue-white energy crackled across his body, holding him against the wall for a moment before it absorbed into the conduits, and he dropped to the ground.

Eden spat blood and struggled to her knees, her ears ringing.

The other guards backed away from their fallen comrade, looking out at the chamber with fear. One bolted down the passage from which they'd come, swiftly followed by a second.

"We need to get free," Eden said, crawling to the fallen guard. She saw the knife on his belt and, with everyone distracted, extended her tied hands across him, fingers straining for a grip.

Another explosion rocked the chamber, the bright white light casting flickering shadows across the stone.

Unable to see what she was grabbing, Eden moved her bound hands down over the guard's shirt. She reached for his belt and found the knife. She grasped it and pulled, twisting the knife as it came free. She flipped the blade awkwardly, her fingers so numb she almost dropped it. She slid the blade in between the zip ties and pushed, the awkward angle sending shooting pains up her wrists.

"Come on, come on," Eden muttered through gritted teeth as the blade barely bit into the plastic. She pushed harder, sawing up and down. Eventually, the tie snapped. Blood rushed back into her hands, pins and needles flooding her fingers. She quickly cut the ties binding Baxter and Hamid.

Another explosion rocked the chamber, sending a shower of sparks across the platform.

Irons was now almost completely obscured by the blinding bright light. The air around him rippled like heat waves rising from scorched earth.

Eden looked at the ball of light and saw ghostly shapes moving within. What looked like a chemical laboratory flickered in and out of focus. A woman in a lab coat appeared for a heartbeat before dissolving back into nothing. Irons stood, his arms spread wide, totally absorbed by the movements inside the ball of light.

"Time moves, and so must we." Hamid rubbed his wrists and glanced at Baxter. "First, we must deal with these rogues." He pointed at the remaining guards, who were too distracted by the lights overhead to have even noticed their captives' escape.

Eden nodded at Hamid and Baxter, then charged at the guard closest to Morales. She slammed her shoulder into the man, sending him flying straight over the edge and into the abyss. The guard's scream faded as he tumbled down, his rifle spinning end over end beside him. The sound cut off abruptly when he hit the chamber floor hundreds of feet below.

"One down, but something tells me they won't all be that easy." Eden spun around as the next captor raised his weapon. She rolled as the guard fired, the shots sparking off the ground. She bobbed back up and swept her leg beneath the shooter, smashing her boot into the back of his knee. The joint buckled with an audible crack.

The brute staggered, his rifle swinging wide as he fought for balance. Eden jumped to her feet and drove her shoulder into his chest. The guard's arms swung frantically as he staggered backward, slamming into a wall.

Eden stayed on him, spun his gun around and drove the

butt down hard against his head. With a crack, the guard fell unconscious.

Another mercenary swung his gun toward Eden, but Baxter grabbed the barrel and shoved it skyward. The man fired, bullets sparking off the ceiling high above.

Baxter yanked the guard forward and cracked a knee into the man's stomach. As the guard doubled over, gasping, Baxter chopped down on the back of his neck, sending him crumpling to the floor.

Hamid slipped up behind another guard, the man too distracted by the lights to notice. Using the blade they'd cut their ties with, he sliced the sling of the guard's rifle. He stepped inside the man's reach, caught his wrist, and flipped him into an arm-breaking fall. The guard hit the floor hard, his head bouncing off the stone with a dull thud. He didn't get up.

"Behind you!" Baxter shouted.

Hamid dropped and rolled as bullets sparked off the floor. Baxter grabbed a fallen rifle and returned fire, forcing the shooter to dive into the mouth of the passageway.

"You're ... you're not with them?" Morales said, peering out from behind the stabilizer as Eden approached. Although pale, her hands remained steady. The machine issued a high-pitched whine, vapor streaming from the vents.

"Dr. Glass sent me. She told me about you," Eden said, stepping up close.

"Dr. Glass got out?" Hope flashed across the woman's face, followed quickly by concern. "Is she safe?"

"She died getting us here." Eden shook her head, then turned back to look at Irons. "We need to stop him."

A shimmer passed through the air, and through the haze Eden saw the chemical laboratory again, clearer this time.

The woman in the lab coat re-appeared, working with chemicals in tubes.

"Anne, I'm here!" Irons roared, his hands spread wide.

Baxter and Hamid took out another pair of guards, sending one falling from the walkway and knocking another unconscious.

"Irons believes he can create a controlled temporal breach to go back and prevent his wife's death in a lab accident," Morales said.

"I knew this guy had crazy written all over him," Eden said.

"Yes, it's totally theoretical," Morales said, nodding at Irons, who took a step toward the ball of light. "I've no idea what will happen once he goes through. If I'm honest, I don't think he does either."

"What's the worst case?" Eden said, already regretting the question.

"The past, the present and the future cease to exist," Morales said. "It's totally ... well, crazy."

"You shut this down," Eden said, pointing at the stabilizer. "And I'll stop Irons."

56

WITH THE LIGHT filling his vision, Irons drew a deep breath. The air tasted of something different—metallic, electric, and filled with possibility. He stared into the light, shapes and shadows materializing within. At first, they appeared as suggestions of form—dark patches swimming through the brilliance like ink drops in water. The shadows sharpened, gained edges and depth. The image of the lab he had known so well appeared. A clock on the laboratory wall hung frozen, beside a whiteboard covered in Anne's handwriting. Morning sunlight streamed through the windows, washing everything like a dream.

"I'm coming for you, Anne," he said, taking another slow step forward. "After all this time, we will once again be together."

The edges of the light writhed as the ball expanded, cracking and snapping as it grew.

Irons's vision blurred, which at first, he put down to the ripples of the light. Sweeping a hand across his face, he realized tears streamed freely.

"I'm here for you, my love," he whispered, taking

another step toward the light. The image expanded to the edge of his vision now. "Just like I promised, we will be together again."

His skin tingled as the energy field intensified, every nerve ending alive with electricity. The hair on his arms stood rigid while static crawled like invisible insects across his body.

He took another step. The temperature spiked from uncomfortable to searing, the air itself hostile. Shimmering distortions flickered around him, showing the disconnected images of a badly tuned television.

Irons saw his laboratory as it had been the morning before the explosion. Anne stood studying her calculations, completely absorbed. Then the same space materialized, now filled with smoke and screaming. Then again, empty and pristine, as if nothing had happened.

"Stop, Irons!" Another voice permeated the noise from behind him, but Irons didn't turn.

The light flickered again, and Anne walked toward the containment unit.

Irons glanced at the clock, which told him he had two minutes until the explosion. Two minutes to get a message to Anne, to get her out of there and save her life.

Anne reached into the unit and started the process that would end so disastrously.

Smoke surrounded him now—the smell of burning fabric mixed with something else, something that reminded him of the moment after lightning strikes.

"Anne! No!" Irons shouted, rushing forward, trying to dive headlong into the scene. He stumbled with outstretched hands.

Anne looked his way, as though she'd seen him. Her facial expression showed nothing, though. No recognition.

No surprise. Just that blank, distracted glance she might give when someone walked past the office window.

"Anne!" Irons screamed, his voice cracking. "Anne, it's me! Get out! You have to leave now!"

She turned back to her work, pouring liquid from one beaker to the next. The portal flickered, the image wavering like a reflection in disturbed water.

Irons saw himself in the distortion—not as he was now, but as he'd been that day. Young, confident, arrogant, flawed. He walked down the corridor, about to open the door. He was close enough for the explosion to take his leg, but not close enough to save his wife.

"Please!" he howled, his voice lost in the electromagnetic storm. "Not like this, stop!"

"No!" another voice shouted from behind him, pulling his focus away. "Irons, stop!"

Eden raced across the walkway, closing in on Irons.

"Stop!" she shouted again, hoping he'd hear her voice over the tortured stream of the overloaded system. "We're shutting it down now. Step away from the light."

Irons turned slowly, his face morphing from an expression of confusion to pure rage.

"I won't stop!" he roared. "She was taken from me once. I won't let it happen again."

"The power's reducing, but too slowly," Morales shouted, darting out of the way as a bolt of energy zipped from one of the conduits. "It's too much!"

"I know about your wife," Eden said, stopping a few feet from Irons, her hands outstretched. "She wouldn't want you to risk all this. There's no knowing what damage you'll do, stripping the energy from—"

"You know nothing!" Irons shouted, lifting his cane and pointing it at Eden. "She died because of my arrogance, because of my belief that I knew it all. All I need to do is get a message to her, to stop her. One small change, and she'll still be here."

Eden took another slow step forward, now close enough to see the madness burning in his eyes. The structure beneath them vibrated, threatening to throw her from the causeway.

"I understand," Eden said, shouting over the electro-magnetic storm. "But you're making the same mistake again ... you don't understand the risks—"

"I've already lost everything." Irons thumped a palm against his chest. "I'm already dead in here. I have nothing left to lose."

"That's not true. You have your memories of her," Eden said, keeping her voice as calm as she could. "Your memories are real. They're yours. No one can take them from you."

Irons's shoulders tensed and his hands trembled.

"This system, and the way you're using it, there's no knowing the damage it'll cause." Eden took another step, inching closer. The portal washed everything in bright white light. "Anne wouldn't want you to risk this for her."

Behind Irons, Eden saw Anne in the light, still working, oblivious to the approaching danger.

"Look at her," Eden said softly, pointing at the portal. "She dedicated her life to making the world better through science. Would she thank you for this? For turning her memory into something that destroys instead of creates?"

The portal pulsed, and for a moment, Anne turned toward it again. Her eyes held no recognition. Concern flickered across her face, as if she'd heard something troubling in the distance.

"It's going down, but too slowly," Morales shouted. "The power has nowhere to go."

"She'd want you to honor her by continuing her work, not with destruction," Eden said, as gently as she could.

"You know nothing about what she'd want!" Irons bellowed, his face contorted in rage and grief. "She died because I was arrogant enough to believe we could control forces beyond our understanding."

"And you're doing it again," Eden said. "Except this time the stakes are higher."

Keeping low, Morales worked at the stabilizer controls, her fingers flying across the panels. Sparks erupted from the unit, racing along the cables and into the crystalline conduits.

"The field's destabilizing!" Morales screamed. "If he enters now—"

"I won't let her go a second time!" Irons roared, spinning to face the portal. He stood silhouetted against the light. "Anne, my love. I've come so far, I must reach you." With his arms outstretched like a swimmer diving into the ocean, he hurled himself into the light.

A sound boomed through the chamber. Energy erupted from the point Irons had touched the light, bolts of lightning spidering out across the tower and the chamber.

A shockwave slammed into Eden like a physical wall, lifting her off her feet and hurling her backward across the walkway. She hit the floor and slid toward the edge. She dug her nails into the surface, stopping inches from the precipice.

The chamber shook as the system overloaded. Cracks

webbed through the structure, and more rocks slammed down.

Eden forced herself to her feet, squinting at the chaos through the blinding light. Against the searing white of the portal, she saw Irons's silhouette. Multiple versions of him existed simultaneously: one stepping forward, one reaching back, one screaming.

Suddenly he stood whole again, straighter than before, younger somehow, as though the years of grief had been stripped away.

Around them, the ancient structure shrieked. Massive cracks split the walls like black lightning.

"The place is coming down," Baxter screamed from behind her. "We need to get out!"

57

IRONS LOOKED AROUND, momentarily confused. He no longer stood in the underground cavern, surrounded by chaos. He took a step forward, realizing he was now somewhere else entirely. He cupped a hand above his eyes to block out the light, and the place came into focus.

He took another step forward, the pain in his leg dissipating to nothing. He looked down and touched his leg. Through the fabric, his skin felt smooth and painless. He reached further, exploring the point at which his leg and prosthetic joined. His leg continued, unbroken, as it had been before the accident. Suddenly, the light dimmed, colors swirling around him. The shapes moved and materialized into images.

It took Irons a few moments to make sense of it all, looking around like a child seeing the world for the first time.

Red and white roses climbed a trellis, and a well-tended lawn spread out underfoot. Butterflies danced and twirled through the warm summer air—their wings catching the light. The air seemed alive, shimmering with pollen and the lazy drone of bees. Somewhere out of sight a blackbird sang.

Irons took another step forward, recognizing their garden as it had been in their happiest moments—Anne's and his.

Painstakingly making his calculations, Irons had expected to meet Anne in the Oxford laboratory. He planned to rush in moments before the disaster and tell her to call the whole thing off. That one tiny change would save her life, reuniting them in the present. The fact that he was now here didn't make sense at all.

Irons stood motionless, breathing in the scent of lavender and roses.

"I thought you might come," came a voice from somewhere to his right.

Irons turned at a speed that would normally send a jarring pain through his injured leg. Sitting on the blue wooden bench they'd bought many years ago, Anne was as beautiful as he remembered. She wore a blue sundress, and the breeze played through her hair.

"I've been waiting for you," she said, sliding a bookmark between the pages of a well-thumbed paperback before placing it on the bench beside her. The gesture was unhurried, as though she had, quite literally, been waiting for his arrival.

"Anne," the word came out as little more than a whisper. His legs, despite their newfound strength, almost gave way beneath him.

"Alistair," she said, her gaze meeting his. "I wondered when you'd finally figure this out. How long did it take you?"

"Six ... six years, in my world," Irons said, moving toward his wife. Although the distance was only a few steps, it seemed to take an age. "I worked at it every day, and here I am."

"I never doubted you would," Anne said, patting the space on the bench beside her. "Come, sit with me. We have much to talk about."

Irons sat beside his wife and exhaled. He took a moment to drink it all in—the warmth of the sun on his face, the sound of the bees, the smell of the roses.

"Is this real? Have I really done it?" he said, his voice cracking. He turned toward Anne, his hands trembling as they rose halfway to her face before dropping back to his sides. A tear traced down his cheek, followed by another.

"It's as real as anything," Anne said, leaning over the bench and running her hand over the stem of a rose growing behind them.

"This isn't how I thought it would go." Irons pressed the heels of his palms against his eyes, trying to stem the flood. "I planned to find you in the laboratory and warn you, then I could—" His words dissolved into a broken sound that was half-laugh, half-sob. "I even practiced what I would say. For years, I practiced the words that would save you." He gestured helplessly at the perfect garden around them. "How is ... when is this?"

"Time is ... let's just say it's not quite as you understand it," Anne said, placing a hand against his cheek. "You're here now, and that's what counts."

"I've missed you so much," Irons said, meeting his wife's gaze. Tears flowed freely now. "Every day without you has been ... empty. Pointless. I tried to continue the work, tried to make it mean something, but without you ..."

"You shouldn't have blamed yourself," Anne said.

"Of course I blamed myself." The ball of emotion rose in his chest. "It was my experiment, my calculations, my arrogance that killed you." He reached up and placed his hands over hers.

"Alistair." Anne's voice carried the same patient tone he remembered so well. "The accident wasn't your fault. We worked in a dangerous field. We all knew the risks."

"But if I hadn't pushed so hard, if I'd listened ..." His voice hardened, his hands fell to the bench and clenched into fists.

"Then you would have been a different person. I fell in love with the person you are, not the person you think you should have been." Anne held his gaze for a moment and then touched the rose again. "Why are you really here?"

"To save you so that we can spend the rest of our lives together."

She turned, and for the first time, he saw sadness in her eyes. "For such an intelligent man, you say some silly things."

"Don't you see, saving you is only the start." Irons slammed his fists into the bench. "This could be so much more. Imagine once I've proved this can work—getting a message to the past—we can do so much good. We could prevent disasters before they happened, save people from accidents, stop shootings before—"

"Stop." Anne placed a hand on Irons's chest. The touch moved through him like a bolt of lightning, killing the words in his mouth.

A butterfly fluttered down and landed on the bench between them. It flexed its yellow and black wings.

"Look at this," Anne said, pointing at the butterfly. "It's a Small Tortoiseshell, and what a beautiful thing it is. Do you know how long this lovely thing will live?"

Irons stared at the creature, its wings opening and closing in a slow, hypnotic rhythm. "I ... no."

"Six weeks if he's lucky. He will enjoy just six weeks in the sun."

Irons watched as the butterfly lifted off, circled once, and settled on a nearby rose.

"But to enjoy those few precious weeks in the sun," Anne continued, "he must first spend months as a caterpillar, eating and growing in the darkness, then weeks wrapped in a chrysalis, morphing into something unrecognizable. All that time preparing, transforming, waiting for those few precious weeks of flight." She turned to Irons, her eyes bright. "He won't rage against the shortness of it, Alistair. He will simply do what he can. He will live his moment in the sun completely, and when it ends, he will let it end."

The butterfly spread its wings once more, catching a current of air, and drifted higher into the garden.

"We had our time in the sun," Anne said softly, her hand returning to Irons's face. "And it was beautiful."

"But ... but I need more. I can't live without you." Irons leaned forward, inhaling her scent as though it were intoxicating.

A crash boomed across the garden, like thunder from a clear sky. The butterfly on the rose dissolved into nothing, scattering like ash.

Irons turned toward the sound and watched as his view of the garden peeled away like old wallpaper. Through the widening gap, harsh strobing light poured in from the chamber. A crack ran through the air, splitting the blue sky like fractured glass.

"My darling man." Anne leaned forward, her lips close to his. "What happened to me was not your fault, and this is not something you can fix. All you must do is learn to live without me."

The garden split in two, revealing the chaos of the chamber. Sparks cascaded down the walls, chunks of crystal fell. In the center of the melee, Eden ran toward him. Behind her, two men fought the last of his guards, their movements stuttering like a film with missing frames.

"I can't," Irons whispered. "I tried. For six years I tried, but every morning when I woke up and you weren't there, it felt like drowning."

"You must. What you're doing here is wrong. The damage you could do is far too great." Anne pointed at the dissolving boundary between the garden and the chamber. "How many more people will suffer because of what you want? Alistair, you must stop this before there's nothing left to save."

The sides of reality peeled away faster now, like a burning film. Through the growing crack, Eden ran in slow motion. Her mouth opened in a warning shout that reached them as a deep, distorted growl.

"Listen, Alistair." Anne's voice held no anger, just sadness. "I died working on something I believed in. That's not a tragedy—that's a life well-lived. But this ..." She gestured toward the fracturing reality around them. "This is not love, this is fear."

"I can't stop. I won't stop," Irons said, anger flaring. "I can't let you go."

"You don't have to let me go." Anne smiled, the expression so achingly familiar it nearly broke him. "You have to let me rest. There's a difference." She leaned forward and kissed his forehead, her lips warm against his skin.

"They're coming for you. It's time to go," Anne whispered. The garden dissolved around them. The roses withered to ash and the golden light faded to a harsh glare.

Anne slid backward, the bench disappearing from beneath them.

"No!" Irons lunged forward, trying to grab her, to pull her with him. His hands swept through empty air as the last traces of the vision disappeared.

He turned, facing the chaos of the collapsing chamber. The crystal blazed in its cradle, flashes of light bouncing around the space. Cracks spider-webbed across the chamber's walls.

"It's over!" Eden shouted, finally reaching him. Her voice came in waves, sometimes clear, sometimes echoing from somewhere far away. "We've got to stop this now!"

Crystal pulsed erratically now, each beat sending out waves that rippled through the air like disturbed water.

"No!" Irons roared, reaching out to grab something, but every recognizable part of the garden faded to nothing. "I'm staying here. You go, leave me."

"Irons, listen to me, we need to stop this!" Eden grabbed Irons around the waist and forced him to the ground. Finally, the light dimmed. "It's over," Eden said.

58

———

"YOU DON'T UNDERSTAND!" Irons struggled beneath her, his face streaked with tears and sweat. "She's there. I want to go back. I need to go back!"

"You can't," Eden said, gesturing at the chaos erupting around them. "The power has done something to the chamber. It's unstable."

Something exploded high above, showering them all with fragments of crystal. The entire chamber shuddered, and a crack worked its way through the walkway.

"Shut it down!" Eden shouted, turning to Morales, who frantically worked the controls of the stabilizer.

Bolts of blue-white energy arced wildly overhead, too powerful now to follow the crystal channels in the walls.

"I'm trying," Morales shouted over the grinding stone. "The power, it's going down too slowly. The system isn't responding."

Eden jumped to her feet, stepped over Irons and reached for the Eye of the Sahara. The crystal strobed, each surge sending spiderweb cracks through the cradle.

"No!" Irons dragged himself along the floor and grabbed Eden's ankle, stopping her a few inches from the crystal. "You don't understand, I just need another minute or two. I can bring her back."

"You can't." Eden spun around and kicked out, striking Irons in the chest. He groaned and his grip loosened. She pulled her foot free and stepped up to the crystal. She grabbed the Eye of the Sahara, and a searing pain shot up her arms. She gritted her teeth against the pain and pulled. The crystal came free with a sound like an ancient machine clunking out of gear. The system groaned, the power continuing to flash overhead.

"Give it to me!" Irons lunged forward, grabbing for Eden. She darted to the side, easily avoiding Irons's grip. She moved around him on the narrow platform, a drop of hundreds of feet disappearing into darkness over the edge.

"Don't make me do this," Irons said, his voice dropping to a growl. Then, almost in slow motion, he pulled a gun from inside his jacket.

Eden glanced down at the weapon, a Walther P99 Compact.

"I've killed before," Irons snarled, sweeping the weapon in a motion that covered Eden and the space behind her where Baxter and Hamid stood. "I'll do it again, too. No bother."

Irons straightened up, the movement clearly a painful one.

"Irons, think about this," Eden said, raising her hands slowly. The Eye of the Sahara burned against her palm, its color now dulled. "Anne wouldn't want this."

She glanced over her shoulder and saw Baxter and Hamid watching the volatile situation.

"Don't you dare say her name!" Irons roared, wildly

aiming the gun. "You don't know what she would want. It's your fault I'm even back here. You dragged me away from her!"

Lights flickered around the chamber, dying out like candles.

"There's too much at stake." Eden pressed the burning crystal against her chest. "You're playing with things you don't—"

"Give me the crystal!" Irons screamed. He lurched forward, putting weight on his damaged leg. His face contorted in pain, his whole body tensing. His finger contracted around the trigger.

The gun roared.

The first shot went wild, the gun bucking in his weakened grip. He held on, pulling the trigger again and again, rage overriding any attempt to aim.

Eden threw herself to the ground, bullets sparking off the walkway on either side and the wall behind.

"Stop!" Baxter shouted. Irons wheeled toward him and fired again, then again, squeezing off rounds in blind panic.

Another gun fired—this one controlled and deliberate.

Irons jerked backward, his eyes widening in surprise. The Walther slipped from his fingers, clattering to the platform and bouncing into the abyss. He glanced down and noticed, almost with surprise, a stain spreading across his chest, blooming like the roses in his garden.

Eden looked over her shoulder and saw Hamid, shouldering a rifle he'd pulled from one of the fallen guards. Registering that Irons had dropped the gun, Hamid lowered the weapon.

"Anne ..." Irons whispered, his eyes losing focus. He reached toward the cradle where the Eye of the Sahara had been a few moments ago. His prosthetic leg, already damaged from the earlier struggle, gave way completely. He stumbled back, his arms swinging frantically as he struggled for balance.

Eden took a step forward, preparing to help him back onto solid ground.

Then, surprisingly, a smile crossed Irons's face—not mad, but peaceful, as if he'd finally found what he was looking for.

"It's time for my moment in the sun," he said, stepping backward. He leaned, as though lying back onto a bed, and fell from the platform and out into the abyss.

Eden lunged forward, her hand stretching out instinctively to catch him. Her fingers slipped through nothing, Irons already far below her. He plummeted down, spinning head over feet until the shadows swallowed him.

The lights around the chamber flickered one last time, then dropped to a deep blue, dying like a closing eye. A sudden silence followed, broken only by their labored breathing and the distant sound of stone grinding against stone.

Then, Eden heard something else—a hiss of pain that wasn't quite a cry. It was the groan of someone mortally wounded and not able to scream. She turned around, a cold shudder working its way up her spine.

"Eden!" Hamid shouted, sudden understanding dawning on his face. He sprinted toward her, his boots pounding against the crystal. Morales followed close behind.

Eden's gaze dropped to a figure sprawled on the walkway a few paces behind her. Even in the dim light cast by the chamber's failing power, she recognized the silhouette immediately.

"No," she breathed, the word barely audible. Her arms

dropped to her sides as the whole chamber seemed to tilt around her.

Baxter lay motionless, sprawled across the walkway, one arm flung out above his head, the other clamped to his chest. A dark stain spread out beneath him. He hissed again, and moved his hand, searching for the place where one of Irons's wild shots had landed.

Eden covered the distance in seconds and slid to her knees.

Baxter looked up at her, the fire already draining from his eyes.

"I think this is going to hurt in the morning," Baxter whispered, managing a weak smile.

"Don't be an idiot, you've had worse hangovers," Eden said, her hands instinctively finding the wound and pressing hard. Warm blood seeped through her fingers—too much, too fast. Above them, the massive crystal pillar cracked like a gunshot, showering them with fragments.

"You can tell me all about how much it hurts tomorrow," Eden said, forcing a laugh that sounded more like a sob. "Maybe I'll even listen to you talking about planes."

A section of the walkway on the other side of the chamber fell away, crashing down into the void. Bolts of energy sparked randomly between the crystals.

"Wow, it must be serious." Baxter's breath hitched, and a trickle of blood appeared at the corner of his mouth.

"I'll listen to every single boring detail about wing specifications and engine types. I mean, I can't promise I'll enjoy it, but ... just ... just stay with me."

"Eden—" Baxter's breath caught. He tried to lift his hand to wipe the blood from his face, but the movement was weak, uncoordinated.

A chunk of crystal the size of a subway car tore free from the ceiling, crashing down into the chasm.

"No." Eden pressed the wound harder, the wet warmth spreading up her wrists. "No speeches. No last words. You're going to be fine."

"We stopped it, right?" Baxter's eyes searched hers with sudden intensity, his bloodied hand finding hers. His grip was frighteningly weak. "The world ... lives on for another day?"

"Of course we did," Eden said, her voice breaking. Tears ran down her face, mixing with the dust and ash falling from the crumbling ceiling. "That's what we do, remember? Save the world, have a drink, moan about it afterwards."

Hamid placed his hand on Eden's shoulder. Eden looked up and met his gaze. She shook her head in a tiny, desperate motion. The wound was catastrophic—she could see it. The bullet had torn through his lung, probably nicked an artery. They both knew what that meant in a place like this.

Another section of the ancient structure gave way, and the platform beneath them tilted a few degrees.

"The system's shutting down. Irons is gone. We did it," Eden said, talking just to fill the silence.

"Good," Baxter said, his eyes drifting closed. "Fair trade."

Eden gasped, thinking for a terrifying moment that was it. Then his eyes snapped open, but she could see the effort it cost him.

"Eden ... I need to tell you ..."

"Save it," she whispered, their faces inches apart. "You can tell me anything you like over a cocktail back at the *Balonia*."

Baxter gurgled something of a laugh. "We both know that's not ..." His voice faded to nothing, but his eyes said everything.

"Yes, it is," Eden said, her body tensing. "It's definitely happening."

Baxter's hand closed more tightly around hers.

His eyes stayed locked on her face, as if memorizing it. Then, between one heartbeat and the next, the light went out of them entirely.

59

A MASSIVE SECTION of the roof fell in, crashing down with a roar that shook the entire structure.

Eden didn't even notice the noise, her gaze focused on Baxter, who now lay completely still. She gripped his hand tight, feeling for any sign of life. Her eyes snapped up with sudden resolve.

"This is not happening." She laid Baxter's hand on his chest and stood so abruptly that Hamid stepped back in surprise. "Morales, I need your help."

"We need to get out," Morales said, gesturing at the collapsing chamber around them. "We barely have time to evacuate, let alone—"

"We need to fire this up again," Eden interrupted, picking up the Eye of the Sahara from the floor beside Baxter's body. The crystal was still warm, pulsing faintly with residual energy, now stained with blood.

Morales focused on Eden with the intensity of a hawk. "You can't be serious. You saw what happened to Irons—"

"This is different," Eden said, her voice breaking. "I only

need to go back two minutes. Just two minutes. Can it be done?"

Morales looked from Eden to the crumbling chamber, calculations running behind her eyes. "The power requirements alone—"

"I have no choice," Eden said, the crystal trembling in her grip.

"I fear you are acting out of desperation," Hamid said, kneeling beside Baxter's motionless form. "You saw what happened when Irons went inside. The stakes are too high to gamble with reality."

Another section of the ceiling crashed down, smashing onto the walkway behind them. A crack snaked through the crystal, tilting the walkway another few degrees.

"This is different," Eden shouted. She turned to Morales, who clung to the wall as a shudder moved through the entire structure. "We won't need as much energy for two minutes, right?"

"Half an hour ago, I would have told you it's impossible." Morales looked up at the central tower, which shed fragments like tears. "But now—"

"Is it possible? Before this place comes down?" Eden said.

"Eden, think about this!" Hamid dropped into a crouch as the platform lurched. "The place is already coming apart. We have to get out of here or we're all—" A rock the size of a refrigerator slammed into the wall behind them.

"Is it possible or not?" Eden shouted, her voice straining against the sound of the structure falling apart.

"Theoretically, yes," Morales said. "You go in, and at the key moment, you shove him to the ground. But do nothing else. Change nothing else. The last thing you want is to make it worse."

"Got it," Eden said, turning and pacing back toward the cradle.

"Wait," Morales said, moving back toward the stabilizer. "For two minutes we'll need ..." She paused as another explosion rocked the chamber, "... at least ninety percent power capacity. The structure can barely maintain its current state."

"I've got to try," Eden said, raising the Eye of the Sahara toward the cradle. She looked back at Morales and then Hamid. "Once I'm in, you two get out of here."

A crack echoed through the chamber, and a split worked its way up the central shaft.

"That's good, the system is still online," Morales said, her fingers flying across the controls. "If we could create a localized reversal, just two or three minutes ..." She looked from Hamid to Eden.

"A wise person should not gamble with forces they do not control," Hamid groaned, crouching again as the walkway shook.

"A wise person doesn't leave a friend to die." Eden glanced at Hamid and then shoved the Eye of the Sahara back into its cradle.

The dying chamber roared back to life. Lightning as thick as a tree trunk shot from the floor to the ceiling, the thunderclap so loud her ears whined. Light flowed across the walls again like liquid electricity, racing in mad patterns and jumping in uncontrolled arcs. Where the power met damaged sections, explosions bloomed like deadly flowers.

"If we get this wrong, we'll—" Hamid said, ducking as a sheet of crystal peeled away from the central shaft and shattered against the platform.

"He's dead!" The words tore from Eden's throat like broken

glass. She turned to face Hamid, each syllable hitting her anew. "Right now, in this moment, Baxter is dead. We get this right, he lives. How is that different from using a defibrillator on someone with heart failure? Both change someone's future!"

"A defibrillator doesn't risk the lives of others!" Hamid shouted over the growing roar of collapsing stone and screaming energy.

The Eye of the Sahara blazed with impossible brightness, its light coalescing into the same portal Irons had stepped through. But this orb was different—unstable, pulsing erratically like a dying heart. It expanded in stuttering bursts, each surge accompanied by a sound like crunching metal.

The sphere grew larger, its surface rippling with disconnected images. Through it, fractured glimpses of the past few minutes flashed—Irons firing his gun, Baxter falling, Eden screaming—all playing simultaneously in a kaleidoscope of moments. The light swelled to ten feet across, then fifteen.

Another support pillar exploded, raining crystal fragments throughout the chamber. The walkway beneath Baxter's body cracked, separating from the main platform.

"Power increasing," Morales roared. "Sixty-five percent ... seventy ... We need at least ninety for a stable field."

The chamber groaned around them, cracks spreading further through the walls.

Eden stepped toward the ball of light, electricity moving through her body as though she'd touched a live wire. The crystals all around the chamber pulsed with increasing speed.

"Not yet. We need at least ninety percent!" Morales shouted.

Another chunk of crystal sheared off the tower overhead.

Eden glanced back at Baxter—her partner, her friend, the man who had saved her life more times than she could count.

"There's no time," Eden said, turning and stepping into the light. Reality twisted around her like a film running backward. The spreading pool of blood beneath Baxter contracted. The cracks in the chamber walls sealed themselves. The echo of gunshots returned, growing louder and louder until it distorted into a single roar.

Then, as though someone had flicked a switch, everything went dark.

Eden stumbled forward, her hands instinctively reaching out for balance. The floor beneath her feet had changed—no longer the tilting crystal platform but something smooth and solid.

A blue pulse ignited high above her. It cascaded downward like a waterfall of light, flooding the surrounding space. The illumination hit her in waves, each pulse revealing more of her surroundings. She spun, trying to orient herself as the blue radiance washed over walls she'd never seen before.

Her eyes adjusted, and she gasped. Cool air touched her skin where moments before she'd felt the heat of explosions. The chaos and destruction had vanished, replaced by an eerie stillness.

She peered up at the space above her, soaring so high that its true size became lost in the blue-tinged darkness. Crystals hung from the ceiling and reached up from the floor like a forest of frozen lightning—some slender as icicles, others thick as ancient tree trunks, all pulsing with the same blue radiance.

Then, looking around the chamber floor, Eden saw the figure. For a moment she reeled back with surprise at seeing another person, but an overwhelming sense of calm settled over her.

She stepped toward the figure who, facing the other way, didn't see her approach. Drawing closer, Eden saw that a long gown flowed across an unnaturally tall frame, reflecting the crystal light. When Eden was a few paces away, the figure turned in a motion like fluid.

"Welcome, Eden," the man said, his voice booming across the vast space. "I have been waiting a long time to see you again."

60

Eden met the man's gaze and froze. He took a step forward, his robes flowing like liquid mercury.

"Who are you?" Eden said, surprised by how steady her voice sounded in this impossible place.

"Now, that is an excellent question," the man said, a smile lighting his face. "We will answer that in time, but for now—"

"We don't have time," Eden said. "My friend, Baxter, he's been shot. I need to—"

The man raised a hand. "Time does not work in the same way here." He pointed up at the crystals. "In many ways, time is all we have."

"Are you one of the people who built this place?" Eden said, looking around the chamber.

The man took another step forward. As he neared, Eden felt a growing energy pulse inside her. "In short, yes. I am of the people who built this place."

"How, I don't ... that's impossible." Speaking the words, Eden realized how hollow they sounded in this place where impossibility was the rule. "I thought the civilization here was destroyed thousands of years ago."

The man smiled, although his expression held something sad.

"This place was destroyed, but we moved on. Those who survived did anyway. Some of us moved across the Sahara to what you now call Egypt, others made their way across the ocean."

"You still live in these places?" Eden said.

"Oh yes, of course," the man said, gesturing to the surrounding crystals. "You don't think you're the only intelligent race to occupy this planet, surely?"

Eden opened her mouth to answer but couldn't find the words.

"I see that you have inherited the most common human trait." He flashed a somber smile. "The ability to over inflate your place in the world. It has in fact, become something of a joke for us. For example, it's astounding how many of our structures you've taken as your own."

"What do you mean?" Eden said.

"The Pyramids at Giza, for instance." He raised his hands to the ceiling. "After this place was built, that was our next civilization." He stepped up to a crystal pillar the size of a tree trunk. The light inside pulsed as he neared. "It's amusing to us how your people accept what your experts say, even though they cannot explain how blocks weighing hundreds of tons were placed with a precision that your modern equipment struggles to match."

Eden tried to focus on the man's words, but all she could think of was Baxter, his lifeblood draining away.

"Or Stonehenge in England—your scholars debate endlessly about how primitive people moved those massive stones hundreds of miles." The man shifted, his robes swishing again. He gestured at the crystal formations above them. "Their theories of wooden rollers and rafts are actually crazier than the truth—"

"You did it?" Eden said.

"Well, not me personally," the man said, placing a hand across his chest. "But yes, our people made them, many thousands of your Earth years ago."

"You're saying ..." Eden started, struggling to process what she heard.

"I'm saying that humanity has been the junior partner in this relationship for far longer than you realize." His pale eyes met hers again. "We have watched humankind grow, guided you when necessary, and intervened when your ambitions threatened to destroy everything."

"Like now," Eden said quietly.

"Indeed, unfortunately that is so," the man said. He reached out and touched one of the crystals. "Although you brought the Eye of the Sahara back to us."

"Dr. Glass told me to return it. She said that would restore the balance," Eden said. "I'm not sure it did any good, though."

"It has, more than you know," the man said, moving his head from side to side. "Your scientists at Los Alamos believed they could use it to create something powerful. They were right about that."

"I wish people would stop calling them *my scientists*." Eden looked from the man to the crystal. "What do you mean by that?"

"That one piece of crystal, the Eye of the Sahara as you call it, contains all we know about the building blocks of the universe, and the code to make and break it at will."

"How? I don't understand."

The man reached out and touched the crystal beside him, its light intensifying at his touch. "Every crystal here has a molecular structure—identical, uniform, repeating patterns that channel energy in predictable ways. But the Eye of the Sahara is different." He looked at Eden again. "Its molecular structure is encoded with information."

"Information?"

"Think of it like computer storage, but at a quantum level. Each molecular bond, each atomic arrangement, carries data about the fundamental forces that govern reality itself." He gestured to the surrounding crystals. "These crystals are like blank pages, but the Eye is an entire library compressed into a single stone."

"How is that possible? How can you encode information into the crystal's structure?"

"The same way nature encodes information into DNA," the man said. "Except we didn't limit ourselves to four base pairs. We used the infinite variations possible in crystalline matrices—angles, bonds, electron spin states." He paused. "Your scientists at Los Alamos barely scratched the surface. They saw it could focus energy. Thankfully, they never realized they were holding the operating manual for ... well ... everything." The man extended his arms.

"That's why the Eye brought me here, and how Irons used it to see into the past," Eden said, understanding dawning.

"Correct. It's an incredibly powerful thing." The man nodded. "It was foolish of Dr. Glass and her team to do what they did. They were messing with things they had no hope of understanding."

"Yes, but now I've returned it, it's all over," Eden said, frustration growing. "All I need now is to help Baxter."

"Maybe you do, maybe you don't." The man looked around the chamber as though enchanted by it. "Don't you find it interesting that you've just saved your people from the same hubris that destroyed this place?"

"Yes, I suppose, but—"

"The problem here is not the situation, it is your understanding," the man said, raising a finger which seemed longer than that of a human.

"I really wish people would stop saying things like that," Eden said, taking a step backward.

"You seek to control something that your species has no business even knowing exists. With the power contained in that crystal, the universe can be rewritten from the ground up." The man nodded slowly, turning somber. "Although this time your people have something we did not."

As the man met her gaze, Eden experienced a totally new sensation. It was as though she knew what he was about to say. She shook her head slowly and took a half-step backward.

"It's not possible," she muttered to herself. The crystals around her now pulsed so brightly they almost became white.

"Oh, it is not only possible, it is the truth," the man said, a playful smile forming. "We have been leaving clues for you for hundreds of years. I'm certain you've seen them?" He placed the palms of his hands together, eliciting another glow from the crystals.

A vision struck Eden so hard and heavy that it felt as though something had fallen from the ceiling and slammed into her.

"The statue in the Hall of Records," she said, her voice sounding unlike her own. "The one that looked like me."

"That's right, but let's be clear." The man extended his finger again. "She didn't *look* like you, she *was* you. The vial around her neck contained your genetic make up."

"And in the garden at Quinta De Regaleira, Portugal," Eden said, her gaze narrowed. "She led us to the Seal of Solomon."

"That's correct, I was especially proud of that one," the man said. "There are many more, which perhaps one day you'll discover. Breadcrumbs, if you will, left for you over millennia to guide the way."

"But why?" Eden said, feeling as though the chamber shifted around her.

"Because, my dear Eden, you are one of us."

61

EDEN STAGGERED BACKWARD, catching her balance on one of the crystal pillars. The moment her palm made contact, the block blazed with a white-hot light. A surge of energy raced through Eden's body—not painful, but overwhelming, like a bolt of adrenaline.

"That's ... that's ..." Eden whispered, fragments of memory flickering through her mind. The visions scrolled backward, like a video playing in reverse. It started with the statue sharing her likeness in the Hall of Records beneath the Giza Plateau, then on to the truth she'd recently learned about Alexander Winslow not being her biological father. Although she hadn't pushed for answers at the time, she knew there was much more to the story than he'd revealed, or even knew.

"How many times have you found yourself in the right place at the right time?" the man asked, tilting his head to the side. "How many times has it felt as though a positive force is watching over you?"

Eden looked closely at the man, a strange sense of recognition rising within her. It was as though she'd seen him before but had somehow forgotten.

"But ... but that doesn't make sense," she said, finding her voice. "I am not like you. I am ... human."

"You are both," the man replied. "You were born of our people but were chosen to move over to the human side. You have learned to be human, to understand their world, but you still retain enough of us to bridge the gap."

Eden looked around the chamber, the whole place glowing like an aurora.

"That is why you are here," the man said, his tone bordering on sadness. "You have been called upon to prevent the same catastrophe that destroyed our civilization from consuming yours."

"Do you mean the fall of Atlantis?" Eden said, the colors dancing around her.

"As you call it, yes," the man said, his hands pressed together. "Many thousands of years ago, we became intoxicated by our own power." He leaned forward as though letting Eden into a secret.

"The power of the Eye of the Sahara," Eden said.

"Correct." The man reached out a hand, and the crystals around them responded with a deep, resonant hum. "We marveled at our genius, because we finally understood how this all worked. But the more we used the Eye, the deeper we went, the more we became corrupted."

"Corrupted, how?" Eden's gaze snapped back to the man. "Wait a second, you're telling me that someone buried this place on purpose?"

"That's right," the man said, a momentary surprise flashing across his face. "It seems that, in our lust for power, we had forgotten one of the life-giving forces we couldn't live without—"

"Water?" Eden said.

"Not just water—but the life force itself. Water was merely its physical manifestation." The man's gaze dropped to the floor, light coloring his pale skin. "Every use of the Eye draws energy from somewhere. We thought we were pulling it from the quantum field, from empty space, but we were wrong. We were draining it from the living earth itself —from the ground, the water, the atmosphere, the very bonds that held everything together."

Eden's eyes widened. "Hamid was right. The Eye converts life energy into power."

"Precisely. And once that energy's spent, it's gone forever. The Eye can bend reality, but it can't create life from nothing. By the time we understood what we'd done, the damage was irreversible. The Sahara you see today? That's not climate change or natural progression. It's a scar because we bled the earth dry to fuel our ambitions."

"But couldn't you use the Eye to alter the past?" Eden said.

"What? Turn back time to before we used it? We'd burned through thousands of years of accumulated life force in a few decades alone."

"A civilization destroyed by its own ambition," Eden said.

"Indeed," the man said, before casually adding, "Plato got that right, but then, he only said what we told him to."

"But he got something wrong," Eden said. "Atlantis never sank beneath the water, but beneath the sand."

"Correct, that's a bit of simple misdirection. We wanted you to learn of our plight, without finding the actual location. We feared you might do the same."

"You feared right," Eden said, a chill moving through her when she realized the implications of what Irons had done and now what she was doing. "Now that energy has started draining again."

"Correct, from the chamber itself, from the surrounding land, and ..." the man paused, "... from the people nearby. Every use requires payment. The energy must come from somewhere."

"By saving Baxter, I'll be—"

"Yes. There is a cost. But you have something others do not." The long finger extended again, pointing directly at Eden. "You can choose to draw the power from yourself— from your life force, your genetic heritage, and your connection to us." He studied her carefully. "That's why only you can do this, and only once."

Eden nodded, understanding finally dawning.

"Don't you think it's a curious human trait that you are able to distort the value of a single human life if it's someone you care for?" The man's tone brightened as though sharing a funny observation. "You'd kill thousands to extend the life of one. When you think about that logically, it's ludicrous, but to you it makes sense."

"And I can do that because I was raised human," Eden said quietly.

"Correct," the man said. "You have perhaps the ultimate superpower—the ability to choose love over power."

"It sort of makes sense now," Eden said, looking up at the surrounding crystals. "I've spent my whole life feeling as though I've been searching for something ... maybe this is it. Maybe this is the answer I've been looking for, but now to save Baxter you're asking me to give it all up."

"I'm not asking for anything." The man shrugged, sending his robes into a dance. "I'm telling you the cost of the decision you're about to make. That's far more than your ancestors had."

"It feels like coming home to a family I never knew I had." Eden closed her eyes, seeing Baxter's face in her mind. Instinctively, she extended her hands and pressed them against one of the crystal towers. A feeling washed through her, as though she were part of something much larger. "But if I save him, I'll lose this connection."

"Yes." The man's tone held no judgment, only observation. "This choice defines the world to which you truly belong."

Eden thought of Winslow, who'd raised her despite knowing she wasn't his. She wished she could speak with someone, to discuss this impossible decision.

The man watched her silently.

"All those times I knew things others didn't, the moments of impossible luck ..." Eden trailed off, pieces of her life clicking into place. "I wasn't imagining it. I really was different."

"You are a bridge between worlds," the man confirmed. "Placed precisely where you needed to be."

Eden's mind raced through the implications. If she kept this connection, she could learn so much. She could access knowledge that would revolutionize science, archaeology, everything. She could help humanity leap forward centuries in understanding. But Baxter would be dead.

"You know the cruelest part?" Eden said, her voice thick with emotion. "Baxter would understand. If I told him the cost, if I explained what I'd be giving up by saving him, he'd tell me not to do it. He'd say that one life isn't worth that kind of sacrifice."

"That's because he is human. His emotional connection to you distorts his understanding of reality."

"Emotional connection?" Eden said.

"Indeed. The fact you're even questioning this decision suggests it's requited."

"I can't imagine a world without him in it," Eden said, blurting the words out. She removed her hands from the crystal and pressed them against her eyes.

The crystals around the chamber pulsed in time with her heartbeat, mirroring her turmoil.

"What will you choose, Eden?" the man said, locking his fingers together.

Eden stood in silence for a long moment, feeling the vast connection pulse through her one last time.

"I need to do it," Eden said, dropping her hands to her sides. "I need to save Baxter."

62

———

"I suspected you would say that," the man said, stepping forward. He placed a hand on Eden's shoulder, a bolt of power moving through her. With it came visions—flashes of knowledge, understanding, connection.

Eden staggered backward, feeling as though she'd been plugged into a vast energy grid. The hand closed more tightly around her as the energy increased.

"But know this, my child," the man said as flashes of knowledge and understanding spun through Eden's vision. "You have done something I could not, and for that I am forever proud of you."

"My child?" Eden said, the words hardly formed as they left her mouth. The man's grip on her shoulder tightened further still.

"Now, you must go back. Your decision has been made." He removed his hand, and the chamber dissolved into streams of light. Colors flowed, pulling her in multiple directions at once. She saw the city as it had been in its prime—not the myth, but the reality. Concentric rings of land and water with crystalline towers and vast structures.

"Atlantis," Eden muttered, her eyes wide.

Then she saw the fall. At first, it happened slowly, almost imperceptibly. The crystal that powered the civilization grew hungry, demanding more energy than the earth could provide. She watched her ancestors make the fatal choice—instead of scaling back, they pushed harder, draining life force from wider and wider circles around the city.

The crops were the first to fail—fields of grain withered to nothing. Orchards that had flourished for centuries turned to ash, lush gardens became dirt. Famine came like a tide. The people who had the knowledge to reshape reality, turned their attention to fighting over the last stores of grain.

The survivors scattered like seeds from a dying flower as the desert grew. What had been the heart of their civilization became the Sahara, expanding year by year, century by century until it stretched from ocean to ocean.

The image dissolved and the Great Pyramid of Egypt rose before her. She stared up at the distant capstone, carved from a single crystal, blazing gold beneath starlight.

The images accelerated, showing Stonehenge, the stones each vibrating at a specific frequency. Machu Picchu, Göbekli Tepe, the monoliths of Rapa Nui all spooled through her vision. Then, the great cathedrals of medieval Europe rose before her. But Eden saw beyond their stone façades to the mathematical principles encoded within. She saw her people, now diluted and scattered, working alongside human craftsmen who thought they were following divine inspiration, never knowing they were being guided by survivors of a fallen civilization.

The images shattered like glass. Reality began bleeding through the cracks—gunshots, shouting, the acrid smell of burning. The chamber flickered between what it had been and what it was: crystalline perfection overlaying ancient ruin, past and present occupying the same space.

The visions fragmented, overlapping and contradicting. Past and present bled together as she saw the chamber as it had been millennia ago, crystalline and perfect. Then she saw Baxter falling—but also standing.

The chamber snapped back into focus—but wrong. Everything crawled as though time ran at half, or quarter its usual speed. Sound stretched and distorted: gunshots became low thunder, shouts turned to deep groans. Dust motes hung suspended like stars.

Eden stood watching bullets cruise lazily through the air.

Irons fired again and Eden ducked easily out of the way. She watched the bullets sailing above her, sliding slowly on rippling trails toward Baxter. She saw him, who despite the danger continued to run toward her, right into the path of the bullets.

"He ran to save me," Eden said, breaking into a sprint. Her feet hit the floor with impossible speed, muscles burning with pure energy. She ducked beneath the slow-moving bullets and slammed into Baxter's midsection. The pair fell to the ground as the shots passed overhead.

More gunfire erupted. Eden glanced up and saw Hamid returning fire. Two shots slammed through Irons's chest, causing him to stagger.

Then, with a sound like thunder, time snapped back to its normal flow. The chamber lurched into full speed—bullets slamming into the walls, dust swirling, shouts echoing.

Eden lay sprawled on top of Baxter. They both gasped. Her muscles throbbed with exertion and her vision blurred, struggling to focus. She lay still for a second, focusing on the beautiful, priceless sensation of Baxter's chest rising and falling beneath her. She clamped her eyes shut and exhaled with pure relief.

"That's a really desperate move, you know," Baxter said, his voice breaking the silence.

The crystal platform beneath them groaned, cracks spreading further through the structure. Somewhere beneath them, a chunk sheared off and fell into the void.

Eden shook her head and rolled to the side, her limbs weak and shaking.

"I ... we ... did it," Eden whispered, looking at her hands.

"You know, if you want a cuddle, all you've got to do is ask," Baxter said, elbowing her playfully in the ribs.

Before Eden could respond, a deep, ominous groan boomed through the chamber. Cracks spider-webbed across the floor beneath them.

"Move, now!" Hamid shouted, grabbing them both and heaving them to their feet. "It's coming down."

As though to emphasize his point, the central column split. A massive fissure raced up its length and a chunk the size of a building tore free. It fell toward them in slow motion, raining debris.

Eden ran, her feet slipping on the walkway. Thousands of tons of rock and crystal raced toward them, closing in on their position.

The platform bucked beneath her—a crack shot between her legs, nearly swallowing her boot. She stumbled, pitching forward. Hamid caught her arm, yanking her upright without breaking stride.

They sprinted flat out across the disintegrating causeway. Hamid led the charge, vaulting fallen chunks of crystal. Baxter ran next, with Eden a step behind.

Morales watched from behind the machine in the mouth of the passageway, still thumping at the controls.

The massive section of the severed central tower punched through the walkway behind them with devastating force. Eden felt the impact through the soles of her feet as the shockwave barreled after her. The walkway dropped, tilting as it fell out of position.

Baxter and Hamid, a few feet ahead, leaped into the mouth of the passage. Baxter landed smoothly, swung around and reached out for Eden.

"Jump, you've got to jump!" Baxter roared, extending his hand.

The walkway beneath Eden's feet tilted—thirty degrees, forty. She looked up at Baxter, now high above her. Suddenly, the walkway jerked to a stop, striking the central pillar. Sparks flew where the surfaces met, grinding crystal against crystal.

Eden sprinted up the incline. On the third step, the walkway snapped free and fell again. She continued running, her feet now hitting the surface as it fell away. Chunks broke from around her feet, tumbling into the abyss.

She looked up at Baxter and jumped, her hands extended. For a heartbeat, she flew—arms outstretched, legs kicking at nothing. The gap yawned impossibly wide.

Baxter leaned out above, Hamid anchoring him from behind.

Eden reached out, her fingertips brushing Baxter's.

Baxter's hand shot forward even further and caught her wrist. The jolt nearly pulled her arm from its socket. Her body slammed against the falling walkway, knees and ribs taking the impact, but Baxter held on. Together, he and

Hamid hauled her up and over the edge as the last of the causeway disintegrated into the darkness below.

Eden collapsed against the wall at the mouth of the passageway, chest heaving, legs trembling.

For a long moment, none of them spoke. She looked out across the chamber as the central pillar crumbled like a sandcastle in the tide. Ancient supports snapped like matchsticks. Through the destruction, she glimpsed the Eye of the Sahara one more time. The crystal remained in its cradle, falling into the darkness, about to be buried under thousands of tons of crystal and rock.

Eden exhaled, pushed off the wall, and then looked at Morales, Hamid, and Baxter.

"In this life there are three things I know for sure," Eden said, steadying herself with Baxter's shoulder, then meeting his gaze. Baxter tensed slightly under her touch, his gaze showing something she couldn't quite read.

"Does the stubborn warrior finally learn to really see the world around her?" Hamid said, a smile creasing his lips.

"Death, taxes and I'll never ask you for a cuddle," Eden said, driving a finger into Baxter's chest.

Baxter caught her hand before she could pull it back, holding it against his chest.

"Although maybe death is not as permanent as I once thought," Eden said, watching Baxter's reaction to see if he knew what she was talking about. When he didn't react, she tried to pull her hand free. Baxter held it in place a moment longer.

"It is true that a leopard crossing the desert will arrive with the same spots," Hamid said, setting off toward the exit.

"As usual, I have no idea what you're talking about," Eden said, striding up to Hamid and placing a hand on his shoulder. She turned and glanced back at Baxter as the final chunk of crystal crashed down behind them, forever sealing the Eye of the Sahara in the earth where it belonged. "But I'm dying to get out of here ... figuratively speaking."

63

Marrakesh, Morocco. The following day.

"WHY DO I always miss the party?" Athena said, looking out over Jemaa el-Fnaa square as the sun slid behind the minaret of the Koutoubia Mosque. "Although in your absence I have got quite into this Moroccan Whisky." She lifted a glass of steaming mint tea to her lips and slurped a good measure.

"That's certainly not for me," Eden said, snatching up a bottle of cold Casablanca Beer.

"Since you guys cut me out of saving the world, I've been living the healthy life," Athena said, stretching out her arms. "Training in the mornings, reading my book in the afternoons." Athena pointed at the copy of *Zen and the Art of Not Giving a...* on the table in front of her.

"Your reading material is something I very much approve of," Hamid said, sipping his tea. "We suffer more in our imagination than in reality. Words of wisdom that ease such suffering are gladly accepted."

"Is that an internet meme?" Eden said, turning to Hamid.

"I have never heard of such a creature. Where might I find a *meme*?" Hamid replied.

"No, it's a—" Athena said, stopping when Hamid's grin suggested he was winding her up.

The door opened and Winslow strode onto the rooftop, followed by Baxter.

"How are you feeling? You look dead ... tired," Eden said, throwing Baxter a smile.

"Thanks, alright, I think," Baxter said, pulling out a chair and joining Athena at the table. He scratched his head, clearly considering but not understanding the subtext of Eden's comment. The call to prayer drifted over the city.

Eden grabbed a beer from the ice bucket and passed it to Baxter. He accepted the bottle, cracked it open, and took a swig.

"The whole thing has been classified at the highest levels," Winslow said, turning his back to the city and leaning on the railing. "I've spoken with our contacts in the Mauritanian authorities. They're calling it a localized seismic event caused by illegal mining operations."

"That's unusually cooperative of them," Eden said, taking another sip.

"Indeed, it is," Winslow said, looking at his daughter. "As I'm sure you've figured out already, they'll no doubt want something in return. But, that's a problem for another day."

"And Morales?" Eden asked.

"On her way back to Los Alamos with a recommendation to head up the Experimental Research Center," Winslow said.

"In exchange for her silence, nice," Athena said.

"A closed mouth gathers no enemies, but an open palm gathers many friends," Hamid said.

"Oh, I like that one." Athena smiled at Hamid.

"She wouldn't talk, anyway." Eden looked out at the horizon as the sun slid out of sight. "But she won't have it easy. Glass left some big shoes to fill."

"And the Eye of the Sahara?" Athena asked.

"Buried under tons of rock," Eden said, her final view of the crystal filling her mind's eye. "You'd need a full-scale operation to get it out of there. Let's add the area to a watch-list, just to make sure that doesn't happen."

"Already done," Baxter said, between sips.

"And the other thing?" Eden said, looking at her father.

"Yes, I didn't quite understand that." Winslow removed a small notebook from his pocket and flicked through the pages. "A Toyota Land Cruiser has been purchased and will be driven to the village of Ouadane, where the driver must search for a man named Khalid. When he finds him—and apparently it won't be difficult, everyone knows Khalid— he's to say ..." Winslow squinted at his own handwriting, "*the friends of the Amazigh have not forgotten the debt.* Then hand over the keys, no questions asked."

"A brand new Land Cruiser?" Athena raised an eyebrow.

"A debt of gold is paid in gold," Hamid said, setting down his tea. "But a debt of life can change the course of generations."

"Good, all's well that ends well, I suppose," Eden said, raising her bottle.

"We cannot control events, only our response," Athena said, taking a deep meditative breath and slurping at the tea. "Clean mind, clean body. You guys really should try this."

Eden looked at her friend, then the tea, before taking another sip of beer.

"After that move Hamid pulled back at the shop, I'm not trusting that," Winslow said, pointing at the teapot.

Eden threw Hamid a grin, not yet willing to let him off the hook for not actually poisoning them.

"The tea reveals only what the drinker brings to it. Some taste mint and sugar, others?" He smiled. "They taste their own suspicions."

"What's that supposed to mean?" Athena said, clocking the knowing glance between Eden and Hamid.

"What you say about control is correct," Hamid said, pointing at Athena. "Irons had all the control in the world, yet he could not control his grief. And how are you feeling, Captain?" Hamid turned to Baxter.

"Still a little confused," Baxter said, scratching his head. "I can't really understand what happened back there. I fell to the floor and came around with you on top of me." He pointed at Eden.

Athena looked at Eden, an eyebrow inching its way up her forehead.

"Not like that," Eden said, playfully slapping Athena's shoulder. "I knocked Captain Clumsy, there, out of the way of a bullet, that's all."

"It must have been quite a knock," Baxter said, rubbing his head. "I've got these weird memories, but it's all a bit mixed up. I'm sure you were on top of me, cry—"

"Yeah, you must have hit your head," Eden said. "It was a stressful time."

"Yeah, maybe," Baxter said, watching Eden closely, something uncertain flickering in his eyes.

Hamid looked from Baxter to Eden. Catching his eye, Eden wasn't sure whether he knew what had happened back in the chamber, or whether the secret was hers alone.

Eden turned away before anyone could read too much in her expression, crossed to the railing and looked down into the square. Below, a group of tourists wandered through the crowds, phones raised, excitedly capturing the scene. They threaded through the vendors, heading toward the food stalls.

Athena and Baxter continued talking, oblivious to Eden's turmoil.

"Sometimes the deepest wounds leave no visible scars," Hamid said, joining Eden at the railing, his voice little more than a whisper.

In Eden's mind's eye she saw the image that had plagued her for the last day—Baxter lying in the chamber, blood spreading across his chest. She saw the life drain from his eyes, the heat already passing from his body.

Leaving the chamber, it had been clear that Baxter couldn't piece together what had happened. That made sense, because now, technically, it hadn't happened at all. The bullets had never found him. That was a figment of another timeline, one that fortunately hadn't come to pass.

Eden was the only one who remembered every heart-breaking second.

"As usual, I have no idea what you're talking about," Eden said, steadying her voice enough to reply. She turned and met the big man's gaze.

"The young warrior knows more than she says," Hamid said gently. "There are stories of those who crossed between the moments. They say that such gifts exact a price that only the giver truly understands. But perhaps," he looked back toward where Baxter sat laughing with Athena, "some prices are worth paying."

"There was no price," Eden said, pausing a beat, "because nothing happened."

"Nothing happened," Hamid agreed softly. "And yet, here we are, discussing nothing with such careful words."

"Oh, I like this one, but I don't quite understand it," Athena said, her voice carrying across the rooftop. "He who fights with monsters should look to it that he himself does not become a monster."

Eden took a deep breath, steadied herself, and turned.

"And what's that supposed to mean?" Baxter said, peering at the book.

"Irons fought his demons so much, that eventually he became one," Athena said, shrugging. "Maybe?"

"Say that again," Eden said, turning and looking at her friend.

"Maybe," Athena said.

"No, the bit before that, about the monsters."

"He who fights with monsters should look to it that he himself does not become a monster," Athena said, reading from the book. "It's a guy called Friedrich Nietzsche."

Eden stood for a moment, something materializing in her mind. She felt as though things were about to click into place when Athena spoke again.

"Impressive stuff, right? As I told you, I've been reading," Athena said, setting down her tea with unusual deliberation.

"I'm glad you now understand that books aren't just for decoration," Winslow said.

"Why didn't you tell me that these pages contained such wealth?" Athena said, dramatically flicking through the book. "This one's good too: everything new excites the mind, but a mind that seeks truth must turn from the new and seek the old."

"She's been doing this for days," Winslow said, looking helplessly at the others.

"That relates to Irons because he was imprisoned by a single moment he couldn't let pass." Athena looked directly at Eden. "Sometimes the bravest thing isn't to fight, but to let go."

"You know what, that sort of makes sense," Eden said, remembering the feelings that had flooded through her in the chamber. She cast a glance at Baxter. "You get one chance to make the right decision, and after that, you've got to live with it."

"Speaking of choices," Winslow said, looking at his bottle of beer. "Who chose this beer? It tastes like dishwater."

"That is Casablanca's finest," Eden said, her tone lightening.

"Then I'd hate to taste their worst," Winslow said. "I'll take a single malt next time."

"I can guarantee it tastes better than this." Eden snatched Athena's glass and took a sip. She winced as the supersweet flavor filled her mouth. "How much sugar have you got in there? That's not healthy at all. You'd be better off with a soda."

"Well, that's how they make it," Athena said, snatching the glass back.

Winslow lifted fresh beers from the bucket and passed them around. "With all that behind us, I'd like to propose a toast."

Athena looked at the beers hungrily, then at her mint tea. "No thanks, I—"

"Wait," Eden said, looking at everyone in turn. "I need you all to know something." She paused, searching for the right words. "Thinking about what Athena said, we've all faced monsters before, and we've all survived."

"Are you trying to express ... feelings?" Athena said in genuine shock.

"What I'm trying to say is ..." Eden looked down at her hands, then up at the others. "I'd be dead a dozen times over without you guys. That's not weakness. Letting you idiots watch my back is the smartest thing I've ever done."

"Thanks, I think," Baxter said.

"If this is what she says to her friends, I don't want to hear the insults," Athena said.

"To watching out for each other," Winslow said, raising his bottle.

"To the secrets worth keeping," Hamid added quietly, his gaze meeting Eden's.

"To second chances," Baxter said, something in his voice making Eden wonder if maybe, somehow, part of him remembered after all.

"Oh, give me that," Athena said, snatching up a beer and taking a greedy sip. "What?" She said, when the others laughed.

"And fighting the monsters," Eden said, looking at the people who kept her both sane and alive.

"And most importantly, not becoming one," Hamid finished, lifting his tea to the group.

64

EDEN STOOD on the rooftop looking across the muted chaos of late-night Marrakesh. With the final call to prayer having faded out hours ago, even the traffic in the square below had thinned to a few diehard tourists and the occasional local on the way home. She sat alone on a bench, a bottle of beer warm and forgotten beside her.

The rooftop door swung open. Someone took a step out and then paused, probably letting their eyes adjust to the low light. The footsteps resumed, crossing the rooftop with what sounded like deliberate slowness.

"You couldn't sleep either?" Baxter said, finally appearing in Eden's peripheral vision. He carried a bottle of beer in each hand, condensation beading on the glass. "I figured you might need a replacement for that one." He nodded at the forgotten bottle, then sat down beside her, placing the two fresh bottles on the table.

"I wouldn't say no," Eden said, taking the bottle. "How did you know where I was?"

"I didn't see you go to bed, and figured you'd need time to decompress after ... you know." Baxter swept the bottle to the side, the gesture encompassing the events of the last few days.

"You know me," Eden said, enjoying the sensation of the cold bottle against her palm. "What's your excuse? You've had an ordeal too and didn't that cute doctor lady tell you to get some rest?"

"And resting is exactly what I'm doing." Baxter lifted the bottle to his lips.

A beat of silence passed between them.

"I've got a horrible feeling you want to talk about something serious," Eden said, turning to meet Baxter's gaze.

"It's all so confusing." Baxter paused, his fingers tightening around the bottle. "I want to remember what happened, but it's ... it's weird."

"There ... there was a lot going on," Eden said.

"I remember the shooting and then everything went dark. I mean, really dark. After that, it didn't hurt anymore. And I thought ..." He stopped, inhaling a shaky breath. "I thought that was it. I thought I was ..."

"You don't need—" Eden said, placing her hand on his forearm.

"No, it's important," Baxter said, steadying himself. "Then, through the darkness, I heard your voice. You told me to stay with you, and somehow, I did. I tuned into your voice, like it was the only thing that mattered."

Several stories below, a motorbike rattled away from the square and off into the medina.

"Were you scared?" Eden said.

"No, weirdly." Baxter turned to face her fully, their knees touching. "At that moment I felt so at peace, with you ..." He paused, struggling with the words. "I don't think I've ever felt that close to anyone in my whole life."

"Or death," Eden said, before she could stop herself.

"What do you ...?" Baxter stopped, and Eden thought for a second that he'd figured the whole thing out. "I remember thinking in that moment about ..." he paused, clearly choosing his words carefully. "I thought about all the walls we put up, all the pretense, and how none of it really matters. I felt exactly how much you ..." He stopped, swallowing. "How much you mean to me ... how much I think we mean ..." He trailed off, unable or unwilling to finish the thought.

Someone shouted in Arabic from the street below, followed by the crash of a bottle hitting the cobblestones.

"The next thing I remember is you lying on top of me," he said, his voice rough with emotion. "But there was no blood, no pain. I was just, better. But, you were shaking as though something had torn you apart. I don't know what you did, but you brought me back, didn't you?"

Eden's fingers closed involuntarily, and Baxter caught the movement.

"And I know it cost you, more than I think you'll ever be able to tell me."

"The brain creates all sorts of hallucinations," Eden said, as lightly as she could. She turned her face away from him as something prickled her eyes.

"I don't want to hide from this," Baxter said, his voice gentle, but firm. "I know you did something, and I know it cost you."

"You don't know. You can't know," Eden said, her tone hardening.

"You saved me, and it cost you," Baxter said, ignoring Eden's interruption.

"Okay, fine. I saved you because we're partners," Eden blurted out. "We watch each other's backs. That's what we do."

"And that's all?"

"What do you mean by that?" Eden shot back. "I was doing what I needed to do for you, for our team."

"You saved me from a bullet, but if it cost you that much, maybe you shouldn't have," Baxter said, looking at his hands. "This has cost you too much."

"No," Eden said. "It was just a bullet. A random bullet amid a lot of chaos. That it found you ..." She trailed off, her mind suddenly picking up on something.

"You know, that's typical of you." Baxter placed his hand over Eden's on the table. "You're not the only one who feels, who gets hurt, or damaged. You face everything like you're going into battle alone, and it's nonsense." His voice took on a painful tone. "Quite frankly, it's an insult."

Eden stared off into the distance, her thoughts running at warp speed. The idea of the bullet randomly striking Baxter had got her thinking. Nothing over the last few days seemed random. Everything they had been through—from the fake poison in the tea, to the collapsing chamber—had been orchestrated, with them stuck in the middle of it.

"Eden?" Baxter said, his hand gripping hers. "I'm sorry, maybe it's too early for this conversation. I'll—"

"No, wait," Eden said, turning to meet his gaze. "The problem is, I do face these things alone." She thought about the moment of connection she'd felt and rejected to save the man now in front of her. The sensation ran through her body, tingling every nerve and synapse.

"Yes, I know you do," Baxter said, shuffling in close. He touched Eden's chin gently, his fingers barely grazing her skin. "I know you do, but you don't need to." The distance between them felt both infinite and paper-thin. His thumb moved slightly against her jaw, a gesture so tender it made her chest ache.

Eden glanced down, the gaze too intense to share. She looked at the bottle of beer on the table in front of them, a drop of moisture running across the glass in the humid night. Suddenly, something occurred to her. A memory flashed into her mind.

"You don't need to face anything alone, not anymore," Baxter said, his hand moving from her chin to her cheek.

Eden continued looking at the bottle as the drop of moisture reached the table.

"It's merely a transition, the water becoming vapor," Eden said, repeating the phrase that had followed her for the last few days.

"I'm here," Baxter whispered, his voice rough with emotion. "Ever since that time in Lebanon, I've been here. Even when you push me away, even when you run. I'm not going anywhere, Eden."

Eden's eyes widened as understanding dawned, but her body remained frozen in position.

"Yes, that's right," Eden said, her mind once again racing. Her gaze slipped past Baxter's shoulder as more pieces clicked into place—not about them, but about everything else. The conspiracy. The orchestration. "Like water becoming vapor," she said, louder this time.

"What?" Baxter said, straightening up.

"You're so right. You're a genius," Eden said, her gaze suddenly bright with revelation. She grabbed Baxter's face between both hands. "You know, you are an absolute genius. I knew it all along."

"Wait, well thanks, but—" Baxter said.

"I don't know why I didn't see it before." Eden leaned in and kissed his cheek, jumped to her feet and ran for the door.

"Eden, wait—" Baxter called, as her footsteps clattered down the steps.

Baxter sat frozen for a moment, then slowly raised his fingers to where her lips had been.

"What a woman," he murmured to the empty rooftop. He picked up his forgotten beer, still half full, and shook his head.

65

───────

Eden picked her way through the narrow lanes of the medina, keeping to the shadows where possible. She paused for a second, remembering the look on Baxter's face the moment before she'd fled. She felt his touch on her face and heard the warmth in his voice.

"Focus," she muttered, darting through an island of light and back into the shadows on the other side. She skirted a small marketplace beside the metal working medina, now shuttered for the night.

She glanced up at a tabby cat with a mangled ear watching her from the top of a crumbling wall. These creatures were the rulers of nighttime Marrakesh—no doubt about that.

Eden ducked into another alleyway, this one leading up a slight incline. Somewhere to her left she heard the rhythmic thump of approaching footsteps. She pressed herself into a doorway as an elderly man shuffled past, navigating his route by instinct alone.

She waited in the shadows for thirty seconds, before pressing on. Soon, the passage became so narrow she had to slip sideways between a parked moped and the wall. She reached the point at which the passage opened into a small square and paused. On the opposite side, the door to the Madrasa Ben Youssef sat locked for the night. A fountain in the center of the open space gurgled softly.

Satisfied no one was watching, Eden crossed the square. She skirted a pile of rubbish and stepped up to the giant door. She had considered using the back route Hamid had showed her, but with no one watching, this way saved time. She slid out her lock-picking tools and got to work on the bulky lock. Although strong, the simple mechanism yielded within a minute. She swung the door open, slipped inside, and secured it behind her.

Darkness hung thick and impenetrable inside the madrasa. If she hadn't known better, Eden would have assumed it was empty for the evening. She moved down the passage, her palm sliding along the wall for guidance. She thought about the flashlight in her pocket, but didn't want to advertise her approach.

She reached a corner and froze. Hearing only her own breathing, she continued, sweeping a foot out before her in search of steps or other obstacles. The passage opened into a small antechamber, lit by a shaft of moonlight streaming in through a high wooden screen. The sound of rippling water drifted from the pool.

Eden took a moment to steady herself, her hand still pressed against the tiles. She crossed through the beams of moonlight and pushed open the giant door. The door swung open, silent despite its weight.

The courtyard was just as she remembered, the intricate tilework mesmerizing in the moonlight. The pool in the center lay perfectly still, the night sky reflected in its surface.

And in the center of it all, sitting on the rug as though

she'd been waiting since Eden left, was Lalla Yasmine. She wore the same indigo robes and sat with her eyes closed, her hennaed hands folded in her lap.

"I wondered when you would return," Yasmine said without opening her eyes. "Although I didn't expect you until tomorrow."

"You knew I'd figure it out?" Eden said, swinging the door closed behind her and crossing the courtyard.

"Oh yes, of course. I told you everything you required. All you needed to do was follow my instructions," Yasmine said, finally opening her eyes and looking at Eden. "It was only a matter of time before you understood what's been in front of you this whole time."

"That sometimes death is merely a transition, like water becoming vapor," Eden said, echoing Yasmine's words—the words that had suddenly unlocked everything.

"And other times, death is something else entirely," Yasmine finished.

"I don't like being played." Eden stopped at the edge of the pool, looking at the dual images of the other woman— one real, the other reflected in the water. Yasmine held her gaze, unblinking.

"You knew everything—every move, every choice," Eden said, folding her arms. "You led me along."

"Don't underestimate yourself," Yasmine said, a knowing smile playing across her face. "I simply understood the patterns that were already in motion."

"Don't," Eden said, striding closer to the other woman. "I'm fed up with this. No more games, no more tests, it's time for the truth."

"And the truth itself is not an illusion?" Yasmine leaned forward and trailed her fingers through the water. Her reflection shattered into a thousand rippling fragments, each one a different version.

"You orchestrated all of it. Irons getting the Eye, us coming to Marrakesh." Eden's voice caught unexpectedly as she realized how close disaster had been. "And Baxter getting shot, was that your work too?" The words came out sharper than she intended, edged with something that might have been fear.

Yasmine tilted her head, studying Eden with a look that gave nothing away. "The young captain. I trust he is recovering well." She traced a line on the rug before her. "I assume you reached the chamber and met the one who waits there?"

"That man," Eden said carefully. "One of your people."

"My people." Yasmine smiled as if Eden had said something amusing. "Such simple categories you use."

"That man, he was my father?" Eden asked, the question coming before she'd realized she'd said it.

"You didn't think to ask?" Yasmine said, her gaze as sharp as ever.

Eden played the memory back. *My child*, the man had said, moments before she'd been swept back to the chamber to save Baxter.

"He is your father, of sorts, yes," Yasmine said, clearly reading Eden's frustration. "Although things are not quite that simple in his world."

"Who is he to you?" Eden said. "An ancestor, or something?"

"Is that what he said?" Yasmine sounded utterly delighted at the description. "How grand. That man has such a weakness for drama." She tapped the rug beside her. "Come, sit with me."

"I don't like being used," Eden said, folding her arms

and frowning at the older woman. "You've been orchestrating this every step of the way. There's only one thing I don't understand—"

"Oh, there is much you don't understand," Yasmine said, shaking her head. "But first, you know you'll sit beside me eventually. Why not do it now and save yourself all this bother?"

Eden groaned, scowled, and stomped around the pool and lowered herself onto the cushion beside Yasmine. The madrasa's reflection shimmered across the water's surface, the arches and columns creating a phantom architecture that seemed to extend beneath the ground.

Yasmine dipped her fingers into the pool again, watching the ripples distort their reflections. For a moment, Eden saw not two women but dozens—overlapping possibilities spreading across the water's surface like alternate versions of the same meeting.

"Now," Yasmine said, withdrawing her hand and shaking the water droplets away. "Your father told you of the Eye's true purpose, didn't he? The information coded in its quasi-crystalline structure."

Eden shifted on the cushion, pulling her knees up defensively. "What does molecular structure have to do with—"

"Oh, everything," Yasmine interrupted. "The Eye stores patterns. Possibilities. Every choice that could be made, every path that might be taken." She traced her finger along the rug. "Once you understand the pattern, you can guide it. Give it a push in the right direction, and the outcome becomes ... inevitable."

Eden stared at the older woman, trying to grasp what she'd said. "You're saying we're all just ... following a pattern? That everything that happened was predetermined?"

"Not predetermined," Yasmine corrected, holding up a finger. "Inevitable once set in motion. There's a difference. A ball at the top of a hill has many potential paths, but once it begins rolling, physics determines its course. We simply ..." She smiled that knowing smile again, "... gave the ball a push."

"You pushed Irons toward the Eye, that makes sense," Eden said, watching the water return to its glassy stillness. "But there's one thing I don't understand."

"Yes, a loose connection if you will," Yasmine said.

"How did—"

The sound of footsteps echoed across the courtyard. Eden looked toward the sound.

"The answer comes this way," Yasmine said.

"We're not alone?" Eden said, her voice dropping to a whisper.

"We never were," Yasmine replied, not even glancing toward the sound. She continued tracing the patterns on the rug with her finger. "Some patterns take longer to complete than others."

A figure emerged from the darkness between the columns. The moonlight caught her face first—sharp cheekbones, dark hair going silver at the temples.

"What?" Eden said, shooting to her feet. "You're dead. I watched them shoot you."

"Hello, Eden." Eva Glass stepped into the moonlight, whole and unharmed. Not a ghost, not a vision—solid and real, a knowing half smile on her face.

66

"Eden," Glass said, crossing the courtyard and standing beside the pool. She now wore dark linen trousers and a loose tunic. Her hair was no longer in its characteristic bun but hung loose around her shoulders, softening her appearance. "I apologize for the deception."

"You ... you were shot," Eden whispered. "You gave me the crystal and sent me—" she stopped, understanding slowly emerging.

"A necessary fiction, I'm afraid," Glass said, her fingers clasped behind her back.

"But ..." Eden's voice trailed off as the pieces continued to stack up. "I asked you, back at the motel in Los Alamos if Irons was working for someone else. You answered with an immediate yes. There's only one way you'd know that for sure. At the time I thought you'd made an assumption, but now ..."

"The ear hears more than the brain understands," Yasmine said.

"The only way you could know that," Eden continued,

pointing at Glass, "is if you were the person in charge. You set him up. You told him to raid the lab, so that you could escape with the Eye."

"Poor Alistair—too heartbroken to see what was happening right in front of him," Glass said, folding her arms.

"But he instructed his men to shoot you," Eden said, the scene scrolling back again through her mind's eye.

"A little bit of theatre," Glass said. "The men were under strict orders to make it look a certain way. They did a good job."

"But why?" Eden said.

"When we recovered the Eye of the Sahara from the Richat Structure ten years ago, we had no idea what we were dealing with," Glass said, her voice carrying a weight of regret. "I was young, ambitious, and certain that science was all we needed to power the future. The more I studied the Eye, though, the more I truly realized what we had. Hidden within that crystal—"

"Are the secrets of a lost civilization," Eden said. "I know, so I heard."

"It's more than knowledge," Glass said, looking down at the pool. "What is encoded there affects people."

"And what you did killed people," Eden said, watching Glass closely.

"Far fewer than would have died if that thing had been weaponized," Glass said, returning Eden's gaze with defiance. "The eye holds a complete blueprint for manipulating reality at the quantum level. Energy-matter conversion, temporal distortion, consciousness transfer—the theoretical frameworks alone would advance human science by centuries." Glass's gaze became distant, troubled.

"We're not ready for that. Imagine giving nuclear weapons to medieval knights." She paused, her reflection wavering in the pool. "Every month we got more pressure from the higher-ups to weaponize it somehow. One researcher calculated that a device based on the Eye's resonance patterns could destabilize molecular bonds across a radius of several miles. Another worked on a method for developing rifts in spacetime. I could only hold them off so long."

"That's horrendous," Eden said.

"The knowledge itself isn't horrendous," Yasmine said. "It is the mind that's too young to wield it wisely."

"That's when I knew I had to act," Glass continued. "If anyone got control of this, we would destroy ourselves before we understood what we had."

"You came back here looking for answers," Eden said, her gaze shifting from Glass to Yasmine.

"Yes, I came looking for someone who could tell me what the crystal was." Glass eyed Yasmine with something approaching reverence. "On my third trip here, I met Yasmine. She let me into their secret—the real importance of the Eye. I knew at that moment I had to stop our research, closing the department down if necessary."

"Well, why didn't you just do that?" Eden asked. "You were the director of that place."

"It doesn't work like that," Glass said. "If I showed so much as a doubt, they would replace me in an instant. There were ten or more people ready to take my place at a moment's notice."

"So you got Irons to raid the place, then took it upon yourself to escape with the Eye," Eden said.

"You have to understand, there was no way I could stop

the program," Glass continued. "Everyone who knew about the crystal was obsessed with unlocking its secrets. The ultimate power ..."

"You manipulated Irons's grief for your own ends," Eden said.

"That's true," Glass said. "I told him it was theoretically possible to use the Eye to change past events."

"You were right," Eden said, once again picturing Baxter splayed out on the ground. "Then you got him into the center and took the crystal before he had the chance, then you had me lead him right to where he needed to be."

"To stop the monster, I had to become the monster," Glass said, looking down at the water.

Glancing at the woman, Eden saw her jaw tightening as though she wished she could take it all back.

The courtyard fell silent except for the gentle lapping of water in the pool. Eden stood up, her hands clenched, processing everything she'd heard. Glass had orchestrated deaths, betrayals, years of lies—but also, possibly, prevented something far worse.

"What happens now?" Eden asked, her voice losing some of its edge. "The Eye is buried, my connection is severed. Is it over?"

Glass and Yasmine exchanged another look.

"Is it ever really over?" Yasmine said, rising to her feet with surprising grace for someone of her age.

"I had a horrible feeling you were going to say that," Eden said, surprising herself with a tired laugh. "For once, couldn't I just get a simple answer?"

"Yes, Eden, evil defeated, world saved, everyone goes home," Yasmine said. Eden looked at the older woman and saw a grin flash across her face.

"If it helps, I'd like that too," Glass said quietly. "But I think you know that this will never truly end."

Eden returned her look and saw something she recognized—the same bone-deep wariness she felt after every mission where the right choice and the good choice weren't the same thing.

"But the Eye of the Sahara is gone. Its secrets are buried," Eden said.

"Not quite," Yasmine said, picking up the lantern. "Come. There's something you need to see."

Eden followed as Yasmine walked to the far side of the courtyard. Glass remained beside the pool, watching with an unreadable expression.

"Tell me, what do you see here?" Yasmine said, holding the lantern close to the intricate tilework.

Eden examined the wall. Thousands of small tiles formed complex geometric patterns—eight-pointed stars interlocking with smaller stars, creating an infinite tessellation. "Zellige. Traditional Moroccan tilework. Geometric patterns based on mathematical principles," she said, giving an answer Winslow would be proud of.

"Look closer." Yasmine moved the lantern slowly across the surface. "Not at the individual tiles, but at the pattern they create. Look at the forest, not the trees."

Eden stepped closer. At first, she saw nothing but tiles and mortar, but then ... She inhaled sharply, running an extended finger over the tiles.

"This pattern," Eden said, looking at Yasmine.

"Yes, it's a quasi-crystalline structure," Yasmine said. "Five-fold symmetry that shouldn't exist in nature, couldn't exist according to classical crystallography."

"The same as the atomic structure of the Eye," Eden said, looking at Yasmine and then Glass.

"Yes," Yasmine said, a hint of surprise flashing across her face. "It's been here for centuries. And before that, it was in another building not far away."

"But this is ..." Eden couldn't finish the sentence. Her legs felt weak. She leaned nearer, squinting at the tiles as the image moved across her vision.

"This is our insurance policy," Yasmine said, moving along the wall. "For seven centuries people have come here, never realizing they are surrounded by the encoded secrets of Atlantis."

"That's impossible," Eden gasped, looking around as the light revealed more—the pattern covered every wall, with subtle variations in colors and spacing. Now that Eden noticed it, she saw it everywhere.

"We don't use the word *impossible*," Glass said, a sad smile lighting her expression. "We look at the evidence and make our own conclusions."

"The builders who designed this weren't merely artisans," Yasmine said, running her hand from one pattern to the next. "They were survivors. Descendants of those who fled when the city sank beneath the sand. They encoded everything they knew into these walls, but in a way that would appear to be nothing more than decorative art."

"The entire building is a textbook," Eden said, turning one way, then the next. "The complete knowledge of a lost civilization."

"Not only here," Yasmine said. "The Alhambra in Granada. The Great Mosque of Córdoba. The Ibn Tulun Mosque in Cairo. Dozens of buildings across the world."

"And nobody knows?" Eden said.

"Some do, of course," Glass said. "The knowledge has been preserved through certain families or schools. The

Pythagoreans knew. The ancient Egyptian priests of Thoth knew."

"This is why you brought me here originally," Eden said to Yasmine. "Not just to tell me about Atlantis, or the Richat Structure, but to show me this." She turned to face the older woman. "And I didn't even notice it."

"You saw what you were ready to see," Yasmine said, nodding in confirmation.

Eden looked around the courtyard with fresh eyes, the patterns covering every surface.

"How many people know about this?" Eden asked.

"Fully know? Perhaps a dozen in the entire world," Yasmine said. "Partially know? A few hundred. Suspect? Thousands. But suspecting and knowing are very different things."

"And now I know," Eden said.

"Now you know," Glass confirmed.

"But that's not what's important," Yasmine said, turning and taking Eden's hands in hers. "The question isn't what you know, it's whether you understand."

"You know what," Eden said, her gaze passing across the sheer number of patterns surrounding her, coalescing and drifting into one. "I think I finally do."

EDEN SLIPPED OUT of the madrasa as dawn painted the eastern sky in shades of red and purple. The muezzin's call would begin soon, and the medina would wake. She needed to be gone before then. She pulled the door closed behind her, the ancient lock clicking back into place. She crossed the square, heading back the way she'd come.

From a rooftop on the other side of the square, a tall figure stood motionless in the shadow of a water tower. A long indigo robe covered his frame, reflecting the dawn light like liquid mercury.

He watched as Eden moved through the narrow alley, her stride purposeful despite the weight of what she'd learned. He had watched her enter hours ago—desperate, angry, and searching for answers. Now as she emerged, she looked different somehow. The set of her shoulders showed she understood what she saw and would help keep it safe.

She picked her way toward him, pausing as a cat wound its way through her legs. After the creature had slunk away, she looked up. Recognizing him, she froze. She looked upon him now, not as the mystical figure from the chamber, not as the voice of ancient wisdom, but as the man who'd given her up. Who'd walked away for reasons she didn't and couldn't understand.

Their eyes met across the distance—two people, separated by years and choices that couldn't be wound back or undone.

Eden's expression didn't change, but she gave the slightest nod. Perhaps the gesture was acknowledgment, or even forgiveness.

Maybe, he wondered, if she really understood—he'd sacrificed fatherhood to save his people, and she'd sacrificed him to save one man. Both had traded power for love, in a manner of speaking, just in opposite directions. Maybe that was the difference between us, he thought. Humans will do anything for love, whatever the cost.

Eden broke the gaze and ducked beneath a low archway, back into the maze of the medina.

The tall figure remained in place as the first call to prayer began, carried by the desert wind across the rooftops.

Somewhere in the city, his daughter was walking back to a man who didn't know he'd died for her. And somewhere beyond that, the patterns continued their inevitable dance, waiting for the next crisis, the next choice, the next sacrifice.

"You chose well, my child," he whispered to the empty air. "Better than I ever could have."

AUTHOR'S NOTE

Thank you so much for joining me on Eden's seventh adventure, The Sahara Event. As with all my books, I had so much fun writing this, a fact that I hope came across in the twists and turns of the story.

Now at the seventh book in the series, I often get asked if I have plans to bring the series to a close. The answer is... no. I'm enjoying hanging out with Eden and her ever-changing band of heroes so much that I already can't wait to get back into writing the next one. That doesn't mean I won't work on other books between Eden releases, though. I have so many other ideas that I want to bring to the page, and of course share with you.

Writing these author's notes has always been one of my favorite parts of the process, as it's my chance to talk to you directly. First, thank you for buying this book—in doing so you're supporting me and my family in leading a life that brings us a lot of happiness. In fact, as I write this, Mrs. R and I are in our campervan enjoying the countryside for a few days. This certainly wouldn't be possible without the support of readers like you.

The inspiration for the Sahara Event struck me while visiting Marrakesh, Morocco, in January 2025. As with all my ideas, I didn't know that it would arrive when it did. In fact, at the time I was taking a couple of weeks away from the keyboard having just finished The Lotus Key. But the idea charged in anyway, and once it materialized, I knew it was too good to ignore.

Marrakesh itself is perfect fodder for an archaeological thriller writer like me—the twisting alleyways, bustling squares, and dark corners, much of which hasn't changed in centuries.

But it's not just the atmosphere that I found captivating; it's the layers of history literally built on top of each other. An example of this, which inspired the secret network of tunnels through which Hamid guides Eden and the crew, are the Saadian Tombs.

This beautiful necropolis, the final resting place for members of the Saadian Dynasty in the 16th and 17th centuries, was "discovered" in 1917 when French officers conducting an aerial survey noticed a patch of land hidden between buildings. Intrigued, they sent a team to investigate. Breaking through the blocked entrance, they found ornate marble tombs carved with flowing Arabic calligraphy, mosaic covered pillars, and cedarwood ceilings in deep reds and blues.

The story goes that after the fall of the Saadians, Sultan Moulay Isma'il of the succeeding dynasty sought to downplay his predecessors' legacy. Rather than destroying their burial site, he had the entrance to the necropolis sealed off, cutting it off from public view. Over time, the tombs slipped from memory, hidden behind the walls of the surrounding buildings.

Visiting the tombs, and learning the story behind their

re-discovery, I couldn't help but imagine what it would have been like to break through that wall and find all those spectacular rooms. Such stories catch my imagination and make me question—if the Saadian dynasty's final resting place could vanish from memory, what else might be waiting down there?

But, as the twists of this story suggest, the idea fully took hold while exploring the passageways and courtyards of the Ben Youssef Madrasa. The walls of which are covered in tiles, arranged in a distinct quasi-crystalline pattern.

Researching this pattern later, I learned that it conforms to a mathematical principle—called aperiodic tiling or Penrose tiling—which wasn't 'discovered' by Western mathematics until the 1970s. Yet here were medieval craftsmen, working hundreds of years ago, creating quasi-crystalline patterns using nothing but traditional tools and inherited knowledge.

Even more intriguing, when scientists finally understood quasicrystals in the 1980s (work that won the 2011 Nobel Prize), they realized these patterns appear in nature at the atomic level. These Islamic artisans somehow coded a fundamental structure of the universe without microscopes or computers, displayed it for all to see on the walls of the madrasa.

Of course, in these pages I imagined these patterns weren't merely decorative, but a sophisticated code that preserved and transmitted ancient wisdom. Add to that the fact that similar patterns appear in Islamic architecture from Spain to India, and it sounds like a hidden network of knowledge transcending borders and centuries.

That brings us to the Eye of the Sahara—the crystal that plays a central role in the book. Although a crystal encoded with the secrets of a lost civilization might sound like a work of my imagination, the science behind it is surprisingly real. Quartz crystals are an essential component of today's technology—every smartphone and computer relies on quartz to keep perfect time and synchronize data processing. Without quartz, the internet wouldn't exist—fiber optic cables use it to transmit light signals across oceans. Even more remarkably, scientists now use synthetic quartz in quantum computers, where its crystalline structure can maintain quantum states at near absolute zero temperatures. Experts now think that data encoded into quartz, and kept in good conditions, could last a billion years.

Considering this, is it really a coincidence that some of the world's most iconic ancient structures are built from quartz-rich stone?

The inner chambers and sarcophagi inside the Pyramids of Giza, for example, are made from granite—a stone that typically contains between twenty and sixty percent quartz. Elsewhere in the ancient world, Angkor Wat is made of sandstone, which contains up to ninety percent quartz and the megaliths of Stonehenge are a mix of sarsen (a silcrete packed with quartz) and bluestone.

Across continents and civilizations, builders gravitated —perhaps unconsciously or maybe purposefully—toward stones that contained this magic mineral. If quartz can store data for billions of years, and ancient builders deliberately chose quartz-rich stones for their most sacred structures... were they trying to tell us something?

In terms of the story you've just read, it took me a while to decide what should be encoded on the crystal. At first, I went down a scientific route with the crystal containing the secret to stable antimatter production. This was a fascinating part of the story, which I enjoyed researching. In the end, however, I felt it was all a bit too technological.

I enjoyed the research, though, learning all about the atomic fossils, which I used in the opening chapters. *Atomic Annie,* as I called the fossil, was inspired by the natural reactor in Oklo, West Africa. Two billion years ago, in what's now Gabon, nature created its own nuclear fission reactor, which ran for hundreds of thousands of years, self-regulating its chain reactions using nothing but natural uranium deposits and groundwater. When scientists discovered it in 1972, they couldn't believe it—nature had beaten us to nuclear technology, and even solved its own nuclear waste problem, containing the radioactive byproducts in place for eons. Of course, there are experts who think such things are too coincidental to be purely a force of nature, but that's a conversation for another day.

In the end, when the character of Dr. Alistair Irons emerged, I thought the idea of controlling the past was a much stronger and more interesting motive. After all, who wouldn't want the chance to do that? Whether it's to change something small—maybe betting on a race or knowing the questions on an exam—or something more meaningful, like reconnecting with a loved one, it's a motive that I feel we can all understand. As always with the antagonists in my books, I feel it's important we understand them and, in some way, see the method in their madness.

With all that said, let's address the elephant in the room, and what a giant elephant it is... Could Atlantis really lie beneath the Sahara?

Well, as Yasmine Amana tells Eden in this story, the Romans certainly thought so. When Roman geographer Pomponius Mela created his world map in 43 CE, working from older documents, he wrote a single word in the desert (suspiciously close to the Richat Structure), *Atlantae.*

Mela wasn't just doodling here—he was one of the

Roman Empire's leading geographical authorities, working from centuries of accumulated knowledge, much of which is now lost to us. His placement was deliberate and specific.

We also know for certain that the Sahara was once a green and verdant place. This isn't speculation—this is scientific fact. Every twenty-thousand years or so, shifts in Earth's axis cause the African monsoons to migrate north, transforming the desert into a lush savanna with lakes, rivers, and abundant wildlife. The last Green Sahara period ended around five thousand years ago—recent enough that early Egyptian hieroglyphs depict giraffes, elephants, and hippos living where there's now only sand. Cave paintings in the Tassili n'Ajjer mountains show people swimming, hunting crocodiles, and herding cattle across grasslands.

What's even more intriguing is that ground-penetrating radar has revealed massive ancient river systems beneath the Sahara, including one as large as the Nile running from the Mauritanian coast (near the Richat Structure) all the way to the Mediterranean. Called the Tamanrasset River valley, it's now buried under sand but once supported thriving populations.

In the Sahara Event, I've taken these facts and asked: if advanced civilizations lived there during the time at which the Sahara was green, what happened to them after the desert took over?

The Richat Structure itself—the Eye of the Sahara—is exactly as I described in the book and remains genuinely puzzling to geologists. This massive bull's-eye formation, forty kilometers across and visible from space, has characteristics that don't quite fit any single explanation. It's not a meteor impact crater, as originally thought. It's not a simple volcanic formation. It has the famous concentric rings, the perfect circular shape, and its location near the Atlantic coast where Plato said Atlantis would be... well, it makes you wonder.

Unfortunately, I've yet to visit the Richat Structure, so had to rely on research for the scenes set there. If you have visited, I hope these parts of the story stacked up for you—I'd love to know what you thought!

Maybe I'll get there on my next visit as the Sahara is certainly part of the world that I'll visit again. There are enough legends to fuel a dozen books or more.

One of the most captivating of the Saharan legends is Zerzura—*the Oasis of Little Birds*. According to Medieval Arabic texts, this mythical white city is supposedly hidden somewhere in the Western Desert. Described as a city of sleeping kings and queens, and guarded by giants, the buildings are said to be made of white stone and filled with treasures beyond imagination. The city appears and disappears like a mirage, revealing itself only to those deemed worthy.

This legend was compelling enough for an expedition in the 1930s to set out in search of Zerzura. Following the Kitab al Kanuz, a 15th-century Arabic treasure hunter's guide, which gives cryptic directions to Zerzura, a team searched the desert with vehicles and aircraft. They found real lost oases and ancient settlements, proving civilization did once exist where there's now only sand, but unfortunately, no Zerzura.

In my thriller, I've woven Zerzura into the Atlantis narrative—perhaps it wasn't one lost city, but many, connected by a civilization that understood the Sahara better than we do today. Whether Atlantis, as described by Plato, lies beneath the sand, I don't know for sure. But I'll tell you this, I'm certain there's a lot we still don't know about that great sea of sand.

As you'll have realized, this is a very personal book for Eden. Once I realized I could tie Morocco and the Sahara into the Atlantean legend, I knew it was time to pull that curtain back just a little.

I did worry that if you're coming to this book without reading the rest of the series, some scenes might not fully resonate. But ultimately, I decided Eden's self-discovery was too important to skip. If that's the case for you, I suggest you grab the Ark Files right now and dive straight in—an adventure awaits!

Aside from my joy at spending time with Eden and her crew in this book, I loved some of the new characters. Hamid quickly became one of my favorites with his collection of wisdom one-liners. Whilst these phrases started off as a joke (I always like a bit of light relief in a story), I felt that he ultimately becomes the book's link between the old world and new—the bridge between ancient wisdom and modern understanding.

As a writer of books set all over the world, it is my responsibility not just to honor the places in my stories, but the people too. I feel that some stories in the adventure thriller genre are built on the stereotype of the local people either being victims or bandits, outsmarted or saved by the strength and cunning of the European or American "savior." I hope I've not been guilty of that in any of my books, and I will continue to work to make sure that's not the case.

To counter that in this book, I wanted Hamid to be thoughtful, clever, and most importantly, to teach Eden (and perhaps me too) something along the way. I also loved coming up with all of Hamid's phrases—*a leopard crossing the desert arrives with the same spots.*

To me, Hamid quietly demonstrates that we in the modern world don't have all the answers. He proves to Eden, and us all, that indigenous knowledge isn't primitive or less-than, but rather a different (and maybe even a deeper) form of understanding.

As to whether Eden and a certain young man will ever be totally open with each other, you'll have to wait and see. One thing I know for sure though: they will be back, they will fight the forces of evil once again, and you're invited along for the ride.

Once again, thank you for joining me on this adventure. A special thanks if you're part of my Adventure Society—this group of readers really helps me keep motivated between book launches. If you're not, you can join here (https://lukerichardsonauthor.com/adventuresociety). I reach out every week or so and would love to thank you personally for your support.

Thanks again. See you on the next adventure!

Luke :D

November 2025

Eden returns in the Alchemist's Codex! Use the link below,
or search online for 'The Alchemist's Codex.'

http://lukerichardsonauthor.com/alchemistscodex

THE ALCHEMIST'S *Codex* will be the eighth book in Eden's adventures, and this time she's heading to France.

What if Notre-Dame's fire wasn't an accident? What if it was a ploy — a way to find something that's lain hidden beneath the cathedral for hundreds of years?

That's where Eden's trail begins, in the shadow of Notre-Dame, chasing a secret someone was willing to burn a cathedral to reach. From there it winds through Renaissance châteaux and down into the Pyrénées. Eden and her crew pursue the ghost of Fulcanelli — the master alchemist who vanished without a trace and left behind only whispers of a lost codex.

But they're not the only ones hunting for it. The man on the other side of the trail has reasons of his own — reasons that run a great deal deeper than gold.

Some say Fulcanelli cracked the oldest secret of all, but Eden's about to find out whether the legend is worth dying for.

http://lukerichardsonauthor.com/alchemistscodex

Are you ready for the adventure of a lifetime?

64% of you read my books without me ever getting the chance to say thank you. I'd love to change that.

If you've ever enjoyed one of my stories, I'd love to welcome you into my *Adventure Society*. This weekly newsletter is your chance to travel to the places that inspire my stories, explore the real-world mysteries, and be the first to know when a new book is ready.

Most of all, it helps me write the stories you love as this way we're connected directly without relying on algorithms or online stores. Believe me when I say that direct connection is so important!

Will you join me for an adventure today?

lukerichardsonauthor.com/adventuresociety

Your next adventure starts here...

HI, I'M LUKE...

...and I'm applying for the job as your next favorite author!

As an Amazon bestselling author, I've had the honor of sharing my stories with readers around the world. My books are a passport to adventure, blending history, intrigue, and suspense into gripping tales that transport you to my favorite places around the world.

From the sun-baked Pyramids of Giza to the glittering skyscrapers of Hong Kong, and from the shadowy back-streets of Kathmandu to the depths of the Atlantic Ocean, my stories will take you somewhere new and exciting. But it's not just about the destinations; you'll meet fascinating characters, encounter unexpected twists, and experience edge-of-your-seat action along the way.

My love for storytelling was ignited during my first trip

to India. As my taxi wove through the streets of Mumbai at dawn, I watched the city unfold like a story. The sight of people going about their daily lives—washing, playing, tending to animals—sparked a desire to capture and share these vivid experiences through writing.

When I'm not globetrotting in search of my next story, you'll find me in Nottingham, England, where I call home. Before embarking on my writing career, I spent years as a high school English teacher, and a nightclub DJ.

Nothing brings me more joy than hearing that my stories have transported someone to a new place or kept them up all night. Whether you're drawn to the lovable characters, intricate plots, or fast-paced storytelling, I'm always working hard to bring you even more thrilling adventures.

So, if you're a history buff, a travel addict, or simply in search of your next literary escape, you're in the right place. I appreciate you being here, now let's hit the road.

Luke :D

CAN A PRICELESS PAINTING VANISH INTO THIN AIR?

Eden Black meets Ernest Dempsey's Adriana Villa

Ten years ago, Bernard Moreau baffled police by stealing a Picasso from the Modern Art Museum. He was arrested and imprisoned, but the painting was never found.

Now, back on the streets, all eyes are on Moreau. But he's a skilled thief and isn't going to make it easy.

EDEN BLACK can't stand corruption and the theft of priceless art. This case reeks of them both. Heading to Paris, she vows to return the Picasso to its rightful home as soon as possible.

ADRIANA VILLA works alone, always, that's the rule. So, when she sees another woman following her mark, things get heated.

To find the painting before a dirty police inspector with a score to settle, the pair must put their egos aside and work together. What they discover shows that nothing is as simple as it first seems.

THE PARIS HEIST is an up-tempo novella which will keep you pinned to the pages until the very end. If you like the sound of a race against the clock, action packed, adventure thriller, set amongst the blissful Parisian streets, you'll love THE PARIS HEIST.

Read The Paris Heist for FREE today!
https://www.lukerichardsonauthor.com/paris

HAVE YOU READ MY
INTERNATIONAL DETECTIVE SERIES?

You visit a restaurant in a far-away city, only to find you're on the menu.

Leo Keane is sent abroad to track down Allissa, a politician's daughter who vanished two years ago in Kathmandu. But with a storm on the horizon and intrigue at every turn, Leo's mission may be more dangerous than he bargained for... A propulsive international thriller!

READ TODAY

https://www.lukerichardsonauthor.com/kathmandu

Copyright © 2025 by Luke Richardson

All rights reserved. No part of this book may be reproduced, distributed, or transmitted in any form or by any means, including photocopying, recording, or other electronic or mechanical methods, without the prior written permission of the publisher, except in the case of brief quotations embodied in critical reviews and certain other non-commercial uses permitted by copyright law. For permission requests, write to the publisher at the address below.

Richa Books

Hello@LukeRichardsonAuthor.com

This is a work of fiction. Names, characters, places, and incidents either are products of the author's imagination or are used fictitiously. Any resemblance to actual persons, living or dead, events, or locales is entirely coincidental.

Cover Design by: https://cover2book.com/

 Formatted with Vellum

www.ingramcontent.com/pod-product-compliance
Lightning Source LLC
Chambersburg PA
CBHW031736180726
48283CB00005B/1535